S0-ADN-118

Richard Temple

PATRICK O'BRIAN

Richard Temple

W. W. NORTON & COMPANY

NEW YORK · LONDON

Copyright © 1962 by Patrick O'Brian
First American Edition 2006
First published as a Norton paperback 2007 .

All rights reserved
Printed in the United States of America

For information about permission to reproduce selections from this book,
write to Permissions, W. W. Norton & Company, Inc., 500 Fifth Avenue,
New York, NY 10110

Manufacturing by RR Donnelley, Bloomsburg
Production manager: Julia Druskin

Library of Congress Cataloging-in-Publication Data

O'Brian, Patrick, 1914–
  Richard Temple / Patrick O'Brian.— 1st American ed.
    p. cm.
  ISBN-13: 978-0-393-06187-1 (hardcover)
  ISBN-10: 0-393-06187-6 (hardcover)
  1. Prisoners of war—Fiction. 2. Painters--Fiction. 3. World War,
1939–1945—France—Fiction. 4. France—Fiction. 5. London
(England)—Fiction. I. Title.
  PR6029.B55R53 2006
  823'.914—dc22

                                2005034884

ISBN 978-0-393-33066-3 pbk.

W. W. Norton & Company, Inc., 500 Fifth Avenue, New York, N.Y. 10110
www.wwnorton.com

W. W. Norton & Company, Ltd., Castle House, 75/76 Wells Street,
London W1T 3QT

1 2 3 4 5 6 7 8 9 0

FOR MARY, WITH LOVE

CHAPTER ONE

TWENTY-SEVEN TILES from wall to wall, thirty-five from floor to roof. Nine hundred and forty-five white tiles upon the wall. He knew them all so well that even now, lying on the concrete floor, he could tell that his shoulder was against the row that ran from two hundred and sixteen to two hundred and fifty-one: indeed, the top of his head must come exactly to the tile of the day, the tile that marked Thursday, the twenty-first. Though he might be several days out in his reckoning: the first days and nights of terror had passed uncounted, uncountable because they outlasted all count of days, and he had worked them out later, by estimation.

But now, although he was aware of his position in relation to the wall, he was not interested in his calendar. He was quite motionless on the ground, still in the place where he had fallen when they pushed him in, and if he did not move his body would not hurt – it would not flame out with annihilating pain. As for the dull wretched sickness, he was used to that: it was a passive, indwelling pain, and he could live with it, and think in spite of it.

He lay there, too, from religious caution and respect. If he were to creep over to the wooden bench (although it was no more than four feet away) to lie there more comfortably and enjoy his victory, it might offend. The omen might change if he was to presume; so he lay there still.

Humble: he was humble. He truckled to fate, and although the darkness could not have been more profound he lay there

on the concrete with the familiar taste of blood in his mouth,
hiding his secret triumph under immobility.

✦

BUT IT GREW in his mind like a fire, and in spite of himself a
smile spread over his face, slowly changing the deep-cut lines of
anxiety and suffering. Two hours earlier they had switched the
light on in his cell: the glare had stabbed into his pale eyes and
he had staggered to attention, blinking and staring. He had heard
them coming, of course, and already, before they had ever
touched the light, he had moved with the heavy blundering haste
of a terrified half-wit – mouth open, hands dangling, uncouth
slouch. Clang, clang, down the corridor praying that they would
grow angry soon – it was so much easier in the turmoil of blows
and shouting.

The knock on the door, the clash and the stamping. There was
another man besides Reinecke and Bauer, a civilian with a briefcase, and they left Temple standing while they finished talking
and handing papers. Reinecke was looking tired and dispirited,
and suddenly very much older. Temple, from behind his moron's
face, watched him with a more eager intensity than a lover: for
this Reinecke was God for him – Jehovah. He was the Almighty,
and Temple had been in the hollow of his hand all these horribly counted days. He was Reinecke's priest and sacrifice: he had
learnt, oh so quickly, how to predict Reinecke's shifting moods,
how to propitiate his wrath and how to be as sparing of his sacrifice as possible: for Temple's own body was the sacrifice.

But now Reinecke had a look that he had never seen before –
could not interpret. Was it fright, apprehension, uneasiness? Was
it age? Was it an aging night out? Could it be that the squalor of
his position had occurred to him? Some idea of his utter corrup-

tion might have come to him suddenly, for Reinecke was not a fool, nor without some insight.

The scream that had been coming in from the other room with the regularity and inhumanity of a steam-engine was suddenly choked off, and at the same time the civilian gathered up his files and began to range them in his briefcase. They were talking in low, rapid German; low, not because of Temple, but because their own words were unwelcome to them. Temple could make nothing of it, partly because he did not know German well enough and partly because his knowledge and his hearing were to some degree obscured by the stupidity of his mask. He could not put on the outward appearance of a dolt without his mind taking on some of the disguise. From next door there was one more bubbling shriek, and a noise of feet.

Perhaps that might have been André, thought Temple: poor devil. Reinecke had mentioned his name. But Temple had little room for active pity at this time: André, if it was the real André and not a shot in the dark, would have to go his own road. He only hoped that André would by now have learnt to scream terribly, to scream long before the point of agony, to scream better than any actor upon a stage.

He had learnt that very early, himself. And he had learnt that Reinecke disliked abjectness – an abject victim irritated him. The way to flatter Reinecke was to be brave. Temple could not provide Reinecke with his ideal prisoner, for there were many moral and physical requirements that he could not fulfil, but he could, by the sharpest observation, find out the minimum acceptable qualities, and offer them. He was a third-rate, but just not too irritating fool, with a core of courage to be broken down.

He was a fool all the time, in his looks, in his stance, in his

long, wandering, garbled, contradictory account of himself, a fool
to all but the smallest, innermost part of himself; and that part
watched the vertiginous performance with agonised intensity.
And all the time he watched Reinecke, to anticipate his reac-
tions, to know his coming state of mind while it was as yet half-
formed. Temple did not hate Reinecke; he did not even wish him
ill, in case the malevolence should somehow leak out across the
space between them; and besides, some of his emotions and per-
ceptions were so sharpened that others – hatred for one – had
dwindled: they were also uneconomical.

The civilian had done; he looked up. He still seemed to want
to say something more, however, and he looked at Reinecke and
Bauer – all three looked at one another with much the same air
– but perhaps he did not trust one or another of them, and after
a moment's silence he left: shaking of hands, little formal bows,
and on his way to the door he looked at Temple with a haunted
expression, or rather his field of vision (haunted vision) took in
the space where Temple stood. It was not the crossing of two
human regards.

'Now,' said Reinecke with a sudden shout, turning towards
Temple: he took a few paces up and down the room, and as he
passed staring, Temple flinched – an involuntary flinch, of
course, an unwilling tribute. Then he recovered himself with a
visible effort and stood docile, obedient and terrified, a man just
this side of collapse, holding on by no more than his nails, but
still holding on.

Reinecke sat down, Bauer passed him the dossier and looking
down at it Reinecke bawled out, 'Name?'

They went through the long rigmarole again, Reinecke following in the dossier with a pencil.

'Name?'

'Richard Temple.'

'Born?'

'April 7th, 1911.'

'Where?'

'Plimpton Rectory, Plimpton, Sussex.'

'Name of father?'

'Llewellyn Temple.'

'Profession or trade?'

'Rector.'

'Place and date of birth?'

'Brickfield Terrace, Cardiff. June 26th, 1860.'

His mother's name was Laura, daughter of the Reverend Mr Richard Gray, formerly vicar of Colpoys in County Durham. Twenty-three more dated facts. It was a strangely unintelligent routine: he had never varied in the last eighteen repetitions and they must be bloody fools if they thought he would do so now. Besides, it was true, as far as literal truth had any meaning: not so much easy to remember as impossible to forget. But Reinecke was completely out of form, and the routine obviously helped him along.

When the passport questions were done with, he led his prisoner through the usual wearisome, slow, time-consuming question-and-answer that built up the unchanging picture of an inefficient, stupid, petty black-marketeer – unchanging, that is, since the first shifty protestations of innocence had been broken down.

Yes, he had crossed the Spanish frontier illegally: yes, he had been engaged in trafficking: the story he had first told about coming over to see a woman had been untrue: he had lived in Barcelona to avoid military service in England. He had not registered with the Spanish police; it was easy to live there by moving from one place

to another. He had never been over to handle a deal before, but
had worked at the other end. The chief was a Levantine Jew called
Sol – was to be found in the café after the opera house, on the
other side. He did not think that Sol ever had anything to do with
passing Frenchmen or Allied agents over the Frontier: there was
not enough money in it to make it interesting. He was only concerned with spare parts of cars and light machinery – merchandise
in the middle price range. He did not touch drugs or girls or cur-
rency, because they were all owned by established concerns. This
was the first time he had sent Temple to meet the French contact
on the frontier. Temple had lost his way in the mountains: he had
been arrested before he had met the Frenchman.

A pause. Was it all so convincing? He had been over and over
it so often that he could no longer see it at all objectively: and
what was the matter with Reinecke?

'You do not suppose we believe all this, do you?' said Reinecke,
in a tired, reasonable voice, as if it really were a question. Goggle-
eyed stupidity: distress.

Reinecke told Bauer to fetch him some files from the other
building: a silence filled the room and suddenly Reinecke did
the cleverest thing that he had ever done in all their horrible intimacy. He pushed Temple gently into a chair and with a voice
filled with human respect and deference he said, 'Mr Temple,
you must put me in touch with an Allied intelligence officer.'

He went on, hurriedly: Temple must help him to meet someone from London or the country HQ. Reinecke could offer several valuable agents – Foster and West, and Claudius – any
number of Frenchmen. He would not abuse the confidence:
Reinecke must, he *must* insure himself – he had a family. Temple
could trust in Reinecke's personal honour. Temple would be free,
free and in luxury, as soon as the meeting was arranged.

The attack was so sudden, so unlike any other, and so skil-
fully delivered (grey face of shameful urgency, trembling insis-
tence) that if Temple had not already had his agonised fool's
uncomprehending face well on he must have shown how jarred
he was. Reinecke had been God for so long and so intensely that
his descent to this plane was very moving. But the fool's face was
on, and all he had to do was to keep it there, gaping.

It was very, very cunning. Yet Reinecke should not have cou-
pled West and Claudius; their organisations were somewhat too
remote from one another.

In the silence Reinecke clasped and unclasped his hands: his
bolting eyes were fixed upon Temple, and Temple saw their
expression change from that first mixture of false forced good
nature, anguish and shame to frustration and anger. Redness was
welling up in Reinecke's face; but before the tension had reached
its height (and the ludicrous undercurrent of embarrassment,
the god's miracle having failed) they heard the clump of Bauer's
return.

Reinecke turned away with the files. Bauer continued the
interrogation. It went along its usual lines, always upon the
assumption that Temple was probably an Allied agent, and its
aim was to induce him or compel him to give information, or to
betray himself. Bauer was not very intelligent, but he was practised, and he pressed hard with his little verbal traps (he was a
lawyer) and he was hot and eager enough to occupy Temple's
entire concentrated mind. Bauer delivered his lumpish, set 'final
appeal' to the prisoner's good sense. 'We know how long you have
been in France and what you are here for. You have been given
away by your friends – thoroughly identified. What we want is
the address of the house where you meet the others. Just that:
nothing more. Just that, and we will let you go. We are bound to

get it in a few days, because we have caught so many of your people. One of them is going to tell us. The first to tell us will be released. Why should it not be you? We would much rather it were you than one of the others. Why let them profit by your resistance? They will beat you to it – they have no scruples. You have resisted long enough; there is no point in it now. They betrayed you, quickly enough.'

But Bauer was a heavy brute: he could not disguise the enmity and dislike and cruelty in his eyes while he produced all this.

'Come, tell me at once. Let us have no more trouble. The address of the house?' He stood up, and looking at Reinecke's back he shouted again, 'The address?'

Silence would not do – too heroic altogether. Rocking his miserable head from side to side Temple blurted out, 'But I don't know. I don't *know* any people. I don't *know* any address. I've told you all I can. I was to meet him by the rock they said but I lost my way. I don't know any house. It was about watches from Switzerland.'

'Where did you meet the others?' snapped Reinecke, turning suddenly. There was a strange feeling of spite mingling with the familiar atmosphere of anger now. Temple breathed deeply, quick, gasping breaths.

'The address, quick,' shouted Bauer, coming up on his right-hand side.

'I don't–' moaned Temple, but the blow cut him short. He screamed as it hit him, a very loud subhuman noise. Oh, oh, oh. Keep close to him and he cannot hit so hard, close in, close in . . .

Then he was in the chair, hawking and choking for breath. He could hardly see. 'Where did you meet the others? Quick.'

'Where did you meet the others?'

'Where did you meet the others?'

Noises of denial, unknowing: helpless.

Reinecke was thoroughly roused now: his mood was changing fast. He was sweating. 'You fool, you fool,' he screamed into Temple's face, slapping him with the full swing of his arms. He fumbled in his desk for his special tool, but in his intense irritation he only hurled the thing down on Temple's head.

'Where did you meet the others?' shouted Bauer, far behind the metallic crash.

'Tell,' they said above him.

'Tell.'

He was on the ground, blubbering now, great shaking sobs: he could not speak.

'Tell.'

'Oh stop it, Bauer,' said Reinecke, empty and discouraged. Bauer aimed one blow more and went to the door. 'Bring the hose and clean this up,' he shouted to the guard. 'Get out, get out, get out,' he bellowed at Temple.

Outside the door Temple fell, and he heard Reinecke say, 'He is only a petty criminal. It is no use going on.'

That was the flower that was opening and glowing in Temple's mind. '*Nur ein gering Verbrecher.*' And the guard with the mop had been between them; Reinecke could not have seen him collapsing gently there along the corridor.

'It is no use going on.' He savoured the words, drawing them out as he repeated them deep in his secret mind.

'*Unnüss...*'

It was victory. He dared not say it yet, but he knew it, he knew it, and the great word echoed about in his head as if it had been shouted from the walls. Reinecke believed him: he had convinced Reinecke: he had won.

Now he would be left in his hole until they cleared him out

of the way. It would be Germany for him, in all likelihood, but there was the possibility of a camp in France – forced labour on the Atlantic wall. These thoughts began to form themselves in his mind, but they had scarcely reached the stage of words before they were wiped out – automatically erased. During this period (it seemed to have neither beginning nor end, in spite of his numbered tiles) his mind had built up curtains or partitions or censors – mechanisms that shut out everything but the essential matter in hand, the struggle with Reinecke's credulity. These other hopes and longings had flittered and flickered like bats whose existence one suspects outside a darkened window – never more concrete than that. Besides, it would have been terribly dangerous to have let them in.

In the same way, but to a far greater degree, he had buried what he had to hide and he had almost pushed it down so far that it was out of his own immediate knowledge: but once, lying there on his bench, he had deliberately dug it up and he had said, forming the actual words in his mouth, 'Number seven, rue de la Cloche d'Or. Knock five times, and three.' And at once he had felt that he had committed the sin against the Holy Ghost; he was appalled, as if everything had escaped and rushed out of him. He was terrified that it might happen again, but in spite of himself, as a punishment; that he might blab it out much as he pissed and shat and vomited when they savaged him upstairs on the dreadful days.

But he was past that now, thank God, thank God. He could remember it without terror, and now he could sleep: there would be freedom in his sleep. He had not known how entirely he had been concentrated, knotted up, to guard himself from even thinking in a way that might betray what he must hide. If he gave anything away, all the rest would follow: and every recollection of the outside world, all external reality, his own identity, they had all been suppressed, but suppressed with unimaginable force.

The effort that it had required: he felt it now, could measure it by the almost unlimited relaxation of his mind – it spread out, rolled out, admitting uncountable forbidden things as he consciously let down the barriers. He could see himself as something apart from pseudo-Temple: he was inhabiting at least part of his own mind again, and pseudo-Temple dwindled to the size of a small, largely fictitious person.

Pseudo-Temple was a little, silly unclean man with skins of pretence that Reinecke had peeled off one by one to reveal the vague shape of the abettor of shady deals, the man of no country but a café table, the minor black-marketeer, the perpetual underling, who had made a stupid failure of his one independent commission. He was a convincing creature: he was also a sort of general confession, for he represented some aspect of every mean, dishonest, ungenerous, discreditable act or thought or even temptation in Temple's life – a life not wanting in materials. He was a convincing creature, however. He had been born slowly, and in pain. It had all had to come out slowly, under blows and wicked pressure (the passionate intensity of those sessions when Reinecke had been almost sure that he had an Allied agent in his hands, a key that could open a great deal if it were properly twisted); it had had to come out slowly, for greater force – each discreditable detail wrenched out of him, the slow, unwilling revelation of what every man would wish to hide. He had had to go low: and yet not too low, for the character had to be acceptable to Reinecke, and Reinecke called for a certain small courage and resistance. The descent had stopped short of rock-bottom; but for all that, and although there were perhaps other mansions unexplored, it had been terribly expensive.

Reinecke had left Temple alone too soon; and in the dark – day and night unseen, the utter blackness of his cell – he had had the time to form the lines of pseudo-Temple's mind. This long period, which Reinecke had thought was softening his prisoner, bringing him to the edge of talking madness, had hardened pseudo-Temple's lines, and Temple was enclosed by his character so firmly that even when he was entirely reduced by interrogation, grovelling on the floor, he still shrieked with pseudo-Temple's voice. Some prisoners could not stand the darkness; they could not stand the deprivation of their sight, and when fifty or a hundred hours had passed they began to feel a desperate need to be re-attached to the visible world. The darkness and the silence pressed in and began to invade them with the enormous hallucination of present death. The invisibility of their bodies – even their hands before their eyes meant nothing – detached them from any reality: they experienced the horror of the gulf, and in a fortnight or a month they were ready for the question.

There was boredom, too. A man could be terrified, appalled by the unending darkness that was dissolving him, undoing his humanity; he could be terrified by the fumbling of a key in his lock, the line of light under the door; a ludicrous and ignominious craving for tobacco could assume almost the same proportions sometimes; but in some men boredom would work just as hard as these, and in conjunction with them. With neither night nor day the prisoner might sleep five hours or ten, he could not tell; and for the rest of the time he must sit or lie, counting his heart-beats or his breathing to feel that he was still in the flow of time, that time was not standing still for him alone, passing elsewhere, passing in the world, but leaving him on some strange, unheard-of island. And when he had said and repeated to himself all that he had to say, then there was the huge and overwhelming boredom. The man would be living on the shore of nothing: he would have nothing to do or say; he would see nothing; but still he would be alive. He would have to live interminably, with no sequence of events.

In spite of several proofs to the contrary, Reinecke (who was frightened of the dark) thought it infallible. Certainly it worked very often, but Temple too was one of the exceptions. It was not a question of virtue or moral strength, but rather of idiosyncrasy – the child he had been had loved the darkness, the kind black ally. And then again, he had needed all his time. He was a slow and imprecise thinker by nature, accustomed to wondering in vague concepts, colours and shapes, and to using emotion more than anything cerebral, and at first, not knowing from hour to hour when they might come for him, he had forced his intellect to work with feverish, exact rapidity; then, as the immediate tension slackened, he had gone over the whole thing again. Again and again he had worked out the pseudo-Temple, and the more he lived inside the man the more the details came – details not only of his life, but of gesture and turn of phrase. He had needed all the time that he was given, and he wasted none; only once a day he allowed himself his ritual counting of the tiles – not only was there a comfort of sorts in their unchanging series, but they provided the basis of an arithmetical divination in which odd and even had the force of omens. He had needed all the time; for such a character, to be of any use, had to be voluminous: he still had nine-tenths of pseudo-Temple quite unused, and even that was scarcely a sufficient reserve.

That was Reinecke's mistake, leaving him so long. It had provided him with his only arm, for he did not possess, never had possessed, that immense courage with which some men and women were able to defeat the inquisition. He had reckoned a certain passive fortitude the highest quality that he could make any claim to, or rather a dull endurance, and he had never attempted bravery – still less any spiritual domination of the brute. He had shrieked at the first blow and at all that followed. It was natural, and it was in character. No doubt it was ignoble; but it had worked. It had worked at last. He smiled again and almost said the words.

Yet it had been a dirty business, inhabiting that man. He had had to be so base for so long. Temple had no particularly strong moral sense, but even so he felt a revulsion against the ugliness of it – so much truckling, so much fawning and cringing for life, so much flattery and lies up to the neck. He was stained through and through with an indeterminate greyish yellow.

Something was coming between him and his triumph. The warmth of the glow in his mind was diminishing. The pseudo-Temple was his own creation, as much as if it had been one of his pictures, or a book that he had written (very like a book) and apart from the fact that in certain aspects it was a naked exposure of himself the whole was a reflection of the mind that fathered it. It was a pity that it was not a more heroic character. But there was nothing heroic in Temple, nor in his desperate war: there was no room for anything but expediency and given his background and the circumstances of his capture pseudo-Temple was the right character for him. It had worked: that was the only criterion. It had worked at last.

I can move now, he said. The obscure time of propitiation was over, and if he stayed lying motionless upon the ground he would grow so stiff that the first movement would be an agony. Already it was painful to tighten the muscles of his left arm and his shoulder: he tensed them for a moment to try and sank back with his face against the damp concrete. He breathed that builder's-yard and morgue-floor smell again, a smell like dust and yet humid, and he smiled again, secretly, into the ground. He was lying, as he had been lying all this time, on his face, lengthways down the cell, with his feet just clear of the arc of the door and his arms up as they had gone to break his fall; his hair was touching the wall and his left arm was doubled a little under his chest; his right arm cushioning his face, keeping it just off the ground. He would have to raise himself on his elbows, his left elbow first; then with a contraction of his belly-muscles he would bring his knees up, pivot round on his right hand and crawl over to the bench. It was the muscles of his stomach that he must spare as much as possible, for it was from there that the huge radiating pain began, the pain that shot pitiless fiery hooks from its red centre and with such power that his whole body would twist and jerk out of control: if once he provoked it into active life it would wrench him into those wild movements that made all the other pains vibrate and scream.

Now he tried again, ready for the inevitable protest of the stiffening weals on his shoulder. He came up on his elbows, and with his unseen face fixed in a mask of concentration, his mouth open and his eyes staring into the dark, he worked his knees under him. A roll over to his left side transferred the strain from his belly to his flank, and with his right hand spread out on the ground he was ready to crawl. But he waited there for a moment, equally balanced on his four supports, waiting to see if the great pain would begin. Besides, there was all the time in the world now; he could nurse himself – indulge in the slowest smooth creeping. There was all the time in the world for the four steps across to the bench.

Two; three; and very slowly the fourth step. He stretched out his hand for the wooden edge of the bench. It was not there. Groping out into the dark, his hand, which had been so unquestioningly sure of the feel of the wood, met nothing but the dark. For the instant he was stunned: then an intolerable suspicion seized him. *They had put him in another cell.* Something was terribly wrong. Quiet, now; quiet, he said to himself, but all the time the disrupting suspicion grew. He remained there without moving, with the surface of his mind blank: for the first time he felt the darkness as an enemy, stretching away to unknown limits, isolating him. Now in the elastic darkness the walls might be anywhere. They might advance, recede, or sweep together and crush him as he knelt. He felt blind, terribly blind, and he made a wild sweeping movement with his right arm, surging forward as he did so. His right shoulder jolted hard against the bench and he realised that he had been moving down rather than across the cell. His mind had wandered again: his orientation had let him down. It had happened before. He remembered it now as he clung to the familiar wood. He should never have forgotten it. Was he so bloody infallible? He was panting, and the beating of his heart struggled against his breath. He waited for a moment, collecting himself, and then, with no precaution, he climbed up on to the bench, still feeling for all the known shapes, the two knot-holes, the polished bolt-head, gripping hard and repeatedly upon them.

Fool, fool, to have let himself go so far: he was still trembling all over and his body was absurdly weak. To have had his triumph taken from him at that moment would have been more than he could bear: he had been so weak and vulnerable at that moment. He must take care, take care. His faculties were declining – they were probably declining more than he knew.

Sanity was coming back. What would it have mattered, any-

way, if they had put him in another cell? It was to be expected
soon enough, in any case.

Sanity was coming back, and the irrational tensions died away.
He eased himself into the curled position on his side – the primitive attitude of the buried dead – where he could lie and protect the centre of his pain, and he let the certitude of victory
come in again and spread; and he nourished it, the re-affirmed
and infinitely precious victory, now far more true.

Up to this time there had been only one end and purpose, and
it had necessarily shut out all other kinds of life; but now shockingly delightful visions thronged his head in spite of all that he
could do. Why should he not come out alive? Why should he not
come out at the other end alive? If he was once booked as a criminal he was almost clear of the firing-squad . . . had that been
the firing-squad, he thought in a very quick parenthesis, that he
had heard just before he woke? Certainly there had been the
sound of shots echoing in his head; but they might have come
from a dream. The likelihood was a camp in Germany. There
would be companionship, men he could trust. Would he survive
it? Surely he would survive it, an ordinary camp.

He was growing restless with the tumult of his thoughts. His
controlling sense was tired with the effort of trying to keep them
down to sober tranquillity and enjoyment – static enjoyment, the
enjoyment of the end achieved, of the thing itself, not of possi-
bilities. An uncontrolled imagining would soon run out into mad
extravagance. The mental effort took physical shape: his body
twitched and jerked; it would no longer lie in peace. He changed
position, but it would not relax: a nervous tic began to pluck at
the corner of his mouth, and as he put his hand up to his face
he let his mind have its way.

Perhaps it was still dangerous to let this ebullience come in unchecked; perhaps it was. He felt it wicked, certainly, but he let it come, a series of racing day-dreams, crowding as fast as the evil visions of delirium, but ecstatic. They all bore towards the idea of perfect felicity in a world at peace.

+

HIS ACCUSTOMED EAR caught the distant sound, and at once he pressed his head against the smooth iron bolt. The faint vibration sounded right into his middle ear: he interpreted it as one man and the trolley. Yes, one man and the steady rumble of the trolley. Was it the big new man or Richter? He could not tell.

He prepared himself, facing the door: if it was the new man he would have to stand. But when the door opened he saw at once through his screwed-up eyelids that it was Richter; and in the moments that passed (his eyes' use coming back to them) he could see that the guard's pale, glabrous face was shining with tears: they ran in shining tracks upon his cheek, and where he had wiped them there was a gleaming patch – the face itself was moist. Richter put down the dish and from his bent head the tears dripped like sweat. He did not speak, and the tears fell silently. Temple put his hand out towards the guard's arm, but checked the movement and looked quickly aside: he said nothing, and the door closed and the darkness came back.

Why? Why? But in this everlasting nightmare Temple's curiosity, still more his sympathy, had atrophied. So many things were commonplace in that world that a man's face wet with tears meant hardly anything at all. There was a certain attenuated kindness between Temple and the guard however. Richter had given him a handkerchief once, and lumps of bread at several times – two sugar cubes, and an aspirin. God only knew how this sympathy had grown up: they had not exchanged five intelligible words.

Perhaps the man's son had been killed. Perhaps his whole family had been wiped out in an air-raid. Temple had no idea of how the war was going. It had been bogged down in Italy when he had been taken; there had seemed no reason why it should ever stop. But he did know that Germany and German Europe was being bombed with tremendous force: even this place had been raided. That was long ago, however, and since those few whistling bombs he had heard nothing: the only sounds of war here were the shrieks of men, a terrible howling, and sometimes the volley of the firing-squad. He had heard other prisoners tapping out messages, at rare intervals, but he had never been able to understand them – he had not even tried very hard, all his energies being used up in his own struggle. Besides, he was not very intelligent, not sharply intelligent, clever and resourceful. His training and the habit of his mind was that of a painter, not called upon to make an intellectual response, and although in this school of war he had learnt to use his brain he still had to keep all his powers for the main issue. His chief quality was that particular sort of endurance that is necessary for a painter, an endurance not incompatible with emotional instability and a tendency to out-run the common range of feeling.

Richter had given him a piece of meat. It was unlikely to have been in the soup to begin with, though indeed the soup was less disgusting, less rancid than usual. It was made of swedes, stringy cubes filled with an insipid pulp that crushed out, leaving fibre to be chewed. This bloated a man's stomach, leaving him with a morbid longing for something hard; but today he had this bone and meat, so large that it took several minutes to get it down. The thought of Richter made a disturbance in his mind, however, and it did not die away very soon.

Now he lay with the meal inside him, as nearly satisfied as he

was ever likely to be in a German prison, and he began to compose himself for his long pause. He had learnt that after this
meal there was a space of time in which he would be left in the
most profound silence, and some internal clock enabled him to
measure this period with great accuracy. At all other times he
had to keep his attention on the stretch not to be taken
unawares: they might come at any other period in the day, and
he must have at least a moment's warning. And although this
continual watching was by now almost wholly unconscious (and
today irrational) still it was wearing, and still, like an officious
dog that could not understand that its zeal was out of place today,
it could prevent him from making a total escape. But during this
particular time, and above all on this particular day, he could
withdraw his sentries, or watch them withdrawing of themselves,
and now he could lie still, profoundly still – a stone at the bottom of a well.

   He was neither in ebullience now nor in a marked reaction:
he was quiet, and his thoughts were ranging to and fro with an
extraordinary and, as it were, a 'civilian' liberty, picking up unrelated incidents, visual images, snatches of action and dialogue,
colours and the smell of things. He was standing in the rain, a
drizzle that swept gently past the street lights in a drifting haze.
The black camber of the road shone in the wet, and on his right
the Thames flowed continually, black too, but its surface curled
with strange unevenness. Before him the embankment lights ran
away in a curve that made tears come into one's eyes, and in the
distance a lighted train and its reflection crossed the bridge. A
few rare lorries ran fast on the broad road, their headlights driving cones into the mist: a half-seen line of barges slipped down
the river on the other side, passing one by one through the red
pool of a neon sign. He had been waiting for an hour in anxiety

and doubt, and when he saw her coming, hurrying under the pavement lights, his heart lifted up and beat; his whole being was filled with a delighted, fragile elation, and he ran.

What was her name? Even now he could see her mouth held up and her happy face: there was rain on her hair, innumerable globules of rain like dew, and her mackintosh crinkled under his hands – the fragility of her shoulders under it. But what was her name?

Then it seemed to him that the young man's name was as unknown to him now as the girl's – the young man who had stood there, loving so much in the rain. But if there really was a chance of his living through, he thought, it was essential to re-establish a contact, some conviction of continuity, with that fellow, before it was too late. His sense of realities was damaged and uncertain, and although that had not mattered yesterday, when he might just as well have been a meaningless figure, a gratuitous act in a vacuum, yet now he was to fish up the line that linked himself to himself. Perhaps it was not necessary – perhaps it was not only rhetoric but presumptuous nonsense – but at least today, in celebration of a private victory, he would indulge in preparation for real life: he would determine who he was, and how he came to be that way. He would remember his past.

It was not easy to see the connection: it was not a connection that was obvious to him. Prison had acted like a forcing-house on his intelligence and cunning; he had been comparatively stupid, slow, unthinking, before he had been caught. It had also acted like the experience of a hard life all concentrated, breeding the mean harsh self-absorption of unhappy age with an unnatural speed. The man that went in (though tolerably experienced even then) was barely recognisable as the man that lay there now. He was barely recognisable to himself and sometimes he looked back with a cold furious contempt at the old weak time-wasting life-eating submissive slob Temple – unbelievably weak, submissive, and silly, *silly*; and sometimes survivors from the past looked at the present hard, competent animal with dismay and even horror.

CHAPTER TWO

PLUNGING BACK INTO these unfrequented memories was something like opening his eyes under water, or coming from a brilliant restaurant into a black street with unconnected lights of varying brilliance in it: quite apart from his 'professional' detachment from himself, he had never been a wanderer in the past. He had always lived minute by minute, in the present – a vivid life, in happiness or misery, like an animal's – and perhaps it was for this reason that he had so little sense of order in time.

In this first period of hesitation, this question of where to begin, a variety of images presented themselves like glowing balloons that he could reach out for as he chose; and presently he chose one that contained the shape and the colours of his first own room.

For it was himself as a child that he could remember best, or best recall: there was no difficulty in that backward jump of twenty years or more, nothing alien in that small body and more rounded face. He had been a commonplace and stupid little boy, but in many ways he was a better person then and certainly a more agreeable one to himself than he had ever been since. In spite of his somewhat thievish and mendacious disposition he had, like most other children, a very delicate sense of honour; and in those days he had a great deal of affection in his heart, affection for the asking. His emotions were brilliant, whole-hearted and direct: and unless he had some positive cause for sorrow, he was happy most of the time. It is true that punishment often came between him and happiness; yet not all punishment succeeded – far from it, for most of it, after the traditional beating, was imprisonment: 'Richard, go to your room.' He had an excellent temperament for that mild confinement, a solitary, idle and unfretting mind; and there was never a pleasanter place of apprenticeship than this room in Plimpton rectory.

There were thirty-nine bands of lyres and roses on the wall that ran from the door to the window. You could imagine them as the conventional bars of a gaol or the magnified wires of a bird-cage: they could also be seen as an abacus and a calendar. They were strips that his mother had pasted over the old, unsatisfactory blue-grey background for his birthday; the old background had frustrated him for as long as he could remember, with its foolish pattern of vague trellises that did not meet at the joints, and thus became doubly meaningless; but the strips had changed all this. Lyres and roses, and the roses were a lovely roughened crimson. The roses and the yellow lyres, which were entwined with the roses' leaves, formed a continuous pattern of whorls, now this way and now that; and yet as well as the pattern each rose and each stringed lyre was a thing in itself. In the first band there were forty-eight roses and forty-seven lyres: this treacherous difference put the calculation of the whole number beyond his powers, for although he delighted in a certain superstitious or perhaps numinous aspect of number he was useless with sums, and in this case he was reduced to counting, one by one. Not that this was any hardship: he spent hours and happy hours in plodding up and down the rows. These were often hours of imprisonment, when he was supposed to be deprived of the pleasure of running about and playing in the open. They did not seem to know that he never ran about voluntarily, at least not

when he was alone, as he always was in the holidays; nor that
he was utterly indifferent to the countryside – he could not tell
a blackbird from a rook, and did not care. In intervals of drawing
he was happiest (when he was at liberty) in mooning vaguely,
counting his slow, lethargic steps in the disused stable-yard,
carefully walking on the cracks, or staring for a pattern or a face
in the crazed roughcast of the wall. So although a kind of sharp-
ness rare in him had early warned him to feign reluctance to 'go
up to your room', he had in fact often been charmed to renew
the spell of slow, timeless incantation by counting. It was a room
that faced the west, and often his mild vacancy was illuminated
by the golden warmth of the declining sun: the wallpaper, the
room and that splendid light were intimately linked in his mind
– it was the recollection of delight.

And yet it was not always so delightful. He remembered a cold
grey morning there: but before he let his recollection go to rein-
habit that time and place he made an effort to find out its date.
It must have been a Monday, and the first Monday of the holidays. Probably the Easter holidays of his last year at his prepara-
tory school. Certainly it must have been at the beginning of the
holidays, because there was the misery of the school report in
its long envelope hanging over him; and it must have been a
Monday, for there had been no punishment, no recrimination
the day before. School had broken up at the end of the week,
and he could remember the extraordinarily enhanced feeling of
liberty when he came home and found that his father was away,
and that he would have his mother to himself until Sunday, a
closed season. But Sunday attitudes could never last, and on
Monday morning he was told to go up to his room. 'Richard, go
up to your room.'

It would be a wretched report, he knew; but he was only nineteenth in twenty-three, which was an improvement, and if they reproached him with smashing the wash-stand he could point to his drawing prize. But he felt nervous and cold; he wished it all over. He began to count off the days of the holiday, starting from the rose that marked the present date. The progression of weeks ran up and up, and on a Wednesday just before the beginning of the term they ran under a picture, to emerge on Thursday week. This picture was a little water-colour of Colpoys rectory, where his mother had been born; he had never been there, but he knew it exceedingly well from his mother's descriptions of her life there, and he could go confidently through the door under the Regency porch and know that if he went along the hall to the left of the stairs he would come to a door that led into a walled garden with a peacock in it. He was standing on an immense stretch of lawn running his finger down the iridescent sheen of the kind peacock's throat when the sound of a door opening below made him jerk. His father was still talking backwards into the room, '..., it is no use arguing, Laura. We must have it out in the open.' And then, loudly, up the stairs, 'Richard.'

He hurried down, his face composed in an expression of dutiful worry, and stood lumpishly in the accepted place, on the edge of the black hairy rug. It was a brown room, yet cold, and the two north-facing windows on his left, with their lower panes covered with translucent paper lozenges, gave on to a scraped grassplot. One was further obscured by a monkey-puzzle tree made of blue-black metal, but in the light of it his mother was sitting in a wicker chair, pretending to sew: she did not catch his eye.

His father enjoyed the due procedure of these court scenes, and it would be some time before the indictment began. Richard felt uneasy and low; but it was a situation that he could cope with – he did not feel desperate.

But then Mr Temple said, 'Have you seen this before, Richard?' and the bottom of his world fell out.

It was a pound note, with the houses of parliament on one side and the grave, bearded king on the other. He had taken it so long ago that he had forgotten it entirely, but in that moment the thrill and terror came back to him, and the impossibility of returning it to the Melanesian box, and the hiding-place under the board.

'No,' he said.

'Richard, dear,' said his mother anxiously; but she had joined the enemy and he had nothing to say to her – would not look in her direction.

The anger was battering around his bowed pale sullen head. It went on and on, booming, growing hotter in the face of dumb opposition, stupid opposition (he was too overwhelmed for any intelligent defence even if it had been possible), refusal to negotiate. He heard the creak of the wicker chair and his mother went quickly out of the room.

In his own place again he passed down through the stages until he reached the point where the reality of his sobs had gone, and although his face was still the face of a child crying, mouth open, eyes screwed up and breath checking in his throat and stomach, there were no more tears and in fact as he leaned his forehead against the cool glass of the window he had already begun talking to himself, although it was in a low, discouraged way.

Downstairs they were quarrelling: not that he could hear any words, but he was quite certain of it. It is impossible to say how he knew. It was certainly not through listening behind doors, for his mother had let him know that eavesdropping was dishonourable and he would have gone to great lengths to avoid it; but he knew it as completely as he knew that his parents did not like one another and that their united front was a kind of pious, necessary fiction, and that she was really on his side against a common enemy. He had gained none of this knowledge directly from her: he had only seen her once or twice, walking up and down behind the house alone after a disagreement, with her mouth compressed into a hard line and the look of an utter stranger on her face: it had terrified him, infinitely more than his father's rages. From this and from those thousands of minute shades of meaning and silences and changes of atmosphere that even the dullest child is aware of, he had reached a fair understanding of the case quite early in his life.

His father, Llewellyn Temple, was an unfortunate man who had succeeded in his early, inexplicable ambition to become a parson: he was of shop-keeping Liverpool-Welsh background, and without the help of any connection, liberal education or apparent vocation he had come to be ordained; and as a curate he had appeared at Colpoys rectory just at the time when Laura, Richard's mother, was in that unsettled, discontented state of agitation in which she would have married a mandrill if he had asked her – her sister Alice, seven years younger, had had her wedding that Easter; the lonely countryside was bare of suitable unmarried men; she was a pretty, high-spirited, highly-sexed woman who would be thirty in November.

The marriage and the interest of his father-in-law had procured Mr Temple the living of Plimpton, and to the day of his death (which happened not long after, when Richard was thirteen) he thought highly of himself for this advancement. But it did not bring him much happiness: even if he had been capable of much, Plimpton would not have brought it, for the place was quite unsuitable for him, and he was quite unsuitable for the place. It was in the deep country, the profoundly conservative and Tory country (Mr Temple was a Liberal and a passionate admirer of Lloyd George): the living was poor; the parishioners were used to a parson with private means and they detested anything new-fangled, such as democracy or enthusiasm. The rectory was isolated – no neighbours except the Hall – and more than usually inconvenient; it had no running water, no electricity, no gas.

Poor man, he was unhappy, and his unhappiness engendered more all round him: he certainly made his wife very unhappy, and she, heaping all her resentment of his coarseness, insensitivity, sexual inadequacy and increasing bad temper upon his Welsh background, made a very unpleasant symbol indeed of the poor Principality.

Richard caught the sense of this, of course – how could he escape it? – but it was not until he was coming along towards adolescence that he began to set it against a wider field of experience, the world outside the house, and to apply it to himself personally. It was a time of elections, and Lloyd George was touring the country: in the opinion of the Hall and of almost everybody else in the vicinity Lloyd George was a hateful person, untrustworthy and unscrupulous, envious, mean and glib; he was a dirty little Welshman, a vulgar, jumped-up attorney overflowing with jealousy and spite, bent on England's ruin. *A common little man*: the final damnation. He was Welsh and he was common. Yet Richard's father was a Welshman: and Richard was his father's son. Was there some unavoidable taint in this? Or did he perhaps belong to his mother's side?

He had always assumed that in the nature of things he was one of the better sort – he would have flung a handful of gold to the respectful peasantry before galloping on to the aid of the king. It was an assumption that he hardly questioned openly, for he was feeling little more than a hint of the immense force of English social pressures and he had only a vague suspicion about how they were to impinge upon him, only the most cloudy doubts about where he fitted in. He scarcely questioned the assumption; but now he would be glad to be confirmed in it, for underlying all this there was the remotely glimpsed possibility that he might be found to belong to the other side, that his mother might learn of this and cast him off.

And then what constituted a gentleman? He had always thought he knew – perfectly obvious – but as he grew older and more concerned he found that the manifold definitions that he had somehow acquired were often contradictory. He was a candid little boy, with remarkably little social sense, and he did not know how to distinguish the cant and the half-cant from the facts. Gentlemen were both good and bad, it seemed, pure and rakish; they were always polite and well-bred, yet look at old Mr Holden of the Hall, to say nothing of Henry VIII. Gentility had nothing to do with wealth, they said: but did it not? Amos came to do the heavy digging on odd days, and when he was preparing the big square bed he came across one strangely shaped seed-potato among the King Edwards that he was setting. 'That's an ash-leaf,' he said, showing it to Richard. 'It won't give you but four or five to one. A real *gentleman's* potato,' he added, in a respectful tone.

✦

SOMEWHERE IN THE present world there was a shuddering noise, a crepitation: could it have been gunfire, or a bomb? But it was not repeated and it only made the slightest check in his meditation, scarcely enough to change the current of his thoughts.

In a few moments his faint questioning had died away; he was back again, and he was remembering school – school, and how he had asked Gay about these things. In this case his visual image was so luminous and strong that if there had been a calendar on the wall of the room he saw he would have read the date: but in fact he could place this time exactly in time, because it was the term before the scholarship fiasco, and the very first day of that term, to be precise.

The first day of term, and yet the place had just the same atmosphere as if the school had never been closed – the ammoniac smell of little boys, the taste and feeling of chalk and dust, the combined odours of deal, ink, school-books and coke. It was a comforting atmosphere, for although the last day of the holidays had been sad, conventionally sad, it had been a holiday particularly full of domestic unpleasantness and punishment, and the old unchanging world of school had been very welcome to him, especially now that he was one of the big boys, in the headmaster's form and beyond the reach of any tyranny. Yet he had not been in the place more than a few hours before change and impermanence showed themselves and dispelled the warmth. The headmaster sent for him and said, 'Well, Richard, and how did you leave your father and mother?'

'Very well, thank you, sir,' said Richard, and the old gentleman gazed at him for some minutes. Mr Fielding was an old friend of his mother's father; he was indeed one of Mrs Temple's very few relatives, though exceedingly remote, and he had known her all his life. He was educating Richard for nothing (not that Richard knew this) and when he was speaking in a private, unofficial capacity he called him by his Christian name; Richard was therefore surprised and aggrieved when the headmaster went on, 'You know, my dear boy, your mother is very worried about your chances of a scholarship. I told her that I had got stupider boys through; but I was obliged to add that your chances were by no means as good as we could wish.'

These words provided him with three very disagreeable reflections at once: the first brought into his unwilling mind the fact that the comfortable everlasting world of school would have an end – that it might go on, but not with him, who must leave quite soon; the second, that his progress to a public school (which he preferred to leave in the vagueness of a remote future) was neither automatic nor certain; and the third, the least important, that he would be compelled to work much harder.

'Why are you looking so mumchance?' asked Gay.

'You must realise that Latin, not drawing or French, is the key to a scholarship,' said Richard, in an imitation of Mr Fielding's voice, as he plucked his books from the desk in the quietest corner at the back where they had elected to sit together. 'I am to go up in front,' he said, with much resentment, 'and am to stay in on Wednesdays to do Common Entrance papers. It's all' – (lowering his voice a little, for he was speaking of a great man) – 'ballocks.'

Of course it was all ballocks, he asserted: anyone could get a sons-of-clergy closed scholarship. Gill had got one, and Gill notoriously wetted his bed – Gill had warts. Besides, everybody went to a public school: it was part of the process and nothing else was thinkable. Most would try for scholarships: Gay was going in for a Winchester scholarship; but he would go there, whether he got it or not. Only cads went to common schools – indeed, they were *called* cads' schools.

It was absurd to think of Gay failing, or Gay's friends, for that matter: Gay was one of those naturally fortunate creatures who never fail. He had bright blue eyes in a round and jolly face, and he did not give a damn for anything. He could have been one of the chief bloods of the school if he had chosen, but he was not at all competitive, and he would not take even cricket seriously. Even so, he remained one of the most popular boys there, and Richard was lucky to have him as a particular friend; for Richard was not a popular boy. Perhaps no boy is ever much liked unless his values are just the same as those of his contemporaries and unless he has the same sense of tact, which Richard had not. There was a curious piece of iron, for example, that lay on a shelf in the hall; one day Richard took it, because he had always coveted its spiny shape. He showed it to his friends, but after some initial excitement they had hesitated and then they had withdrawn their moral support. Many things could be taken, such as elastic bands and things from the laboratory, but somehow meteorites were not among them and they all knew it, except Richard. There were many things like that that he got just wrong. But his unpopularity, at its worst, was never more than a mild unpopularity, being mitigated by his good looks and his courage: he was far more aggressive than Gay, and it would not do to meddle with him. Most little boys are cowards, and when they fight it is upon the tacit understanding that neither will go too far; but Richard could not be relied upon to keep in bounds.

He and Gay had always got along well together, but it was only in the last year that they had been such close friends, drawn together, it must be admitted, by the abominable vice of sodomy. Gay very much admired Richard's talent for drawing, and Richard had illustrated most of his books: Richard also made drawings for Gay's primitive, mediæval jokes – some few of them were clean, but Gay's mind was very like a sink, and most of them had to circulate under double oaths of secrecy. Not that Gay was exceptional in this; Grafton was a rather dirty school at that time, and it was not particularly Gay's influence that had turned the top form into a little suburb of Sodom – a cheerful and unselfconscious Sodom, however, for it was an unusually happy school.

It was from Gay, too, that Richard had caught the habit of reading. But it was unfortunate for Richard that Kipling should have been Gay's favourite author, for Kipling's curious image of the world was not the most reassuring one for him. To enjoy Kipling you need a strong stomach, a certainty of the Herrenvolk's existence, and an unshaken conviction that you belong to it.

And Gay had always been a fount of worldly knowledge. Long before this, when they were both little boys in the lowest form, he had been able to give Richard some idea of what was *the thing* in that particular community: in the kindest way he had said, 'You don't want to be a blooming arse with your French, you know, going on like a foreigner. The chaps are laughing at you.' Laura Temple had been educated at Lausanne; she spoke beautiful French and had taught Richard very early and very well, but even after he had been at school for some time he had still not grasped the atmosphere of the place better than to go on angering Mr Frisby and the rest of the class with this odious perfection.

Richard would never make such a gaffe now – he was too well attuned, at last, to the feelings of the upper school – but Gay remained his authority for nearly all matters outside it. Gay could explain books; Gay could explain dark passages. And yet in this relationship there was no striving for place, no first and second fiddle; it was a singularly sweet mutual liking, and the wearisome domination that is part of so many adult friendships was not there at all. They could speak to one another openly, with an ingenuous lack of dignity that would never come again.

When Gay had helped him move his books they went out to a place beyond the cricket pitches called Starve-Acre, where they had the habit of sitting upon a bank in the evening sun. Richard was carving a lump of chalk into the likeness of the school porter while Gay told him of the events in his holidays, which were always filled with parties, picnics, excursions and so on, because he had a large family and his people lived in a thickly-populated part of the country – and because they were rich. Richard was deeply engrossed with the porter's ear, but through it he heard Gay's spirited imitation of his aunt, shrieking in a cross falsetto, '. . . a dreadfully vulgar man in a screaming bookie's suit.'

'But wasn't that Brown's father?' asked Richard.

'Yes. But she didn't know it at first. Then she did.'

'She didn't mean he was really common?'

'Of course she did. He is, too.'

'But he's a colonel.'

'What's that got to do with it?'

'Can officers be common, Gay?'

'Oh yes,' said Gay, with conviction. 'There are some rotten regiments, who just get the dregs . . .'

He went on; but Richard, half listening and half reflecting, found that one of the props of his tentative system, that of gentility by office, was giving way. Gay was going on from the Army Service Corps and the like to bodies of his own invention, such as the Brothel Corps, and he was enjoying his own wit to a high degree when Richard interrupted him and said confidentially, 'But I say, Gay, that's not the same for parsons, is it?'

'Oh no,' said Gay, as earnestly as he could manage, 'parsons are always all right, I dare say.'

CHAPTER THREE

H E DID NOT win any scholarship, not even the smallest; the recollection of this time arose cold and dark in his mind – the first adult, whole and irremediable unhappiness. It mingled with that of his father's death, though this was an emotion that also overflowed into diffuse awe, agitation and excitement, as well as sorrow and dread of the void; and the visual image for both was the same. It was the cross-piece of his window, black against the shining grey of the sky, while the cold twilight filled the room behind him and all comfort drained out of it: he sat there so long on the floor gazing up in that wretched time between the examinations and the results and so long when all his worst suspicions (although they had been exaggerated to take off the curse) became the facts that he was to go to bed with; and in the same way he sat there some weeks later, in the same silent, cold, uncoloured light, during those unending hours when there were strangers in the house and his father was to be buried.

Llewelyn Temple had been kind when the news came. 'Well, I'm sorry, Richard bâch, but there it is. Perhaps it is all for the best. We must try not to be too disappointed.' It was the kindest thing he had ever said, and the sudden spurt of tremulous affection that Richard had felt then had not died away in twenty years.

Perhaps it was all for the best: it was certainly not entirely for the worst. At all events it turned out to be nothing like the terri-

fying fate that he had imagined. Before the new rector came to
take his dead father's place they moved to a cottage within bicy-
cling distance of Easton Colborough, and he went to the local
grammar school.

The school at Easton had remained very much what it was
when it was founded, some four hundred years before, a place
of instruction for the boys of the town and the immediate countryside. Its meagre endowment had tempted no man's cupidity,
and it had neither become a minor public school nor part of the
state's system of education. It was a grammar school: the chief
subject was grammar, Latin grammar, and the boys bawled their
way through *hic haec hoc* as their predecessors had always done.
The great part of the school was housed in one vast barn-like
hall which had three classes in it, three separate classes with
three masters and three distinguishable pandemoniums; the
noise in this hall seemed to be quite chaotic, but somewhere in
the din there would always be a pack of boys going through their
hic haec hoc. The cobwebs in the bare rafters had stirred to this
noise for centuries, and it was not likely that the school would
change its ways now: in all these years it had never turned out a
classical scholar of any reputation, but perhaps that had never
been its intention – although up to the end of the eighteenth
century it still sent a few boys on to the university. It was certainly not its intention now. Its intentions, as far as it was conscious of having any, were simple and direct: for a small fee it
sold a small amount of information. It taught the boys a certain
amount of Latin and a little history and geography: it prepared
them for no examination, and it no longer had any notion of their
going any further; it took the boys in at any age their parents saw
fit to send them and it kept them until they were thought wise
enough, which was usually between the ages of fourteen and

sixteen. The cleverest boys might come to read Cicero or Ovid with some degree of ease, though scarcely with enjoyment, but the dull boys would learn nothing but their copy-books and the majority went off with little more than the three Rs. However, this satisfied the town; and certainly the boys were a very decent lot, upon the whole. They were far more tolerant than the boys of Grafton, and they received him without any of the inquisition or ill-treatment that he had dreaded. They formed an almost classless society, in which parents' status was accidental and of little importance; and in this society accent counted for nothing – some of the country boys spoke broad and some of the town boys spoke with a nasal whine, but it made no odds: after a week it was imperceptible.

In its way it was a very restful school. There were no games at all except those which the boys played by themselves for fun, and with scarcely a sigh Richard abandoned the tightly-organised ritual of cricket and football (as well as the more sophisticated delights of Grafton) and took to the ancient, common, childish games of marbles (called alleys here), conquerors and tops. He had never spun a top in his life before, but presently he learnt, being taught by a broad-faced, kind, hoarse boy, a love-child who was brought up with the son of the farm where the love-token had passed, and who looked exactly like a Flemish Boor.

Out of the vagueness of musing recollection, while he was trying to build up the brown planes of Jocelyn's face there came a sudden precise detailed brilliant image of the market at Easton Colborough, of himself standing there with Jocelyn and the boy who shared his desk – Ham, the posthumous son of a turncock, a mother's boy with a girlish nature and a sweet and gentle look. It was the half-holiday, and Richard was coming from Miss Theobald's drawing-class through the market-place, where the

week-long desert was cram-packed with sheep, pigs, cattle, poultry, bright red ploughs, blue harrows, pedlars, hucksters, bone-
setters and respectable long-established stalls that sold harness,
saddles, brasses, girths, curry-combs and plaited whips.

It was one of those days full of limpid air, when white clouds
pass across the sky, and the light changes. They were standing
on the north side of the market, between the part where the
horses were and the outer range of stalls. On the right there was
a flimsy trestle set out with cards of celluloid studs and cuff-
links, brilliantly striped, penknives with many blades, patent
glasscutters and frail inventions for slicing beans; and on the left,
on the other side of the cobbled way, in a pen by himself stood
an enormous horse, a bright bay Shire gelding with his mane and
tail done up with scarlet ribbons. Jocelyn, the boor-like boy,
stared with love and admiration at the horse; Ham and Richard,
turning from the bean-slicers, looked at it without much understanding, and while they stood there the horse straddled and
staled. It stared intently straight before it, and from its huge
extruded mottled yard gushed a foaming jet of piss, inordinate
in quantity. Jocelyn laughed, chuckled hoarsely: he was
delighted. He said, 'You ought to draw him. He would be worth
drawing.' Ham walked on, blushing; but Richard stared – he was
amazed, not only by the particular grandeur of this horse, but
also because he had never seen a gelding stale before, and
because it was indeed worth drawing. Partly because of its size
and its rigid, unaccustomed pose, partly because of its dangling
penis (so startling) and partly because of some quality of the light
he was suddenly seeing a horse for the first time – an intimation
of the ideal horse.

They moved on, lingering past a man who wished to sell them
a gold watch wrapped in a ten-shilling note for sixpence, provid-

ing they could tell the right packet from the packets full of chaff, and dawdled through the penetrating reek of swine to the herbalist's, where a grave, attentive crowd looked at a picture of a transparent man, or rather of a partially transparent man, for where none of his vitals were concerned he was solid enough: only here and there his purple liver, his spleen and bowels showed through. His bearded face, however, with its serious and evangelical expression was scarcely one that could rightly belong to an undressed body, far less to a transparent one; it floated on another plane, surrounded by pinned-up shrivelled plants, a dusty halo; and there were other bunches round the body below, with ribbons leading from them to the parts they healed, and with a wand the herbalist pointed them out as he described the diseases. Rising of the lights; strangury; horseshoehead and head-mouldshot; dropsy, marthambles, the strong fives and the moon-pall; stone; gravel; pox. Some of the audience were willing to pay their money early on – there were shillings and half-crowns held up in the air – but the herbalist would not stop or spare them anything; in a high, unfriendly, didactic voice he went right on through cancer, consumption, bloody flux, the quinsy and worms. Jocelyn and Ham, shocked and fascinated, stayed on; but Richard was still amazed by his discovery of the horse and he was unreceptive; and as he also had a message to deliver he left them standing there.

He went up one of the steep lanes that led towards the High Street, and as he turned the corner the bawling of the calves, the squealing, baaing, roaring and shouting of the market place died to a mild composite hum: only by some freak of acoustics a single voice pursued him up the lane, calling out with passionate conviction, 'Honest Bill Podpiece. Honest Bill Podpiece gives everyone a chance. Some has a watch, some has chaff. I will not deceive you, gents: pick the right one and you get a valuable prize. Come on, gents, a gold watch for a tanner – you only have to pick the right one, gents . . .'

He turned into the broad, mild splendour of the High Street and stood looking up and down it, for his message was to Mr Atherton, who would be painting there: on the left was the barbican, then the pink brick and white stone court-house with its curving flight of steps and the royal arms in its pediment, then a long row of bow-fronted shops; on the right the Harp and Crown with its enormous sign, the Palladian corn-exchange and the little Regency theatre, followed by a recessed line of the grander houses of the town, with white steps, green doors and brass knockers. The pavement in front of these houses was remarkably broad, wider than the street, and this allowed one to see round the ascending curve to the Norman towers of Saint John's, which closed the vista. Mr Atherton's easel was there, far off on the corner of Butter Lane, and the back of his canvas could be seen, a sudden white square against the soft, diversified background; from time to time little knots of people gathered behind it, to look with that invariable penetrating knowing glance from the canvas to the view and back again. But there were not many of them, and they did not stay – the town had known Mr Atherton, man and boy, for more than seventy years: he was an Academician, and they were proud of him; furthermore he had a way of lunging backwards and stabbing the air (and sometimes those who bored him) with a loaded brush.

It was to avoid this that Richard stepped forward and delivered his message: Miss Theobald was sure that Mr Atherton would not forget Mrs James at five o'clock.

'Oh, it is you, is it? Thank you, thank you, Richard,' he said. 'I shall not forget her. What did you say her name was?' He stared

shrewdly at his picture, with both Richard and Mrs James receding from his mind: he could pin the floating tower by making the
tree much more determined. He worked else to the easel for five
minutes and then stood back again. 'No. It was a mistake,' he
said, resuming the low monologue that always accompanied his
painting, 'a bloody error – should have left it alone – that silly
green – vexed. Now I shall have to start again. Why did the old
fool daub on the green?'

Richard gazed at the picture. The High Street itself did not
move him – the High Street pure remained unseen: but the High
Street on canvas, filtered through Mr Atherton, stirred him profoundly – once he had seen it in pictorial terms it acquired a new
prestige. The picture seemed to him excellent: he could not see
why Mr Atherton was unsatisfied. And indeed no one could deny
that the picture was wonderfully accomplished, from the technical point of view: as for the Venetian light that bathed Easton
Colborough's corn-exchange, Richard thought it a great improvement. But whereas Richard at that time knew nothing about
Guardi, Mr Atherton did, and he turned away from his easel with
a sigh. 'I shall not do any more today,' he said. 'Would you like to
come back with me? We can do a little drawing until this woman
arrives.'

They walked off, with Richard carrying the easel respectfully
and attentively, a symbol of their religion, and at the next turning they left the gentle business of the High Street for the tree-
lined quiet of Hog Lane and the alley labelled No Thoroughfare
that led to the green garden door in the wall.

'Mind the easel in the fig,' said Mr Atherton. 'That reminds
me, I must tell you about fig-tree sap as a medium. You use the
milk from the young shoots on the south side. Cenino says . . .'

They came to the door, a lumpish green door in a brick wall

his belief in hard work as something of more than rational value; and by hard work he meant primarily drawing, all kinds of drawing, from plaster cones and prisms to the most elaborate anatomical studies. In an appropriate, tall cupboard he kept a skeleton, mounted upon lead-alloy wire; he encouraged Richard to draw it from every angle, and he often joined in the holy exercise himself. But he also attached great importance to the crafts of the studio, and Richard ground colours until he was first blistered and then calloused from the wear of the pestle. He grew intimately acquainted not only with linseed, sunflower and poppy-seed oil, egg tempera, wax emulsions and so on, but also with the more recondite preparations of honey, rabbit-skin size and Armenian bole; and he was obliged to make his own stretcher and stretch his own canvas upon it before ever he was allowed to begin to lay on the paints that he himself had ground. Mr Atherton could do all these things well: his manual dexterity could have earned him a comfortable living as a handyman if a revolution had made it necessary, and he valued it highly in others. His aesthetics were much simpler, being summed up in the expression, 'Theory is all stuff.' The only exceptions to this broad statement were some parts of Reynolds's *Discourses*; but as far as Richard was concerned no exception was called for – he worked for the delight of working and wasting no time in asking why some shapes, colours, textures made him happy. Indeed, Mr Atherton had never had a harder-working pupil, one who came voluntarily all through the summer holidays; and once, when he found that Richard was unable to construe Sir Joshua's *serpens nisi serpentem comederit non fit draco*, he warned him solemnly that he must not neglect his Latin and his sums, and all that sort of thing, as being of the greatest use in after-life.

So his time went by, in a golden haze, and memory did not

serve to break it down into its elements: it remained an infinitely distant period of normality, when happiness was in the natural order of events. In those days he passed continually from one world to another (or even between three, if his low school, his upper-middle-class Philistine home and Mr Atherton's studio were all to be set at equal intervals) but it scarcely worried him, and if at odd moments he had a suspicion that he did not entirely belong to any one of them, that he did not quite seem to belong anywhere, it did not then seem to have any immediate importance. After all, his mother was always there at home; school was not at all unpleasant, but for the confinement and the waste of time; and he could at least aspire to Mr Atherton's spacious way of life.

In this golden haze he could not now distinguish near and far: he could scarcely make out its most general chronology, even after probing back to link events with the seasons in which they occurred; but it must have lasted for years – perhaps for three. Most of the time, as he remembered it, seemed to have been summer; and certainly it was summer when first he began painting the backgrounds to Mr Atherton's big commissioned canvases. The umber landscape came back to him, the first one he ever did, with its four brown trees in the distance: then again he was painting Mrs Foster's shoes, handbag and parasol, left for the purpose; and at another time Apollo's hams, under the admiring gaze of Colonel Apse, who was to occupy the middle of the heroic picture, a more gentlemanly Mars, and who posed to that effect, in moistened drapery, all August through. But there must have been winters too, for he saw the lonely pond again, and felt the thin ice bow as he skated round and round in the gathering darkness. He was alone and it was perfectly silent except for his skates and the strange pervasive sighing of the ice as it bent; the

CHAPTER FOUR

Y ET QUITE SUDDENLY and with no clear warning his life
went bad: in those days he could not see why it was so
nor tell exactly how it began, yet now as he looked backwards the division was as sharp as that between light and dark.

The first, the most obvious but by far the least important
cause was that by mere seniority he was moved up into the headmaster's form. Old Mott had the usual schoolmaster's perversion
and he was an ugly man with a cane; Richard was a fine juicy
boy, which was provocation enough, but his ignorance of Latin
was also a real, almost legitimate, offence to Mott, who, with a
dirty gleam in his eye, began to call him out almost every day.
There had always been a great deal of beating at Easton school,
but up to that time Richard had escaped: he would have gone
on escaping, however much he excited Mott, if the man, who
was very close to the shopkeeping gossip of the town, had not
heard things that made him sure that Richard would have no
protectors to resent this treatment, and that in any case he would
not be staying long.

When it became clear that Richard was to be this year's scape-
goat, there was a movement away from him, as from one who
attracted ill-luck. One or two of his friends continued to sympa-
thise with him, and to the very end Ham would whisper him the
word; but few of the boys were really on his side, and as Mott
beat to an audience, being sensitive in his own way to public
opinion, this meant that he was beaten more often and more

viciously. Before this time he had been neither particularly liked nor disliked in the school, but now he became unpopular. He was aware that he was cut off from the support of the class: it is a wretched thing to learn that the unfortunate are often disliked, but this was almost the only thing that he did learn in this school, apart from the fact that he had much more fortitude of a passive kind than he had known, and that the limits of endurance were a great deal farther off than seemed likely.

+

THE DARK STAGNANT air of the cell vibrated with a tremor so deep that it lay somewhere between feeling and sound, a huge explosion far away. Three times it was repeated, with intervals of great solemnity; and while Richard Temple was still poised up on the echo of the third there was a burst of fire much closer to – not quite so close as the usual firing-squad perhaps, but he put it down to that until it grew ragged, no longer volleys but an almost continuous firing that went on for several minutes. Nothing but percussive noises ever came down here from the outside and when the firing stopped it stopped without any explanatory shouting or the stamp of troops: the rare intrusions from the other world were generally inexplicable and as they were always irrelevant to Temple's own battle in principle he did not try to account for them – he had little more curiosity left than he had humour, and what curiosity he had he dared not indulge: a dispersion of energy. But today the case was altered: he wondered, surmised, brought up ingenious explanations; but if he had hit upon the truth he would have run mad with mingled joy and even greater apprehension.

The Allied armies were deep in France: the French forces of the interior had risen and they were attacking from within, disrupting the Germans' communications and harassing their retreat. In this region their initial attack had been very successful and the Germans were in a state of confusion: in some places they were withdrawing without a shot, abandoning everything; in others they were systematically destroying their fortifications, stores and records and killing their prisoners before pulling out; in others they retreated with lorry-loads of paper and as many hostages as they could lay their hands on; and in others again the different commands acted without any attempt at co-ordination, some following one policy and some another. The situation was worst wherever there were large numbers of those armed French collaborators called Miliciens; they were vicious, stupid people in any case, and now they were quite desperate, out of hand, panic-stricken, and dangerous. Here in Villefranche, a strategically unimportant town, the garrison was largely made up of these creatures, together with a half-company of Vlassov's Russians and a few Mongols; they were in a state of frantic disorder; for a small local group of maquisards, over-excited by the blowing-up of the ammunition-dump at Combray, had begun a totally unexpected attack. Even the Germans were infected by this feeling of being trapped: only half an hour earlier they had been at peace, at a sort of back-line peace; the war had been a hundred and seventy kilometres away and even if the worst should happen the road to the north was perfectly secure: now everything was turned upside down. There was no order any more.

+

RICHARD DID NOT divine this, however; his final answer was army exercises, and some time after the noise had died away he returned. That is to say, he sank back to the edge of the place where he had been interrupted; but he stayed for a long time on this edge alone, without advancing. For although in this course of identification, or re-identification, he was dealing only with the truth, not with apology nor scarcely with comment even, and although he was no longer moved by old shame and humiliation (the last things to die in recollection) being so far removed, yet still there was this unbearably painful area. With him remembrance was largely a matter of images which followed one another with a logic of their own (not unlike dreams) and although many of them were vague enough, filled out with words and exposition, some were extraordinarily brilliant – the sudden sight, from a darkened place, of a person, or a head, or a whole series of incidents that would go on, outside his control and in a wonderfully vivid light, so that every colour and detail was there unblurred; and in the case of his mother he could not permit this undisciplined recall. The most he could do, even now, with all his removal and all his adult experience and nearer comprehension, was to state the facts, in an impersonal, almost statistical manner, with no dwelling upon them and above all no seeing the things he talked about – no true recall, indeed.

It had been an unsavoury nine days' wonder in Easton Colborough and it had caused a great deal of talk; but it was not really very rare or extraordinary and if Mrs Temple had not been a clergyman's widow she would have been quietly shut up with very little of the noise that in fact occurred. Briefly, when she reached her critical years she took to drunkenness, and from drunkenness to promiscuity: her mind, her nature, even her heart became estranged.

Everything had been against poor Mrs Temple; everything, her frustrated married years and her restless widowhood; and she had retired from life too young. The cottage that her brother-in-law had found for her was dark, poky and damp, and it did not have a single one of the amenities of civilised life – but Canon Harler had not been concerned with her convenience: only with getting her firmly anchored at such a distance from his own home that she could not be a burden nor her poverty a reproach to him. (On the same reasoning he had refused to let her touch the capital of her little trust-fund to send Richard to a better school: besides, he had never approved of her marriage and would lend its results no countenance.) It is ludicrous to cite earth-closets, well-water and paraffin-lamps; but they were not without their effect, particularly as Mrs Temple was a pretty woman. She felt that this incessant, ineffectual charring (for however she worked the place could never be anything but a rural slum) was adding, as indeed it was, to the irreparable insults of time; and this caused one resentment more.

And she was unfortunate in her neighbours. She and Richard now lived on the other side of Easton Colborough, nearly twenty miles from Plimpton, and in a sparsely inhabited region. The big house belonged to a man who only came down for the shooting, with expensive parties of City friends; and the distant parsonage contained a hard-faced celibate who trailed incense and the smell of candles and required her to call him Father. Otherwise, there was only the one very large farm, run by a sharp, efficient businessman, and the labourers' cottages, in the immediate vicinity. The hearse-like Daimler from Plimpton Hall came winding through the narrow lanes from time to time, and a few women came to see her from Easton Colborough, but on the whole she was very lonely and when Richard began to spend all his free time at the studio she felt that she was giving away her last beautiful years for nothing. She suffered much from his pre-occupation with Mr Atherton, and in her moments of depression Richard seemed to her a selfish boy, taking with both hands and giving nothing.

He had of course no conception of the extent or even the nature of her sacrifices: but equally she had no idea of the degree to which she was the centre of his universe. You do not praise the daily sun nor say thank you for your daily bread, unless they seem precarious. She did not know how he regarded her as a fixed principle (although in fact she was changing almost as much as himself, even before the disaster occurred), nor that almost his whole way of life was an attempt to come over so firmly, so recognisably on to her side that she could never throw him off as she had thrown off his father.

Laura Temple was a woman who really needed a husband, a proper husband; and when the people of Easton Colborough had said she would marry again it was their way of saying that she was an eminently feminine woman, that in no bad sense she was particularly fitted for marriage (being incomplete alone), and that she was likely to attract a husband. The most censorious mind could not at that time have accused her of the least impropriety, but a naturally warm temperament is clearly different from a flaccid indifference, and they said, 'Mrs Temple will marry again.'

Later it was, 'It would be nice if she were to marry again and settle down,' or even, 'Somebody ought to find a husband for Mrs Temple.' Then there was a silence about her, the significant silence of the high-principled, which was soon broken, however, by whisperings, at first indignant and incredulous, then stern and angry and more and more medical in their nature.

She was terribly open to her body's betrayal: she suffered very much from headaches and turmoil of spirits whose nature she could not determine, and once casting about for some relief from her migraine and depression she tried a glass of cooking-sherry.

It was not very good to taste, but it worked. She had no head for alcohol, and she never acquired much of a tolerance, so that even on her income she was able to become an alcoholic – rows and rows of South African sherry (it was two shillings a bottle then) hidden in cupboards, behind bushes, clanking on the out-house shelves. Her progress was unbelievably rapid, and the dis-solution of her personality was a matter of weeks, not of years. Sometimes it was replaced by an extraordinary 'modern' substi-tute, hard, brassy and confident; sometimes it was replaced by nothing but a fog with no one behind it, an impersonal body of suffering; and sometimes, though rarely, she would reappear, herself whole and gentle, and it was inexpressibly painful.

The disease ran fast; yet although he did not see or know the half of it, this period seemed to Richard a boundless everlasting state, in which anxious misery became the normal condition – grey apprehension at the best, in the intervals between crises. It went on and on, from the time when he first found her incapable, her words a slurred mixture of incoherent dignity, lachrymose pre-cepts and weird jollity, until the last day when they took her off in a terrible drugged-sober state, quite withdrawn, yellow-faced, huddled in an old black dress with her peroxide hair straggling its dead colour over the dusty lightless cloth.

The course was rapid indeed; but not so break-neck that each gradation did not prepare him for the next. In some ways the very beginning was the most difficult time, for then he could not tell how remote from normality this was – was his feeling that everything was hideously astray quite justified? The bald police-man, shining on the cottage step without his helmet and stand-ing there to tell him that 'she was taken poorly at the bus stop' said it with an appearance of normality. Everybody was still polite: the world continued, apparently unmoved.

But there is external and internal normality, and here too it was the beginning that was the most difficult: his inner world cracked irreparably when first he heard her singing a dirty song. It was more destructive than many of the later stages; more wounding, for example, than the lewd accusation about Mr Atherton, which came to him prepared. Besides, they were shouted out by an enemy, a queer rakish manifestation of another self that seemed to possess her, invade her, from time to time, an intruder from another, later generation and another, unknown, class: the same which caused her to dye her hair. This being was openly hostile: shrieked 'Prig' at him and smashed things: but it lacked authority and even its most evilly calculated words – *dirty little Welshman* or *Liverpool guttersnipe* – caused no more than a dull wound; and some of the time it was afraid of him.

Later he realised that he had not seen or understood many aspects: the odd bookie or bookie's clerk, the vague men hanging about the shadows, they never meant anything. He was protected by his own ignorance (forty-five was old age for him) and by people's kindness – a kindness which had at one time puzzled him. Very early he had noticed that the occasional invitations to proper Easton Colborough houses had stopped, invitations that had always been very irksome to him, by the way; but in the town he still sometimes met the people, and they would speak to him with a particular earnestness, trying to inject an unusual degree of sympathy or benevolence into words that of course remained utterly commonplace.

It was a very difficult case for interference – no family doctor, no near relatives who could be spoken to and no one with the authority to write to them. Mrs Temple had no close friends in the town, and those of her acquaintances who might have come forward in any other circumstances could not in these. There were eccentrics by the dozen in Easton Colborough and certifiable lunatics like Miss Hodson, who sometimes ran about in her nightgown with her long hair trailing down her back, and they were all very kindly treated – perfectly acceptable. But the good women would not tolerate the least unchastity: a hint of riggishness with labourers wiped Mrs Temple's name out of the list of human beings. The nightmare ran on, therefore, a longer time than would be thought credible: yet it had its end – ignominious and violent, but still an end, as far as anything can have an end.

+

BY THE KINDNESS of his friends, Richard was sent almost directly away to France, to live as a resident pupil in the house of a Monsieur Durand, a respectable and conscientious person long known to Mr Atherton. He was the only pupil; no one in the house spoke a word of English, and the change could hardly have been more complete. His window looked out not on to the lush green of Grimmond's meadow, but on to a stark plain of vines: the light that surrounded him, the air he breathed, the food, drink, language, smells, manners – all these were entirely different. And yet it is possible that even without this immense assistance he would have recovered fairly soon: one of the most striking sights upon a sheep-farm is the castration of the ram-lambs; they undergo their mutilation with a few little inward groans and stand as it were amazed for one or two minutes; then they start to graze again. And although they do not play that day, nor the next, after some time they do, almost as if the thing had never been done to them. In any case, after the mingled shock of travel and exhaustion was over, Richard found himself as much at home in this new house as ever he was likely to be, familiar with its hours, the arrangement of his room and the distance from this place to that, and he was not without taking pleasure from it.

During his life there, other pupils appeared from time to time – once there were as many as four together – but they usually stayed only a few months, to cram for a Beaux Arts examination; and the regular inhabitants were Monsieur and Madame Durand, Fifine the maid, and himself. It was difficult to believe that the desiccated, fussy, pedantic Monsieur Durand could ever have been a boon-companion of Mr Atherton's youth, an habitué of the Lapin Agile and a friend of some of the best, most hopelessly disreputable painters in Paris before the '14 war; and looking at his competent, frigid, official pictures it was difficult to believe that he had ever seen any painting since Puvis de Chavannes – difficult, that is, for one who had no experience of the chilling force of virtue. Monsieur Durand was nine parts dead from self-imposed rectitude and conscience; but he was a capable teacher of official art, and in his dry, pompous manner he was not unkind. (He looked like a piano-tuner.) Madame was less amiable, a big, strong, moustachioed woman with too great a love for economy; she was an ardent church-goer, and there were several others who looked just like her in the local charitable society. The sight of a congregation of them made one wonder how the Church had lasted so long. Both Monsieur and Madame Durand avoided any close contact with the pupils: they cultivated the high degree of formality usual in bourgeois circles in the France of that time, and Richard remained Monsieur Temple to the end.

The other permanent face in the household was that of Fifine, the maid. It was a pale, bald, waxy face with a nose, a Gothic face, a universal peasant face, shrewd and ignorant. She was employed for all duties, and Madame Durand's all meant everything; fortunately, Fifine had been brought up in a mountain village of the dry Corbières, a little to the south, where they work fourteen hours a day to keep alive, and she was constitutionally very strong. She was not only willing but also able to clean the house, wash and iron all the laundry, prepare the food and then take a heavy two-pronged mattock and labour the kitchen-garden before dealing with the poultry and cutting the wood for the next day's fires. She was of some age between thirty and fifty, and she spoke the harsh patois of her region more easily than French. She was a deeply pious woman: her earthy and often superficially irreverent religion informed her whole life: it was an immensely practical religion, and yet it was lit with a fine unselfconscious mysticism. She answered the question that her mistress raised, for a church of Fifines was likely to outlast time.

It was a pity that she was no better a cook, however: though indeed a high degree of talent would have been wasted on the penitential fare that passed through the Durand kitchen – haricots, stockfish, blood-pudding and chick peas, for the most part. She did not take to Richard for some time: it needed weeks and even months for her kindness to overcome her suspicion of anything new, above all foreign as well as new; but after that she became his frequent companion, and she was certainly the best friend he made in France, the most interesting and agreeable person in that house.

The house itself was built of glazed purple bricks, and it had a high-pitched slate roof; it stood in a vineyard about a mile outside the town, a striking contrast to the usual houses of the neighbourhood, with their white walls, low pink-tiled roofs and small grilled windows. Madame Durand always referred to it as 'my house', just as she spoke of 'my garden' and 'my vineyard'.

The vineyard was a broad flat expanse of some twelve acres, although it looked larger because there were no hedges to prevent it seeming to merge with the precisely similar vineyards beyond it and to either side: it was planted with seventy-five thousand vines in hundreds and hundreds of perfectly regular rows, an industrial exploitation of the unwilling earth for the manufacture of the lowest grade of common wine. The vineyard came right up to the house on three sides – the house swam naked in the field – and it was let on the usual share-cropping basis. Cheating was a major occupation both on the Durands' and the tenant's side; but the tenant, although he had less courage and less tenacity than Madame Durand, always came out on top; for every year, just at the crucial season of the vintage, the family was obliged to go up to Paris for three months. Monsieur Durand sat on two official juries and several ministerial committees; he also conducted a course of appreciation and the history of art at the Institute, and he renewed his contacts with the official world, the galleries and the auction rooms; it was a necessary and a profitable voyage, but the leer on the tenant's face was a flood of gall in Madame's heart, and the certainty that she was *being rolled* embittered her existence. On the fourth side of the house there was a kitchen-garden, maintained by Fifine; and this garden, too, came right up to the very wall of the house, taking away nothing of its naked irrelevance. It was a harsh house and it stood jaggedly in a harsh and arid landscape, unrelated to it and indifferent.

The landscape was an indefinite repetition of the vineyard – field after flat field of vines going on and on to the vague horizon, or on the south to the remote line of the Corbières, the division between the Languedoc and the Roussillon – and he remembered it under two aspects only, summer and winter. In summer it was a sea of coarse, dusty, sulphured and sulphated leaves drooping under the weight of the heat while an infinity of cicadas filled the quivering air with an omnipresent metallic din that seemed to emanate from the sun or the brilliant sky: and its winter aspect was that of a naked plain with rows upon rows of twisted amputated black stumps that bowed under the shrieking assault of the wind from the north – dust whirling under a pale and cloudless sky. It was an uncompromising landscape and an uncompromising house – both equally devoid of comfort. Yet Richard was not unhappy there. He either did not notice or did not mind the absence of country (in the English sense), books, comfort, bathroom, decent food or intelligent companionship: in many ways his values were essentially those of a painter and curiously enough of a modern painter – he was already indifferent to the picturesque, and where a young man of a predominantly literary cast might have deplored a howling desert, he saw order and a world of light. And indifferent though the house was, to be sure, it was here that he had his cardinal experience.

He had been there a year and more – they had been up to Paris twice – and all this time he had worked according to Monsieur Durand's rigid and exacting plan: it must have been the winter of his second year when he decided to paint a picture as a first-communion present for Fifine's nephew Sebastien – a martyrdom of the saint. He had always heard a great deal about this nephew, who was *chez les Frères*, and he had been told every stage in the poor child's long drawn out agony with the multiplication table, but his primary object was to give pleasure to Fifine and therefore his intention was to paint a perfectly direct saint undergoing a really painful martyrdom, with the arrows sticking into him right up to their feathers, and those feathers wet with scarlet blood. But for some time before this his mind had also been haunted by a curious formal pattern, and he determined to include it in the picture.

The Durand's house stood within the range of the last of the municipality's lights, a swan-necked, cast-iron brute that stood in charming incongruity among the vines and shone a beam through Richard's window in the night. The shadow that it projected on the ceiling was the pattern in question, and it was a very subtle pattern, being composed not only of the crosses of the casement and two fortuitous diagonals made by hanging cables, but doubled and trebled by reflections whose origin he could not determine, and multiplied, at certain times, by the moon: these crosses and planes lay upon one another in different intensities of grey, and not only did they present a singular and to him fascinating technical exercise, but they seemed to him ominously important – he had an obscure feeling that it was necessary for him to acknowledge them. The notion of luck, possibly of religion, entered into this, and there was some indefinite association between the pattern and his love of the kind darkness – that darkness which his most private fantasies represented as containing a hundred unknown nameless colours of marvellous intensity.

When he came to it he found it much more difficult than he had supposed. He was using a thin wooden panel, and in the bottom right-hand corner he had already painted three crossbow men, very close to the observer and crowded together, pointing their bows at the saint, who was tied to a low cross on the left of the picture and who had already received a great many arrows, or bolts: he was a little farther away than is usual in such a case – at the back of the foreground rather than in the middle of it. The light came from the bottom left-hand corner, the strong cold light of a declining January day in the south, and it lit the intent, crowded bowmen side-face, and their gleaming horizontal metal bows. The saint stared back at them with a harsh fortitude and in the pale space between, parched by winter, the ground was spotted with crimson flowers that showed the arrows' path: the bowmen, their pointing, the flowers and the cross formed a right to left diagonal in the lower half of the picture, and he intended to fill the top right-hand part with his pattern, which in its main axis would form the other diagonal, pinning and suspending the martyr at the crossing of the two lines. The picture was lit from the bottom left-hand, and the pattern (which was essentially one of crosses) would start with the shadow of the saint's gibbet stretching up towards the right-hand top; from this shadow others would arise, multiply, and superimposed fill the receding air.

He had already painted the crossbow men, a villainous set of brutes, all with faces that Fifine would recognise (he was clever with likenesses), and he had already done the saint, a painstaking anatomical study: so far the picture was a competent piece of work that he had worked over with great industry in his spare time during the past few weeks – it was a little dull, even rather laborious, and it showed the uncertainty of his literal taste, for whereas the bowmen derived ultimately from Bosch, the saint had a faint air of Géricault, and they existed in different kinds of reality, in different states of mind. But now he was to attack the upper part of the picture: this pattern, which preoccupied his mind, was to provide the force of counterpoise and contrast that would draw the cross into the centre of the picture and make it rise and glow – give it a far greater significance and perhaps harmonise the incongruity that he sensed but could not see.

He had the whole of the day – it was a Thursday – and he hoped to finish this piece and with it the whole picture before the evening. Yet it was far more difficult than he had supposed:

parabola that he would presently touch with vermilion, he gave them a unity that they had never possessed in his idea before. It was a vital line, one that had never physically existed in the pattern, although his mind must have postulated it, and it did wonders; but he was not content, and standing back with narrowed eyes and screwed-up lips he saw why. His pattern was supposed to repeat the first cross, and certainly crosses were there, receding into infinity: but they were the reflection, the repetition, of something that did not appear in the first place – the first cross itself was wrong. The beautifully painted martyr and his cross were in the wrong place. In a moment he abolished the patient craftsmanship, and in another moment the martyrdom was re-enacting in another focus, in another shape.

As far as he was conscious of himself he felt a tightness in his stomach, a trembling; and as he bent over his palette mixing he heard the sound of his own breath in his throat. He could not work fast enough and he had a furious need to go faster, although in fact his hand was working with a greater speed and happiness and ability than it ever had done before. He was not *thinking*: he directed his hand and the paint by an urgent spiritual pressure, and he not only prolonged his being beyond his hand to the brush but actually into the paint itself as it curled – he was himself the surface, the junction of the resilient brush and the unyielding wood: there were no ordinary limits to his being. The light increased to the impartial glare of noon: very slowly in the afternoon it declined; and in the evening it began to go in little pulsing beats lower every ten minutes, every five.

At the bottom right-hand corner where the crossbow men had been he drew the last firm curve and stepped away. As he fumbled with his brushes and the paint-rag, blindly cleaning them, he began to smile: the tension was dying, and it was being replaced by a remarkable happiness. He was quite limp, and this happiness was of the passive kind: it kept flooding in, quite filling him. This was the picture that he had meant to paint, and whether it was good or bad it was the most complete thing he had ever done. It was probably very good, he thought; but that was a little beside the point: it was the wholeness that was the base of his satisfaction.

✦

IT WAS NOT an experience that often repeated itself: indeed, throughout the year that followed he had scarcely more than one or two hints of it, but they were enough to tinge all the great long stretches of grey routine (life at the Durands' was lived *en grisaille*) with lapis lazuli and gold; and it remained the most significant thing that happened to him in France, even including his acquaintance with the power of love.

It was strange how late he came to this: Madame Durand's ascetic diet may have helped, but it had not prevented his beard from growing, and it had never kept any other pupil from romance, far less from fornication.

One of the few favourable conditions of Fifine's servitude, if not the only one, was that she was let out for the saint's day of her native village: the fête included a pilgrimage, a feast of snails and a visit to the sea, and in this last year of his she invited Richard to accompany her. He had leave to go, for although Monsieur Durand was a tyrant in the matter of holidays, which he hated, Richard had recently met him in the little local brothel, and although Monsieur Durand had carried it off pretty well, with high and distant formality – a remark upon the likelihood of rain – his Roman authority had cracked. They set out at four in the morning to catch a train that would intercept the village bus in its course, and when they arrived at the station a brisk shower overtook them. Fifine thought this an excellent sign, and with her best skirt tucked well up she strode about among the deserted railway shrubs catching the snails that the rain called forth, and called out in her strong voice to the dim forms among the churns, telling them (by way of feast-day merriment) not to piss in the milk and asking them for continual reassurance about the train. Richard, cold and wan without his breakfast, thought her excessively Gothic for a railway-station: but in the bus, which was conducted in the spirit of a mediæval wagon, she was much more in place. It was crammed with the inhabitants of Saint-Modeste in their Sunday clothes and with their provisions; they had no intention of buying food from any untrustworthy strange shops and they carried everything, including a huge quantity of bread and four barrels of wine. The snails were on the roof for the benefit of the air during the early hours of the journey, but as the sun climbed to its strength they were brought down, the younger men being sent up to make room for them. Fifine knew everybody there – she was related, more or less, to all of them except the curé and the new baker – and she shouted to them all in turn and they all shouted to her in the highest good humour, although they had been travelling since dawn and although at this time most of France and the western world as well as the whole of America was looking with horror upon the undoing of society – the dissolution of its wealth. This was the time when million-aires were killing themselves in Wall Street and the shape of the slump and the depression was beginning to be clear to all but the simplest of the land, among them Fifine and Richard. He did not see Mireille as he got in, for she was stuffed in at the back behind a big spotty girl who would be leaning forward to shriek out of the window; he did not see her at the pilgrimage either, because

Fifine took him in hand and explained everything to him, in an unusual, didactic and particularly loud voice, as if his Protestantism would make him deaf and stubborn for this occasion and blind him to the virtue of the miraculous water that dripped from a Gallo-Roman sarcophagus – the fairly miraculous water, for the Church was half-hearted about it and it owed its bottled reputation to Fifine and her kind. The true object of the pilgrimage was a splendid black Romanesque Madonna, as tender as a she-wolf; but Fifine was more interested in filling a bottle for the family – she had a duty to the Durand household.

He saw her at the feast, however, when they were all sitting round a fire of vine-cuttings, with the flames ghostly in the whiteness of the sun and the snails hissing, bubbling and dribbling on the embers at the edge, and he was amazed – a girl like a dark peach. There were no glasses except one for the curé, and they used the spouted pots of the region called pourous, passing them from hand to hand; and when he saw her take the pourou and tilt back her head and pour a long curved scarlet jet of wine from a height into her open mouth, her long curved throat and her pretty breasts held up, his heart fainted – there was an emptiness for a moment, as if it were not there, or had died.

But he was a modest creature then, and he did not suppose that he could ever presume so high; and in his simplicity he did not even notice that she was unattached, that the lads of the village were either clustered round the girls with bad reputations or chained to their public loves. He climbed back into the bus for the next long lap, melancholy and low in his spirits.

The blazing dusty miles went by; his head ached from too much wine; Fifine still read the names of all the villages they passed and all the shops, but with declining zeal. Apart from the reviving burst of jollity at the necessary halts it was a party chastened by the heat, best clothes, holiday wine and food and fatigue, that trundled over the jolting landscape of bare rocks, rosemary and scrubby trees that separates the Languedoc from the Roussillon, and so down the hilly roads to the sea.

He had once heard that the great object of travelling was to see the shores of the Mediterranean, and he had formed some vague notion of a liquid pearl; but as he staggered out of the suffocating bus into the pitiless glare of three o'clock it seemed to him that these sterile shores were commonplace indeed. The hot wind blew eddies of dust and paper along the beach; the shallow, waveless water, all flattened by the wind, had no grandeur, magnitude or shape. This corner of the village was organised for the exploitation of trippers, and strong inimical women shook paper hats, pea-nuts, dying-pig balloons: the traders, a little more in touch with the world than the peasants, were anxious, uneasy and obscurely hostile.

The village stood on a rocky bay, with a huge castle jutting out into the middle, and a path led round underneath this castle to a farther beach and farther rocks; Fifine and most of the elders stayed to paddle their tormented feet in the nearest water, but she urged him to go with the others – to enjoy himself, to profit by the occasion; he was only young once. The rest of the busload hurried along this path to join the other trippers (three other buses had already arrived) in their search for crabs, winkles, mussels, anything living within reach of the shore or among the pools; the curé had brought a rod, but the others contented themselves with throwing stones at the gulls and the uncomplicated murder of what few moving creatures the holiday had left up to this time – someone found a small octopus.

Most of the recesses in the baking rock were filled with excrement; the shallow waters of the bay were covered with the débris

of many picnics. Children howled on the dirty pebbles of the
beach, and their parents, exasperated by heat, tiredness and holiday, bullied them with automatic threats; old women stood
shin-deep in the water and comic groups changed hats to be pho-
tographed; soldiers in the castle shrieked and whistled, and knots
of plain girls all clinging together with their shoulders hunched,
shrieked back in a state of sweating excitement. The wind had
no freshness, and it was filled with dust. He saw Mireille quite
suddenly, walking back to the bus alone: she did not repulse his
tentative, easily-retracted smile – there was nothing haughty or
unkind about Mireille.

A jetty ran out at the far end of the second beach, and as he
handed her up the steps he noticed the extraordinary clarity of
the air; and as he walked along the jetty with her scent in the
drawing of his breath he took in a host of vivid impressions – the
brilliance of the open sea, white horses, the violet shadows of
the clouds. From the end of the jetty the whole village could be
seen, arranged in two curves; the sun had softened the colour of
the tiled roofs to a more or less uniform pale strawberry, but all
the flat-fronted houses were washed or painted different colours,
and they might all have been chosen by an angel of the Lord.
There was a blood-red house far over on the other side, with
chocolate shutters (the colours of an old German lithograph) but
by a particular dispensation of grace its neighbour was of a faded
blue and peeling rose – the happiest result. The high-prowed
open fishing-boats were also painted with astonishing and successful colours: they lay in two rows that repeated the curves of
the bay, and their long, arched, archaic lateen yards crossed their
short leaning masts like a complexity of wings.

At the reassembly by the bus Richard's shining face, his animation and Mireille's conscious looks required no great degree

of penetration, and Fifine, willing to do her friend the friendliest office, adroitly set them down together in her former seat and went to join her cousin Fabre with the car-sick baby.

The backward journey began – a journey (as far as Richard was concerned) towards a letter that told him that his days in France were done and that assignations were in vain – and on this road the bus no longer jolted and the heat no longer beat on his head: presently the sun set, and he found that by bracing his right foot against the seat in front and leaning over sideways he could put his hand upon Mireille's without appearing to do so and without being seen; and in this ridiculous, cramped and painful attitude he travelled until one in the morning, when the bus put Fifine and him down alone at a remote and doubtful crossroads.

CHAPTER FIVE

ROM THOSE EARLY days in Chelsea when he was a student at the Reynolds he recalled – what? A confused jumble of impressions: parties, keen but unreal poverty (an allowance stood between him and the world): a variety of living places: but over all there floated a general feeling of impatience and dissatisfaction. The period was nearer to him, as far as anything could be near to this strangely isolated present, which scarcely had the ordinary dimensions – but it was the part of his life that he had revisited the least; the person he met there was sometimes barely recognisable, and although he did feel a kind of impatient pity for him sometimes, it was difficult as well as humiliating even at this distance to be identified with that person's more embarrassing excesses.

However, that young stupid man's maladies of growth were perhaps not so much worse than those of the general run: at any rate they should be looked at impartially; and in an attempt at putting order into his thoughts he tried to recall the sequence of his rooms, from that first enchanted den with a window on the Thames to the house with the pigeon-loft on the King's Road which saw the last days of his protracted adolescence. He remembered leather-aproned Hare, the removing man, who lived with Burke, his little horse, in a green triangular place, a hay- and stable-scented vestige of the rural village, near the sad walls of the workhouse, and how he had walked so many times by Hare's van: Dovehouse Street; Smith Terrace with its monstrous bugs, immune to sulphur-fumes; the World's End; the lower end of Redcliffe Road.

At the lower end of Redcliffe Road there was a cat-haunted landing: in front of him there was a cupboard and directly to his right the door of a room with a tea-party going on in it. There came back to him the nature of the dim, filtered light on the landing, the shadowy colour of the door, the smell of that London staircase in the winter and the sound of the tea-party, to which they had asked him. He was rather late, in so far as it was possible to be late for one of these indefinite meetings, which took place at night: later, at any rate, than he intended; for in that rabbit-warren of a house, now abandoned to a multitude of people with one room apiece, the servants' staircase forked into three, and dark passages wandered here and there among the cisterns, promising short cuts. However, he had reached the door and he was in the act of feeling for the handle when on the other side of the matchboard partition a voice as clear as a bell said, 'Richard Temple.'

'Richard Temple, the new person in Andromeda's old room, is also a painter.'

'So she told me. Tell us about him.'

'Oh, he is not so bad, really,' said a man, as if he had been appealed to; and content with this tepid recommendation Richard would have opened the door if another voice had not cried out passionately, 'No, no, no. He is a silly bastard. Temple is a very silly bastard.'

Richard could not for the moment decide what face to put on this, and he stayed where he was.

'That is no news,' said Julia (and the treachery pierced him where he stood). 'He told me he was the illegitimate son of somebody or other, but it was a great secret, and not to be known. By way of keeping it dark he told Kate Hassel, too.'

'I mean bastard in the sense you say *he's a bastard*. If you want to be literal you say basstard.'

'Everybody has hoped they were illegits or foundlings at some period.'

'Yes, but they do not go on with their mysterious nods and becks after sixteen. Missing heirs and strawberry marks are not grown up.'

'Who is this? Who is your bastard?'

'Richard Temple. The young man who has Andromeda's old room.'

'I know him. He is one of those popular phalluses.'

'I do not know him.'

'Of course you do. He is the young man who got Anne with child, the one she said practically invented art.'

'He is at the Reynolds. They say he is very good.'

'No they do not,' said Spado, a fellow-student. 'He is very slick and clever, if you like, but nobody says he is very good except the duller members of the staff. He came as protégé of Atherton's, so naturally old Dover and old Wilson loved him from the first. He is just their cup of tea: very dainty and competent.'

'No one could call poor Spado competent. Everybody else at the school says Temple is very good – he won the Haydon.'

'Exactly,' cried Spado, with an immense sneer in his voice to show how discreditable it was to win an official prize. 'Nihil tetigit quod non ornavit: that's exactly what I object to. Painting is not an *amusement*.' There was a great deal of confused noise at this, and the conversation broke up into several parts; there was movement, changing of seats, and suddenly, right next to the door, so near that his voice resonated in Richard's ear like the diaphragm of an earphone, a new man said very confidentially, 'There are always contacts, isn't it absurd? I heard of him a great while ago, from my aunt's cousins: an extraordinary fellow, who burgled his school, and set fire to it.'

'Who?'

'This chap they are talking about – Temple.'

'Oh? I do not know anything about him. But I am glad he set fire to his school; it sounds spirited. Most of these people are so wet.'

At a little distance the bell-like voice called out, 'Plage, Plage, come and sit with us, and tell us about our new neighbour. Plage knows him well.'

'He has, I am afraid, no settled system of any sort,' said Plage, 'so that his conduct must not be strictly scrutinised. His affections are social and generous, perhaps; but his desire for imaginary consequence predominates over his attention to truth.'

'He is also a frightful snob.'

'He says that he has been at Munich, a fiction so easily detected that it is wonderful how he should have been so inconsiderate as to hazard it.'

'He told me that he had visited the Isles of Langerhans too.'

'The trouble with him . . .' began Spado trenchantly, but he was overborne and no more could be heard except 'Nihil tetigit quod non ornavit' again and, 'It is one of these little showy talents that fizzle out in a flood of decoration. He reminds me of Sert.'

'We will not attend to poor jealous Spado. They all say that he is good but they all admit he is an ass; which is very strange.'

'Why do you find it strange? What makes you think there is any relation between painting and common intelligence?'

Spado repeated, 'One of these talents that fizzle out in decoration,' and an electric light, turned on by some lower switch, suddenly illuminated Richard, while a couple of even later guests came swarming up the stairs, peering upwards and hooting: retreat was impossible, and with as even a countenance as he could manage he opened the door and walked in. It was strange to see how the voices paired with the faces and how their knowing looks were all dissembled. Judas Julia smiled at him; his hosts looked welcoming; and it occurred to him that people often spoke like this behind his back.

He had suspected for some time that he was not doing very well, but this whole-hearted, unequivocal confirmation went far beyond the worst of his dim, vague apprehension. (As for their praise, he did not reckon it any comfort; he scarcely noticed it – there was not one of them whose good opinion of his work meant anything at all.)

Yet now from this remote impartial view what surprised him was not the way some of them ganged up on him while they let still more offensive youths get away with more, but rather the tolerance of others; for indeed he must have been a monster at that stage.

Such elaborate, unnecessary poses, such attitudes . . . through the prodigious distance he could still see some of them. He beheld them without any tenderness, for the person back there was so disguised by fermenting youth, so drunk with it and removed from his ordinary nature, that he could feel little responsibility; he looked at them rather with astonishment, for he could no longer make out what some of the attitudes were meant to signify. Perhaps they were literally meaningless, like those profound looks of the young, in which it is hoped that someone else will supply the significance: perhaps they only meant that to épater les bourgeois was the highest aim in life.

It was this ferment that caused him to depart from his natural solitude and to dread the loneliness that he had always accepted: he was a natural solitary, and he had little social talent or discrimination. How much was nature and how much circumstance? He had been brought up alone and he had passed many of his formative years without the ordinary contacts; yet on the other hand his father, with a totally different upbringing, had much the same want of tact. Whatever the cause, the result was much the same: he danced with the grace of a half-taught bear. Just as homosexuals often find life in a heterosexual society difficult because the heterosexual culture is concerned with handing on heterosexual experience, discussing heterosexual attitudes and providing literary bases for conduct, so that the homosexual has no great corpus of information and accepted attitudes to draw upon but is obliged to work out everything for himself from the start (a task beyond the capacity of most), so the solitary finds life in a gregarious society laborious and baffling. He is not provided with some of the natural qualities of the rest, and he does not understand the wider sense of the common social rules but clings to them as arbitrary formulæ: though indeed the comparison is not very just, for the solitary is rarely as committed to his solitude as the pederast to his boys. Yet however lame the comparison, Richard certainly found reality difficult to make out, and he certainly floundered more than most.

The world in which he lived, it is true, was concerned more with things of the spirit than was the Stock Exchange; but this did not make it all of a piece nor prevent it from being pretty phoney in a great many of its aspects – there were the inevitable hordes of silly and dirty people in search of a literary justification for silliness and dirt, the uncircumcised Jews and the white Negroes, as well as the lechers – and there was a strong sense of class distinction, which ran, apart from a few obvious inversions, upon exactly the same lines as those which divided Easton

Colborough into its unnumbered castes. Indeed it would have been necessary to escape from England altogether to escape from this pressure: he was more conscious of it now, and he coped with it as well as he could, with little regard for honesty and without much skill . . . he must often have made himself ridiculous, and he certainly made himself disliked.

Yet though his prating, his dogmatism, his violence and his affectation rather told against him in gatherings of more than a few people, he could be agreeable in a simple relationship, a tête à tête; and upon the whole he enjoyed those last years of play. He was, in some respects, an undifferentiated youth, scarcely to be distinguished from the herd of his contemporaries, who all looked very much alike; and in the same way the greater part of his young women (the principal source of his joys and pains) were undifferentiated girls. Though indeed there were some lovely exceptions. He had abounding health and vitality and the energy usual at his age; the smell of the streets and the plane trees were aphrodisiac, and he was as amorous as a dove. Love had come late to him, but this was obviously through no irremediable block, for the emotion was very strong – a great turbulence of spirit; yet it was less an exclusive desire for any one girl than for all nubile womankind and although the affectionate and sentimental side of his nature attempted to disguise this from him in fact he often behaved with so shocking a degree of two-faced promiscuity that it was surprising that he was able to maintain his conviction that he was an excellent and virtuous man.

He rarely knew any of them well: he was barely acquainted with them as people, and indeed most of them were vague enough to be mistaken for one another in the dark. Perhaps there is not often much friendship between young men and women, and certainly there cannot be much intimacy of mind where each is preoccupied by a rôle. He did not *know* many of them, and now in the course of a somewhat caddish enumeration he found that many of them he could not remember except as part of a picture: their names, unbacked by any definite character, had faded, and they were replaced by the shape of hands, body, face and colour. *A likely wench may be told by the jut of her bum*: it really meant her likeliness, no doubt; but it was very true in another sense. He saw the lovely pearly buttocks of a round blonde girl, nacreous in the light of dawn, and himself so drained of desire that he could consider them then as objectively as he did now – a question then of light and surface; now of identification. Did not know them: and what is more, although he was passionate and sentimental he doubted whether he had even really liked the most part of them.

It was a rather subhuman activity: but most of these grapplings had another end as well – at this period he was a great talker, and his loquacity suffered from a night alone. How much he talked, and what balls; and when mendacity sickened him, he fell into the other extreme of candour; but he never would be quiet or continent. There were only two things which showed that he was capable of reticence at all: from superstitious motives as well as from piety he did not speak much of his occasional visitation, and those he did tell he told in confidence – he expected a high degree of honour in others, and discretion. The thing itself, the presence, the eudaemon, the possessor or the breath of God (as he privately considered it) had not been with him for a long time; hardly since he was in France, and only once with the same overwhelming certainty. He did not understand its laws: it would never come without industry, yet no amount of industry could bring it; it could not be surprised or forced. Yet he was sure that it had nothing to do with common goodness and that the God whose breath it was had no relation to the God he had been told about – nothing to do with religion, to which he was profoundly indifferent, if not hostile.

And then even at his most garrulous he kept his essential privacy untouched, his real nakedness. He might even have been able to bar it out of his own recollection if only every month, every Christmas, Easter and birthday had not brought a letter. At first the envelopes were typed by the people at the place where his mother was kept, but then they started coming in her hand, so completely unaltered that the sight of it made him tremble. He had opened them at first. They were odd, prim letters, obviously written under direction, impersonal and uninterested; and he had answered them in agony with trite phrases that concealed a burning prayer to be forgotten. But in time he left them unopened and answered with set phrases and a mechanical account of his progress, so far as it was acceptable. There was no difficulty in this, particularly at first: he started at the Reynolds as well as his friends could have wished – his technical abilities were far above the average and his training fitted him perfectly for the old-fashioned academic official standards reigning there. It was the best school, in that it was the oldest and that it had the most prestige; it had Academicians as lecturers and its diploma was the best qualification an art-teacher could possess; but it was an unpolished place, with an almost medical roughness, and there was nothing in its traditions to make Richard any less barbarous: worse, the best students, and particularly the painters, despised its methods and its aims after their first few terms. However, he began well. There were only two or three who could rival him, and in his first year he won the Haydon prize, which was the best the school could offer, apart from the leaving premium. Yet it was never much satisfaction to him; and even that little evaporated as he wrote it down in these dreadful letters – he could scarcely bear to look at the envelopes as he addressed them: and as for hers, he no longer opened them. Yet he could not bring himself to burn them as they came, and one after another they piled up on the far side of his mantelpiece, with his name turned down.

At the other end of the mantelpiece there was a little pile of white postcards: these came every week from Canon Harler's bank, and he was supposed to post them back, acknowledging the thirty shillings that accompanied them, but he never did, and indeed he had some vague notion of steaming off the halfpenny stamps in time and selling them to a person in an office.

Canon Harler had cut up very ugly, very rough, when he found that he had a whore in the family and a whoreson thievish incendiary for a nephew. 'The evil brute must have set it alight in half a dozen places at least,' he said bitterly: yet there were people who seemed to entertain a very curious view of the whole affair, even to the extent of perverting the course of justice to protect the boy from the rightful consequences of his own actions. It was the status of these allies that staggered Canon Harler: Mr Holden of Plimpton Hall was not only a magistrate and an intimate friend of the chief constable but a deputy lieutenant, Atherton was an R.A. and Colonel Apse the cousin of an important politician. Yet these people were not only willing to square the police and the schoolmaster, but even to maintain the boy in France. As a good committee-man he felt the sense of the house and he very smoothly overrode his personal views which were strictly of the whip, cold water and Antipodes variety; for he was a man who would sell his soul for a mitre, and he did not wish to offend any man who might have interest. The canon conceived a sort of respect for Richard, because of these allies, and it lasted even after Richard's patrons were scattered by death and the depression – Plimpton Hall empty, grass tall on the drive and in all the grey windows broken glass, the Holdens gone; and Colonel Apse, still uncertain of what had happened, trying to live on the uncommuted quarter of his pension in a boarding-house – and it made him speak humanely to Richard at the time: he had not committed himself to any personal expenditure, but he had spoken kindly and with hope – vague, indefinable semi-promises. More than that, he had later undertaken to allow Richard seventy-eight pounds a year against Mr Atherton's legacy, though not without a very high degree of anxiety lest it should involve him in a loss; for although Mr Atherton had written Richard down for a sum that should have seen him handsomely through his studies the estate was much confused – it was extremely difficult to realise in this, the worst phase of the slump, and as far as the executors could see they would not be able to pay more than half the stated sum, and that not for several years. He was still reasonably polite when they met: the Reynolds School was well known, it was old, and it was creditable to have a connection elected to a scholarship there. When Richard won the Haydon, Canon Harler took him to the Café Royal instead of Lyons, and gave him a pound with less moral gesticulation than he usually employed over half a crown. He also said that the world was an oyster, with the general intention of alluding gracefully to a palette-knife.

The oyster is a creature much held up to youth: Mrs Dover had told Richard about oysters, rather as if she owned them; so had Mr Wilson, his other respectable acquaintance. He knew nothing about oysters except that a palette-knife was not much use: and now on reflection he did not seem to have evoked a very satisfactory picture of youth, either. That far-off, almost unrecognisable namesake of his, the silly creature, swamped by sex and

sociability, was true enough in a way, but it was an over-simplifi-
cation and it left out a host of factors which were exceedingly
difficult to name but which he summed up by the statement,
There is something antiseptic in the quality of youth. There was
something that took the curse off the callowness and squalor, or
at least diminished it. There were so many contradictions: for
example, the generosity and honourability that withers away so
soon. He had known so many cases of it, subsisting alongside
great unwholesomeness – the generous response was as common then as calculated meanness later on. He had suffered from
it himself: at quite an early stage he had thrown away his sacred
first commission for love or rather out of kindness for such a disagreeable young woman, a frigid shrew at heart, who was not
even pretty.

She lived down the corridor in that house in Redcliffe Road,
and nearness, opportunity and a lingering amiability in her were
enough to bring them into a very close connection. Doris was
her name, and she was employed in a decorating firm: she was
unlike most of his acquaintance in being self-supporting, clean,
neat and efficient; she was also pathologically jealous and sexu-
ally inept, but until they were lovers he did not know that and it
was in the earlier days that she was particularly kind to him and
used her contacts to get him a commission. Later on he exploited
women's kindness in a most odious and deliberate way, but he
never had it so good as this first time, when his approach was
entirely disinterested and ingenuous.

The work in question was to be done in a house in
Hampstead, the home of a widowed plaster-manufacturer called
Mrs Limberham; and it was to be a fresco of the seven deadly
sins, at four pounds ten the sin, with a ceiling to be painted later,
on terms to be agreed.

Mrs Limberham had always, from her distant childhood, embodied all the sins except for Sloth; but it was only recently that she had begun to break out in the direction of art, and her house was as yet scarcely affected. The hall was large and white, with a copper bed-warmer and folk-weave mats, just as it was when she first reached suburban refinement, and it was only when one passed through the lounge, with its little bar, and into the new wing, that one became aware of art. Mrs Limberham had no use for dead artists: she liked them to be alive and she liked them to call her Peggy, and her gallery consisted of portraits of herself. But it was the garden room that concerned Richard. This was a kidney-shaped affair of glass and chrome, with a copper floor; the front was glass, but the back was to be plastered and it was this back wall that interested him: its sinuous line was broken by seven niches, each about five feet high and prettily arched; and he was to have a free hand. In its way it was a terrifying commission. The room was so extraordinarily hollow and empty that everything would be focused upon these pictures; and then true fresco is a most inhibiting medium – it allows no second thoughts: you must paint directly on to the wet plaster and succeed or fail in one bout. And in this case it was necessary to succeed seven times running: one failure would wreck six successes.

But he accepted it with the same unreflecting confidence that he would have felt if they had asked him to take over the Creation or to rebuild London from its ashes: this was a sort of trust in the kindness of the world that had very strangely survived from his childhood. Yet towards the end of the week (he allowed the sins one day apiece) as he stood there waiting for the plaster of the middle arch to grow firm enough to bear the brush he felt a sinking cold qualm of fear: he had taken so much

pleasure in the three to the left and the three to the right, and
he took so much pleasure still, as he looked at them, that the
dreadful question naturally arose – what if he should not do so
well for the seventh?

Everything had gone so well up till now that if the connecting
link were anything less than remarkably accomplished it would
be a disaster: Luxury, the central sin, must have not only all his
abilities but also all the luck he could command. It was not that
he had been aiming very high – this was not particularly serious
painting, and he was well within his limits – but every level of
accomplishment has its own difficulties, and he had overcome
them so well hitherto that for a moment he felt that it could not
last. The urbane figures to his right and his left looked as if they
had been born in their niches; they were thoroughly at home in
their own scheme of things, perfectly balanced and secure,
whereas in his moment of doubt he was not, even though he had
his brushes in his hand – he felt inferior to his own creations.

The plaster would not dry. He had particularly wished to start
early, not only to attack the danger as soon as possible but also to
get away as soon as he could: Doris had a private celebration that
evening – its exact sentimental significance escaped him and he
did not like to ask, but he believed it to be of great importance to
her. He thought angrily about the plasterer, a burly middle-aged
man in a cap, with no more than mediocre skill: he, like the plaster and a great many other things in the house, came from Mrs
Limberham's works, and when Mrs Limberham was there he
called Richard Mister: when she was not he referred to him as a
poor unfortunate bugger. 'Poor unfortunate buggers like you and
me,' he would say, to Richard's intense annoyance; and all the
time he worked he would preach in a nagging whine against the
rich and fate and God, who ground down poor unfortunate

buggers like Richard and him. Only that morning half a valuable hour had been lost in a long, muddled account of what God would feel like if He had been born in a working-class district.

Mrs Limberham and her companion, a pale, obscurely vicious-looking girl named Pake, had also tended to be a nuisance at the beginning of the week, but fortunately there had been labour trouble at the works and he had not seen much of either of them since Gluttony; which was just as well, because he made a point of doing each niche without a joint in the plaster, and that area was all that he could managed in an uninterrupted day.

One sin every twenty-four hours. As to the sins themselves he had nothing much to say – no new light to throw upon sin – and he had not attempted anything of the kind. Under Monsieur Durand he had done plenty of Sins and Virtues; he had copied Baldovinetti and Luini in the Louvre and he was familiar with dozens of other pictures; and this time he had done no more than take one of the usual sets from the general stock in trade, with the usual mildly offensive attitudes, the usual symbols of depravity, and he had confined his own personal contribution to a statement about the colour of the sins that he was particularly acquainted with and to a very cunning and elaborate pattern of light and drapery worked out from right to left clean across the seven. They did not make up a very important set of pictures, and they were never intended to do so; but so far they were very pleasant, refreshing and cheerful, and for all the exacting, meticulous work that had preceded them, they had a charming air of spontaneity.

The plaster was firm enough: he pinned up his cartoon, squared off the niche, and began to work. And in work, as in some of his dreams, he reverted to his old and habitual self (which was incidentally a sexless state); he was alone and happy in his solitude, unaware of himself and conscious of little but the slide of the brush on the plaster, the immediate technical problems of the continually changing surface. It was an awkward piece of plaster, first too wet and now drying patchily, but within a few minutes of beginning he was on the top of his form; the anxiety dropped away, and if anything the difficulty spurred him on. He worked extremely fast.

The niche was rapidly peopling itself: the lower part, the swirl of drapery that connected with the pictures to the right and the left, was finished, and he was working up the high lights on the old lecher's robe with an almost excessive virtuosity when Mrs Limberham and Miss Pake came in.

'Boo! Surprise!' cried Mrs Limberham, with a girlish skip. But they quickly resumed the solemn and religious faces that they had come in with, and this made Richard suspect that the thing that Mrs Limberham was carrying was Art.

It was indeed; far more so than usual. In some unimaginable recess Mrs L. had discovered a twelfth-century sin, a black, bald ithyphallic Luxuria; and she wanted him there, with his monstrous member, right there in the middle.

'Pretty please,' cooed Mrs Limberham, as he tried to explain that it was impossible to include the Romanesque gentleman: she cooed and stroked his arm, but he could see that she was likely to turn awkward at any moment.

'It is very beautiful,' said Miss Pake in a prim voice, as if he were objecting on prudish grounds: and she added, with a chuckle, 'Jolly old Dick, the pride of the Admiralty,' in a more natural undertone.

It was too late in the day to start upon Mrs Limberham's æsthetic education, and even then, in his green and inexperienced condition, he suspected that he should never have begun this interminable argument.

The light faded; the plaster dried. He cut away the old lecher's unfinished upper half, and the plaster made a sad threatening dump as it fell. 'I can make a perfect joint tomorrow,' he said to himself, but without conviction. Still talking they drifted into the dining-room, where Mrs Limberham poured out the gin: the only time she ever deviated into generosity was when she poured out the gin, and the snorting tumbler made him wink again.

She was very much excited by her discovery and by the successful outcome of her battle with the union; Richard became aware of this quite early in the evening, but he still thought she was primarily interested in the decoration of her garden room and as he desperately wanted to preserve his fresco and the commission for the ceiling he tried to win his way by kindness. Very much against his will he stayed to dinner.

The hours passed, and he suspected that he was making the worst of both worlds; but he was young, diffident and polite then – hamstrung by civility – and he was still pinned there when after a brief disappearance Mrs Limberham threw open the door, and clad in a diaphanous (mistakenly diaphanous) nightgown cried, 'Una, I am going to make Richard happy.' Una was Miss Pake's Christian name.

What unprophetic words! She was neither going to make Richard happy nor be made happy herself, for in the momentary pause that followed his curious sense of honour came into play. Why? It was not as though he were ordinarily faithful to Doris, nor indeed much chaster than the next baboon. But it seemed obvious enough to him at the time, and as he walked the echoing miles that separate Hampstead from civilisation he wondered only about Miss Pake. Why had she helped him escape through the lavatory window? What was the nature of Miss Pake?

He walked for hours and hours, and when he did reach home

he found that he had in fact made the very worst of both worlds. Doris had got drunk out of self-pity and then had sobered up cold, to meet him with the most concentrated shrewishness – she was immovably convinced that he had been whoring. The whole thing degenerated into a squalid brawl that had to be broken up by their furious neighbours.

He hurried away down one street and across another, and presently he came to rest leaning against the parapet of the Embankment: he was full of emotion, physically shaking with it; but the nature of the emotion was not clear; it had no distinct line; it was just emotion, and in a little while the smooth run of the water calmed its extreme agitation. The dawn had been gathering itself for some time past, and now it came up over Battersea, grey and prosaic; and by imperceptible degrees the ordinary world began again. The river grew commonplace, and he walked away, towards an eating-house in the King's Road called the English Rose. It was a low place that often stayed open until broad daylight, existing in a private, artificially prolonged night of its own, underground.

There was no one there but Barbara Celarent, regal in a black evening gown: she was sitting in front of a picture of his – a gouache of the Albert Bridge that he had given to Pozzo, the owner of the place. He scarcely knew her, for he still belonged most in the student world, whereas she was a medical woman in her thirties, married to a Jewish musicologist of some renown, and ordinarily he would not have said much; but now he was exalted by fatigue and amazed by the expanse that had been crammed into so small a space of hours, that he told her about it with a remarkable simplicity, as one might relate an astonishing catastrophe that had happened to someone else.

'Poor old soul,' she said, 'you have had a crowded night: you had better wipe the egg off your chin and come and get some sleep on our spare bed.'

She thought he must be dreadfully moved, and so he was; but one of the chief factors in his emotion did not become clear to him until he was on the very edge of sleep – it was an incongruous guilty delight at the loss of Doris. He would never have to put up with her any more, nor be grateful, orderly or clean: all qualities that she prized far, far too much.

Yet all this was very trivial: the emotions, apart from disappointment, were so superficial and muddled – they hardly belonged to a full-fledged person: and it occurred to him that he might define humanity as the feeling of entire and pure emotion. His mind wandered about this point, but it brought up no clear, sharp statement of position, and in parenthesis he observed that in the whole of this piece of recollection there was scarcely anything that might not have belonged to any spotted contemporary; nothing, indeed, except for the brisk competence of the paintings at Hampstead and their gaiety and lightness of touch. He remembered them perfectly well: for whereas his connection with his own larval state was tenuous in the extreme his connection with his paintings was not. He took full responsibility for them. Yet how could that silly youth have painted a human being's pictures? He reflected upon the difference between the painter and the person as he had seen it in others: but surely, he thought, to the man himself the two must coincide in time? And he looked through a mass of disordered recollections to see whether he could not fix a date for the re-emergence of the Temple that interested him – that is to say, of the whole person with real emotions, rather than the vapid creature whose feelings were mostly froth, and who was, for nearly all the time, a most appalling bore.

With the Celarents he was human enough: they were dear
people, and their grown-up deference to his painting was mar-
vellously tonic. Barbara was an exceptional woman –

> I know a reasonable woman
> Handsome and witty, yet a friend –

and nothing pleased him more than finding that she thought him
ill-used. He admired her very much: yet clearly admiration and
affection (though great maturers of the mind) were not in themselves enough to bring his lurking humanity into the open, for he
also admired another frequenter of the English Rose, a man
called Torrance – yet on the whole his behaviour with Torrance
was something less than manly. Torrance had this in common
with the Celarents, that he stood out from the ordinary run of
habitués by a particular sort of composure and self-possession
and the aura of money; but he did not belong to the Celarents'
world, and whereas they used the Rose as an occasional restaurant, it being open all hours and practically next door to their
house, he treated it more as a club. Barbara disliked him
intensely. In general she was a very tolerant woman – too tolerant
of bum painters, in Richard's opinion – but she could not abide
Torrance, and she would sometimes refer to him in a womanly
tone as 'your friend Machiavel' or 'What has old Mephistopheles
been up to lately?' and 'What news from Hell?'

What news from Hell? He had once had a dream that he was
in a huge city, colourless and grey under a perpetual artificial
light, and the unhappy, agitated people who filled every street
and bus and small gateway so that they spilled over into the running gutters, had all died at the age of twelve, with never any
resurrection. But if the feeling of direct and strong emotion, as
pure (in the sense that a colour is pure) as a child's up to the age

of twelve, is a proof of continuing humanity, why should he not cite Diana? Her name had been hovering there ever since the word 'exceptions' had run through his mind.

He still could not strike upon a date, though it must have been very late, when he was painting those blue tempera pictures – immense skies – and he had an invincible repugnance for placing her in reference to other girls, before or after, because she was quite exceptional: exceptional not only in that their relationship was 'pure' but also in that he knew her very well – it would be difficult to define love in any way that did not come very near his feelings for her. And when they were separated by an ugly, unscrupulous piece of parental blackmail which neither of them were old enough or hard enough to resist, they thought they would part in a place that had been particularly kind to them, far up the river, near Kew. They mismanaged the parting – butchered it, indeed – and instead of one going one way and one the other they went to and fro, so that it was drawn out in an exquisitely painful manner. But it came to an end somehow and he set off to walk back to London; and if any one thing marked the end of his submerged, disconnected state it was this, for in the man hurrying through the anonymous grey streets of houses with porches and steps and dustbins ranged in a nightmarish repeating perspective as if he were continually re-entering the same series, he recognised himself entire, hurrying, losing his way, asking unqualified people; losing his way in his distress and becoming confused to the point of being uncertain of even what it was that he was trying to reach.

CHAPTER SIX

THAT WAS TEMPLE all right, walking on the bottom of the river: and that person, essentially the same, called out to him (if to nobody else) in his own voice. The distress was still a little tender and naïve, but the language was the same language that he used today. This was almost the first time that his own figure came wholly into view again since his childhood; and although after that it sometimes vanished again into the fog of forgotten circumstances and attitudes this was the point at which he could begin his really personal history again.

But although it was on the bottom of the river that he was most easily recognisable and earliest recognised, he did not have to be there to be known: it was not his necessary habitat. Far from it, indeed: for this early period included the highest days of his life and a more pure happiness than any man could ask for or expect – those days when he was quite free in the world and he lived by himself near the Roebuck.

His mind was ranged with cupboards that were not to be opened because of pain or shame or because the things were too good for handling often; and the recollection of those days was wonderfully sharp and vivid and unused. With no effort he rein-habited that time and place.

He could feel the very grain of the wood under his hands as he leant on the unpainted window-sill high up over the King's Road: the lack of paint had raised the grain in ridges, and at the corners of the window-frame the dowels had dried and shaken out: the right-hand dowel had been replaced by a cushion of moss and a little dark fern-like plant. Ferns also grew in the leaf-choked gutters. The house was going to pieces and nobody cared because its ultimate landlords were going to pull it down: there was a tumble of long leases falling in and sometimes for a month, sometimes for half a year, the place was the technical property of some vague and uninterested reversionary; they all abandoned it, even to the extent, on one occasion between Lady Day and Michaelmas, of neglecting to collect the rent. The pigeon-loft was abandoned, too. Some working-class tenant had once started pigeons there, but no one had looked after them these many years – perhaps for generations – and now the loft was ankle deep in dirt and feathers. The pigeons did not mind it, however, and in spite of the mice and the vermin and the occasional rat at least a dozen pairs bred and cooed and paraded on fine days, dipping and bowing in the little privet-waste below.

The pigeons came and went as freely as the tenants in this delightful period of abandon: they came and went by a pigeon-hole just over Richard's window, and now as he leaned there one shot out and planed down over the tree in the privet-bushes to land beyond the buses on the other side of the street. The noise of its wings brought him out of his vacancy, and he looked up into the winter sky; the light was receding from it, but in the pale pure bowl that was left he saw, with intense satisfaction, all the promise of a well-lit day tomorrow: there were no clouds, and the veils of smoke that lay here and there were themselves luminous. Presently the roofs and chimneys would begin to be detached in sharp hard lines from the distant sky, and the leaf-less tree would rear up with extra-ordinary significance. It was winter, but winter at its best; and although the woman walking along on the far pavement had a fur coat on she had no need of

it. Even in this monastic seclusion (for he had long ago done
with the monkey-hill) a fur coat stirred his carnal mind and with
the faintest velleity in the world he regretted that he had never
known a girl in one; but when it reached the pillar-box opposite
his window the fur coat looked up and waved. It was a girl called
Pamela, said to be a poet. Barbara Celarent, no less, said she
was a poet and a good one, but he was not interested in poetry –
never read it and could not see why anybody ever wrote it – and
he was not interested in clean, bright, intelligent Pamela either,
even if she did come wrapped in fur. He waved back faintly, and
withdrew a little from the window-sill. He had no clearly-defined
attitude towards women any more than he had coherent politi-
cal ideas, but he had done with first love and now he resented
the goat who had come to replace the ingenuous calf. Though
for that matter his diet was telling on the goat at last, and he was
by no means the untiring leaper that he had been, not on bread
and milk.

He was hardening very fast, and it was just as well, though
rather late; for there was no liberty without it. It was an abject
thing to be chained by one's prick, he thought, remembering
Jacqueline, who by this chain alone had twitched him from a
high austerity to an anguished concupiscence for three agonis-
ing weeks. Not that she was not a disguised blessing, however,
like so many others.

Carlotta, for example, was one of these blessings in disguise.
It was she who had confirmed his mind when in his diploma year
the final examination had rushed upon him – he being as entirely
unprepared as if he had never learnt to read a calendar. He had
hardly been near the school in those last terms except to keep
himself enrolled, and he had completely abandoned figurative
painting: he declared to her that he would not be judged by a

reactionary crew, a gang of Academicians; but this was a rather wild statement, made partly for effect (he was still a great ninny in his moments then) and partly out of a vague notion that it might let him out. At the time that he said this the feeling of the depression and something of the terror of it had filtered down even to the level of the students – there had never been such a meek, worried, dutiful set of diploma candidates before – and although he personally had little notion of what it was all about (the slump was as unreal as politics to him: words and words in the dreary newspapers that he never read except by chance) some of the panic had overflowed into his mind. Two million men were unemployed: but ever since he had taken notice of the outside world two million men had been unemployed and it could not strike him with the same force as people a few years older; but even so the sight of so many frightened men made the earth shift and creep beneath him. It was not only a shamefaced longing for a passport to safety (the diploma was the best teaching qualification in England) that worried him, but also a straightforward appetite for the hundred guineas awarded for the best diploma show – a sum that he had always considered his by rights.

But he dared not show abstract paintings, and the other work he had by him was all of a very special nature – a number of pictures 'after the manner of so-and-so'. It would have been acceptable if they had all been dead the right number of years, but this was not the case: he had begun them for fun, but having begun them he felt his conscience involved and he had finished by spending great pains. The result was a little ponderous as a joke, but together they constituted evidence of a minute technical study of the originals and proof of a remarkable degree of competence and ability; and competence, after all, was the subject of the examination. Apart from these he had only a Last Judgment, an elaborate performance with some charming passages. The composition and the drawing were not likely to be faulted and he knew that no one in his year could touch the virtuosity of the central figure's robe. But he regretted now that the central figure's face was that of Braque and that the damned should so exactly resemble the staff, in spite of their cuckold's horns and blubber lips: he regretted the naked Academic wives.

He was in two or three minds at once: he wanted to show; he dared not show; he suspected that he was ashamed of what he had to show. But Carlotta had no doubts at all – she was all for boldness. She said that the judges could not in decency take notice of anything personal, and that they were obliged to judge by the quality of the painting alone. Torrance was there during one of these colloquies, and with real pleasure Richard saw that he was impressed by the paintings and by his high and independent stand. He said little – no one could say much when Carlotta was airing her views – but he did observe, 'It would be a remarkable show if you decided to risk it. I should like to see their faces.'

Richard had always valued notoriety at the school; but this time he had to pay for the notoriety more highly than he had expected. He was the only pupil within living memory who had been threatened with prosecution for a criminal libel or told never to present himself again. The rest of the show was very, very tame; the weight of the depression crushed down all originality, and the competing canvases were so tame, so little competitive, so safe and ordinary that even the judges sickened and the terminal prize was not awarded at all: it was held over until another year. But at least the prudent competitors got their diplomas; and in time they all vanished into respectable obscurity.

It was certainly for the best. If he had had the wretched piece of paper – it was imitation parchment, in point of fact – he would never have withstood the temptation: he too would have crawled thankfully off to breed up another generation of earnest daubers. It was all for the best, but at the time his soul went pale with terror.

Canon Harler (as he still was at that time) never heard more than a cautious version of the whole thing, but even so he made an ugly scene. He told Richard that he was a worthless wastrel, of course, and made a good many more of those personal reflections that will occur naturally to a vulgar mind: he also offered the following considerations about art – 'that the true artist does not pollute his canvas with deformity – that there is enough unhappiness in the world without creating any more – that we do not wish to see more ugliness. That the whole duty of the artist is to represent, to depict the Beautiful in as accurate and tasteful a manner as possible: and that in any case *Richard would not get a brass farthing out of him.*' And when he had vented all his spontaneous bile he cast around in his mind for something more that would really hurt, and he said that he *hoped* that the news of this criminal failure would not *completely* undo the improvement that was reported in Richard's mother.

But the canon was in London after a bishopric, and he had so schooled himself to universal civility that he was not himself in a battle, even when the enemy was bound and gagged, and the whole thing ended, if not amicably, at least with the two still on speaking terms; and when the newly-appointed bishop sailed for Limbobo (it was only a colonial mitre, but it would lead to higher things) he left Richard's affairs in the hands of his solicitor, uttering at the same time an expression of guarded interest in his nephew's future – an expression so hedged about with qualifications that it had almost no meaning at all; but a generous mind would have understood it as a promise of eventual succour: or perhaps not so much a promise as a notice that read, *This way to the life-belts.*

Carlotta, as far as he could trace her in his memory and assess the ghost with his maturer mind, never did come out of her cloud of unknowing herself, although she had certainly helped him to emerge a little way from his. It would have been quite unfair to blame her for his vagueness about what people would or would not accept and in fact he did not do so: if he associated her name with that *débâcle* it only meant that he dated things by women, they being central to his life at that time. Carlotta was the name of an early stage in his toughening: Jacqueline was another, much later and far more important. A blessing whose disguise was quite impenetrable at the time.

It was not that she was a person of much size or importance (Carlotta had more to her, and she was a blockhead) but for a combination of reasons, a centimetre here, a centimetre there, she instantly made you think of bed. She was the embodiment of English fantasies about France, and she brought him acquainted with some emotions that he never knew existed – the violent far extremes of jealousy, humiliation and unsatisfied desire.

She appeared at a very happy time in his life, the bitch, when the Celarents were still there and when he had Old Gobbo's studio: these were not his great days of the pigeony house which his memory was now inhabiting and from which it ranged backwards and made wide parentheses, some of which never closed but looked in others in a series of vanishing perspectives so deep that no logical way out was possible and he accomplished his transitions by gaps of mere unconsciousness. They were very happy days, and he had met Gay again, the same cheerful, affectionate, obscene creature of Mr Fielding's school: it was as if Winchester and New College had had no effect on him, or rather as if he had reached his definitive condition very early in his life. His face had changed so little that there was no possibility of mistaking him, even across a crowded gallery, with nothing reminiscent of Mr Fielding's anywhere near it. He was taller and thinner, and he was now enthusiastically heterosexual, but otherwise one could hardly tell the difference, and they took up their friendship where they had left it off. Gay was a diplomat, at the Foreign Office for the moment; and the consequential ring of this pleased Richard, for although he was essentially concerned with paint he loved pompous sounds and he looked upon social clichés with gratitude and esteem, as cardinal points in the uncertain world that began at the edge of his area of competence, an extensive world that contained almost everything that was not mixed with linseed oil; and many delights, no doubt. As a diplomat, according to Richard's lurid convention, Gay was colourless, but as a friend he was all that one could ask – kind, enlivening and confidential; and he added to these qualities a fine new zeal for modern art.

Indeed, he had all the virtues, except that of permanence. He was on the wing, camping in a huge old-fashioned brown flat behind Victoria lent him by an absent colleague, because it was not worth while getting a place of his own. He had been in Paris until the end of the year before, and now he expected to be posted at any moment to Monrovia or San Salvador; so he was making the most of his time. His enthusiasm had brought him into contact with some very weird painters and his kindness prevented him from throwing them off, but Gay also had some delightful acquaintances – an attaché from the French Embassy who not only knew most of the Ecole de Paris, but who brought the more amenable part of it to the flat, having persuaded the government to pay its fares on the occasion of a cultural feast; some other civil servants and a few mixed politicians. There was also an outstandingly rich young man who was going to open a gallery.

He took an immediate interest in Richard and sat by him on the sofa, asking him about himself and about his views on all the painters in the public eye, and listening with grave attention to his judgment. His name was Drome, and under his elegant waistcoat, his double-breasted waistcoat, there beat a tender heart for boys. It was difficult to say how this became apparent, for Drome was something of a prig and a formalist, but it was apparent, and Richard felt a distinct relief when, Gay having made it clear by a well-timed indiscretion that Richard was a follower of drabs, Drome showed no unfavourable reaction.

'In my opinion,' he said, waving his hand towards the wall, 'society ought to provide him with a room-full of trollops, if he can paint such sweet things, and if his tastes lie in that direction.'

'In my opinion,' he said, with a shrug – for the bell had rung, and it might have caused the loss of his first remark – 'anyone who can paint such sweet things ought to be provided with as many trollops as he likes, by society.'

The wall to which he waved his plump white hand was papered with a biscuit-coloured paper that imitated damask, and among the faded Bartolozzis that hung upon it there were three of Richard's pictures. Two were small squares, acid yellow, with a lake-lined purple shape rising to the right in one and to the left in the other, and between them a long thin picture, an infinity of rectangles of all kinds of blue, a completely static composition. They were abstract paintings, without any modelling or hint of depth, and their colour was exceptionally strong and pure: in those surroundings they looked like a beautiful rude word.

'Sweet things,' repeated Drome, and he spent the evening being agreeable to Richard: at the end of it he begged him not to forget to get into touch with him, saying that he hoped to be quite clear about his plans for the gallery quite soon – by the New Year, or February at the latest.

It was a pleasant evening even though it had its overtones of strain and although Drome was something of a pomposity, with his money hanging down under the hem of his coat and with his huge face already beginning to show signs of that lofty petulance which is so usual in rich men who engage in publishing or paint: but it was always pleasant at Gay's; there was the exciting air of success there, as if life were naturally a going forward from one excellent thing to another. And at Gay's, feeling successful and knowing that he was liked and even admired he quite sloughed off the incipient tough sullen reserve that had been beginning to come over him. In French, particularly, he slipped naturally into a civil and even a mature way of speaking: it is easier to be civil in French. Gay had many French or French-speaking friends, and it was after an evening spent in this tongue that he met Jacqueline. It had been a very long evening – an art-critic from Paris who had told them about his trade in all its scabrous detail – and Gay had offered to put him up. But he had gone: there was a half-coherent idea moving in his mind about his current picture and he wanted to get straight at it in the morning, without formal getting up, breakfast, good mornings and travelling back through streets of moving people. It was a very quiet night and it seemed even later than it was, for the fog had come down again: an almost silent night, white where the fog was lit up, and utterly black above.

He cut down behind the station as usual and threaded through the frozen side-streets of Pimlico, making for the river, which he would reach very near Old Gobbo's place.

The Pimlicites were all dead or lying there in dreadful silence behind the black walls; none of them uttered a human sound to mingle with the steady thumping of his feet. He was on a long, long dark line of road that vanished into fog in front and now on either side, fog that closed behind him, so that he was a moving point on an infinity and for a profoundly disturbing moment he had the feeling that he was part of a painting of the thing that he had imagined – this line, and the moving spot. But the recurring lamp-posts broke up this pattern and the train of thought, and a long way off he heard the uncertain click of her heels, the click-click of high heels stopping and turning and starting again, and automatically he stared about, like a dog sniffing. But it was only an unconscious reaction; he was not really interested. In spite of what Gay had said to Drome, he was quite chaste at this time, for the sake of seeing what it would do for his painting, and he had avoided temptation for several weeks.

But when she called out, 'Monsieur, oh monsieur! Mister – dear sir,' in such a shipwrecked tone, 'Sir dear, please,' he stopped in common humanity, and under the street-lamp he saw a young woman with dark red hair.

This was Miss Porny, Miss Jacqueline Porny, the answer to the ponce's prayer, and she was lost. Her great determination and her courage, already tried by the journey, the language (which was not the same as the English she had learnt) and the nourishment on the train from Dover, were beginning to tremble at the prospect of a never-ending emptiness through which she was apparently condemned to carry her suitcases for all eternity and if they had met ten minutes later her eyes would have been bunged up with tears and smeared with mascara and her nose would have swollen, a disastrous red. She would have looked like a drunken tart (which she was not) and there would have been no danger.

Anybody, an old lady, a Salvation Army field-marshal, would have been welcome to Miss Porny at that moment; but a civil though shabby young man who spoke French and who had a home and two hands was something beyond the call of providence. She put her luggage in his hands and hurried straight off into his bed.

How she came to be half-way down Wanhope street he never knew for sure, but her most likely account was that she had crossed that day, travelling in the company of an elderly woman known to her family, and that she had come to England with the intention of improving her mind. At Victoria she had given her companion the slip, but she had lost herself into the bargain. She did not seem to think that her disappearance would cause anybody any concern – she spoke vaguely of a family consisting of old female unfriendly cousins and of some remote connection at a hostel for girls in Gloucester Road, but he soon found that there was no truth in Jacqueline; none, except in her bosom, which you would have sworn was padded.

There was no truth in her, and he never thought there was: but even now he kept her portrait turned to the wall. It was the most decided erotic outcry, and it still moved his amorous propensities. He had worked on it all the time that she had stayed; and although he had worked very fast, as he could on occasion, she still found time to deceive him with his friends from Aaronson to Younghusband, passing by Gay, and with his enemies, from Abrahams to Williams. By the time of the last sittings she had grown rather prudish towards him and even a little patronising – meat for your master, but I do not mind letting you finish my picture – and at the Arts Ball he lost her altogether. She went into keeping somewhere in the region of Maidenhead; and long afterwards he heard that she had married an elderly gentleman who owned a gold-mine and a diamond-mine and an oil-well.

It had not lasted very long on the calendar, but it was almost unlimited in shame and he had fed himself with as much ignominy as if he had spent a year in the pit: he had passed through all the hoops: he had not only been fighting mad but also feebly lachrymose – a dreadful stage unique in his career at which he abandoned pride and common sense entirely and begged people to leave her alone.

She did not mean any sort of harm by him at first, although he was not at all her type; but he soon irritated her by being poor, by trying to keep her in, and by being hurt; and once vexed she was pitiless. Of course he vexed her more and more and of course she deceived him (though *deceived* is scarcely the word when he con-tributed to it so much by ludicrous wishful gullibility on the one hand and crack-brained suspicion on the other) with tales of friends who lived in the country and relatives who had asked her out; and of course she went off in the direction that she had always intended to take, as soon as she possibly could.

It was usual enough; and there was nothing wildly exceptional in his fight with a richer rival – a public, squalid, and very painful battle which led to his being taken up for assault and bound over to keep the peace – nor in the fact that he should have been tossed out of the Paradise, or that he should have spent a great deal of money on buying agony. After all, he had been false enough in his time to have deserved all that and more: but although at some level of his spirit he acknowledged this, the chief result struck him as completely abnormal, unexpected and wicked – a more-than-pox: not a dropped nose but his hand sawed off. His painting was completely stopped.

Before she appeared he had been working hard. His adolescent froth and passion for minor lechery had largely died away, and staying with the Celarents and seeing them very often after he had left he had learnt something of the adult values outside painting. Not many, God knows; but something had seeped in. And he had heard a great deal of music. They had put up with him because they thought it their duty to good painting: but they must have been cruelly tried sometimes . . . he remembered telling Ludwig dreadful little glib things about Bach. 'Bach always makes me think of the higher mathematics' et cetera. And yet at that time he really did know something about Bach. Perhaps Ludwig divined this. He remembered an unlimited vast afternoon at their house when Ludwig played the whole of a new recording of the St John Passion for him, winding the gramophone, sharpening the needles, turning the discs, while Richard stood in the bay of the middle window, gazing into a kaleidoscope. In the small illuminated round there were these brilliant particles, existing in some other space and light, invested with some other significance, perpetually changing and perpetually almost apprehended; and all the time great curves and waves of sound filled the audible world and combined with the angularities of what he saw.

Something of all this, the Celarents, their music, his happiness, was in the heart of his painting at that time – something indefinably related to it – and he thought it the most valid painting he had ever done; almost the only valid painting, and his certain road. And yet when Jacqueline was gone at last and he thought of something other than his loins he found that it all meant nothing. Or very little. As he had suspected there was a good deal of falsity and affectation in his younger work, sometimes painted over with surprising cleverness; and now that he could look sharply at it (there being such a wedge of experience between then and now) he saw that it did not amount to anything much: too much cleverness and at the same time too much artful open-faced simplicity. However, it was of no great importance one way or another – juvenilia. Of his recent work the portrait, the obscene nude, was quite good: it would stand up to any amount of melancholy reaction. But he looked with real horror at the abstract work that had occupied him for the whole of this very active period. How could he have been so deceived? He had felt the urge to paint them with great fervour and sincerity, and on at least two pictures he had thought that he had that wonderful presence filling him, the comforter which never could be wrong. Could he have mistaken the nature of the being? Were they really the sterile posturing that they seemed to be? Fakes?

He looked hard, very hard, to find the truth; but staring he grew stupid, and worse than that he lost interest. After all it was not as though he were ever going to make another picture, he thought: it was as if his heart had run out of a hole that someone had made in his body.

It was a discouraging time, by any reckoning, although it was so valuable. His occupation was gone. And with his occupation a dozen subsidiary forms of order, among them the curiosly fascinating employment of managing a very small income so as to make it last far longer than was human. Porny had not only blasted a hole in his budget, but she had taken away the basis of his cherished economy; he was surprised to find how much he missed it. There was no point in contriving: there was no point in eating on seven-and-three-pence a week any more. But

equally there was no pleasure in relaxing his strict observances —
he had no pleasure in smoking again, for example, but only a
confused and gloomy sense of guilt.

It was a necessary experience, for there is no doubt that a
painter must be tough; and there is no doubt that any artist
needs a particular kind of selfishness, which can come not only
from total dedication but also from being kicked so often that
the artist cares more for his private, kinder world than anything
outside. As for toughening, there was a great deal of room for it:
he had been disastrously soft before.

How had he reached this stage, how had he managed to come
so far without getting himself married or plunged into Commu-
nism, or even Fascism for that matter? He had started out so
sentimental and tender-hearted that he might easily at this time
have been surrounded by the smell of rancid babies. And
although he could never possibly have become a Liberal or a
Socialist, any amiable Communist could then have converted
him by a factual account of working-class life. Fascism was a
more obvious danger, because it was a natural home for certain
forms of uneasiness and because at that time it was very busy in
the neighbourhood, with a few remarkably pretty girls in the local
ranks; but these girls were all bespoken, and the men he knew
were such obvious blackguards. But in any case there would have
had to be an outside force to over-come his heavy-witted indifference, and as there was none he remained unmoved by the
spirit of the world, ignorant even to the pitch of scarcely knowing the difference between the sides in Spain. He had been told
that Franco was a rebel, and that he was a 'Catholic gentleman'
— a term used in some of the papers at that time — and these
qualifications seemed pretty good to him. He could not see what
the fuss was about; and this was presumably why the Celarents

did not make an anarchist of him, which they could have done with no trouble at all. They may have thought it unfair to argue with a mind of such a very different kind, and with the advantages they had, the advantages of affection and respect, for they were scrupulous people; or they may have thought that his conversion would not add greatly to the intellectual value of their party.

In any case, they were exceedingly busy at the time of his overthrow by Porny, hurrying about and addressing meetings, collecting funds and rallying informed support for what they passionately believed to be the cause of freedom in the whole world: however little he went along with them, he could not but feel that he was only a side-issue; and apart from that the exceedingly violent erotic feelings involved belonged to an atmosphere that was not the Celarents' and which he would hesitate to make clear to them; for although they were as 'civilised' as could be wished, they were, like so many committed people, distinctly puritan. So this time nobody held his hand.

One of the most shocking things about a suddenly disrupted life is its appalling tedium. There are a very great many very long moments in the day and each one must be lived through; and each moment is long enough to be filled with a thousand unwelcome thoughts. Each day lasts for ever. He stayed in bed until noon, dawdled interminably over breakfast among a general filthy huddle of heavily crusted paint, crumbs, forgotten milk bottles with hideous translucent liquid in rings within, and over all the smell of mice, while on the table he spread the local paper, consisting entirely of police-court news. He would read it through and through, the factual and the jocular alike, and he derived from it all a feeling of hopeless wretchedness, made up of bullying, prison, spite and jeering; a grey, mean world without any sort of excuse.

He could not get over the idea that what he had thought so

good now seemed commonplace if not forced or even totally insincere; Jacqueline faded from his mind far earlier than this profound dismay. He could not understand it, and every time his mind was rested it came back for some easily comprehended solution. 'What is truth?' he asked, and the nearest he could come to any reply was, 'You had better be careful; very careful, because if you make a mistake you will certainly be sent to hell.' These painful, necessary cogitations, this naïve rumbling about in an unfurnished mind took place in the day-time; out of habit and an obscure superstition he stayed in Old Gobbo's freezing studio until the evening, drooling about in the long intervals of thought with the practised lethargy of an old lag: but in fact this prison of meaningless leisure and insignificance was harder to bear than most he had inhabited.

In the evenings he was allowed out, however, and as he could not bear pubs because of their very recent association with Porny, who had delighted in them, and as he was afraid of being an object of amusement for some fortunate oaf at the usual bottle parties and tea-drinkings that had until then occupied so many of his nights, he generally went to the English Rose. This was an unbelievably decayed tea-shop that had been taken over by an Italian named Pozzo. He was a wretched cook and would never be anything else, but he would stay open until the last customer drained his last cup of inferior coffee, whatever the hour, and this pleased his regular clientele. They were a mixed lot, but generally speaking they were occupied with the arts, or more or less literary; they certainly had a common love of talking, and the place was a Babel when more than one was present; and as Pozzo (to his utter bewilderment) could not serve even so much as a glass of wine, it could be fairly assumed that they were not of the drinking sort. They belonged to all sexes, and on the whole they were of the older kind; older, that is to say, than students.

It was in these dreary days, and at the Rose, that he became a particularly close acquaintance of Torrance's.

✦

JUST WHERE PAMELA Crandison had walked he saw Torrance; there was no mistaking him, for he had a very distinctive walk. He held his head high and went along quite slowly, in a line from which he would not for anything deviate; and as that younger Temple watched he saw Torrance stand still upon his imaginary line while a perambulator made its way round him: then a little way beyond the pillar-box he stopped, moved to the kerb and stood there a moment, as if in doubt. Richard made a gesture from the window, but Torrance did not look up, and in another moment he stepped off the pavement with peculiar deliberation, so near to the wheels of a crimson Rolls as to interrupt its smooth progress and even shake the occupants like peas in a bladder; he glanced at the mooing of its horn and continued his procession to the other side. He affected a high formal civility in his ordinary contacts; but he would risk his neck at any time to vex a Rolls.

He was an uncommon-looking man, with yellow-reddish hair and pale eyes like a young fox, and he gave the impression of being tall. He might perhaps have been called handsome, but whenever he opened his mouth he showed a gapped line of blackened teeth. He was completely self-possessed; he wore his clothes however old with great distinction; and he might have been almost any age – in fact he was little older than Richard. He had lived in the neighbourhood for some years, and as he had already been established as an impressive, settled figure when Richard was a floundering bumpkin, he seemed to him even more ageless and permanent: Torrance knew everybody, but he had no intimate friends. He belonged rather to the literary division, and he was said to be an authority on Rochester – he certainly quoted him fluently enough – but as he seldom mentioned his affairs little was known about him; he was not the sort of person one would ply with questions. He lived in Tite Street, but no one had ever been invited to his rooms.

This was the man in whose company Richard spent much of the time that it took to recover from his disgust. It was difficult to see what they might have in common, but Richard enjoyed his impersonal conversation and his indifference to time, and he was gratified by his acquaintance – Torrance courted nobody, and formed no part of any of the groups that Pozzo's customers naturally fell into. And at this conjecture Richard did not derive much comfort from the Celarents; he loved them very much, and he admitted that their 'politics' legitimately preoccupied them; but he could not help feeling a little wounded, and at a certain level he wished they were not quite so perfect – that Barbara would betray a certain frumpishness or that Ludwig would be found constuprating the refugee servant. At this time, too, he tended to keep himself to himself; for although he needed company, the noise and the talk, he was obsessed by the idea that he had made himself ridiculous over Jacqueline and he was unwilling to have anyone make game of him. He miscalculated in both directions, however: nearly all the ignominy had been within, and what little showed had been outweighed by the prestige of ever having had such a remarkable mount. And as for making game, there were few who would undertake it now. He had the reputation of a fighter, and with the taciturn sullenness that a consciousness of his present state (some qualified variety of universal cuckold) affected him with, he looked one; he was quite safe from meddling. He did not know this, however, but supposed that he looked as young, as dismayed and as vulnerable as he felt.

It was difficult to see why they should have gravitated together; although Torrance did have the negative quality of being the only one of the bloods of his acquaintance – the dominant and car-borne and whiskey-drinking people – who had not lain with Porny, even in her keeper's imagination. He had been unmoved by her advances: and he had been away for most of her career. But they did, and from time to time Torrance invited him out for a drive. The intention was not to go anywhere, but to travel very fast, and usually they went out by the Kingston by-pass or the Great West Road. Torrance was not a good driver, although he seemed very much at home behind the wheel and even somewhat naked without a car round him – a dismounted Centaur; he had little feeling for the mechanism, and he drove dangerously as well as very fast. As a form of catharsis the rides were a great success. But sometimes, having got down into Hampshire, he would cruise slowly along the small lanes and even cart-tracks that led to the chalk-streams of that county, or ran bordering along them. 'I fished that water last year,' he said, nodding towards a very beautiful stretch of the Test itself.

'Oh, yes?' said Richard, looking at it attentively.

But this was apparently not the answer that Torrance thought satisfactory, for he drove off without saying any more until they reached the main road again and one of the booths with which it was so freely studded – Hot Pies, Tea, Good Pull-in. He was a passionate drinker of tea, and they stopped to refresh several times a day; and while drinking the tea he would always play on the pin-table machines, shooting the balls about with the same intensity, recklessness and lack of scruple that he showed in his driving. Generally he left the table tilted.

Richard had long ago abandoned solemnity with regard to the plastic arts, if indeed he had ever suffered from it, but he still expected a sort of earnest behaviour from intellectuals, and Torrance's absorption with pin-tables disturbed him. He was a great one for pigeon-holes, and for months he had been unable to reconcile the double placing of Barbara Celarent – a person wrongfully inhabiting two holes at once, music and medicine, which was almost as monstrous as being both good and bad – and it had only been accomplished by habit in the end, no intellectual process. But in the evenings Torrance returned to his pigeon-hole: Richard's demands for classing a man as an intellectual were not exacting – he was not to be a painter; he was to be able to talk over Richard's head; and he was to be quietly obscene, that is, he was to use rude words without guffawing – and Torrance fulfilled these many times over. On that particular evening he shone at the Rose, where the discussion hinged on two themes, the delights available in the streets of Berlin as opposed to London, and the moral worth of painters – what relation it had to the value of their work.

Torrance scarcely ever talked bawdy; it was not his style to be so personal as to talk bawdy; but he was exceedingly well documented upon perversion; and as his opponent was a widely ignorant young man who knew almost nothing of Berlin and scarcely anything of London, Torrance had the field to himself. 'As far as I can see,' he said, 'you know nothing whatever about the matter. You have come back from this perfectly commonplace pederasts' pub in Shepherd Market all amazed, like a yokel who has just seen his first giraffe; and you have brought back nothing from your more or less imaginary travels but the woollen statement, "the Nazis have cleaned up the Kurfürstendam". You are like these lady novelists who are obliged to talk about *nameless orgies* because they do not know what gives out.'

No one likes to be accused of ignorance, still less of purity, and Webber, the authority on German mores, made a rash plunge into the language, by way of rehabilitating himself. He had suspected Torrance of playing from weakness before this, and he risked the bluff. The result was disastrous. Torrance in fact knew Berlin and the language spoken there remarkably well, and the poor young man was reduced to silent hatred, the more so as a new girl was in the corner, listening with her pink ears pricked. And Torrance sat swilling his tea and grinning with insolence: he seemed to take a delight in making his position more dangerous, for there were half a dozen people there besides Webber who would be delighted to see him down, and who would have no mercy, at the slightest slip. It was a sort of game in which he had to win every time.

And later, when someone raised this other point, Torrance, who was in a talking mood, maintained that a painter's moral character had nothing whatever to do with his painting. He spoke with surprising earnestness, not as if he were talking for victory alone, but as if he were speaking from conviction. 'A man can do whatever he likes and still be an excellent painter or sculptor or whatever. You have only to read a few pages of Vasari. Look at Cellini, for God's sake; or if you do not think he is much good, think about Beethoven – a pretty moral character, I believe. What did Titian die of? Take Fuseli; or almost anyone you like to mention. There are hundreds of examples in every gallery – fornicating brutes, horrible people – only there is this holy mouthing about Culture that makes even the Tate like a Methody Sunday-school. They do not know what the hell it is all about, and they call it Beauty and look glum and pious and purse up their mouths like the arse of a hen; they have it all con-

fused with tidiness and worthiness and keeping out of other people's beds and pockets. It is all irrelevant. I do not have to reach
out – the names come in dozens. Gauguin. Utrillo, and his mum.
Even Cézanne, making little bastards all over Provence: and his
buddy doing the same in Anjou, or wherever it was.'

'Who?'

'Renoir, of course,' said Torrance, with a cold stare.

'He never did,' cried Webber eagerly. 'He never did anything
of the kind. Renoir was perfectly happily married, and never did
anything of the kind. Besides, Cézanne married the girl: there
was only one, and he married her afterwards; it does not count.
But even if it did, *Renoir* did nothing of the kind. You have got it
wrong.'

'He certainly did,' said Torrance. 'It may not be set out in
Culture for All, in five easy lessons, but you must not expect too
much for fourpence. Among people who know anything about
painting, it is notorious. Is it not, Temple?'

'What?'

'Everyone knows that Renoir was a rapist?'

Richard had some reputation: what he said was likely to be
believed. He valued his reputation for accuracy, and he loved
Renoir; but Torrance had gauged his reaction quite exactly. And
on another occasion he affirmed that there was too a quattro-
cento Moroni.

They neither of them referred to these lifelines afterwards,
nor acknowledged them, other than by a certain apologetic air
in Richard for having thrown them, and a slight stiffness in
Torrance which showed that he was quite unweakened by having received them. It was an odd alliance, with curious formali-
ties; and it was quite unusual in its tacit kindness. Richard
valued it highly.

But it was not Torrance's friendship nor even the effect of his terrifying car that undid Richard's melancholy knot: the immediate cause was a letter from Drome. He said that his arrangements were taking longer than he had thought, but that he was reasonably sure of opening his gallery by Michaelmas, and might he come and see Richard's work again? He was thinking – although with a great many uncommitting qualifications – he was *thinking* of having a show of five non-figurative painters in the spring. He had four names lined up, three of whom were already known to Richard from the reviews of shows in Paris, and the fourth was presumably a German.

The first distinct emotion that he experienced was cupidity – how delightful it would be to be rich – and this was almost instantly followed by reviving ambition and a host of mixed feelings, exhilarating but shot through with regret. He still could not decide whether the bright mosaics and arabesques that stood along the wainscot were valid or not; he only knew that he would never paint like that any more. There was no particular moral issue involved, as he understood moral issues: he would have no hesitation in selling them to a private person, but he would not exhibit them. As far as he was concerned it was all decided by the fact that he could not paint any more pictures like that, except by copying; and that was not what was required.

It was a pity; but he remained excited rather than depressed. The mention of a show sent all sorts of currents running through him, exciting a great many rational and irrational emotions, for a show is almost everything to a painter. It is what publication is to a poet, and performance to a composer; and the word *show* made everything that was most real in his world spring into vivid life.

At the same time, or within a few hours of the same time,

Hyacinth Briggs, a little sad man in a beard, an etcher, told him of the house with the pigeon-loft; and that evening Richard walked along the road with Leather Apron and his dwarfish horse – an easy cart-load, accustomed to removal. His canvases, those that paired in size, were pinned face to face with double-pointed pins; but Porny voyaged alone, wrapped in a sheet. Leather Apron, on being desired to load her, had stared for some time, and then with a hoarse, unknown, leathery guffaw, had said, 'You'll 'ave to cover it. I wouldn't answer for it, else.' Afterwards he observed that he had seen a bit of everything, and that he had carried some pretty old-fashioned objects in his time: but he had been young himself, and you might as well enjoy it while it lasts. And as they walked along through the gentle rain he sang in a whispering monotone, 'Cover it over quick, Jemina, cover it over quick.'

Gobbo had signalled his return from Cornwall some weeks before this: he could not bear the disgusting rotting warmth and damp and the slugs in his bath any longer. But until that day Richard had done nothing about finding another place. He merely watched the date coming nearer with stupid, dull concern. Now he moved about in a completely different manner, as if on springs, and he settled into the top floor with much more zeal than usual, sweeping it with Hyacinth's broom (the Briggses lived on the bottom floor, with some incongruous children) and cleaning the inside of the windows. He was in quite a flutter, as though he were to be married in the morning.

Torrance came to see him, walking up the stairs with some disgust and opening other people's doors on the landings as he passed and staring in. Torrance was in a bloody-minded mood, and Richard was aware of it at once; and even if he had not been Torrance would have made it plain within the first few minutes.

It seemed that 'your friend Major Barbara' had been making a nuisance of herself in the Six Bells.

'If she wants to go a-Godly recruiting, why doesn't she turn to her native suburb? Her style is perfectly suited to Balham or Peckham or William Morris on the Thames, or wherever it is.'

Richard had already heard an account of the incident, in which Barbara had said to three men, including Torrance, 'If you really dislike the Nazis so much, why do you not go to Spain?' But he had not thought it of any importance – certainly nothing to rankle twenty-four hours – and with his usual tact he said, 'But she is really very kind, you know.'

'Of course, one is obliged to say so. Very proper. But that is exactly what I complain of: that is the whole source of the trouble. This compulsive benevolence. I can just tolerate her worthiness, but not her perpetually bleeding heart. If you really wish to stand well with her – if you would really like to do her a kindness – you would loot her house in her absence, or inform the police about Ludwig's activities. She cannot bear to see herself unless she is in an aura of good works, martyred by ungrateful people – do you remember Davidge? No; he was before your time. But he was the one who was so ungrateful as to – but really, that was not very pretty. Do you know that need to be always right, always done badly by? However, that is not what I came for.' But he did not go on to say what his purpose was, contenting himself with walking about the room and grinding the knob of a mahl-stick into Jacqueline's yielding belly.

Torrance was in a bloody mind, and Barbara Celarent was probably no more than an additional irritation; but even so Richard was too full of his personal excitement to contain it, and he told him about Drome.

Torrance seemed puzzled and even in a curious way suspicious; it was as if he were being asked for sympathy in an unnec-essary and even bogus situation, and was irritated by it: and partly as if he were not going to be had.

'Do you mean that abstract painting is no good?' he asked, and he listened in silence to Richard's rambling, diffuse account of what he meant – an unconnected and at times contradictory statement in which only one or two positions emerged with any certainty: that it might provide a real language for some few peo-ple, particularly for some of the clever ones, but that he was not one of them; and that as far as he was concerned he could only see it leading to a blank canvas or to decoration, if persisted in. But that it might have been sound enough at a certain moment, to say a few very special things: perhaps: but there was nothing more easily faked.

Torrance listened with cold attention. It was not exactly that he was hostile, or he could have taken advantage of any one of the many places where Richard opened himself to ridicule or logical objection, but rather as if he did not understand the basis of the whole thing, but was determined not to let this be known; and as if he did not believe that the discussion had any real importance.

But although he resented having the confidence inflicted upon him, he maintained his poise with no great difficulty: he said politely enough that Richard clearly knew his own business best, and that he would only suggest framing some sort of a short, civil statement – a clarification of his ideas – in order to persuade Drome, who was obviously such a valuable contact. But then having got below the surface of the business and find-ing that Richard had no alternative to offer to Drome, he grew positively irritated. For himself Torrance was a man who attached uncommon importance to privacy and non-involvement: it was not only that he was unusually reserved and had created an

atmosphere of impersonality for himself in that vulgar, gossiping
little world; and now that he abandoned this natural attitude in
his irritation and as it were profited by his enforced involvement
to interrogate Richard about his ability to make such a gesture,
his background, his prospects of inheritance and so on, the effect
was quite brutal.

'. . . but your mother is still alive?' he said again, rearranging
the facts.

'Yes,' said Richard, thinking with confused pain and distress
of the cardboard box on the mantelpiece, where he had put her
letters, sorting his things as they came out of the van. The oldest, the few that were opened, were yellow and dog-eared; the
most recent, (which announced her approaching release) was as
crisp and white as it had been when the postman delivered it,
just before the move: and between the two extremes there were
at least two changes of stamp and one of colour, visible on the
neat corners of the unopened envelopes.

He would have been much more upset by the question and
he would have resented it very much more if it had not been for
this strange flutter in his spirits, but even so his heart beat abnormally and an ugly, sullen look came over his face; his surly shoulders seemed to grow heavier and he jerked his chin forward.

Torrance could adopt a very charming manner when he chose.
'Of course, it is an intensely personal judgment,' he said with a
quick glance at Richard's face, offering him a cigarette, 'and I am
not remotely qualified to . . . But it would astonish me if you did
not find these – (indicating his most recent pictures) – entirely
valid, when you see them in perspective. I do not pretend that
they are immensely important – I mean, not necessarily your last
word – but you cannot possibly deny that this one, for example,
would be delightful to have hanging on the wall.' He picked up

an arrangement of red and yellow planes with a big peach-shaped
form over on the right – a black line enclosing a crimson which
was scraped right down to the coarse grain of the canvas. It was
'meant to be' (*what is it meant to be?* they ask in tones ranging
from fat condescension to a starved anxious longing not to be
left out) a picture of red, a portrait of the colour red; and if it did
not go all that distance at least it was an unusually cheerful, amiable picture. It was one of the two that Richard suspected most:
could this mean that Torrance really knew something about
painting, he wondered.

'Tell me about prices? I should like to buy it if I can.'

'Oh, you can have it,' said Richard. 'No, do. It would give me
pleasure. It was one that Drome liked, when he came.'

'What did he say?'

'I don't remember. It was at Gobbo's. Jacqueline was there at
the time.'

Torrance looked at his watch and said, 'I came to see whether
you would like to come to the dogs. You said you had never seen
them. If we go now we shall be in time.'

Richard had not been brought up with a car: they were rarer
then, in any case: and when he was in any sort of an automobile,
let alone a great open throbbing affair like Torrance's, he tended
to swell and to despise the foot-passengers; but that evening he
did not even notice their passage through the crowded streets.
Nor was he much affected by the hot crowd and the roaring, the
lights and the dogs racing by, and the mechanical jerking swoop
of the hare; for he was obsessed by a thought that had come to
him in the studio, just as they were leaving it – that the portrait
of red was not a picture but *part* of a picture, the basis, or one of
the bases, of an earth-shaking great picture.

+

AFTER THIS CAME the best of his life as a painter; not a very long period in time, but a great length measured by intensity of life and experience; and all this time he spent in the house with the pigeon-loft. And at the end of it, leaning out of this same window, also in the evening, he saw the tree in leaf and the red buses against the wet black of the road with such unexpected calm brilliance that he laughed. In the room – poorly lit, with nothing from the roof – it had grown too dark, and as well as that he had been working on an obscure red piece of background; and now the contrast was enough to make anybody smile. Richard, being already very happy, laughed outright.

The light out of doors and most of the colours were pale, cool, serene; and as he settled his weight comfortably on the window-sill it occurred to him that they too were all liberated and free of passion. For his part he was not only suffused with happiness but he was also removed from most ordinary and conflicting emotions. This was the blessed time of his life, when it seemed to him that he had come to a proper and permanent understanding of his function; he saw provision for some time to come and at the end of that time an exhibition; and more than that he could not ask. It seemed to him that he had reached normality, and that normality was the earthly paradise. He had taken up his physical way of life where it had been before the days of Porny, and he had improved upon it as a means of satisfaction: but infinitely beyond this there was the comforter with him. Often and often he had prayed for it and sometimes he had persuaded himself that the presence was there although in fact it was no more liable to mistake than a naked fire in one's hand.

He had often prayed for it, but now without praying it was there and would not leave him, and the fierce activity of his mind far outran his hand. The walls of the room were covered with fragmentary dashed-off schemes, a few strokes of charcoal, brief reminders of a whole gallery of pictures yet unpainted: for he painted on his knees nowadays, with very little of his old easy confidence; it was a very dangerous proceeding, in which a mistake would have shocking results. It was as if he were walking along a continuous tightrope: and not only that, but he had to unlearn artfulness at the same time, and the cruel discipline of throwing away hundreds of hitherto cherished opportunities, and restraining emotion in the harshest way. This was not a painting that could go along very fast; and the big Homage to John Atherton behind him had taken . . .

A pigeon that lived in the loft above came gliding in over the roof, but on seeing his head out of the window it shot away with a clap of its wings and took refuge in the tree. At the sound and the sight he shrieked and flung himself back into the room, hitting his head on the upraised sash so hard that some wizened strips of putty fell out. Presently he reappeared, panting, and arranged himself on the sill again: some drops of blood ran from his scalp, and rebounding from the greasy stuff of his collar splashed on to the wooden surface, where he drew them into a crimson omega. The pigeon watched him suspiciously from among the leaves, craning an uneasy neck: this was one of the few pigeons left, for Richard was painting in tempera now, and he used their eggs. He had also taken to eating their young for economy, the warm, half-naked, grey-skinned squabs, which he smothered in their nests, and now the pigeon looked upon him as something in the nature of an ogre, whereas before he had been trusted by the birds.

His flayed nerves stopped jerking, and his breathing quietened down: after all, he reflected, he saw that pigeon every day, and half a dozen times a day. It was an excellent life, none better, the Good Life itself, the normal life before the Fall, but he was probably not taking enough exercise. From the remote areas of his childhood survived unquestioned the worship of cold water, exercise and draughts; he disliked them all and practised no worship, but he now reproached himself for being *out of shape*. His only exercise was grinding burnt bones or colours of the cheaper sort in a brass mortar, an enterprise that made him gasp and brought up blisters on his hand, but which was apparently not enough to keep him as well-balanced and phlegmatic as an ox.

Besides, he had had another wretched night. He had woken up to find himself standing against the wall, facing it and oppressed by a terrible anxiety – what about the mauve? And for a long time he had been unable to find the switch of the electric light.

But nights were often pretty bad, although if they were the price of his days as he sometimes supposed, they were infinitely worth the paying. They were not a negligible price, however. His sleep was broken by half-waking dreams of perpetually forming and dissolving colour; it was essential to note some passing phase before it should change, but he would be forced to lie still and follow the next building-up. One of his most often-repeated dreams, full of anxious delight, was that he was on the very edge of an immense discovery, no less a discovery than a whole colour hitherto unknown: and he had a feeling that in one dream, a dream overlaid by stupid inactivity and not to be recaptured, he had actually seen the colour, clear across the background of a huge, soaring apocalyptic canvas, presumably an unknown El Greco.

These nights, and they grew more and more frequent, were followed by days of intense activity; then towards the evening, when the necessary tension of work should have relaxed it did not. It lived in his stomach, and he could make it relax by a conscious effort; but as soon as he was not thinking about it it would be there again, something of the feeling that one has when a rocket is climbing up and up and up and is going to burst, a breath-holding that becomes hard, tight and straining, a knot in the end, when the rocket climbs on for ever. It was a perfectly acceptable feeling during work and during the planning of work and indeed not only welcome but indispensable; but it seemed to him that it was the same thing, or a cousin of the thing, that would attack him in the nights when he really paid. Then he would wake up, knowing what was coming, and a gentle pressure would begin where he ordinarily felt the tension, and it would build up to a huge irresistible force that would double him up on his face, not allowing him to breathe while he ground into the bed with his feet and hands to disperse the pain; and then slowly let him go, to start again in five minutes' time. This would generally go on until dawn, but hitherto the light had always stopped it, and as he set his tin alarm-clock to the earliest hour in order that he should not lose any of the day, he sometimes went very short of sleep. But when he did sleep he had the rare compensation of waking and knowing that it was actively delightful to be alive.

The light was fading now. In the street below a thin line of people went by, among them Weenix, dressed as an artist. The poor sod was already done. Richard had always disliked him, but Weenix had had talent: now he had nothing more to say – nothing whatever – and when he did not imitate others he imitated himself. It was horrible to see. But Weenix did not seem to mind it very much: he had a teaching job and he talked on the BBC.

Then after a blank space in the frieze came two young women pushing go-carts, and behind them Bolton, hurrying along in pale corduroy trousers that gathered the fading light. They were stiff, and they smelt. He had made one of his now rare sorties as far as Bolton's studio some days before and there he had smelt them as they warmed in front of the stove. Bolton was a very vulgar man, always cheerful, with a beautiful innocent bright blue eye; he painted tubular factory-hands and work men in corduroys, and he appeared untroubled by thought, doubt or even his dreadful artistic wife. He was a Lancashire Catholic – another of the reasons why Richard was vaguely away to the Right. The corduroys twinkled, hurried after the go-carts, and Bolton pinched the nearest rounded bottom before turning into the tobacconist's.

But in general most of his friends were away. The Celarents had gone to Spain: Gay's letters bore the outlandish stamps of Sissavang Vong. Torrance was away, and he had been away for months. Several people had asked Richard when Torrance would be back, but although he had been rather pleased by the assumption of intimacy he had not been able to answer: the elegant Bullingdon had asked him, with the added civility of an offered drink, and the notorious glazed young rich woman who was always appearing in the Sunday papers.

For that matter he was away himself most of the time, shut up at the top of the stairs; and sometimes for long stretches at a time his only contact with the outside was this evening gaze from the window-sill. He needed this isolation and now that his particular friends were away there was almost nobody left who had the right to walk up into his room uninvited: he had been growing much less familiar, and at this time he asked nobody, no painters – he did not wish to talk to them: why should he? – only Drome and by night a few odd girls.

Pamela went by, and he kissed his hand. 'Ha, ha,' he cried in the exultation of his heart, 'I can take it or leave it alone. How strong I am!'

Drome was something of an anxiety, however. It was not that he was not reasonably appreciative, even enthusiastic on the two or three occasions that he came, nor that he had been out of measure annoyed by Richard's curious decision: but he had a partner now, and to this person he would attribute all sorts of commercial motives and incomprehensions. '"The abstract-expressionists are only just getting into their stride as a selling line"' he reported with prim humour, '"and the buying public will not be ready for this sort of neo-realism for another fifteen years, even if there is not another war."'

'It is not neo-realism.'

'No,' said Drome thoughtfully, looking at the Homage to Mr Atherton, in which all that Richard had learnt from his passionate excursion into the abstract was combined with at least one passage of startlingly precise architectural drawing, the Town Hall of Easton Colborough. 'But he calls anything in which he can recognise the figures realism, unless they are upside-down, in which case it is surrealism, or fubsy, which is impressionism. It must be admitted that he has great business acumen, however. What would you call it yourself?'

'I don't know,' said Richard. 'Does it have to have a name?'

'A name – a theory and an ism. It is a great comfort to people.'

'You could call it representationalism.'

'Oh, come!'

'Represents what is really there.'

'A sort of expressionism?'

'No, no. The *thing* that is there . . . the thing itself.'

'Well, I must say you do very prettily without an ism,' said Drome, gathering himself together. 'You would not mind showing this nude? I am really very enthusiastic about it, and I know my partner would be – a curious common ground. Such morbidezza, my dear. We really must see whether anything can be managed in November or December.'

'I shall certainly have enough for a show by then.'

'Splendid,' said Drome in a tone that Richard thought definitive as he engaged in the dark stairway: and which he presently considered so firm that it was the equivalent of a contract, and the only problems were how to work fast enough and how to survive until that time.

It was then that his archaic training came in so very useful, for after Porny's depredations and his own extravagance he had very little money left, almost none to spend upon materials if he was to live a year. Fortunately he could do almost anything short of spinning his own canvas, and his own abilities, his own old pictures scraped down, and his own ancient preparations served for a great many of his needs: the unfortunate pigeons served for some that remained, but still certain colours (that afternoon's cadium yellow, for example) could not be made at home, and when he could not fit these into his rigid budget he usually stole them from Rapin and Crab, who had a large open counter in their shop.

His shifts, his hours of grinding, rarely saved more than a few shillings here and there; but half a crown saved at this end meant an extra day of life at that end. Or at least it did in theory: but in fact there was the show to come; there was the possibility of private sales – Gay would have home leave in a year's time, and he had sworn that he would oblige his aunts to buy and to stir their whole acquaintance; and there was the Lord, by means of His servant George, bishop of Limbobo. Meanwhile Messrs. Ellis and Grice sent him a cheque at the end of every month: this month it would be unusually welcome, and it would arrive tomorrow.

A person moved in the twilight under the tree and looking up called, 'Oh, Temple.'

'Who's there?' cried Richard, with his voice fluting up and down: he gripped the window-sill and craned far out in an agonised cramp.

'Only Gobbo,' said the up-turned white blob of face. 'The char says there was a woman asking for you this morning. She did not let on. There are some letters for you, too.'

'Thank you very much.'

In the spasm of hearing his name when he was thinking of something else he had torn a hole in his blouse. He thought for an anxious moment that it was his coat, which he wore underneath, for warmth; but he found on switching on the light that it was only one of the familiar three-cornered tears in the paint-covered cotton. He had one good coat now; his clothes were all old, student clothes or even his last schoolboy clothes, and they were very thin, shabby, and easy to be torn. The discovery that it was not his coat quite restored his happiness.

'I am enormously strong,' he said, plucking off his blouse with his trembling hands; and he reflected upon his strength and his freedom. 'I am tough and immovable.'

He was no longer avid for company, nor for girls: he was not obliged to run away from them. He could take them or leave them. 'I am free of childishness and unselfishness,' he said. He had resisted Hilda's attempt to move in on his solitude. His relationships with Hilda, Pamela and Prue were more or less casual, more or less masculine – no commitments.

He attributed this new strength to the rock-like basis of his present painting, and he was pleased to detect in his present calm, tough attitude towards other people a further proof of the value of his work.

'It would take an earthquake to move me,' he said, feeling through the pockets of his other trousers for another half-penny to add to the fourpence in his hand; and perhaps from the aesthetic point of view this was true, but physically he was hardly holding together at all.

It was his intention now to go and have a glass of beer, to bathe himself in the light and clash and smelly din of the pub, and then to go to the Rose and settle the beer with a mass of spaghetti, at tenpence the mass: he always did this at the end of the month – beer and noise for his last fourpence ha'penny and spaghetti on tick.

'But I cannot go there,' he reflected: yet after a pause he said, 'Oh, it will be all right. He will have forgotten; he always does. I can certainly go.'

Pozzo had banned him again not a week ago, this time for beating one Poate and breaking a chair. 'You are making my select café a brawly-house: you are a 'orrible gorillo.' This Poate was a big, fleshy moon-calf whose favourite sport was counting dukes. 'Let's count dukes,' he would propose, with shining eyes; and on this evening he was explaining the English social system to a Swede, with particular reference to rank and schooling, but he had branched off to the subjects of death-duties and Lloyd George when his braying voice reached Richard's ears. '. . . a dirty little Welshman, from some impossible board-school.'

However immovable Richard might have become in painting he was still acutely sensitive to common worldly status: but in this case he fell upon Poate out of delight in living, as well as a need to punish him for his blubberish great face and his fatuity.

The half-penny was necessary to his plan, however: there was no tick at the pub. He knew the coin existed, and this was not a room in which a halfpenny could easily be lost. It was rigidly and even fanatically bare, rectilinear and clean; where the old walls bowed and the angles sagged he had ruled hard lines – he had also ruled them on the floor. His sketches and reminders were pinned up in an order that joined with that other order of coloured squares which formed at once his calendar and diary and a private system of divination upon arithmetical principles. His friends' pictures, drawings, casts, sculptures were ranged in a brutal, strictly regimented group outside this order along one wall, and his odd hideous bits of furniture stood in certain fixed attitudes that made a transition. The almost compulsive neatness reached its height on the old marble-topped washstand that supported his colours, tools and brushes, and this was the place from which it had radiated; even at his most slobbish stage, now far behind, his first years in London, he had kept his materials superstitiously clean and trim, and with the continual change in his work, its enormously growing intensity and his much greater happiness, this order had spread. Now it reached the limits of the room, where even his plate and cup stood as exactly as the plate and cup in the cell of a disciplinary prison. It was a bitterly uncosy room and it was turned entirely towards work; but it was not a room in which a half-penny could hide for long and presently he ran it down on the mantelpiece, shining like a good omen.

'I can certainly go. How delightful about the ha'penny,' said Richard. He gathered himself together, put out the light and crept down the stairs, smiling in a rather cunning way as he circumvented the difficulties in the dark, the rotten board, the missing hand-rail. Since the intelligent Webster had left the floor under Richard's nobody had known how to mend the electric light.

He walked along King's Road in the gathering darkness; the air was soft and pleasant on his face, but almost certainly it would rain again presently: the air could be thought of as a liquid and apart from that walking in the dark was not unlike swimming. If the rain held off he would go for a walk after the Rose, right along the river, and the night would be all the better for no moon; in the enveloping dark, one could see ideal colours; and besides there was the exercise: in a very solemn internal voice he was speaking of the benefits of exercise when he found that he was in the middle of the road with a bus rushing furiously upon him. His disjointed movement of self-preservation was complicated by the shattering horn of a van coming in the other direction, and after leaping about for some little time on the crown of the road he found himself back on the pavement that he had started from.

'I knew it was you as soon as I heard the brakes,' cried an odious girl named Marjorie.

'You'll come unstuck one of these days, mate,' said the van, which had come to a stop.

'When I heard the screeching of the brakes I knew it was you,' said Marjorie, grasping at his arm. In order to be done with the incident he plunged into the pub on this side of the road rather than the one he had intended. It was full in front, clots of people at the bar and an unformed mass behind them: he pushed through to the room at the back, where he found a place for himself on the stuffed benches that ran round the wall, at a corner table that had just been left: the bench under him was still warm, and although he was somewhat isolated, barricaded off by the table and a little space to either side, he was aswim in other people's warmth and breath and in a huge general noise from which odd words and phrases detached themselves as you got used to it. Presently he would go to the little bar that curved into this retreat and buy his pot of beer; but for the moment he would sit down.

Three bitters, miss. Miss, three bitters, please.

And the innumerable sibilants of English in such expressions as *So I said – so 'e said.*

So Myrna Loy goes into the room and there is this man and he says . . .

One Guinness and an Old Bushmills.

Female chastity is much praised; but the women inherit nothing, and are classed with the hyaena. The hyaena is the least valued animal in Eritrea.

I assure you, Ma, it is a perfectly good cheque, a very good cheque.

Yet we read in Ludolphus of the were-hyaena.

No language gents please.

And Schweinfurth says that Bongo music is like the raging of the elements.

A voice sang:

> 'With one accord they all refuse
> The bleeding offspring of his muse,'

and the singer cast a false look at a group of strangers, who might be tourists. This was the pub for tourists, and the pub most haunted by the objects of tourism.

The first drunk began an interminable account of the wrongs of the blacks; and all around the confidential esses of reported conversation hissed gently on.

It was indeed very much like being in a sea, sitting at the bottom while it soughed and boomed: he had come just for this immersion, but now his mood was dropping, and he wished he had not. He thought that perhaps the beer would improve this state, and as a preliminary to fetching it he began to move the empty glasses in front of him; but his hands were so shaking and uncertain that he was afraid he would knock them over and he stopped. He deliberately relaxed the tension in his stomach and with studied calmness he gazed mildly about. From his corner he could see beyond the little triangular bar (a continuation of the main one) to the partition that separated the parlour from the saloon, a mahogany partition of excellent workmanship with small heavy panes of bevelled glass that gave a series of square glimpses of the detached world beyond. The middle of a man: an isolated arm, with the hand of it marking off the points of an argument and with each point descending into the prismatic area of the bevel – the Seraphic Doctor. Some way back in the room the figure of a respectable sculptor, talking with great animation, exactly framed by the wood as he harangued his listeners; they could not be seen, he could not be heard; for only the nearer sounds made their way into intelligibility or even separate existence. The people who had just pushed their way up to the bar on the other side were quite audible, however, loud-mouthed pub-men whose voices would always be heard through the mahogany. The sound and some unwanted vistas of them made them known, nasty businessmen in suits who were often seen there, but even more often in drinking-clubs later on – middle-aged roaring laughter, a kind of obligatory booming; some of them got into bottle-parties sometimes. One was a colour-merchant, one a contractor, one the proprietor of a garage, one was to do with furniture-removal: the worst of hangers-on, comparatively pulling out ends of pencil, charcoal, a few dead pawn-tickets, handkerchiefs; but no forgotten money.

He ran downstairs and burst into Webster's room; in the shocking emptiness he searched and called, with his voice resounding, before he remembered that Webster had moved away long ago. Downstairs again to the Briggs's door; he listened intently, but there was only the whining of the children locked in alone. Hurrying out he tried one or two other houses; but this was not the time for finding his friends. And having lost the thread of his intention he let his overwhelming desire have its way and ran from the place – from the whole neighbourhood where he was known. He followed the direction that he had intended when he thought of a walk along the river, and in fact he ran most of the way at first, so that by the time the rain started he was far down, far below the Tate, where the small rich streets behind the Abbey came down to the Embankment.

A squall of wind staggered him and broke his mechanical stride; he realised that the rain was beginning to come down very hard, and he took shelter in a doorway, under a hooded seventeenth-century porch with a lantern in it.

There was a dinner-party still going on inside the house – a golden light in the windows, voices, laughter, three cars parked outside the door. The rain increased in wild gusts, and after half an hour of it the spouts were jetting solid columns from the roof and the gutters ran in high swollen streams almost level with the pavement. By the light of the lantern he watched the rain drumming madly on the cars: he also watched the matchboxes and odd pieces of paper racing across the lit-up stretch of gutter, appearing from the left and vanishing into the darkness on the right. It was very much colder now.

Then the changing wind began to drive the rain into his shelter, and the drops splashed up knee-high all round him and rebounded from the door. Turning up an inch of coat collar he ducked across the pavement and sprang into the nearest car. Not only was its door unlocked, but a warm pink light went on in the roof as he opened it. Presently, having noticed the ignition key, he started the engine.

To a person who has little notion of driving and who has not the habit of a car, the handling of the machine is intensely absorbing: he crouched over the controls and peered out into the darkness filled with sloping rain, and he felt the engine respond, and the wheels answer the movement of his hands or even their barely-moving pressure. The whole great formidable heavy thing and himself in it moved away, faster and faster.

He became more accustomed to it; it was a powerful car and it put up with his treatment of it; the controls were simple, and after some time he could manœuvre it tolerably well. No traffic, no policemen, no lights had come to disturb his progress, and he circulated in a void. He wanted to go out on to the Great West Road, which he knew; but in learning he had been obliged to go where the car chose, or where the turn was easiest, and he could come no nearer to it than the way that led out to Hemel Hempstead.

But it was all one, so long as he was on an open road, with the rain falling and his headlights boring into the rain, and the only clear opening on to that world the triangle made by the windscreen wiper; and inside the car he had switched on a small glowing dashboard light, which tended to solidify the inside at the expense of the outside. It was the perfect solution, the ideal life; and he noted with satisfaction that there was a full tank of petrol.

The hours passed; he hummed steadily on, never so confident as to be able to relax his complete physical attention, but suffi-

ciently confident to stop the car at a roadside café and spend his
fourpence ha'penny on a pie and a cup of tea. This was the first
food that he had had in the day, and it had the effect of diminishing the dream-like feeling that had been with him: partly
because of this he drove badly on starting again, and made an
inept turn in the village, then two more, one at a crossroads,
which upset his sense of direction and sent him heading back
towards London, although he thought he was still driving
towards the west. But soon the excellent solitude returned, the
sense of being a completely isolated, faintly lit-up thing flying
through the darkness; and this went on for miles and miles and
miles of unwinding perfect road all black and very much
deserted, a shining road with the continual rain, which was
exactly what he wanted until he came to great sparse sodium
lights like the outskirts of some unhappy town. He could not tell
what town it was: still he thought he was running west. But it
looked very much like the far end of the Edgware Road, and it
grew more and more like it, so like it that he determined to turn
round at the next road-junction. A police-car picked him up at
this point, and although at first he did not recognise the flashing
headlights behind him and the warning going, he was still well
enough ahead to have a fair chance, in his opinion, by the time
he knew that he was being chased.

It was his intention to get away, back into the darkness of the
road that he had left, the country night; and he had some vague
notion that the police could not go over the border of the county.
The road was straight and empty, but for a single distant lorry on
the other side; he crouched a little more forward over the wheel
and pressed his right foot down. The instant response of the car
was like a force pressing him from behind, and the sound of the
gong faded away. The flick-flick of the following lights grew less

CHAPTER SEVEN

THEY HAD IMPRISONED him, and that was his first literal cell. It had a certain likeness to this, thought the prisoner; as if men's cages were necessarily of the same basic pattern, and as if the righteousness of being a keeper infected the good with the same smell as the bad and even the unutterably evil.

The physical smell of the prisons was similar, too, the same filth and carbolic acid mixed; and he himself squatting in that distant white-tiled cell was recognisable as himself and above all as a prisoner, a fellow-prisoner, with his mind retreated into a kind of winter's lethargy: of course in that relatively decent prison (though inhuman enough) he had been able to abdicate all responsibility and decision – an essential difference; but there was also this likeness between the two prisoners, that neither of them was oppressed by any sense of guilt. To be sure he was not at that time supported by the same forces that supported him now; indeed he was not supported by anything but moral insensibility; but moral insensibility can produce an effect wonderfully like that of innocence.

But himself afterwards was a strange figure, himself released. It was not moral insensibility that accounted for this, nor his remaining simplicity – though indeed that went very far. It tumbled him into the hands of his enemies at the very beginning, and although the concussion that he received when the car turned over might account for something, want of sense accounted for a great deal more. The police, professional thief-takers, smelt out his odd thievishness at once; and although it could not be said that they *framed* him in the full meaning of the term they certainly abused his confidence and distorted the course of justice to make it arrive at a conclusion that they thought just. It was easy to take him in: after he had been badgered and humiliated for some time a fat, kind-faced sergeant who spoke civilly and who assumed that it was all a lark – 'young gents will sometimes have a lark' – was able to get anything he wanted out of him; except, in the nature of things, the truth; but the sergeant had only the remotest interest in the truth. He was condemned, of course, for the car (for no ingenuity or lack of moral scruple on his part could deny it) but he was condemned too on a number of side-issues; and although nothing was admitted in evidence that ought not to have been admitted in evidence the court was left with the impression that he had assaulted the police, obstructed the police and threatened the police; that he was a dangerously violent character, rowdy and probably Communist and certainly most undesirable. And when after his condemnation he was found to have been already convicted of assault and battery, this impression was very much confirmed.

However that was all quite tolerable, the relative injustice and the imprisonment: it was afterwards that he lost his balance. He had been heavily fined, and because of this and his family's attitude he became first entirely impoverished and then, because of a complete deviation from what seemed to be his own natural character, entirely destitute. Conceivably the extraordinary tension of his long happy period had undermined his fortitude: he could think of no other solution.

But whatever it was, he became entirely destitute, in money and in everything else. His common good sense left him and none of his faint and ill-directed attempts at escape had a chance of succeeding. He became totally bewildered and he blundered from place to place like a child that is blind with emotion or a wild animal let out in a market-place. It was scarcely himself that suffered; but for all that he remembered the exact colour of those days and their taste.

+

HE REMEMBERED A night down near the Houses of Parliament. He lingered down there. The weeks and the months passed, and that was his centre. It was night, and it had been night for an uncountable time, the inhumanly cold indifferent darkness that begins after midnight in London with the death of all movement. Again he looked up at the clock, although he had promised not to do so until he had walked five hundred steps. They had not moved perceptibly – the hands were still awkwardly merged together at a quarter-past three. Once he would have thought that the clock had stopped, but he knew better now. They all behaved like that.

He had learnt so much, and most of it seemed entirely useless. What was the use of knowing that all the street lights begin to flicker wildly about their centres when you have reached a certain point of tiredness? From his earliest childhood he had always felt at home in the night, and that if the day were hateful, if he had no good place in the day, at least he had one in the dark; but now the night was no longer friendly.

He had also learnt that after a certain time you think of nothing but food – that nothing matters, nothing in the world, in comparison with food. He had learnt that his toughness had not amounted to so very much.

Some of his learning was confirmation: *There is nothing in poverty more cruel than its power to make a man ridiculous*: that he had suspected before; and now he knew it with deep conviction, and he could add *ridiculous, contemptible and an object of repulsion and disgust*. He had learnt that a man can die of shame, which was new to him, and that the words about the poor helping the poor were nonsense, at least as far as he was concerned. He had been cheated and abused by the poor as much as by the others: even now the other derelicts saw in him a prey, not a fellow-bum. In the Adelphi, for example, when this very night he had wanted to lie in the malodorous and frigid shelter (but shelter) of the Arches, three horrible old tramps had closed in upon him, at first with some exploratory hesitation, then much faster.

At the very beginning one of the oldest and cruellest tricks had been played upon him. He had been looking for a bed, very late at night, and this pair had talked to him in the snack-bar near Charing Cross. Oh, yes, they knew of a bed – they knew of a very cheap room: they were friends of the house – it could be arranged. Richard gave the price to the woman, for it all had to be *arranged*. Ten minutes later the man said he would see what was keeping her.

And so it had gone on. They never accepted him as one of themselves, on any level. He had lodged once in the East End; it was the last place where he had had a bed. A very poor place – the people seemed kindly enough and God knows he had given himself no airs. But the girl of the house coming up to sit on his bed and talk to him had robbed him steadily throughout his stay while there remained anything unpawned to take; and the day when he could not find the rent he had been locked out and his remaining oddments kept 'until he should pay and what did he want to try to bilk a working-man for?' They would have liked a scene; their voices and attitudes were prepared and the girl leaned out of the window with a mincing air, completely hostile. But he walked away. He could not bear a scene – he could not bear the humiliation of another scene.

The least important had been that with his uncle, who spoke with a gasping viciousness that was almost frightening, it was so naked. 'Worthless, flagitious life – always knew it – the publicity – "bishop's nephew" forsooth – *poured* out money – you and your mother between you – rot in your own iniquity.' In another burst, 'Never think of others – unexampled selfishness – just at a time when certain negotiations – when I might have been induced to take up certain grave responsibilities.' And then again, much more decent because of the presence of the lawyer, 'There are other deductions that I could have made but this compensation to the unfortunate innocent owner of the motor-car I insist on. Check the subtraction. Sign the receipt.'

But there had been others; and all these things seemed to accumulate. The court itself, of course, the police; the handling, the pushing, the deliberate offensiveness, the calculated humiliation. The lies rankled: they *knew* that he had taken nothing from the car; they *knew* that he had not been really violent; they *knew* that he had no felonious intent. Their oaths rattled off, and they upright and pink without their helmets. When he had been taken up he had been searched: in his coat pocket there were several paint-rags, stuffed in without a reason, and one of these had been a pair of knickers – he had no idea of how they came to be there, except that no doubt some girl must have left them – and this was continually mentioned, not for any true purpose but merely to blood the magistrate: no candour and yet the sergeant had spoken to him with real friendliness, most candidly.

It had not been much to bear at the time, but it came back on him. The staring and the sniggering and indeed an infamy that his uncle had no conception of, for all his eloquence on the subject.

He had learnt this too, that at a given stage you become hyper-sensitive; and although the immediate past does not mean very much (and the old past nothing at all) the immediate future does, enormously. Sense of proportion goes. It is ludicrous to stand watching people after lunch throwing good bread and but-ter to the sea-gulls – whole sandwiches – and to pretend to be watching the birds; but that is what you do, and you pick up the pitiful remains when they have gone. Not only hypersensitive, but desperately complicated: the lives and minds of the very poor are unbelievably complicated, full of complex shifts and deeply involved perplexities, when so little means so much.

There was a policeman coming now: to move him on, no doubt. Your wonderful policemen. You should see them in the station with their helmets off. You should see them working up a case in order to get a day's holiday in court; or listen to them talk-ing to a suspect in old and dirty clothes; or learn what happens to the whores who do not pay; then you would see that the civil fellow who tells you the way when you lean out of your car is all of one wonderful piece. And always the righteousness, the offi-cial Crown righteousness that by definition never can do wrong, that seeps so readily into the figure dressed in uniform.

He had lived some time in the East End. He had not been kindly treated there by anyone, but he had seen something of their lives from the inside and although he loathed nearly every-thing he knew about them, he passionately abominated the injustice and oppression of their lives – where that was con-cerned he was in complete solidarity with the working-class, and so of course he shared their hatred of the police. He knew what they thought: he thought the same.

As the policeman approached, the slop, the rozzer, the—, he sidled away. High over his head there was a click and a whirr, and the half-hour struck, with an inconclusive note. A little more than ten minutes had gone by. In a hundred more the night would begin to end, at least at Covent Garden, where the lights and the noise would begin a fictitious day and an appearance of warmth. He drifted off the bridge and wandered over the ghostly space of Parliament Square. These lights lit nothing; there was only the cold glare on emptiness, a darkness visible, and all round it this flickering. It seemed incredible that this should ever be alive again, a swirl of violent traffic, with busy people dodging through the lanes. He was alone in a dead city, with the police and the cats and a few wrecks who had not found shelter from the cold. Cold. Oh he was cold, so cold that there was no part of him that was not cold: and in his cold mouth the bad taste of hunger mounted. Ten minutes had taken an almost immeasurable expense of spirit to live through, how would he last through a hundred more?

There was something that moved in the corner of his field of vision, but he knew it was an illusion: there were several of that kind, and it was not always easy, particularly at night, to separate them from the facts. The lamps did not in fact flicker; the clocks did not really stop; these things were illusions: and eight million bastards were in bed.

He might get warm by walking, although this in a way was an illusion, or something that had as it were got left over from real life, for it did not seem to happen any more: however, he would try. He stepped out and at once he fell on the edge of the pavement. His sole had come flapping off again: he had forgotten to walk with care – the string that tied it on needed a slow, careful pace.

Poverty makes men cruelly ridiculous. For weeks he had been ashamed to lie on the grass in the park because it would show the holes in his shoes. And now his coat was out at elbow, obviously torn, which marked him with a mark as clear as Cain's but also funny, at least by the convention that regarded a crucifixion as a treat for the little ones – We'll take a picnic out to Calvary, ha, ha. It also put an end to his search for work – a search that had started with ignorant hopelessness and had ended with informed hopelessness.

The worst of the depression was over, but the state of mind that it had engendered was very strong; and still there were close on two million men unemployed, terrible anxious queues of them everywhere, grey and humourless. The strong, very highly skilled miners from the Rhondda were still singing in the streets in desolate choirs all day. In those days if a firm advertised for a clerk at twenty-five shillings a week there would be between two and three hundred letters by the morning post and perhaps another fifty in the evening or the next day, from the provinces; and naturally the firm would not answer more than a few of them. The only people who answered regularly were those who wanted to help you make good money by a little light work at home in your spare time, designing chintz, making boiled sweets (no elaborate apparatus necessary) or running a mail-order business; but these, for hard unscrupulous cruelty, did not reach the same class as the vacuum-cleaner and refrigerator firms who relied with well-placed confidence upon a constantly renewed succession of desperate men who on commission only would manage to survive as their representatives for a few weeks, by selling the vacuum-cleaners or refrigerators to their relatives and friends.

It was a hopeless search, but he went through the motions of it while it was possible.

'What experience – have you had any experience? Of course
you have your diploma? What school were you at – no, no, I
mean what school were you educated at before taking up art?
Who do you suggest as references? Well, I will show your application to the governors – there is an interview in a couple of
months' time. But there is a great deal of competition.'

That was almost the only job that he was in any way suited
for, the only one where he really had anything to offer other than
a general willingness shared by every one of the two million: with
most of the other jobs the questions hardly ever passed
'Experience?' And when it came to manual work or labouring
they usually said, 'Are you a union member?' or merely shook
their heads.

There was indeed a little casual labour, when you had learnt
your way about: for example at Billingsgate you could earn
'fourpence an up' by running a barrowload of fish from the market to the bumarees' places behind Eastcheap. But Love Lane
was steep, and it had to be done at a run; and even if you were
strong enough to do it the regular shovers resented newcomers,
and even on Thursdays sometimes (the heavy day of the week)
they would check your barrow at the top of the hill so that it
would roll back on you, spilling the boxes of fish as it came,
which was one of the reasons why the bumarees preferred
employing men they knew. The regulars would also tell you how
they would kick your parlins out, and on light days two or three
of them would chase you through the dark lanes behind the market, hoping to run you into a blind alley.

One of the rare cars of the night passed, pushing back the gla-
cial timelessness of the night for a moment, but only for a
moment. In the absence of any other movement the emptiness
returned. As something of an occupation and as it were to feel a

certain warmth somewhere he thought of the things that he hated: he hated the labour exchanges, their official smell, the clerks' wicked rudeness to the men; he hated the police of course; and he hated the unmeaning thunder of the world. But all this was very faint, by way of hate. He had cared terribly about being verminous at first: but now he cared about nothing very much, except the coming of the day.

The day would never come. Life was so much easier in the day: there was warmth in the Underground stations, warmth in many places; and the people moving about the streets reflected real life into you. But the day would never come: this was to be an eternal night, the cold and aimless wandering for ever.

Dear God: oh God, would it never end? A car sped by, running through a puddle, and the thin mud splashed his leg: there was no point in dodging it now, and he let it splash.

He was slowly dying of shame – a particular kind of shame reinforced first by want of intelligence and now by apathy. There were friends, dozens of acquaintances in Chelsea who would have helped him, but he had not been there: the area was taboo. And he had very early reached that stage of hypersensitivity where reason and logic have very little importance, where kindness is all, and where the danger of meeting a known face and of accumulating one more slight or humiliation is too great to face, whatever the advantage. But indeed he never considered the possibility of going there – almost forgot its existence.

Yet even if Chelsea had in fact ceased to exist, there were dozens of organisations that would have helped him – existed to help – but he did not know or would not ask. After a certain point the price of asking is too great. He was ashamed to beg. That afternoon he had formed the words, but they had stuck in his throat and the man he had stopped had supposed that he wanted

to know the time. 'Half-past,' he had said, walking off and carrying with him loose change that would have brought Richard out
of the gutter and a disposition to give it, if he had understood.

He was ashamed to beg. He could have gone into any baker's
shop and asked plainly for a loaf – the gift of a loaf – and they
would have been few and very strange bakers who would have
refused. But of course he never did: sometimes he stood outside, staring at the bread and smelling the bread, inventing long
involved harangues, but he never went in although bread, not
much noticed in ordinary life, becomes the most valued food of
the very poor, much more desired than meat or fish or vegeta-
bles. The simple request is almost undeniable. But simplicity
vanishes with poverty: everything becomes involved, everything
is a tortuous scheme. Nobody is less simple than a man long
tried by want, as if involution were his last defence.

He was not ashamed to steal, but stealing food (and he was
soon far too shabby to have a chance of stealing anything else) is
rarely practicable – that is to say cooked food, immediately edi-
ble – and the few oranges that he had picked up in Covent
Garden were very far from supplying his needs.

He passed by a seat, and on it there was a bulky figure, lying
full length, the middle and lower part wrapped in newspaper:
hair and beard showed in a mixed whispy bush at the top. How
long can this go on? he thought. Years? That tramp has gone on
for years. The thought appalled him even through his growing
indifference and he moved on somewhat faster.

A slow car came throbbing up behind him, and passed, and
for some reason he thought of the added ghastliness of blue light.
Some streets were lit with sodium lights and they rendered the
unfeeling part of the night hellish to a pitch that could not be
borne. The car had stopped some way along the embankment

and he had the curious impression that it was coming backwards. This appeared to be an illusion for some moments but it was not; a man leaned out and he saw with a great thump of his heart that it was Torrance.

'Temple?' he said.

Richard stopped, but did not go any nearer.

'Temple?'

Richard answered with an indistinct 'Yes.' He was trembling violently, but he felt that his face was perfectly calm.

'I have not seen you for a long time,' said Torrance, getting slowly out of the car and looking at him with very much of a question in his face and the tilt of his head.

'Torrance,' said Richard with a bursting of life, 'will you lend me – a pound, if you can. I am very down . . .'

'Yes, of course,' said Torrance.

CHAPTER EIGHT

TORRANCE TOOK HIM in, fed him and clothed him; and when he was set up he gave him the money to find a new room, for his old place no longer existed.

It did not surprise him to find that the house had been pulled down. The tree still stood, but behind it there was only an open space: the shattered branches of the tree, so broken as to look chewed when he stared close, were veiled now by a flush of new leaves; its scored trunk had healed; and in the open space where the house had been there was a faint mist of green. It did not surprise him much to find that most of his things had been taken; for if he could steal impersonally and without much inner strife he could also be stolen from without feeling rancour – it seemed to him one of those things that happen, and if he had ever reflected upon it he would have expected others to regard it in the same impersonal light, quite without malice. He regretted the loss of his easel, a big heavy solid versatile easel – Mr Atherton's second best – whose ratchet's temperament he had understood from his earliest days, and he was sorry for the loss of some of his pictures, a few because he liked them as objects and others because they either marked stages that he had passed or because they were imperfect versions of something that was yet to be realised. But he did not feel particularly censorious about this; he did not accuse fate.

And then Bolton had rescued not only three of his most recent pictures, including the big almost-finished Homage, but also by a very happy chance, his brushes, which were exceedingly valuable to him and which he welcomed as much as if they had been undeserved presents from another land.

'I did ought to of fetched more,' said Bolton, 'because there were a lot of people cooming and going even then – the big nude had gone already – but I had to travel on the Tuesday, and by the time I was back the roof was off the house. The only thing left was this, which they hoong on tree.' He held out a picture of his own, a picture of tubular purple boors.

'I can't understand it,' said Richard.

'They are not oop to it, man,' said Bolton, frowning. 'They are not bloody oop to it.'

'Bolton's work is very near the earth,' said his wife. 'The Londoner has no folk-roots.'

Briggs was also said to have saved some canvases, but he had run away from his wife and children and there was no telling what he had done with them.

'He had probably painted over them,' said Eunice Briggs, 'or else he will daub in little silly figures and try to pass them off as his own – it would be just like him. Oh, be quiet, Rudolph, when Mummy is talking. But he has probably painted them over, out of spite.'

'Was that portrait of Jacqueline among them?'

'No,' said Eunice, drawing up her shoulders and compressing her lips, 'though I remember him sniggering about it. I can't see what you saw in her. But it was when Bolton said that it was gone that he said he ought to look after what was left, and he went up and fetched some: I forget what, but I dare say it was just the sizes he wanted himself and he has used them for his own daubs. It would be just like him, because he is mean; and it would be just like him because he was always jealous of you. You know that, don't you? Shut up, *shut up*, Celia, while grown-ups are talking. He was always jealous of you. He was always pretending to be tall and virile, with that silly pipe . . .'

Richard listened gloomily, while the watery children crawled silently about: they were dressed in thick, blubbered wool, and the one Richard thought of as the urine child kept trying to climb up on his knee. Eunice was preoccupied by her drama: she gave examples of how she would not have minded 'if he had come to me openly and said . . .' and of her replies, which were sad, wise and generous; she gave an account of the various jobs at which she had *worked her fingers to the bone* to keep him.

But for all that her nose was too long and she reminded him a good deal of Beatrice: and presently, when she had discharged some part of her bile and began to grow more than comradely, she reminded him even more. It was terribly depressing. But the needs of the other child obliged her to carry it out of the room, and she came back at the moment when he gave his tormentor a strong push with his foot. It was perhaps the best service that he could have done her, because the sight of her baby kicked into the fire raised up in her bosom the Virtuous Mother who had been lurking quite out of sight, not to say the termagant, and she sent him off with a flea in his ear. He was glad to be out; he was glad to have got away; yet still it was depressing: he had seen Eunice arrive, and had seen her take up with Briggs when she was a fresh and lively girl who loved to dance; and now she was a yellow-faced, long-nosed slut and her tiny mind was as strong as a horse and unalterable now. Ill-used; and so a shrew and righteous for ever after.

He came down the mean streets of Fulham to the King's Road and walked up it: he felt no particular emotion, for the taboo had not lasted – it had scarcely outlasted one substantial meal, as if a sense of proportion could be eaten up, or found lying at the bottom of a second helping; and although he had at first walked about watching for rudeness nobody had been rude. Mrs Temple had been taken away almost at once, and even among the few who had connected them, one more alcoholic middle-aged woman was scarcely a nine-days' wonder: as for his own out- break, people had been surprised and had talked a fair amount; but now it was all quite remote – too far past even for conscious looks. In expecting people to take much of a stand over it, one way or another, he had over-estimated his own importance; yet this was one of the reasons why he had decided to live some way off, out of his usual haunts in a peripheral area that was almost Pimlico – a straggling and undecided thing between a street and a road, on the way to Victoria.

+

HE WAS VERY much better – he felt quite restored – but even so the road seemed a weary length; it was a very long way right up to the far end, particularly with the wind buffeting the can- vases under his arm, and he was half decided to turn back to the Rose for a rest when he saw Torrance cross the street with the obvious intention of going there himself.

They went in together; and although this was not a time when one would have expected it there were several people down below – a writer named Plage with three of his friends at the round table in the middle, and some chess-players in a wordless struggle by the kitchen door.

Plage had a deep, resonant voice, and in a complete silence he said,

> 'The delinquent and felonious traveller
> Sucking the last drops of vital blood
> From the unfortunate and innocent traveller.'

Richard pushed from behind Torrance and stumbled quickly through the crowded chairs. He said, 'What is the matter with you?' A flat conventional phrase, in the form of a question; a challenge that required a climb-down and of course assumed an attitude from which climbing down was possible.

'Nothing,' said Plage quickly. 'It is a quotation.'

'What from?'

'Here,' said Plage, busily finding the place: and he read, in fact,

> *The delinquent and felonious traveller*
> *Sucking the last drops of vital blood*
> *From the unfortunate and innocent traveller.*

'Oh do be quiet, can't you,' cried the losing chess-player, 'and let a man think.'

His ludicrous passionate sincerity lowered the tension at once and the whole thing passed away in a flood of tea. Torrance took no notice of it at the time and did not refer to it later, except perhaps by two obscure remarks, one about humour and the other about his ability to look after himself. 'I am quite good at looking after myself, you know.'

As for a sense of humour, reflected Richard – as for my sense of humour, is it declining? Is it less? And the thought struck him suddenly as being perhaps unusually significant, as he sat there gasping on the edge of his bed, while the rescued pictures leaned up over against him on the wall; because he had been looking for something that had gone out of his painting or rather out of his approach to painting, for he was hardly getting anything down at this time; and up to the present he had been unable to find what it was. Something was missing, for sure: conceivably it was his sense of humour.

By way of finding out whether this could be true he launched
into an analysis of himself and his recent conduct; but this was
not a pursuit that was at all usual with him then – he was not
accustomed to thinking about himself and he did not do so with
much acuity; he came up with no more than a general idea that
it might indeed be the case: he certainly could not remember
laughing recently. On the other hand, there was nothing so very
much to laugh about.

The situation was not brilliant. It was uncountably better than
the worst; but reckoned as a human situation (whereas the other
was not a human situation) it was far from brilliant. In his
absence something had happened to Drome. He had became
elusive, difficult to see, and when seen less enthusiastic (he was
apt to complain that people had no *idea* of the difficulties
involved in running a gallery, the incessant cost and the disappointments); and he seemed strangely vague about the past, the
not so very distant past; and perhaps this was designed vagueness on his part; but Richard dared not press him, to prove or
disprove it. For Drome had grown a little temperamental; not so
much flighty, perhaps, as pettish; and he needed management.
Richard thought that it would be best to confront him with a
whole series of pictures, a gallery-full of excellent pictures, rather
than tempt him to be disagreeable over little groups of two or
three: it was essential not to let Drome commit himself under
the influence of passing ill-temper. A whole series was the thing:
it only remained to paint them.

And in his absence Gay had come and gone, leaving two or
three letters – the last with a rendezvous for the very day he left
again, this time for Bogotá. Richard bitterly regretted missing
him: on one plane there was affection, on another there was
interest – at this juncture Gay would have been so useful: he

having the right to say it, and he glanced up at the ceiling and
round the walls; he looked at the door at the far end which he
himself could open and close as he saw fit, and his spirits began
to rise. He reached out for the loaf, and the bread in his mouth
had the clean slightly bitter and salted taste of thorough goodness; there was a long solid loaf of the holy stuff, and while he
savoured the particular taste and texture of separate pieces of
crust, he looked at the room, considering it in the light of an
enclosed piece of sheltered private air with himself in it. It was
a beautiful shelter: it had a bed in it, a junk-shop divan, and the
blaring of the traffic outside emphasised the beauty of its privacy. Considered only physically it was one of the ugliest spaces
that could very well have been imagined, being long and thin
and much too high, in two sections that looked each like a kind
of corridor; it had a sloping roof at two different levels, both of
them slabby, and the whole of it had been painted long ago by a
man with a pot of dark green shining paint. Then somebody had
given it a chocolate dado and had made an unsuccessful attempt
at covering the paint at the end by the door with some kind of
commercial distemper, which had turned a sick ochre where it
had not peeled off, and now it lay in flaky drifts at the foot of
the wall: perhaps it had been sick ochre to begin with. And considered from the magical or ominous point of view it was not very
fortunate: no amount of ingenuity could make his numbered
paces in it come to any sort of harmony; and in this it was unique
among his living places, for all the others had had some good
number or proportion about them. But in fact this was not a living place: so emphatically was it not a living place that it was
illegal to let it as one and the proprietor of the decaying bootshop below had said with a leer, 'It is a storage space; I let it as a
storage space – a warehouse. But it is none of my business what

you want to store in it or when you come and go; and there is the separate entrance.'

It had no lavatory, but there was a tap on the landing downstairs, and by climbing on to the parapet outside the window one could reach a blackened plateau, a plot of zinc some fifteen feet by ten, from which one could empty a pot. It was bounded on three sides by sheer blank walls of yellow brick soaring blindly up and on the north by a sea of air – an ocean whose bottom was the uneven ancient higgledy-piggledy crowd of roofs, never meant to be seen, any more than the back of the huge advertisement away to the left, peopled by a host of chimneys, huge and portentous and all different, and all testifying, with their various cowls and prolongations, to a desperate anxiety down below to keep warm – to have a fire that drew. Perhaps the plateau would make an excellent place for painting, when the summer came, if he could anchor his easel: there would certainly be all the light in the world up there. The room itself was rather poor in light, though what there was was good.

He was lucky to have found it; it was the cheapest place he had had so far; and if it was a little squalid, inconvenient and smelly, he had had others worse. The smell was not the smell of dirt, either: in more prosperous days this had in fact been the shop's upper store-room, and on the walls one could still make out notes such as *Gents tan oxfords* or *Fancy ladies' boots*; the smell was that of cardboard, dye and bootshop, and it would soon change when he had had time to saturate the place with paint. When would that be? Presently, presently he would get going: at this stage it would be stupid to try to rush into paint, for this was a dangerous situation in which he had to succeed; it would be fatal to begin badly. Yet it might also be fatal to delay much longer.

But he had the essentials: he had more than the essentials.

There was no need for him to be eating bread alone – there were eggs in a paper bag – and he was doing so at present to recapture the essential delight of having bread: but he had used this stimulus a little too often recently and the response was beginning to have something literary and second-hand about it.

Why was he so hipped about the squalor, then? He had put up with more and had only been amused: was it lack of humour now? Was that the trouble?

He tried to remember some jokes, to see whether he would laugh, but he could bring up nothing better than the beginning of a limerick and in any case he suspected that the test was too simple-minded and abandoned it. It was something more complex, he decided: perhaps the thing ought to have been called gaiety, rather than a sense of humour. Can you paint without gaiety? Certainly you can. Can you paint with a certain kind of colour without gaiety? A question.

'I know what I shall do,' he said aloud, stuffing the heel of the loaf into his pocket. 'I shall do my own portrait.' He had reached this age without ever having looked at himself in this light and now the idea excited him. 'I shall make a few drawings first,' he said, searching through his portfolio for a good piece of paper and pinning it to the portfolio's propped-up cover. 'No doubt I shall see what the poor unfortunate bugger lacks.'

+

YET THIS PERIOD was not one of unrelieved squalor and anxiety; until the want of rain in July prematurely closed the season it contained some of the purest days of his life, while Torrance fished and he painted or wandered vaguely in the meadows along the bank.

There was one such day, perhaps in the month of June, when

the sky was a tenderer, more luminous blue than he had ever
known it; an enormous bowl-shaped sky, unbelievably deep and
enormous; and white clouds passed over it. It was a soft day, and
so warm that you could walk in the water and hardly notice it; it
was a day when everything was relaxed, in the morning and in the
afternoon – the sound of the water had no urgency, the warmth
of the sun no fire: it was more like a piece taken out of eternity
than a day and yet it seemed to be the normal time, the sort of
time, weather, serenity, warmth, by which others are judged.

They were also in a place where he could relax, and for his
part he had been lying in the tall grass of the bank of what had
once been a well-tended water-meadow and which was now
reverting to something not unlike Eden. He had been lying
sometimes with his face turned to the sky, watching the clouds
in their mild procession, sometimes with his face in his arms,
breathing the smell of earth and hay; and through all this time
the air was filled with a murmurous hum, unidentifiable, but
benign. This bank was on a lost bend of a well-known stream,
where for once in its expensive course it ran through a derelict
strip of land lying between a great ducal estate on the one hand
and the water of a syndicate on the other. It lay far from the road,
although Torrance had managed to get the car along an overgrown cart-track to within a hundred yards of the water, and it
was so quiet that you could not easily believe in the existence of
a great many other people. They had been here before, and he
knew its limits well: on the left there was a dabchick's nest,
moored in a clump of weeds, wet through and curiously warm
in its wetness: it had a warm egg in it. This was the first
dabchick's nest he had ever seen, and he would not have seen it
at all if Torrance had not pointed it out. Then travelling along to
the right, going up the stream, one came to a wood, big bosomy

trees still brilliantly fresh, so many Rubenses struck with green; and all this wood stood on the far side, on a rising land that made the curve of the stream and shut in this private world: but before arriving at the wood one passed a short stretch of the stream that ran quite straight between banks of turf kept short by the rabbits, without so much as a bush on either side, and here the water ran so clear and yet so smooth that you could see the smallest detail on the bed, and even more clearly, as if it were glazed. Here the weed did not reach the surface, but lay as it were in beds, clean and perfect waving beds, while in the gravelly channels between them one saw trout like torpedoes, sometimes quite still in mid-water, sometimes cruising gently up through the lanes, and sometimes floating downstream, to turn again and bring up in some new clearing farther down: and sometimes one would see the explosion of a crayfish in the sand, or a flight of minnows.

And then, on the extreme right, where the wood darkened, there was a pool, formed by a stone weir at the bottom and at the top by some sort of an ancient sluice or water-gate that led off into a ruined channel that now had young trees growing in it, and a forest of nettles. Beyond that there was another pool, but this was strongly wired off, being within the ducal pale.

Several times the kingfisher, cutting off the curve of the stream in its journeys up and down, had passed over the meadow behind him, and now it went by again, a blue spark travelling on a ruled line; and as he followed it he saw the flash of Torrance's rod, just where the kingfisher's course rejoined the river. Torrance was fishing far and fine, and his cast curled out a great way backwards, an immense length gleaming for an instant before it snaked forward; he was fishing with great concentration and skill, but there was not a breath of air and the water was clearer than gin. An occasional trout rose on the far side under the trees, but most of them were asleep as they swam: at any rate, none would trouble himself for an artificial fly.

Richard's rôle, at this particular stream, was confined to wading over to the other side to unhook the fly on the rare occasions when Torrance was hung up, and (on more fortunate days) to wielding the landing-net: there was no need for him to keep at all close, and indeed at this juncture he preferred to be some way off. If today's fishing followed the usual pattern Torrance would search scrupulously along under the wooded bank, then, reaching the pool, he would try the best places in it from below and perhaps he would catch one or two fish; but if he did not (and today he would not) he would pause for some time, change his tapering cast for something altogether more substantial, and then with a look at once defiant, apologetic and furtive he would thread a lob-worm on to his hook: with this, fishing it over the fall, he would sometimes heave up Leviathan.

In principle and in conversation Torrance was a dry-fly fisherman of the extreme right wing; he was very contemptuous of those cads who hurled a drowned tangle of lures in the hope of catching some unseen, unknown fish far downstream – foulhooked, as often as not; and it was to avoid Torrance's uneasy blush that Richard kept his distance.

After all, Torrance had been very considerate of Richard's feelings in this matter of fishing: the religious sort of fishing. There is a curious subsidiary form of worship in England, and it is emphatically termed *fishing* as opposed to angling; trout and salmon are the only sacrifices acceptable to the unnamed deity and they must be caught by certain extraordinarily difficult ritual gestures nothing much to do with reason; and excellence in the catching is a high mark of gentility. The god has the highest sense of caste. Richard was perfectly well aware of the social implications, and when first Torrance had invited him to come he had been extremely unwilling to let his ignorance appear. He was growing adult enough in many respects, but still in this he found that the idea of showing at a disadvantage, especially before Torrance, irked him inexpressibly. But no amount of spiritual energy will suddenly turn a man into a fisherman: and although it is not impossible to pretend to be able to throw a fly it is quite impossible to maintain the pretence; and here Torrance was remarkably delicate and forbearing. 'Perhaps the rod don't suit. – It is a very stiff action. Try the greenheart; the line is rather heavy on that rod. – Never mind, there is a spare top in the bag.'

Richard's descent to the position of an unskilled labourer was brought about quickly (for the Windrush and the Evenlode are no place for a beginner), but without any acknowledgement of the facts, and when it was over Richard was rather glad than otherwise. He was and he had always been comparatively indifferent to the things of the country, but he loved the trout streams: trout never live in ugly places; the better the trout the more beautiful its surroundings; and Torrance went after the best trout in England. He loved the peace and the running water, and in every way his inglorious wandering in the background was more suitable for him.

But although he did not wish to embarrass Torrance, even by not looking sufficiently solemn at the ritual piece about 'ridding the pool of a pike' or 'of a hulking great cannibal', on the other hand he did not want to be out of the way just at the one moment when his hand with the net might be wanted. So allowing a suitable pause for Torrance's passage up the stream and his struggle with his principles, Richard walked along by the open water and along by the side of the wood. But Torrance was not above the pool, dibbling over the sluice: he was in the pool itself, poised crouching between the two main boils of the fall; he was in up to his waist, and his shirt-tail streamed out on the water behind him. His head was low to the surface and he was bent as though he were searching slowly in the strength of the current: for a moment Richard thought that he had lost his rod, but then he saw it on the bank, by Torrance's trousers.

Torrance looked up cautiously – it was all he could do to stand in the thrust of the water – and seeing Richard he nodded, formed a silent, incomprehensible word with his lips and returned to his quiet, perilous groping.

Then from the long slow quietness of the still figure and the perpetually flowing falling water there was a sort of slow explosion, a slow violence of movement – Torrance straightening, rearing himself up out of the water, turning and lurching with a great slow splashing and froth along the spit that ran down the middle of the pool: then with his face and his eyes blazing he turned to the bank and Richard saw that the violent foam in front was a trout locked between his hands. Off the spit the water ran deeper; Torrance tried it, but then, crying, 'Hey, Temple,' he hurled the fish up on the bank.

Gasping and dripping he stood over the fish and two or three times he said, 'He would not take a fly, and he would not take a worm.' The trout bounded on the grass, and its golden fins were spread like hands: sometimes it lay still, with its gills pumping irregularly and its expressionless eye gleaming up at them.

Torrance was singularly modest of his person at ordinary times, but now he stood in a Gothic nakedness, absorbed in staring at the fish; it was clearly a very strong emotion, and there was a long pause before he bent down to kill it.

Then, no longer panting, and speaking in an ordinary, level, amused voice, he said, 'How strange it is that you should be so squeamish, Temple! Dozens of people kill them like that – parsons and all. It is good for the flesh. Look at his tongue – he will be as pink as a virgin's tits. What do you say he is? Three pounds? Over three pounds: oh yes, he must be well over three pounds. Would you like to put him in the bag? The cigarettes are under the small bottle.'

He put on his trousers, turned decently away, and they sat with their legs dangling over the edge of the pool. The broken peace came closing in over them again and the smaller creatures, with short memories, began to move about as if nothing had happened: some of Torrance's intense satisfaction seeped over into Richard as they sat there smoking in silence, with the smell of trout on their hands and the smoke drifting and lying in a blue skein as if they were in a room; and all the while the fall boomed on their right and the weir made its high running sound on their left. Torrance told him, with slow pauses for exacter recollection, the story of a shattering battle that he had with a salmon in the steep-banked Avon, and had lost him in the end for want of a friend with a gaff. The kingfisher returned in a sudden blaze, and supposing they were cows, sitting there so quiet in the sun, took up its habitual place, bolt upright and blue on a dark green mossy stump. Richard felt the gentle flood of an indescribable happiness – a boyhood feeling, of an almost forgotten kind.

But fishing with Torrance was not always nor even usually a sweet-minded occupation; wandering and dreaming along the scented rushes of the Evenlode was rare indeed, for it was no satisfaction to Torrance to fish legally, and as he would not put up with the third-rate sort of stream which can be guarded by a notice board because the temptation to poach is very slight –

few trout, and those few determined bottom-feeders – there was always the likelihood of trouble. This may have been because he did not have the money needed to hire a beat on a suitable stream, or it may have been lack of foresight, for these things have to be arranged the season before; it may have been a love of variety (not to be bound to any one water), or it may have been connected with his dislike of paying. Torrance could be very generous and on occasion he would spend magnificently; but in general he was rather close-fisted. Yet however that may have been (and obviously other factors were also involved) he took a particular delight in fishing some of the most pompous water as nearly as possible to the owners' noses, and although he always (and perhaps more naturally) fished like a Christian he was not above any heresy short of the too noisy dynamite if the fish did not yield to reason. Richard had the most vivid recollection of standing by a little ornamental bridge in somebody's park, explaining to a deaf water-bailiff first how he came to be painting there, then (in a kinder but interminable interchange) the general theory and technique of painting in oils, and then the art of literal representation, with the bridge itself and a small herd of park sheep as examples, while all the time under the bridge's shade there splashed and thundered the huge worm-hooked trout that 'his friend, who had just come along for the walk' was holding on a line under his foot. A sketching easel was a piece of fishing equipment, in Torrance's view; and strictly as a fishing operation Richard was required to suit his painting to the tastes of water-bailiffs – to conform to what they would expect 'a real artist' to produce.

He remembered, and would not easily forget, being seized with a cramp high up in a benighted tree, while Torrance waited for the keeper down below to finish his cigarette – all this some fifty feet above a pool in a show place near Guildford, where the trout, hand-fed and familiar, ancient and cunning, run up to a prodigious weight – trout which had been denied to the King, no less. The arc of the cigarette-stub, its dying hiss, and the departing feet; then the descent of an impaled white moth through the branches to the dark water, where an occasional ripple made the starlight come and go, and the surge and ring of a rising trout. And he remembered the yews at Dives Abbey, where the Test runs at the bottom of the lawn, and a house-party approaching from behind the yews, very early in the morning, with the intention of fishing: apparently no way of escape except by swimming – but he had not thought of walking straight up to the house along the other side of the clipped yew hedge and so by way of the open breakfast-room and the hall to the drive and so, in spite of his urgent prayers, back to the waterside.

Richard was not by nature a fisherman: he did not mind about catching the trout and as often as not he was on the fish's side – glad if it escaped – and just as he could not really appreciate Torrance's uncommon skill, so he could not share in his predatory delight. He could not understand the pleasure of fishing in these circumstances and although he was always ready for a battle if it was necessary (having voluntarily enlisted in this war) the keen edge of the delight escaped him; and it was only by the grace of poverty that he did not sicken of the taste of trout.

The delight of gambling escaped him, too. He loved and revered money far too much to bear even the thought of losing any of it, whereas Torrance had a fanatical streak and sometimes on a race-course he would suddenly become three times more alive than usual – so much so that his impersonal calm would crack in all directions and show the vivid turmoil within, at least to a knowing eye; and he would persist to a shocking degree. Once he appeared

at Richard's place, late in the afternoon, after one of his charac-
teristic absences, and proposed that they should go to a dog-track
out beyond the East End, a hole-in-the-corner muddy field with a
second-hand hare, shifty-looking dogs and an all-male audience.
He was in a tearing flow of spirits and he moved about among the
bookies on the rail with an almost exaggerated assurance; he had
always affected a certain mystery – a liking for showing himself to
be at home in unexpected places – but Richard had never seen
him so free with Christian names, applied for the most part to
men in cloth caps and chokers or men with narrow foreheads
and long thin faces, dressed in narrow-brimmed hats and long
thin overcoats.

Nothing much happened during the early races, but Torrance
seemed to be doing fairly well, and in the long intervals he talked
continuously, explaining the whole system of keeping a book and
pointing out the merits of the dogs as they paraded. After the
fourth race the excitement rose, and on the last he betted outra-
geously. There was no tote and Richard helped him place bets
among the bookies: pushing along the line on his errands he saw
extraordinary quantities of money, dirty-faced men peeling off
rolls of notes that made him sick, and himself he carried money
that he could hardly bear to deliver up to be stuffed promiscu-
ously, carelessly, into those open leather bags. He could scarcely
have done so without the noise of the bookies bawling the odds
and the surging hot pressure of the crowd, the chalking and
scribbling of the odds, the violent eagerness, and the intense
activity which overwhelmed his desires and scruples. He was
dull-witted that day (he had spent the whole of it until tea-time
in an unavailing struggle with a rose – in useless stupefying
industry) and the necessity for hurry and precision confused him
even more than the bellowing and the press so that in the

momentary silence of the start he was hardly sure of what he ought to hope for – which number, which colour among the band of dogs that stretched along at such a pace, but he felt an immense and intolerably mounting tension and, in the instant of the last shrieking of the race when Torrance turned to him with a gleam of triumph on his tight-closed face, a huge relief.

Torrance collected his winnings himself, cramming the notes indifferently into his trouser pockets or his wallet. He said to Richard, 'Keep close, will you? A little behind me. There are a lot of thoroughly undesirable people around.' And when they sat eating fish and chips and drinking tea in the reeking shop outside the ground he pulled out one pocketful, smoothed it and separated it into different values. Richard had never seen so much real spending money in one place before, and the sight at once excited and depressed him. It is terribly depressing to see the price of so much underprized. As if divining his thought (which must have been tolerably obvious, for in his emotion he was unable to eat) Torrance deliberately laid out a small bed of notes and passed them over, saying, 'That is my debt,' and then another, adding, 'And that is your bet: I put half a bar on for you.'

He did it so pleasantly that it would have taken a more umbrageous temperament than Richard's to object or to be anything but pleased. Torrance was in one of his most pleasant moods, and after they had driven back to London and when they had been cruising slowly through the deserted City for some time he suggested that they should finish the evening at the Knocker. This was a very low place in Soho, a kind of sub-nightclub or inferior brothel, and its only merit was that someone there had the sense to prepare fried chicken in the American style: he said that it would do him good to treat Richard to a chicken and a tart.

'You do prefer girls, don't you?' he asked, as an afterthought, when they were actually on the stairs.

They sat in an atmosphere of yesterday's cigarettes and drank a bottle of watered whiskey: they talked about Corvo, and the Catholic Church. Torrance was one of Corvo's then rare admirers, and with Corvo and the chicken the evening passed along very well, although the place was nearly empty apart from the people of the house and the two or three couples of shop-girls who gyrated together when the sad little piano played.

But at the beginning of the second bottle Torrance grew somewhat contradictory: they had switched from Corvo's artistic ability to the springs of artistic impulse in general and Torrance broke into Richard's surmise with an unusually rude and petulant, 'Oh, Plato. Yes. Plato, hot potato.' Richard was pleased to hear that his ideas were Platonic, but he was sorry to learn immediately afterwards that nobody believed in them any more and that it had been shown – scientifically proved – that the artistic impulse was always traumatic in origin; writers, painters and musicians were sexual, spiritual or social misfits, impelled to create a more acceptable world. Who had ever heard of a considerable poet et cetera who was of even tolerably good family – that is to say, well-based and pleased with himself? With one or two exceptions they were all freedmen or tradesmen's sons, terrae filii, bandmaster's brood; it was only very recently that their activities had become at all respectable – or rather, their persons. Torrance was very much against 'all this bloody art stuff', by which he meant the modern self-consciousness about it and the modern romanticism, which provided an all-too-easy means of escape for perverted clods who should be at the tail of a plough. Life should not be easy for them: it should be hard, and probably made artificially harder, on Darwinian principles, to crush the host of malignant mediocrity. At present everything possible was done to bring them on, the unlimited subsidised spawning of art-schools, the insane encouragement of charlatans – there was a horrible man named Podpiece creeping about now – had been seen at Morrell House – who would never have escaped from Bridewell in a more enlightened age. 'Give me the eighteenth century,' said Torrance, and went on to observe that the creative writer was not in himself worthy of any respect, whatever the independent value of his creations: only the *man of letters* was respectable – Dr Johnson, who had never felt the slightest breath of inspiration in the whole course of his life, was eminently respectable. Torrance had a great respect for Dr Johnson, but none – how could he have? – for Dickens or Thackeray, for example. He took these examples apart and handled them severely; they were great perverts, both of them – most unsavoury. Thackeray could not write either, but on the whole he was preferable to Dickens, whose descriptions of gents were the most crawling pieces of snobbery that Torrance had ever read, far more obscene than the openly obscene passages in the more notorious books, such as *Bleak House*. Torrance was very much against snobbery. He then came to modern instances; and to his great surprise Richard noticed that Torrance was drunk: he had never seen him so much as garrulous before. For his own part he had a very high natural tolerance, so long as he was not already drunk with youth, which was no longer the case these days, and there was no movement in his head; but even so the Connemara Dew before them was so very much more dew than anything else that he would not have expected anyone to be much affected.

Yet Torrance certainly was affected, and this grew more obvious when it came to choosing their girls: they were common lit-

tle stupid short-legged very young drabs without much in the
way of looks and no one could pretend to be passionately enam-
oured of them, but common humanity demanded a certain
cheerfulness and complaisance. It demanded in vain as far as
Torrance was concerned: he did not pretend to respond to their
formalised sallies, and presently he took to speaking to Richard
only in French, referring to his dreary dreary little whore as 'this
here machine' and describing her imperfections in detail. He
took a pleasure in humiliating the girls, and quite soon what fes-
tal air had lasted to this point faded entirely away.

Although it was clear from the behaviour of the woman of the
place that Torrance was a valuable customer Richard expected
trouble, and to avoid it he fell in with Torrance's merely bloody-
minded suggestion that they should exchange choices, just before
they left. It was not very difficult, for he did not feel at all strongly
about his charmer and indeed would much rather have had the
money than the girl – an unpromising beginning for even such
unimportant joys as a cross, jaded, essentially frigid strumpet
could offer, she having to be up again at seven to get to her shop.

They drove most of the way back in a melancholy silence:
Richard's mind was taken up with dark thoughts of the pox – how
wretched it would be to undergo softening of the brain – the car-
tilage of one's nose eaten away – loathsome sores – mumbling –
general paralysis of the insane – and the poison already running
in his blood no doubt – but he was not so preoccupied that he
did not notice the stateliness of Torrance's demeanour, a restraint
now and a withdrawal that defied him to presume upon this tem-
porary intimacy.

And the next time they met, which was some days later and
by chance, he was equally remote, as it were abolishing that particular piece of the past: yet in spite of his high air the past would

not be abolished, for of the two it was Torrance who suffered as a result of that evening's jollity. He retired to bed for the necessary seclusion and treatment with a decent composure, for he took his pleasures almost entirely in this way and he was not unaccustomed to the consequences. Even when he had a free and equal choice he seemed to go for the nastier trollop every time.

Something of the same kind though to a very much less important degree had happened to Richard, for now he would not be bothered with the preliminaries and the ceremonies (however brief) of an affair with a girl on his own level except where his motives were interested; and as his appetite grew more goatish and direct so his girls became more sluttish and wanton – odd pick-ups who knew exactly why they were picked up.

On his return from destitution he had not bothered to look for the girls whose favours he had enjoyed before his departure; he knew very well (who better) that a young woman is not a thing to leave lying about unattended for much more than a week, even in cases of unusual constancy, and as far as Hilda and Prue were concerned he was quite right. But Pamela had not provided herself with a new lover: not that they had exactly been lovers – they had no particular understanding and their relationship was quite undefined – and all that could really be said was that no other person walked into her flat with the same degree of ease: other men walked in, and she had a great many friends: but a difference remained. In a way he was pleased; in a way he was furious. She had a place that could be called a flat without too great a stretch of the word – clean, trim, a carpet underfoot, smooth, smooth; a bathroom; curtains: and in a gust of indignation it seemed to him monstrous and that for some reason she was highly blamable, though he would only have shrugged if she had behaved like Prue.

Pamela was a young woman with very strong feelings about independence and exploitation. She always even violently paid her share of everything, whoever took her out (she would make a tedious scene about a twopenny bus ticket) and she continuously stated in this way and in many others that she was not there to be taken advantage of. She was quite good-looking, but she had little confidence in her reflection which seemed to her to be banality itself mixed with some lingering remains of the priggish and overwholesome prefect at a girls' public school which she had been; and in spite of her rather desperately black-and-white manner she liked to be often reassured. She was a vulnerable creature and in fact she had once been very much abused in her purse (as well as hurt in her tenderest heart) by Plage, but this was not the *cause* of her phobia – it was only one of the things that so often happen to people who are determined not to be exploited.

Their association had begun when both Richard and she had begun to grow a little wary of the warmth of unguarded sentiment, when both were growing jealous of their independence and reasonably aware of the traps laid by the heart; but in spite of her caution she had begun the association at a disadvantage – she had sought the acquaintance and although he had liked her very well as a person neither particularly male or female, a person he could go and see with a welcome – whose records he could play and who would talk pleasantly without the eternal facetious badinage of most of his acquaintance – he had thought of her as being on 'an equal but perceptibly inferior' level. He did not understand her verse, but he was perfectly certain that his work was infinitely more important than hers. Sometimes in those days, when they had talked late, far into the night, he would stay until the morning; and at first he had been rather surprised by the vigour of her detachment, the reiterated assertion of an independence that it had never occurred to him to challenge; an assertion that he took at its face value.

But then they had been essentially equal. Her advertising agency paid her well, but then he too had been wealthy as he counted wealth, and his only feeling about it was pleasure in the fact that she could produce a bottle of wine when she invited him to dinner. Now the situation was radically different, and so was their relationship. It was very much more a relationship between a man and a woman, and a difficult one in that the man was now inferior and resentful, and potentially desperate and wicked. It is a disturbing business having a friend who is really poor when you are comfortably off: hundreds of new factors come in to complicate the situation and not the least of them is your friend's hostility – he is enrolled among the wolves, unless you are exceptionally endowed.

Pamela was certainly endowed – her verse had a real sensibility beneath its hermetic coverings – but she was not equipped to deal with this situation. She was worried by it and made wretched; but by this time, this particular present among so many, the worst was over and Richard was now losing her rapidly and almost wantonly by perhaps the most ignominious manner open to him. She defended not so much her purse as her concept of a rightful love, but it came to much the same thing in the end and their unedifying quarrels were as dirty and as envenomed as if they had had the most directly sordid motives; particularly as he, being so very much reduced, had as many moral trumps as a Jew or a colonised black.

It was ugly – an unnecessary ugliness – but he minded less than she did. Somewhere, at some indefinable stage between his wonderful days and this, he had come to the conviction that so many men start their careers with: that women are the enemy.

There are two species, each the natural prey of the other: sometimes he was aggressively aware of this – he was aware of it all through the period when however hard he worked he could accomplish nothing, a period long enough to destroy the kindness between him and Pamela (which died hard, nevertheless); but when, as it sometimes happened, a picture would flower suddenly out of the desert, for no reason that he could see, or when some project began to take shape in his mind, comforting its aridity and giving him at least a remote sense of excellence (an intimation of immortality) the principle faded into a mere theory, and his natural amiability would come to the surface again.

This did not happen very often, however. These were laborious days, upon the whole, with very little to show for them; the time out, the pure escape with Torrance, was rare enough, and in a way it was harmful – for one thing because these expeditions, which were never planned with reference to him, broke in upon the slow process in which his pictures or his thoughts about pictures moved quietly about in a sea of colour somewhere between his conscious and his unconscious mind that ebbed and flowed according to some obscure laws; and for another, because coming back from that atmosphere of easy money, of money so easy that it was only the time and place of food that was in question, never its existence, was a chilling jar each time.

Real poverty is a very frightening thing when you are not used to it and a terrifying thing when you are; and although he could paint in spite of poverty he needed all the fortitude that he could bring into play, and his fortitude was of the kind that works much better if it is kept continually on the stretch. His fortitude was called upon to do a great many other things as well; not only had it to serve as a substitute for a system of social ethics and moral-

ity and for what religion that painting did not supply, but it also
had to stand for wealth, and it was not surprising that spread so
thin and worked so hard it was so often ineffective. There is *no*
substitute for wealth, especially wealth as he defined it: in his
mind richness was having so much money that you could not see
the end of it, or so much that it would last beyond that time in
which time has its meaning and into those days which you regard
with equanimity because you do not believe in them any more
than in your own death day or because they are so distant and
mild that they cannot have any inconveniences – they will not
bite: very far off dogs are all as kind as puppies. With Richard
the sum was something over fifty pounds and the period somewhere between six months and a year. The amount of money and
time, used as he knew how to use it, was wealth indeed; or it
would have been if he had had it; smaller sums were different in
nature – no number of them could ever constitute wealth. Once
he had an extraordinarily vivid dream in which he was restored
to that enviable state, placed right back in the uninterrupted
course of those wonderful days that he had once thought of as
normal; and in it he was assured that everything that had happened since was an illusion. There was a painting to be begun
in this dream and it was probably the excitement of starting it
that woke him up. A suspicion of the real state must have woken
with him, because he dared not move for some moments in case
it should be unlucky; but even so, when he was fully awake and
almost filled with bitterness the dream was still so strong that
he was disturbed to find that he was in a strange room, and
astonished that his old easel was not in its accustomed place. It
was a dreadful bitterness, of the kind that can make one cry if it
comes unawares; but it was of the kind that money can cure, if
only that can be come by. It was not Richard's way to come by

money, however; people praised his work – many kind words for his recent river-paintings – and they were charmed to have them as presents; but they did not buy. He was not then a person who attracted money, although he loved it so desperately. He did not win bets; he lost at cards; he rarely picked up so much as a penny piece. During Torrance's illness he sat with him in the evenings, and they played innumerable games of piquet; and although piquet is far from being a mere game of chance, luck certainly enters into it. Yet he never won a single partie; and piqued, repiqued and capotted, he was often obliged to look sneaking and mean about the stakes, to 'owe' them, low as they were.

It was a perfectly assured, discreet-looking house that Torrance lived in, built long ago to be let in chambers, and Torrance's set was furnished in an old-fashioned way that might have been very comfortable – Turkey carpet, brass fire-irons, deep red leather arm-chairs; something between a superior boarding-house and a modest London house of before the '14 war; but he did not appear to *live* in it, to make his home there: his area of occupation did not extend beyond his bedroom, and even that had a little of a public air – trunks and fishing-bags lying about, pictures with their faces to the wall, piles of magazines. And this inn-like feeling persisted in spite of the presence of his books. There were some hundreds of them, nearly all new and still in their jackets and nearly all, as far as Richard could see in the dim light, to do with sex, in one way or another. It was not that he did not have some fine things of his own – there was a Regency dressing-table, and a low red-lacquer bench which served as a shrine for a case with a pair of guns in its beautifully padded interior that would have done credit to an Indian prince – but they were unassimilated, and the place was not as much of a home as Gay had managed to make in a couple of weeks in

his cavernous borrowed flat beyond Victoria. A respectable char-
woman came in in the mornings, but she did not seem to be
allowed to do more than make the bed in Torrance's own retreat,
and one sensed a certain amount of conflict, for whereas the rest
of the set was as neat as the char's own parlour, the bedroom had
more of the higgledy-piggledy look of a pawn-shop – an incongruous assortment of objects in arbitrary positions, rapidly collecting dust.

One of the reasons why Torrance's place looked like an inn
was that he used it as an inn: he was often away – sometimes he
spoke of a country cottage, but without precision, and it may not
have been his. He also spoke of a friend who lived in the north,
within reach of the Spey, and it was there that Richard thought
he had gone when he vanished at the latter end of the summer.
He did not say that he was going, and Richard was very sorry for
it, because they had parted on indifferent terms.

Torrance had come to Richard's studio, which was by then
beginning to smell something less like a disused bankrupt store,
just as a picture was finishing: a stream ran into a pool surrounded by trees and above it was a sky of the earliest morning,
filled with vapours that rose to join an immensity of cloud –
vapours that also floated between the pool and the observer's
eye. It was obviously an impossible picture to describe, and any
remote suggestion of Turner or Redon might call up an idea of
redness or rose, whereas this picture was essentially green.

Richard was working out the last transparency of wet luminous air, and as this was technically exceedingly difficult he
crouched right up against the picture with his head almost
upside down, droning:

> *La peinture à Phuile*
> *C'est bien difficile.*

Mais c'est tellement plus beau
Que la peinture à l'eau

over and over again, on two flat notes. He was aware that
Torrance had said, 'So you did find some canvas?' and that for a
moment his mind had been unpleasantly jarred by the recollection of where he had found the canvas – hints and platitudes to
a stupidly intense young woman, false melancholy blandish-
ments, but with his grunt of an answer he had dismissed it.

'There,' he said, standing away and looking at the picture with
a long stare of concentrated judgment. He nodded, and observ-
ing that 'it was done; it was quite good' he unclamped it from the
rickety little easel and set it on an inclined rack of his own invention, against the dust – he was fanatical about dust on his paint
– and began to clean his brushes. The assurance of his attitude
appeared to irritate Torrance, who said, 'You have not signed it.'
Richard had a suspicion that Torrance was not in his most con-
ciliating mood, but he was particularly well satisfied with himself at that moment – the satisfaction of technical excellence,
hitting the bull with three successive darts, quite apart from the
finishing of the picture, which made his heart glow mildly; certainly it was in the right line though conceivably a little *small* –
and he carelessly replied, 'Oh, I think it is all balls, signing pictures. You do not want a bloody great *word* curving about in the
corner, unless you have made a place for it. But if anyone
thought it made the picture any prettier to have it signed, I would
write my name on the back, like a cheque.'

'How nice to feel superior to Picasso!' said Torrance, opening
and closing the window as if he owned the place. 'I could see
what you mean if it were an abstract – tightly composed. I have
always thought it a pity, by the way, that you gave it up. But to

say it of this – well, I would not say cant, because cant is a rude word . . .'

'But it *is* very tightly composed,' cried Richard. 'Don't you see it is? Don't you see it is almost entirely abstract – all this rising mass – the curve here?'

In order to make his point and also to make his peace – for he disliked quarrelling with Torrance – he showed several of his recent pictures and drew out the essential abstract basis of them in charcoal on the wall: but Torrance only said, 'Well, to tell you the truth, Temple, I far preferred your last approach.' Richard had been experimenting with canvases out of the square and the delib-erate clash of colours to try to break his way back into a strong positive line of painting that would chime in with his present state, but had given it up as an expressionist mistake. 'They seemed to me, as poor Julie would say, so very much more *modern.*'

'Don't you think these are modern?'

'Well, yes: of course. But you misunderstand me. Still . . .' He lit a cigarette, and observed, 'Everything is modern once. Landseer was modern, once upon a time. *Modern – modern.* It is a silly word. But what I mean by modern is not just contem-porary, not just the use of a few contemporary clichés, like your friend Bolton and his tubes, or all these mandolines you see about. I mean something harsh and bloody, and bellowing: some-thing like good flamenco. And this, you know – I do not mean that it is not charming and of course very accomplished – but don't you agree that it is something gentler? Less in a way archaic – not quite so much blood and shit? Something more perhaps in the line of Debussy than someone howling in the gutter?'

Torrance knew nothing about painting; he was no more than a reasonably informed spectator with a fair knowledge of the jar-gon, the names and the recent fashions; Gay knew three times

Torrance had, in effect, been staying in Scotland, with a sort of an old relative, an excellent fisherman, though rather past it now, and although the water had been low they had caught a few grilse between them and had lost one capital salmon; he had often wished that Richard had been there. There would not only have been the pleasure of fishing calmly, but the old gentleman also had some pictures. He had bought the Impressionists when he was young and they were still to be had by Christians, and he had gone on buying so long as to possess a Utrillo, which he prized above all the rest: he bought no pictures now, however.

'I had very much hoped to tempt him, by telling him about you,' said Torrance, in his most obliging way, 'and I dare say that even ten years ago he would have chaffered for a couple of your rivers: he never went wrong in finding the great men early. But now he lives entirely in the past. Still, he was very much interested in you – laughed madly when I told him about the show you had when you were a student; your diploma show; and he asked me with a great deal of typical caution, over two or three evenings, whether you were really very able, whether you would do it, and what you would want in the way of a fee – I told you he was a Campbell, a kind of Scotch Jew, and in his time he has bought Gauguins for a fiver. I do not suppose he has ever paid more than ten pounds for a picture in his life and would consider it a wicked extravagance to do so, although he loves pictures entirely. But to come to the point. The point is, do you see, that he is a curiously sentimental old man; and although he would happily trip a blind beggar into a well for the pleasure of his screams, he fairly weeps blood about his vanished youth, which he identifies very much with this same Utrillo.' He unwrapped the parcel. 'There. I thought that would amaze you. He would not trust it with anybody but me.' Richard suppressed a violent need to giggle and in the same bland, kind voice Torrance continued, 'What he wants is to have it absolutely exactly copied, but with another figure in the corner, by my thumb, with its back to the beholder, which he could imagine was himself. He would enter a Utrillo, do you see? He would give his younger days some kind of a ghostly permanence: and I dare say there are a lot of motives that Freud would discover as well. I said I couldn't tell, I was sure, but that I would put it to you. You are not offended?'

'No. Not at all.'

'Of course, I quite understand. I should never have asked you. But I have a particular regard for the old boy, and it would have given me great pleasure.'

'Oh, I will do it all right. Only–' He hesitated and looked a little sideways at Torrance, '–of course *you* know that it is not a Utrillo.'

'It most certainly is,' cried Torrance, quickly taking the picture from him. 'It is signed.' Then feeling that this was somewhat naïve he looked anxiously at the picture, and said in a low voice. 'It came from a most respectable gallery.'

'What a ham-handed bastard!' said Richard, taking the picture back and walking to the window. He frowned and shook his head, genuinely vexed at such a blundering imposture. 'It is not a Utrillo,' he repeated, 'and it does not even look like one from nearer than the end of the room, and not even that for more than a minute.'

'That is a matter of opinion,' said Torrance, bridling.

'No, it isn't,' said Richard mildly. 'There are lots of these things about – you can see them all over the place. They are like the Mantegnas and Correggios that people used to bring back from the grand tour. Gay, the man I was telling you about, bought two in Paris; a Bonnard and a Pisarro. There is a kind of Bonnard factory just outside Nice. But usually they are much better done than this. This man has not even taken the trouble to use zinc white. Utrillo always used zinc white. This is not zinc white. This picture is supposed to be something out of the *période de plâtre* and yet the bum has not the wit to use *blanc de zinc*, which is the one thing everybody knows. This must be the rue des Saules, looking up.'

'Well,' said Torrance, in a grieved and moral voice, but Richard went on. 'And look at these figures. He put them in at the same time as this house, ha, ha, ha. And then, you know, if you were to add another, that would make an even number, seeing that there are three already; which would never do. Besides, a figure here would make a most horrible mess. Not that it could be much worse, but still . . . Oh, I will do it, if it will give you any pleasure; but what I should like to know is, do you want a copy of this *croûte*, or do you want something like a Utrillo? Because although I could copy this thing out of hand, I would need much longer to turn out something like a Utrillo.'

'Could you really do something that would pass for a Utrillo?'

'Yes.' Richard mused for a while, gazing absently at the canvas. 'I was always very fond of Utrillo. The man I was trained by in France knew him well before the war and used to watch him paint: he did not like his painting, but he admired the way he used the paint. He could do extraordinary things: I did dozens of things in his manner, at one time, trying to follow his ideas. Utrillo, I mean. He put plaster and glue in the paint during this period, you know, and sand and eggshells as well, in some of them, and when you put it on with your knife you feel a kind of sludgy crunch. In a way it is the very heart of paint. I am very fond of him.'

'And you could do something that would pass for him?'

Richard nodded, and with a reflective air he added, 'It

would not be a good *Utrillo*. It could not be, naturally. But it could look exactly like something he did on an off day when he was not thinking about it or when he was thinking about the next picture. It would certainly be good enough for a merchant, or an expert, or anyone who–' he was going to say, 'could take this for genuine' but changed it to 'anyone like that. It could not be faulted technically; and at least it would be a respectable composition.' He picked up the picture, with renewed disapproval.

'Would you?' asked Torrance.

'Oh yes,' said Richard, rather vaguely.

'Would you?' said Torrance again, and when Richard nodded, went on, 'from the moral point of view, I mean?'

'Yes,' said Richard, as if no particular difficulty or question were involved; as indeed it was not, for him.

'Well,' said Torrance, with a curious look. But not wishing to raise difficulties where they were so strangely and to him unexpectedly absent, he coughed and hurried on, 'Well, I would be infinitely obliged to you if you would exert your best efforts, in the cause we all have so much at heart.' When Torrance was embarrassed he became facetious; it happened rarely and it sounded unnatural, but at this moment he was making several readjustments in his ideas, which diminished his assurance. 'Are there any materials that you will need? Sand? Plaster? Glue, ha, ha? I need not ask about skill.'

'If you want it on canvas, I ought to have the right stuff, a rather coarser grain than this piece here, and it should be on a French stretcher – a good keyed stretcher. And strictly speaking I ought to use French colours.'

'Where are they to be had? Give me a list, and I will fill the car with them.'

Every man likes to have his efforts appreciated, and it was a real pleasure to Richard to display his skill to such a sharply attentive audience. He primed the canvas as soon as Torrance brought it, and with the first strokes he began to explain the technique. 'I think one ought to consider it more as a sort of small mason's trowel than a knife,' he said. 'It is the back of the blade that does the work.' And at the same time he noticed with a different kind of pleasure that although he had not used this technique for years his hand had forgotten none of it, and without any conscious guidance from him the palette-knife ran through and through the ground-up paste as though it did so every day. 'And now that I have put it on I shall knead it all over with my thumbs, round and round . . . I work it right in, do you see? Now I shall brush it over roughly: and let it dry for a fortnight. That is where this booby fell down – he could not resist the temptation of painting straight on to it. Or really I should say one of the places where he fell down. He was hardly ever on his feet at all, except for the signature, which is quite well done. I dare say someone else did it for him,' he added, looking at it narrowly in the best light at the window. 'Though it is not impossible Utrillo signed it himself – he sometimes did. Stupid little fakes with a genuine signature.'

In a fortnight he said, 'Now I shall draw the chief masses of the picture upon this enduit. In charcoal. No details.'

'Isn't it cheating to use a ruler?'

'No. Not at all. He used a ruler and a set-square and a plumb-line. Do you see it taking shape? It is that street at the bottom of the rue Norvins: a friend of Durand's had a studio just there, on the corner. I can do it perfectly well from memory. He did most of his from memory at this period: he was shut up, poor soul. And indeed it might even be a mistake to be too exact. Do you see, the symmetry of the whole thing is already established: but when I begin to paint it will seem to overbalance at first. Now I am going to cover the masses in aplat: a *flat* house . . . another *flat* house. See how it spreads. This slab will be the roof of the bistrot: flat walls. Look how strong this line is with the ropey white. That is really a delightful line – what a pleasure it is to use paint like this! He could not have done better himself. So much for the masses. But you see that the whole thing is unsatisfactory here? And this whole area? It is because there is a space you can't see for the details – I am going to put them *over* this. Watch this sign-board: the blue square brings down the line of the roof and anchors the whole of this side; and that blue answers this blue up here – it ties the whole thing up: relates it. You notice the courage of this ultramarine? It is almost his only blue. All these details mean something, as well as representing something . . . if only one could make the fools understand that. Window. I must take care not to be too pedantic with this window. Tree. Emerald, according to him. Do you see these gaps? A kind of blankness here and here? Last thing I shall put the figures there: one here and two there, and they will bring everything into balance. An odd number of figures. He had a curious feeling for numbers, in that way; and he liked to count his paces and other things; which I am very glad of. It is enormously important, I have always thought. Pattern and order. Will you pass me that rag? Now the solitary figure. Do you have any feeling about odd and even, both excellent in their way, but entirely different? When I was a child I used to love the night – counting in the darkness. It is related. There: no more. It is finished. Yes, that's finished. You don't want to go on any longer – it must not look careful, as if you had been licking it over for a week. What a pleasant little thing it is; I did not think I could have done it so

Marx Brothers film, and listened to a Negro trumpeter; they finished the evening by driving almost silently through the motionless and rigid City in the moonlight and up and down the black Embankment: the river was at flood. And when they parted Torrance said, looking up at the moon, setting now, at the bottom of the street, 'When she is full again, we must see whether we can get some duck.'

Shooting with Torrance was a less anxious business than fishing with him; for one thing almost any evening field would produce a rabbit – it did not necessarily have to be a grand and fanatically preserved shoot; and for another Richard was by nature a tolerable shot and he was therefore able to bear an active part. This too took him sometimes into a country of a kind and of a beauty that he had never suspected: huge Cambridgeshire fields with pheasants round the ricks like so many hens, and hares racing in the stubble; Constable's own Stour, with snipe along the meadows; and the endless reedbeds and the mixture of water and mud, half land and half sea, day and night mixed together, where the duck came whistling in over the bright water and sometimes geese rose with a thundering out of an unseen cut. But he could not cook the unfortunate creatures and he often regretted both their deaths and the shivering hours and the caution required for their killing: and for him the most interesting thing about all this was the door it opened upon Torrance's various lives.

It was in shooting that he met some of Torrance's friends, people from a completely different world, that had no contacts with his own; as far as he was aware he was the only person of their set who had made this migration, and he found it peculiarly flattering when Torrance first suggested the encounter.

It was on a yellow day on the verge of winter, too dark to work even leaning against the window, and he was not sorry to be interrupted. It was an icy day, and although he derived some warmth from the picture that he was working on, a nude on a red and ochre ground, the knowledge that he had only three weeks' life in his pocket kept adding itself to the cold to make the picture more a painstaking example of obstinacy than a delight. It was little use going on: the girl had already huddled on her clothes and had crept perishing away, determined to find a more comfortable lover.

Torrance had the expressionless face that he reserved for distaste or emergency or surprise, and watching Richard for the effect he laid down a thin bundle of notes in an elastic band, saying, 'Here are the wages of sin.'

Richard looked startled and said, 'What sin?' He had almost forgotten the Utrillo, classing it in fact (after the first day's uneasiness) as something in the nature of an over-sized practical joke, rather blundering and painful, as these things so often are.

'Any sin you like,' said Torrance. 'The sin of attaching too much importance to a name is my choice: or collector's gripe.'

'Thank you very much,' said Richard, stuffing the notes into his pocket and trying to count them by feel, unseen.

'I am going into the country with some friends after lunch,' said Torrance, relapsing into cheerfulness. 'They have some partridge shooting, and I thought you might like to come. You are invited.'

'Could I go like this?' asked Richard. He was wearing a mackintosh over all his clothes and he looked fairly respectable.

'Oh, it will do for the country,' said Torrance, after a momentary pause. 'A Burberry covers anything.' Then, still obviously thinking of the same subject after a few civil remarks about the work in progress, he said, 'What I cannot understand is why you do not correct fortune more – more heartily. I mean, speaking as one citizen of Carnal Policy to another, it is ever so much more comfortable, ever so much better in every way, to be well dressed. Or if not *well* dressed, at least you know *tolerably*. Herod's have perfectly presentable men's things, in a modest way, and your uncle must have an account there.'

'Yes. They bought me a suit from Herod's once.'

'It would not be decent if he had not: I doubt if it would be canonical. You must set yourself up – expressed in richness, not in fancy – I am sure he would wish it. And if he does not, tell him a few Christian truths: Saint Paul advises us to let no man seek his own, but every man another's wealth. No man in his position can conceivably make a fuss: that is a thing worth remembering.'

They went in two cars, the friends in a smaller, lower machine, three of them with one crammed into the dickey, and after a very shocking drive they came into the deep country off the high roads in the neighbourhood of Six Mile Bottom. Torrance either had a slower car or less skill than the leader, and he did not speak between Puckeridge and Trumpington; but he arrived at the remote and deserted cart-gate just behind the other car in excellent spirits, and passing Richard his spare gun and a pocketful of cartridges he muttered in an eager half-tone, 'We shall wipe their eyes.'

They walked a long field of villainous sugar-beet (a very ugly green) in the mizzle of the expiring afternoon and they flushed three coveys; of these they knocked down several birds which for want of dogs they lost, and some which they picked up; and Richard, unused to shooting in a line, took his neighbour's bird, swinging round in such a fashion as to make him duck – his only contribution to the day. Shortly after this, soaked to the loins, they went back to the cars and so began their hurtling return. It seemed a poor afternoon's sport to Richard, and he never knew whether they were poaching or not: on the balance it seemed to him that they were probably not – they had gone quite near a very large house in the trees behind a park wall on the left of the long field and they would scarcely have done this if they had been poaching; for another thing Torrance, who ordinarily stared cautiously into any field before he entered it and then went in with a wildcat's or a lurcher's silent approach, had had none of that air: and for another these friends seemed perfectly capable of owning a shoot.

There were three of them, Mowbray, Crichton-Meddow and Lynch; and when Richard had them sorted out he found that of the three Mowbray was by far the most important. He was a cheerful pink and white fairly young man with yellow curly hair; he dressed particularly well, and he had even more than the others the appearance of wealth. He was almost illiterate: he preferred to have even a race-card read aloud and when he was obliged to communicate by the written word he did so by dictating telegrams over the telephone. But Charlemagne could not read either, and Mowbray was in no way inferior to Torrance; he was not in the least degree submissive or deferential, and Torrance, usually so eager for mastery, was content to leave it so. Mowbray belonged to an old Catholic family, not so strict that it objected to sending him to Eton, but strict enough that divorce was unthinkable without the interminable process and most improbable consent of the Rota: in spite of some shocking reverses on the Stock Exchange he would still have had a good deal of available money if he had not locked it all up in a trust fund for his wife and children (his father-in-law's prophetic soul) and as he was separated from them, and she blameless, he could not get at any of it; so for some time past he had been reduced to living on his wits. The reduction was rather moral than physical, however, and he looked fat and contented. His credit and standing were almost unimpaired; he still had many excellent connections.

Crichton was also a Catholic, but he had been to Downside, at least for as long as the monks' patience could bear the strain: this had been astonishingly long, because Crichton had had no parents since the war, and his guardian (a righteous man of high degree) could not stand the sight of him. Torrance had first met him in one of those homes for unwanted adolescents that then flourished in Germany under a variety of more or less cultural names and with a variety of ambitious programmes – carrots, Gautama and Jung, the power of music or handicrafts. He was now a strong, hairy man, very dark, and his eyebrows ran jointly a little way down his nose: although he had the physique and except on formal occasions (when they could be very pretty) the manners and vocabulary of a porter there was no doubt that he belonged to the upper sort – the sub-human section of the upper sort – and one had the impression that he would have been far happier in the army. He had some private means and the reason for his presence was his attachment to Mowbray rather than necessity. He had also been very fond of Torrance, in his dark and surly way, but now he was divided in his allegiance and he did not always know where he was. Sometimes if there was a disagreement between Mowbray and Torrance – carried out in hints and tolerably fine work rather than the plainer method of a kick in the groin – he would look anxiously from one to the other: and they were not above playing on his feelings, either.

Lynch was a younger man, decorative and of the same kind, but merely vicious and stupid. His only distinction was that he had gone directly from his public school to Borstal, but this experience had apparently left him quite unmarked. He was of no importance and from an unguarded remark Richard gathered that he was a 'stooge'. But what exactly the speaker thought the word meant in its native idiom was far from clear and to Richard it conveyed no more than a general impression of contempt. Lynch was often replaced by others remarkably like him, Barclay-Browne and Holland, for example; and eventually he disappeared.

At this first meeting, after their return to London, they went to a club in Shepherd Market, a very luxurious slum with dim pink lights. There was a cashiered officer of the Guards behind the bar (a pathetically agile man with an automatic laugh, anxiously undignified, fifty-five) and in front of it several young ladies alone. They were made up in rather a whorish way, but in that quarter this was far from conclusive evidence; they were so very proud and high, and bored, that he could not pronounce within himself, even after a good deal of reflection.

He had plenty of time for reflection, for the conversation was entirely about cars. To begin with, Mowbray had been quite civil, and had asked him what he would drink; but the other two, having stared at him heavily enough, had ignored him. Once Torrance, to bring him in, had observed that 'it was when Temple here was with me – we were fishing that day below Fullerton.'

'Well, I hope he fishes better than he shoots,' said Crichton, who had been thinking about this for three hours. 'He nearly blew my head off.'

Richard had it in his mouth to say that that could have made only a very unimportant difference, but he was impressed by his surroundings, and at a push Crichton's tone could have been called jocular. The talk went on, therefore, without this piece of repartee, and Richard gazed at the long smooth legs at the bar and lusted a little, spinning out his luke-warm drink. The talk was excruciatingly stupid, and though he was qualified for talking stupidly himself this was a different stupidity and one that he had not learnt at all: he had nothing to say. He knew that he was infinitely more of a person that Crichton or Lynch, but he was equally certain that they were ignorant of this superiority and it would have needed greater wisdom than he possessed not to find this painful; for in a way, and in part unwillingly, he admired them. It was not directly their insolence and assurance that he admired but rather some underlying quality that he saw more clearly as he knew them longer, something that had to do with dash and ferocity – an ability to attack and a love for attacking that he did not possess himself; for his variety of courage was more a capacity for endurance, and although he had made himself into a fighter his aggression did not come unprovoked from his nature. Whereas in them he felt its spontancity.

Generally they robbed country houses which they knew and which they knew to be worth robbing: sometimes hotels: and because of their position they and their friends could sell jewellery and such things with an ease and at a profit unknown to common thieves. At this time, from the commercial point of view, they were doing extremely well; but sometimes they would vary their tactics out of sheer bloodiness of mind, and once, soon after their first meeting, Richard found himself, without any necessity, sitting among the spewed-out sawdust that had packed the walls of an old-fashioned and, as it had proved, inefficient safe while they lingered, talking much too much and much too loudly, in the little room behind the upstairs bar of the Swan Embowered, a pub in a country town, where they had stopped by chance. It was the great inn of the place, and in the assembly rooms below a dance was going on; a loud but muffled thumping and sometimes applause came to them all the while, and much more clearly each time the door up the service stairs was opened. This happened several times, and now and then a servant could be seen hurrying through the bar – darkened and closed at this time of night – on some tray-laden mission, and once the landlord, clearly recognisable through the curtained half-glass door, stopped to light his pipe, a long process, with jets of flame that lit up his face for the watchers: he stood there staring straight at the door when his pipe was going and he presumably meant to come in at the end of his meditation, for his hand was on the flap of the bar when a voice on the stairs called him down.

Yet in spite of this deliverance they would not go. Their car (a hired Daimler on this occasion) stood in the stable yard outside clearly visible to Richard at the corner of the window; but Mowbray had to make a slow tour of all the shelves and cupboards in the room and Torrance and Crichton leafed through a volume of comic sporting prints by the light of a shaded torch, sipping from the landlord's private bottle as they did so.

He did not like it and they knew he did not like it; he said nothing, but even very stupid men are aware of these currents in times of accelerated life and as far as Crichton was concerned it was this very reluctance in Richard that made him exaggerate his bravado and on that night delay the going intolerably. That night at the Swan was, as it happened, clean contrary to Torrance's principles, which abhorred unnecessary risk: they were sensible, cold-blooded principles, and he usually insisted upon them with a puritanical harsh righteousness, but sometimes, unpredictably, he would be bored, and he would fly off at the most extravagant tangent.

This was rare, however: usually he found his more extreme emotions on the racecourse or in driving, and a more usual expedition was the carefully timed and arranged descent upon a house that belonged to Lynch's godparents. A huge house, of which Richard saw nothing but the vague loom through the trees and the rain in the trees, but whose pictures he was called upon to judge later, after some miserable and dripping hours of watch, at least those of them that had passed Torrance's preliminary inspection.

It was difficult to see how much Torrance was influenced by Mowbray and how much of it was the other way about: they certainly disagreed upon many points, but where the compromise lay – nearer whose side – was a delicate and a varying point except in one or two instances. Torrance, for example, completely ruled out all physical violence, whereas Mowbray did not; but here Mowbray gave way. On the other hand Torrance bowed to their loathing of tea, fish and chips and mutton pies, and they frequented road-houses, where the food, if not necessarily better, was a little less repulsive to look at and where they could drink: the tea, the nameless reptiles and the sodden chips, the pies with their brilliant encrusted peas, were reserved for the increasingly rare occasions when Torrance and Richard were alone together. But it was clear enough that Richard needed all Torrance's protection to keep him in the band, in the face of Crichton's continuing hostility and Mowbray's indifference; and it was clear that his talents, as they appeared in this context, were scarcely of a kind that raised him above the rank of stooge.

CHAPTER NINE

A DISGUSTING VISCERAL PAIN and an extreme foulness came welling up to destroy the order of his mind: the years and days of his recollection that filled this dark present cell were thrown out of all sequence by the assault, and they almost vanished to their former hidden place. But this was a pain that he could circumvent or shorten (an old pain, known ever since his first interrogation) and in time it passed, leaving him to grope his way slowly back to that point at which the chain had been broken. He did not reach his place easily or quickly; it was a humiliating, disagreeable place to inhabit, for all his cynicism and detachment.

There is very little known about sin. And if sin is not only what is described as loathsome and shameful in works of piety but also what is loathed and contemned in living fact then even less is known about it, because at this point communications break down: the plain word no longer suffices and poetry and parable are needed to throw their indirect brilliance; but there are few poets, and those few do not have many listeners.

The direct account is not enough, if only because of the rule of custom. In ordinary circumstances the mean sin is never acknowledged, so that when it is the effect is excessive and disgusting: Bunyan was *the chief of sinners*, but he furiously denied any particular fault; Christian was a little better than his author, but he never mentions bilking the tradesmen of Destruction before his departure; spite and vanity have no place in any man's

Confessions. There is something like a parallel in the difficulty with reported conversation: many ordinary men say such words as fuck and cunt, but until recently they have scarcely ever been printed and even now they tend to leap right out of the page when they are seen although they may have been said in a mild and commonplace voice. Or in the description of a person: to say of a boy that he picks his nose is to present a more than ordinarily unpleasant little brute, and to say that self-abuse is his delight is to hold up a monster; whereas the boy may be ordinary enough, and even amiable.

And even in ordinary circumstances the communication is still imperfect, cold, formal and inefficient: how far can a man go and still confess? Confess the doing rather than only the name of the deed? Not very far, even with the fear of Hell behind him, because language is not designed to convey information about sin. Language and the whole habit of mind of a lifetime make anything much more than the 'miserable sinners' nearly impossible in direct terms, even with the best of will.

'. . . and Father, I have committed impurity.'

'Yes, my son; with women or with men?'

'Oh,' (in a shocked voice), 'only with *men*, Father.' (Or only with women, as the case may be.)

But *impurity*, even when it has been related how many times and whether adultery or fornication, does not get you very near the fact. There are so very many more sins than names of sins; and the names do not often fit the sins. There are two difficulties, and if one is avoided the other is not: the near-impossibility of communicating for want of medium and skill, and the near-impossibility of receiving; for in the matter of sin it is to be presumed than the intuition which conveys magnificence and beauty from one mind to another is largely inoperative, if only because of the meanness of scale in the emotions usually involved. Yet it is a break-down only in communication, for the sinner's private and personal and only too portable Hell is equipped with apparatus that can revive the entirety, without any civil generalising or artistic selection or even common good taste – every nuance of false intonation and every lancinating jet of shame. Fiction cannot go very far in recounting meanness or caddishness, unless it is concerned with villains; but the agenbite of inwit knows no such restraint.

He was waiting for Valerie, or if not exactly waiting for her (for she had been trained to punctuality) preparing for her; and he moved about the long and hideous room increasing the untidiness. It had been squalid enough in the first place, for of all the austere and even fanatical order of his best days nothing remained but the arrangement of his colours and his tools – all the rest could go to hell and indeed had gone in that direction if hell is filled with dank grey dust, but it was not the right kind of squalor, not sufficiently picturesque. Increasing experience had taught him what people expected of the *vie de Bohème*, and he set the stage accordingly. Different kinds of women called for different kinds of mess.

The room was less bare than it had been once, but not so well supplied as it had been just before he was dropped – then, at the modest, barely perceptible height of his criminal prosperity, it had contained a gramophone, as well as many other portable objects which were now represented by a sheaf of pawn-tickets. Still, he had an excellent easel and almost all that he could wish for in that way: a dozen canvases, heavily primed, hung drying on the rail and below them there was an impressive array of French colours, brushes, pots and little bottles; beyond them there were three or four current things of his own, unfinished, very slow and unsatisfactory in some ways, but still containing enough of a strange value to encourage him whenever he saw them objectively. One of them was to do with the bridge over the Saint James's water, and in the spring of the arch, leaping through a flood of green and yellow light, he thought he had one of the purest statements that he had ever made. There were some preliminary sketches of the place pinned up near it, and in one of them the figure on the right was Valerie. She had been sitting there, reading *True Confessions*, while he was working, and something of the kind was needed in that place: when she got up he called out very roughly and told her to sit down again, and she had sat there without so much as turning a page or altering the rather startled expression on her face until he had finished.

Not far off there was a study of her, just a few lines of her head – extraordinarily recognisable – but principally her pink back and bottom, for she was the only person directly out of Ruben's world he had ever seen and the ample, dimpled, abundant flesh with its unbelievable nacreous green shadows fascinated him. For years she had tried to starve this body out of existence and she was more disappointed and ashamed than gratified by the picture. But she was pretty gratified, too, and recently she had been pestering him to do her portrait, which naturally enough was the only painting that had anything to say to her. He was not interested in portraits: he never had been, and at present a portrait would be clean contrary to his line of work. In any case he worked so terribly slowly now and missed the way so easily if there were a distraction: and his reproductions or forgeries took so much of his time now that they were done without any pleasure: he would say something about portraits being *bad for his art*, or some such stuff.

His constantly attentive ear thought it caught the slam of a taxi's door and he walked over to the window with a frown and an ugly expression on his face; she ought to have learnt by now that he hated early visits as much as he hated unappointed ones. It was only a delivery van, much lower down.

But in general the set of a man's face – its ordinary look, its unconscious general expression – lags far behind the set of his mind (it may take years of celibacy to rule the lines in a clerical face) and although Richard had been roughly used by life, and although he had enjoyed it on occasion far more intensely than most, he still looked untouched. He had been much terrified and shaken; he had been ill; and recently he had been bitterly humiliated by his exclusion and disappointed in his hopes: his mind and spirit were setting in hardness and resentment and unaffection, but for all that his face looked young and pleasant, and quite handsome enough for his purposes.

This lag may be the cause of many mistaken judgments: it had certainly deceived Richard in the case of Drome, who even now did not have the typical appearance of the sour kind of sodomite, but who could nevertheless run into a shrill unprovoked malignance that took away all hope. Though indeed Drome's ill-temper had not been altogether unprovoked; it was not always one of those apparently wanton fits of dislike that come so cruelly between the sexes from time to time.

Richard had been dropped. 'The truth of the matter, my dear fellow,' said Torrance, 'is that the others look upon you rather in the line of a Jonah.' There was no denying it: whenever he had been with them they had had bad luck. They had not been taken, it was true, but they had prised open safes with infinite pains only to find them empty (or in one case containing an inexplicable bag of moth-balls); they had risked a great deal to steal a rope of Woolworth pearls; and the ancestral Lely turned out to be

RICHARD TEMPLE   213

ancestral only as far back as Victoria's reign. Sometimes they had done a little better than this, but never so well that his personal share had ever amounted to twenty pounds – and they were people who thought in hundreds. Still, for his part, he had not gone along primarily for the gain, and almost all the time he had hated the whole thing; so it was difficult to see why he should have resented what he also considered a deliverance. Partly, of course, because of the pain of rejection – they had preferred a person called Motherless Porter, who understood the changing of the numbers inside an engine and whose skill and dialect appealed to them much more than his; and partly because he knew that there was a deep, cunning competition between Mowbray and Torrance for the possession of Crichton, and that he had been thrown over in the course of it; and partly because he knew that Jonah, though true, was not the whole truth, unless perhaps Jonah was also slightly middle class, a man who did not know how to dress, who was rather uneasy in the Ritz and polite to the waiter, who never had the look of one with fifty pounds in his pocket – a man who was wanting in dash.

It had not been done very brutally nor done completely; for some time he had gone on doing odd subsidiary jobs, pawning and selling, and he was still the art-expert. But now on those occasions when Torrance asked him out and they joined the rest at some road-house he found that he did not understand their talk, no longer caught their allusions and did not know what was afoot; sometimes he would see strange faces – Motherless Porter came and went – and he knew that they were *in* and he was *out*: bookies sometimes, and once, in a particularly discreet restaurant, a well-known dealer.

He had been relegated to the manufacture of Utrillos, and this was now his chief livelihood; an uncertain, vacillating kind of support. It was an enterprise that belonged entirely to Torrance; it was not even mentioned to the others; and Torrance controlled the coming and going of the pictures, their number and their price. The number was variable but generally small; the price was always very low. Torrance admitted this and regretted it, but he said that they had to pass through many hands; and now Richard found that the affectation of mystery that he had always noticed in Torrance was not so much an affectation as a stroke of deep policy – he had no idea of where or how Torrance disposed of the pictures, which were not readily saleable objects, and he was quite unable to dispense with him even if he had wanted to.

He did not want to do so, though sometimes he wondered why not, for Torrance could be very disagreeable. And besides he was sick of London and everything in it and everybody, and he had a great longing to escape to Paris. He had a great deal to escape from, and he felt that if only he could get there and settle down he would be painting again within a month. He had been over twice with Torrance on what could be termed business, and each time, going into France, he had felt that he was coming home – he slipped into the language as if he were waking from a dream. It was a harsh, severe, dirty and parsimonious country, which he knew perfectly well, like an extremely valuable and often unpleasant relative, crammed with character; and it contained none of his wretched middle stretch of life and filthy memories. It seemed to him the only country worth living in. It was ten times more alive than England. He knew many people now working in Paris or still working there – there was everything to be said for it: and one thing among all the others was that it was not a facetious country – a sense of humour was not obligatorily hung out all day long. He was sick of simpering.

He would go out in Paris. Here he hardly ever went out any more, except on those violent, hideously expressive jaunts in which everybody but himself seemed to be brooding the deathwish.

He would paint there: he would find out the line that now he kept just touching, only to lose it in five minutes, and he would paint until he was back at that marvellous stage that he had reached once, and beyond it. And if in fact Drome was intractable in the face of what he could accomplish, given the space and time and a breathable air, there were other galleries, for God's sake.

The thing that made the air unbreathable was fear. Fear was there all the time, waiting for him to be conscious of it; and although he could put up with a great deal, poverty and cold and noise and irregularity, as well as discouragement and hope deferred, he could not paint when he was afraid. To work he needed a certain detachment from immediate impressions, a kind of peace in which his mind could revolve in its own way for a long time before each picture and during the painting of it, a time that grew longer and longer as he became more hard to please; but fear is of all the emotions the wildest and the most immediate, and the most insistent. That was why his painting was so slow and why it so rarely gave him any of that full satis-faction, that feeling which not only persuaded him that he was alive and ten times more alive than the sleepwalkers in the streets and half the studios he knew – not only that he was alive but that he ought to be alive – that he had a place in an appar-ently indifferent world. He would be standing there in front of his easel, working deep in the shifting colour with a hundred nec-essary recollections in his mind about the poise and mass of this coming shape and the necessity for that curve to be foreseen when an unexpected knock would make it burst into life, an explosion of fear. Or sometimes it would come without any knock, just seeping up into his consciousness to destroy his peace. It was the same thing that made his Utrillos a great burden now, a heavy, time-consuming grind, an anxious application of technical mastery, instead of a light-hearted nonsense that he could toss off in an hour or two.

He had forfeited his liberty and all the decency that his life possessed; and his fear was the fear that he might at any minute be called upon to pay. The unexpected knock might be a request for payment, not to be denied.

It is a bad thing to be hunted, even when you know that most of your pursuers are slow, heavy, stupid men; for you also know that there may be some clever ones among them – there are so many, a pack of thousands. And the thousands are all backed by the strength of the law and the far greater strength of their own approval and the approval of the world, a whole world full of people morally behind them and against you. And if they catch you they will inflict an infinity of humiliation, ignominy and suffering upon you, very gladly and with universal support. The older he grew the more he reckoned the annihilating force of public punishment – the hiss of the world; and he was getting much older now, so much so that he had no difficulty, alas, in knowing himself from that time to this present, this other prison: it was, for some impressions, some ways of thinking, only yesterday.

And his fear was not exaggerated: he knew that the others shared it, and that although they were better equipped to cope with it, they were driven from one living moment of intense danger to the next, and that in the intervals it was necessary for them to move about in a band from one noisy place to another. It was a real fear. There was always the possibility of a mistake, some

overlooked trifle that would blow up everything, privacy, seclusion, human dignity (such as it was), all in one hideous and very
long-drawn-out explosion of misery.

His fate was not in his own hands: it was not even in
Torrance's. However cautious they might be a failure in any
remote associate could be fatal; and there had been too many
associates. Torrance was careful, but not always; yet even if he
had been Solomon he could only have chosen among the sort of
men who were available. There were certainly fools among them,
and a fool might so easily get drunk and blab. His freedom
depended upon the sobriety of some remote and forgotten fool.
But he did not have to look so far as that – there was Crichton
at hand. Torrance and Mowbray almost never drank enough to
move them, but Crichton could sometimes hardly see. He had
been drunk when they had had their fight: he was quarrelsome
and talkative when he was drunk. However, they kept Crichton
very much under control: a greater danger was Lynch, who had
been dropped when all the information that he could supply had
been supplied. He had taken up with a far more stupid, brutal
and notorious set – the fellows (actually related to Crichton, as
it happened) who had very nearly beaten an old jeweller to death.
Lynch was in prison for seven years now, and there was no knowing what revelations he might not make for good-conduct marks,
after the system had been working over him for some time. The
natural world of thieves was said to have a rigid law of silence:
but this half-world of vicious misfits and strange exceptions had
no particular code that he had ever been able to detect, and they
must rely upon Lynch's ideas of right and wrong – an uneasy
basis.

The fear was with him all the time. He could not see a policeman without mistrust, nor a plain-clothes man without a miser-

able turn of dread. He had often heard as a child that *the wicked flee when no man pursueth*, but he had never understood how *often* the wicked fled, nor how the world was filled with pursuers, most of them imaginary, but each one potentially real. He had not then known that the pursued hated the pursuer with a venomous hatred that turns him wicked – that in the degradation of the pursuit he becomes wicked, independently of the initial crime.

No one had told him then that it was wrong to transgress because nothing in the world was so ugly as the sight of a man in the hands of his righteous enemies – that nothing was so ugly, miserable and boring as fear – that a man kept in a cage was liable to become an ugly beast, his soul having evaporated between the pages of the *Police Gazette* – that it was immoral to be treated as a thief. He was arriving the hard way at last, by himself and by means of aesthetics, expediency and repulsion at something in the nature of a conventional morality, at least a civic morality. But he still hated the police and the thief-takers: on one of their last really agreeable days together Torrance had said, 'Power corrupts; and the spiritual corruption of the police is something inconceivable to people who do not know anything about it. It is not only that they are inverted criminals, but they never have the criminal's saving sense of sin,' and Richard went right along with that.

But that evening, waiting for the flighting to begin, was already months and months ago, at the far tail-end of last winter, and since then he had not seen a great deal of Torrance; at least not of the Torrance that he had been so intimate with.

Richard was growing up; his spring and vitality were going, together with a natural cheerfulness and good-temper that had resisted a surprisingly long while, but on the other hand he was at last beginning to arrange his values outside painting, and to earn some expensive common sense; yet he did not see that Torrance was also changing. It was as though he thought Torrance too impressive, too monolithic, to be subject to development – indeed, it was impossible to imagine him as a child.

But Torrance had not reached his definitive form either, for he was only slowly being eaten by Ishmael, and somewhere between their first meeting and this time he had undergone an apparently radical change, in that he had completely lost any real interest in the arts. He never had much feeling for painting or music, but some writing, some poetry, had once moved him profoundly, and as he had a great deal of restless mental energy he had amassed an extraordinary stock of learning for an uneducated man. He had outlived that, and it had vanished gradually as he became more and more committed to his present way of life with its more obvious satisfactions: of course he had retained the jargon and he kept his vocabulary very much up to date – he could still be very impressive at the Rose, when he happened to drop in. Not that he went there much any more: some of the younger people hardly knew him, he was so rare a visitor. He could he impressive, there and at the occasional studio party or wrangle in a pub, but he was always *against*; his talk was all denigration, or if by way of contradiction he did uphold anything it was always some bizarre and perverse, consciously 'modern' manifestation: and in this generally glum or railing attitude he was carrying one world to another, for Crichton and his friends and hangers-on were not people who admired anything. Nothing was any good; and as though to admire anyone were to diminish in honour, they filled the world exclusively with knaves and fools, legitimate objects of their all-pervading contempt; which made their conversation so unspeakably mean and dull that after some

'Not at all,' said Torrance, in a stuffy, offended tone.

'Yes, you are,' cried Richard. 'Last time it was *communication*, and the time before that, "did I really believe that making marks on a piece of canvas was the most important way of passing through life?" As it happens, I do.'

'It is common form,' said Torrance, 'to take criticism for hostility: but I did not think you would keep up so much rancour. Obviously I must not speak candidly: I must confine myself to undiluted praise. But as for communication, what would you have me retract? I thought communication the essence of painting, and I think so still: I did not find that the picture in question communicated anything to me, and I concluded that either I was dull, or that you were losing yourself in hermetic mystery, or that in fact you had nothing to communicate. After all, why should you have? It is not given to everybody to be an extraordinary exception. Methinks sometimes I have no more wit than a Christian or an ordinary man has. And as I understand it you have never set up shop as a lonely titanic genius. As for the other thing, you seem to have lost all sense of humour: it was merely a quip because you were being so portentous and disproportionately solemn – and, to tell the truth, such a Goddamned bore. But I really have not the time to go into all the grievances you may have worked up, because I have an appointment; and I only want to make it clear that as you have not finished this little piece it had better count as next month's picture and next month's need not be done.'

He had used almost exactly the same words after their disagreement over Fux. He had always somehow resented Richard's knowledge of music – conceivably as deriving from the Celarents – and he disliked Richard's setting of himself up with a pompous kind of gramophone; but when Bolton brought a man to see

Richard's work and the man bought a gouache, which thus turned, in part, into records, Torrance was irritated beyond his usual equable incivility. 'Of course, you know that this whole fugue is lifted bodily from Buxtehude? It is not Bach at all. I remember longing to tell that fool Simmins that it was mere presumption on his part to listen to Bach without a musical education. Exactly like those skinny unwashed girls with their Joyce and Eliot and no more foundation of literature than The Madcap of St Bede's: and all their talk about sex, based on nothing more than a little furtive grappling among themselves. Don't you think all this talk about Bach being so cerebral is overdone? An old-fashioned provincial pose, like saying that he is *mathematical*, for Christ's sake. A living woman actually said that to me, once. I thought it had died with the old Queen. It is the label, the signature. If the record was blank, how many people would know whether it was Buxtehude or Fux or Telemann or perhaps one of the little Bachs instead of the fashionable one?' And he was so vexed and so confident of what he had said that he put it to the test, which was incautious and unsuccessful. There followed a long stoppage of funds: the picture was eaten; the records vanished one by one, and the gramophone followed them.

It was an uncomfortable life; but the absurd thing was that with all these vagaries Richard's income, the actual sum that he spent over the year, was considerably higher than it had been in his happy days. But there was no certainty in it: it had very little real existence, and so nothing was more pointless than starving his heart out for a cigarette (as he had done before) in order to manage these phantasmal pennies. A capital sum would have been real; but economy over anything less, of this nature, was stupid, particularly as Torrance might clap down on supplies at any moment. There was no certainty. Even with great submission there was no relying upon his mood; and what had once been a kind and even an affectionate alliance had come to resemble something not unlike a hostile domination.

Or was he mistaken? Was he too prickly – assuming too much – giving himself the airs of a great painter? Was he abnormally ungrateful? He was unwilling to believe and anxious to doubt his conclusion, for if that went bad on him he was indeed adrift. At times, with his fear, his terrible inability to work or struggle to get through the block, his disgust at sponging on women, and his disappointments he felt himself slipping down to a moral equivalent of the Embankment.

These thoughts were interrupted – and with what incisive vigour – by a strong, authoritative knock.

It was not Valerie's knock. There was half an hour to go before Valerie: it could not be Valerie. He looked very quickly round the room, and with a stony face walked over and pulled back the bolt.

It was only one Karipos, a young man with a remarkable sense of colour and a dangerous degree of ability, who came again and again, with very little encouragement, to see his work. There were some others like him, and usually he would not let them in unless they had asked to come before and had named a day.

Karipos wanted two things, to look at Richard's St James's Bridge again, and to hear his views on women – on concubinage, to be exact. He had brought a present of a pot of oriental ultramarine, lapis-lazuli ground by his aunt in Constantinople.

'Don't let them in,' said Richard, putting away the ultramarine. 'No,' he cried, 'never *live* with one – it will not do. Even if she can keep you,' he said, seeing Karipos's disappointment. 'You can't draw, you know, Karipos: you are no bloody good at drawing. But you are a marvellous colourist – you know a great deal about colour. Now as I see it, you can learn something about drawing – drawing is intellectual. But you can never learn anything about colour, because it comes from nowhere that you can touch. It is unintellectual: infinitely more important. So it would never do for you, you understand – you could not cope. There is a voice there, a person there, bawling about eat your pie *now* – drink – wash – just in the hours where you need everything in your hand. She is going to object if you bring other girls in or go away without saying anything – everything has to be arranged. Slopping pails of water – broom. No. It is convenient, I admit, but it will not do. Think of poor Dürer. Did you know a man called Briggs? No. They swell up directly: you look round, and there is a woman with a big belly, knitting, and the next thing you know there is a little Urine or a little Slime running up and down shrieking. I must push you out, you don't mind? Thank you for the ultramarine. I am expecting someone – a person.'

He had talked very much at random to young Karipos, his nerves being all a-jangle, and now he walked up and down the room for calmness. There was a good quarter of an hour to go. Admiration was very well; it was comforting; but it was immaterial. He walked over to the edge of the window: it was raining outside with a sulky air of never having stopped; and Valerie was there already. She wandered rather uncertainly to and fro on the opposite pavement and from time to time she looked at the silly little watch she had on her wrist. He saw the flash of the big sapphire as she peered under her fur sleeve – fur that was now tipped with innumerable drops of rain.

'I shall bite off that finger, sooner or later,' he said, watching her coldly. It was a ring that he always noticed – it was a ring that forced itself upon his notice, because she pulled and twisted it whenever she was uneasy, and it made him so furious to see escape and liberty more or less disregarded among three other rings on a plump and foolish hand that sometimes he could not be civil – the object there in the same room as himself, separated only by a little air, a little decency, a little fear of the consequences.

But as she turned he saw that she was sheltering a box of cakes under her coat and that the coat was beginning to get wet – dark streaks and rats' tails appearing on the surface. She looked particularly lost and inept and in an unexpected surge of kind feeling he threw up the sash and called out: they met on the stairs, and he brought her in.

The rain went on and on, and with a shift in the wind it beat against the window-pane, making the twilight room almost comfortable by contrast; he had an electric stove, precariously wired to the light, and he had propped it on its back to boil the tea-kettle. Its pink glow lit the ceiling, the steam, and the smoke of his cigar.

The last time he had smoked one of these had been shortly before a visit by Torrance, who, sniffing the air, had broken his usual rule of discretion to say, 'What ho, for Cuckold's Point.' It was true enough: Havanas at half a guinea apiece could only come from a cuckold's cabinet, slightly damaged by their voyage in the powder-smelling handbag of a guilty wife.

Valerie sat by the box of cakes, picking up the crumbs with a moistened finger: formerly she had felt obliged to make conversation of an unrestful kind – 'I always feel that yoga must be a great help – you know, to catch the harmonious radiations. Our vicar's wife was born in India. Do you think it is given us to know all? – What do you suppose will happen in Czechoslovakia? What do you think of this Hitler?' but all this was against her nature and had died away, and now she was far happier eating éclairs and telling him about Mrs Tooth and the pretentious Mrs Irens, who owned culture in her part of Chorley Wood, or so she thought; and Valerie was particularly pleased by the secret knowledge that she in fact knew more about the inside of a studio than Mrs Irens could ever hope to know. Yet this evening the quiescent pause was not altogether peaceful; he felt, rather than saw, that she was twisting her ring round and round her finger, and he guessed that when his ash fell, or when he moved, she would speak about her portrait.

'I have told Mr Hewer about you,' said Valerie, and at this news Richard's ash fell in one solid piece. He had always understood Valerie's husband (she had a delicacy in naming him) to live somewhere in the murkier recesses of 1890, a roaring disciplinarian, who kept her very short of spending money, and although he knew him to be matrimonially null he still had a distinct picture of a mottled, hairy, choleric citizen, not at all likely to be pleased with such a mark of confidence. He said nothing, however, and after a pause Valerie continued, 'You remember about Uncle Fred, who gave me this ring? His money has come through and *he* said I might have a hundred pounds as a present. It was my own money, after all; but he said I might spend up to a hundred pounds, and I thought of a picture at once.'

She described the gliding success of her first monumental lie to her husband, by which she accounted for their acquaintance; he caught the name *Molly Woodman* (a sure support) but his mind went running fast until it was brought up by the expectant silence after her question, 'Would you do my portrait?'

'Portrait? You would not like it if I did. You can have two or three of these, if you like; or you could go to the Rapin Gallery and buy one there – they have some of my things and they look worth much more in a smooth gallery with a carpet.'

He knew Valerie pretty well, yet even so he could form no conception of her indifference to all painting that was not a likeness: but she had an excellent escape in Mr Hewer. 'That would be ever so nice, but he would not understand it. He knows a portrait costs money; Mr Fleshman had his wife done by an R. A. But he would think buying just a picture a terrible sin.'

Richard digested this, and while he thought what to say the time slipped by; his mind was active, tumultuously active, but it did not seem able to come to the point – any point. Then he noticed that she was crying, very quietly, with suppressed heaves, and the tears pattered on her knee. She said, 'I should not have asked. I am not pretty enough, I know: he said himself, "You're no oil painting." And too fat. But I did so hope you would; and I could have asked you to make me not quite so fat.'

'No, no,' said Richard in the calm voice that he thought the kindest, for although he had withstood tears from girls in plenty with cold indifference or unappeasable rage Valerie was so open to wounds from every side, genuine wounds, and so humble under them, that he could not refrain from hurrying forward with some armour. 'It is not a question of that at all. I will do it – oh, I'll *do* it all right. But you probably won't like it when it is done, that's all. That's all I was thinking about.'

'Oh, but I will,' cried Valerie, embracing him warmly and drying her tears at once – so fast that an unvoiced suspicion that he had been manœuvred flickered in his mind – 'and Mr Hewer will come with me on Saturday to arrange the terms. He would have to come, you know, or it would not be right. And you will let me come on Friday and bring you an artist's smock, to look better, with just a little ruching here? Could I bring a little broom, Richard? I am so excited.'

CHAPTER TEN

Y ET IN THE end it was nothing that Torrance did then that liberated him; it was no part of the current oppression, but rather the discovery of an old betrayal.

It was one of those unforeseeable chance encounters that always precede this kind of discovery. He was sitting in a bus, upstairs and in the front seat, thinking vaguely about Paris, and just after the bus had passed Victoria another person came up on to the empty top deck to sit exulting in the front and view the city. Richard glanced at him as he sat there leaning forward with his hands clasped between his knees and noticed the delight with which he gazed at the yellow brick of the mean side of Buckingham Palace Road and at the railway shunting yard on the other hand, and almost at the same moment he recognised him as a man who had been seen in Chelsea some years before, at the richer sort of parties. There were several like him, tall, florid, pink-and-white young men who hurried into the milieu strictly for the fun: now he was thinner and rather yellow, but still cheerful and elegant. He caught Richard's glance and said, 'Why, it's Temple, isn't it? I don't suppose you will remember me: my name's Bullingdon.'

Richard was surprised at his claiming acquaintance, for it had been slight and fortuitous; and Bullingdon had been a great deal of a blood. But it appeared that Bullingdon had only recently come back from a horrible exile in Palestine, – 'knocking the Jews on the head – I wish we would leave them to stew in their own ungrateful juice, and let the Arabs cut their throats: the Arabs are all right' – and that he was therefore apt to love London and all its inhabitants. Besides, he had been speaking of Richard only a little while before.

'I suppose you are pretty famous by now?' he said with a kind, an almost deferential air.

Richard shook his head.

'But you must be doing pretty well,' said Bullingdon. 'I was staying with Andrew Bentley – you remember Andrew Bentley, of course? Yes. You had a little trouble with him at the Coconut Grove. And he showed me your picture of Jacky Porny – Lady Berg as is. I must say I thought it was a terrific picture. He has it hanging in his bedroom. Of course, I don't know anything about these things, but when he told me what he had paid for it I was amazed: I thought you only paid that sort of price for old masters. So you must be pretty famous. I don't mean it was too much – nothing like that – because it really is a smashing picture, ha, ha. And then of course Andrew is very rich.' He sighed. 'By the way, do you see anything of Jacky now?'

'No,' said Richard.

After thinking for a while Bullingdom laughed. 'No,' he said, 'She doesn't know me any more, either.' He lapsed into a silent and apparently comforting reminiscence, but came out of it to ask, 'How is that chap who had the big Lagonda? The man Andrew got the picture through – Torrance?'

'Oh,' said Richard, 'I see him sometimes.'

'Will you come and have a drink?'

'Thank you very much, but I am afraid I have an appointment. This is my stop. Good-bye.'

The excuse was an excuse, but it was also true: he had to meet Mr Hewer in half an hour. After he had absorbed the first shock he was not sorry to have this necessary occupation, and he hurried along to his studio with a great many small immediate problems turning one about the other – size of canvas, pose, lighting. There was no urgency in his emotion – his mind was cold – and as well as this he felt a sinking cowardly unwillingness to look at the situation, its shockingly painful meaning and its dreary consequences.

But it occupied a great deal of him, nevertheless, and he was so far from being in the ordinary present that when he came into his swept and tidied room he could not for the moment tell why it was so unfamiliar, nor what the new model-throne was doing there at the far end. Pulling himself together he put on his new blouse; and as he had always worn one of the same colour in France this reinforced the thoughts of Monsieur Durand which had been running in the technical part of his mind.

'Never let them become familiar,' he had said, 'or they will know no bounds – they will grow more and more reluctant to pay. They will expect to be given things, on the ground of friendship: do they bring you loaves, cutlets of pork? Always remain aloof, correct and professional, impassible.'

Mr Hewer was a thick-haired, grey man; hair grew from his ears, and his deep-set close grey eyes gleamed with suspicious cunning among his eyebrows. He was somewhat out of his element (which was the wholesale tallow market in the City) and he had dressed a little better than usual to offset this: Richard could not know it, but this was Mr Hewer's best bowler, this the glossier of his two black overcoats, and the heavy silver-mounted umbrella that was soon to avenge the cuckold's honour – his efficient horns – was the best umbrella.

Valerie, who came in well behind her husband, had fortified herself with beer at lunch and she was rather coarsely pleased with the situation; but in spite of the beer she was also very nervous and she would probably have spoken foolishly if she had been called upon to say anything. But in Mr Hewer's view of the world women had nothing to say out of doors, and she was put down in a corner while he addressed himself to Mr Temple.

Mr Hewer had intended to take a high hand, but it is impossible to take a high hand with an indifferent or an absent competitor; Monsieur Durand's tactics were effective enough, but far more effective was Richard's fundamental lack of interest in the whole thing: most of his attention was withdrawn, and his reserves about portraiture gathered force from his inattention. Mr Hewer was a businessman, a thoroughly commercial man; he knew nothing about his tallow, never handled or loved his tallow, but he did understand money; he had thought about it hard and close since he was fourteen, and after a lifetime's cupidity he could tell perfectly well whether his opponent was eager for money or not – whether he was weakly avid for the bargain.

Richard's terms were high – 'A hundred guineas is my fee,' he said, with no particular warmth – but many curious factors were involved, including that of gentility, and Mr Hewer found himself capable of stipulating only that, 'there should be no art – none of this', turning his back to his wife and indicating a deep décolleté on his waistcoat, and that there should be the usual number of features.

'If you don't like it when it is done, you need not pay for it,' said Richard.

'Well, that's fair enough,' said the cuckold, with amazed glee, unable to conceal it in spite of his principles. 'That's fair enough, haw, haw.'

Richard set Valerie in the pose and began to sweep out the main lines of the portrait: it took him some little while to get the feel of the canvas, the distance he could pace backwards and the set of his easel, which was in an unusual place, but when these points were settled he sank into his habitual movements, and he was beginning to find great comfort in this sinking down when he noticed an odious tendency in Mr Hewer to move about, breathing and staring like a little malicious ox.

'Perhaps Mr Hewer would like to sit down and look at these,' he said, passing him a portfolio of drawings. 'Are you comfortable, Mrs–?' He could not connect her with her married name. 'We will have a rest soon, if you are not comfortable.'

Valerie was not comfortable. Tidying, she had put an explicit, unmistakable nude of herself in that portfolio. She tried to convey this to Richard by means of a series of agonised expressions and silent words but he was concentrating upon her middle and missed them all: the discipline of the pose (connected with a memory of the time when a camera took a long time to fix a likeness and the photographer clamped your head into an iron band) and the discipline of her husband's not far distant eye and her own indecisive flurry prevented her from waving her hands or gesturing with them. Automatically she held herself rigidly upright with her breath drawn in in what she considered her most advantageous shape and all the time her agony went on while Mr Hewer slowly grunted through the drawings one by one, turning the sketches, narrowing his eyes and pursing his lips. In the same silence Richard touched the canvas, backed, cocked his head to consider the stroke and came forward again, lunging, while he arranged her left forearm and a fold of velvet to his satisfaction. It lasted; and she had almost gathered the courage to scream and make an insane diversion when the storm broke.

'The saucy 'ound,' said Mr Hewer in a low voice, setting the sketch the right way up. 'You saucy 'ound,' he shrieked, realising how he had been abused and how nearly he had had to pay for

the privilege. 'You saucy 'ound,' he shouted into Richard's astonished uncomprehending face, throwing the portfolio in an explosion of paper.

He rushed forward with his umbrella and Richard darted
behind the easel. They ran up the room, turned about the model-
throne and ran down it again.

The form of the room and the disposition of the furniture were
such that this could go on and on: as he ran Richard tried to
think of some way of bringing it to an end, but there seemed to
be no reason why it should ever stop. Valerie was no use. She
was petrified into a condition of utter uselessness, and she only
moaned from time to time as Mr Hewer lashed out at Richard
or slapped her in his passage by the chair.

Richard was obliged to suit his pace to Mr Hewer's: it would
have been indecent to get too far ahead – an intolerably embarrassing situation – and so they trundled up and down, not very
fast even to begin with and progressively more and more slowly.
In his care for decency Richard received several stinging blows,
but the alternatives that came into his mind were all unaccept-
able; he could not turn ugly, and so must necessarily run, or trot,
as long as Mr Hewer's stamina would endure.

This was not more than another half-dozen turns, however,
half a dozen more turns up and down and Mr Hewer fell into a
grey fit, and was obliged to be helped into a chair. His rage was
run out, and in a cold chill of recovery he began to be a little
afraid of the man he had been beating. They helped him silently
downstairs into a cab; but although his rage was run out his vin-
dictiveness was not and when he was safe in the cab he leaned
up to the window and called out 'Call yourself a gentleman? You
are only a dirty ponce.

✦

AT THIS TIME Richard had two ways of reaching the ataraxy
that he so highly valued, and under the shock of these such different crises he did not find it difficult to follow either or both
of them. The first consisted of letting his mind go along very
calmly wherever it chose, as if the dreadful place did not exist,
and if his mind strayed he turned it with the smallest possible
gesture so that it skirted the pit and reassumed its conventional
ignorance. The second was a form of denial: acceptance of the
fact, denial of the consequences alleged by his sensibility.

As far as the vanished guineas were concerned, it was not any
great discipline to remove them from the plane of reality, where
they had never had any sort of freehold property; he had never
believed very strongly in their eventual existence – it was too
great a sum; it was too good to be true; there were so many fore-
seeable things that could go wrong, apart from malignant fortune – and he only had to suppress the incautious passionate
longings that had in spite of himself taken some sort of shadowy
uncertain lodging in his mind for everything to revert to its ordinary, ungilt appearance, for his ordinary prosaic mind to ignore
the loss in fact.

But this was the unimportant thing, although it had been so
noisy: quite another exertion of spirit was called for to say, 'He
stole Jacqueline's portrait and when I was on the bottom of the
river he sold it for a great deal of money; and since then he has
lived with me on terms of the closest friendship; but I merely
record the fact, which does not move me. To say that I am shockingly wounded or to call it a betrayal is a foolish mistake – irrelevant as well as untrue. It is a piece of dung on the road which I
look at; I say nothing; there is nothing to say.' It was more difficult, but in the circumstances of that evening it was far from
impossible, particularly as a host of hitherto stifled intuitions,

happy outcome of a long and grinding labour) but you may have committed some dreadful blatant vulgarity that will make you shudder for ever after, or perhaps worse, something embarrassing; which is a thing you can only do three or four times once you are mature – as if it were a game in which you had so many lives and no more, a game in which self-disgust disqualifies.

Some of those pictures he had recovered from his early days seemed to him less exciting now than they must have been when they were painted, and some were juvenile nonsense that had unnecessarily survived; but on the whole he found them far better than he remembered. In those days he seemed to have had extraordinary luck, a wonderful capacity for plunging into dangers that he did not recognise and yet coming out unharmed; but with every allowance he was proud of having painted some of them, and even elated. This made the confrontation of now and then more anxious, for all his indifference; and he turned abruptly to his most recent picture, looking harshly at it, with none of the gentleness that he had had for the others.

It was not a very large picture, and yet it gave the impression of size, partly, no doubt, because of the clarity of its colour – pure intense colours in which he had succeeded in keeping the cleanliness and even something of the strange light of tempera. He looked at it in the most strictly 'painterly' manner, and as unkindly as a hanging judge at first, almost willing to condemn it. Its figurative and its literary aspects aside, it consisted in the main of two upright forms connected by a receding curve: on the left a tawny rectangle filled the bottom corner; from it arose a great violet plane, cut by the curve, which in its turn rose in a diagonal flight towards the right-hand edge, being supported on the left by a hard bar, a dark column raised and sustained by the fire of crimson lake. The other form rose on the right-hand side at a slight angle to the edge, converging inwards and coming from an area of mauve, not unlike a platform. This form (which had its origin in one of the piers of the little bridge) was in two parts, a green upright that rose steadily into a still more intense green and the other silver-white with a dashing stroke of cobalt-blue and a vivid, almost invisible vermilion line, just far enough from the green not to move. These rose towards the high end of the leaping curve: it was essential that they should join, for there, in that junction, was the whole point of the matter; yet a junction alone would not suffice. His eye, travelling up the curve, followed it with rising tension to the top; and there, exactly balanced and poised by the opposing movements, was the sun, holding the entire picture together as one natural whole.

Once seen it was the obvious solution, the only answer; it looked so easy now, to crown the complexity of movement in the middle of the picture and to resolve the tensions with the sun, and yet he had blundered through several versions, always knowing that some essential was not there, but unable to name it, supplying busy non-essentials and almost spoiling it for ever in the gouaches he had made, some of which had been terribly commonplace and dull laboured things: depressing industry. Two had fallen victim to Mr Hewer. Yet the final oil had been implicit in the earliest drawing, the sketch in which Valerie figured, for their greater unhappiness.

It was good. High, remote and pure; no gesticulation. He put his hand over the sun and the picture fell to pieces. He took his hand away and covered the vermilion line: this was less spectacular; the balance shifted, the picture lost something of its vitality and the sun its fire. With the vermilion restored it glowed again. That stroke was the last he had given, and he had hesitated so long that the paint had thickened on his slab; it was a

remarkably successful stroke, and it was perhaps the most valuable thing that had ever come out of his long excursion into the
use of clashing colours, for this vermilion, swearing with the
carmine sun, gave it a life and a thrust that nothing else could
ever have done.

Upon this he went to bed, but going supperless – and he had
forgotten tea – he woke from hunger in the dead hour of night.
There was a loaf and a half-full tin of sardines in his cupboard,
and when he had eaten these he climbed out of the window and
on to the parapet. It was a warm, still night with no moon, over-
cast and as black as a London night can ever be, with the reflection of street lights and railways from the sky: this was the kind
of night he liked best, and when he had stood there for some
time, poised high over the street, he walked along the parapet to
the place from which he could reach his flat piece of roof. He
had a tin trunk up there, moored with bricks, in which he kept a
sack, to be able to sit on the sooty flat without too much filth,
and his current forgeries – not that there was any danger from
the police, for whereas in France a picture is criminal as soon as
it intends to deceive, criminal from the first immoral stroke, in
England it is an innocent mass of paint until the moment of the
signature; and even if there had been he was not so simple by
now as to suppose that a trunk on the roof was any protection.
But his acquaintance, reduced though it was, was still among
painters, and he did not choose to have any knowledgeable man
come in unexpectedly upon an example of his diligence.

He sat there on his sack, leaning against the trunk: the sky
was lit here and there by the effulgence of some marshalling
yard or night-working factory south of the river, and by the
power-station. There was also a factory away to the right: one of
its chimneys could be seen, with the underneath of its smoke

just tinged with crimson; and far over towards Battersea Bridge another sent up a plume that was in itself faintly luminous. But these were as remote, in their way, as the planets, and his particular neighbourhood was undisturbed: he sat hour after hour, sunk into the darkness. When he was a little boy he had done this, and even then he had felt this accretion of strength as he sat, with his mind still, watching.

On the sheltered part of the roof there were little pieces of mortar, lying where they had fallen from the pointing of the wall behind, and from time to time he tossed one out over the edge: even the heaviest never sent up a sound again in the silence, and they could be imagined curving through the darkness for ever.

A little before dawn the earliest trams began to cross the bridge, sending great sparks like lightning from their masts: he climbed down again, and descending into the street he walked until he came to the back lane where the baker's grating sent up a glow all permeated with the smell of new bread: they would always let you have a loaf if you had the right change.

Moved by some obscure impulse (for his usual breakfast was a summary hunk of bread) he turned round as he came out of the baker's and made a long circuit until he found a milkman with his trolley, from whom he bought eggs, butter, and, as an afterthought, a pot of cream.

With these he made an excellent, even a luxurious breakfast, and he was still eating it when the police arrived.

'Good morning,' he said with a neutral face, and his heart quite still.

'Good morning, sir,' they said. 'Are you the occupier of this here floor?'

'Yes,' said he.

'We have called in consequence of a complaint,' said the constable. 'Number fourteen in Rodger's Mews, behind, complains of a nuisance, somebody emptying what you might call slops or fee-cees into his yard at night. No window behind on this floor, sir?'

'No. My window is on the street. All the windows in this house give on to the street, I believe.'

'"Windows look on street,'" breathed the constable, writing. 'Then we must look elsewhere, it seems: thank you very much. Good day, sir. Pardon us, I'm sure.'

'Good day to you,' said Richard.

He finished his coffee, with an appearance of the utmost phlegm and even with some of the calmness of it, and he resumed his search for an answer to the insistent question, 'What shall I do next'

He could come to no satisfactory conclusion. One thing was clear, from the immediate and practical point of view, however, and that was that he must take extreme care of Torrance. He knew two things about the criminal world: first, that no band ever willingly let one of its members cut loose, for a hundred reasons, a sour jealousy being one of them and common caution another; and secondly, that a great many successful prosecutions were based upon denunciation – a great many policemen began their testimony with the words *acting upon information received*.

When Torrance found that Richard was no longer a devoted adherent, how would he react? What weapons did he possess? For Richard had no doubt that Torrance would instantly become aware of the situation as soon as they met: he did not think it possible to out-Macchiavel him, and he did not intend to try.

He passed their various exploits over in his mind, to see whether there was anything in which he alone was implicated; for although he was indifferent enough indifference is a relative to plan and think clearly. But on the other hand it made him think himself stronger than he was – quite impregnable – and when in the evening his natural emotions took him from behind his armour, he being by then very tired and at the lowest ebb, they hurt him very much more than he had supposed possible.

Finally, admitting that he was weak, he indulged himself in a very painful and very profitless indictment of Torrance, looking for things to condemn in him, and for other signs of his treachery; he had little doubt that Torrance had used him from the beginning – he remembered Torrance's contemptuous reference to Crichton as 'Mowbray's strong-arm man' and at the time he had wondered just what his own rôle might be, since he had heard himself spoken of as 'Torrance's apache'. It had not amounted to more than a tumble with a gamekeeper and a hurried scuffle with some racecourse toughs, but he had always been ready for more, if more had been necessary. And after that as a profitable hack: Torrance had known his skill in imitation years before. But there were so many hints and tokens that he had ignored or left unexplained which all pointed to the same unscrupulous exploitation that his list would have gone on almost indefinitely if towards the end of the night he had not fallen into the greater and even more painful weakness of trying to find proof that a real liking had at one time existed, even if it had existed alongside the interested cozening – something to show that he had not been deceived in quite every respect.

He was willing to find it, and he found enough to have made him give up any idea of revenge, if he had ever considered it: but he felt that they were quits, quits and done, and he hoped never to have to see Torrance again. For if they did meet he would be ashamed of his moral superiority, and ashamed for Torrance's face; and if they did meet there might well be a fight, and he could not bear it if Torrance turned out to be shy of a fight.

The next day, calm again, he pursued his inquiry, but he knew no more what he should do next than the day before; on Thursday he finished his painting (a dull and laboured performance) with no clearer idea in his head, and he went out in the evening to see what a change of surroundings and voices would do. He went in spite of a ridiculous, almost panic fear that he had of meeting Torrance; he felt that he had already betrayed him, and he was very unwilling to run into him without preparation. He joined a late party in Karipos's rooms, cheerful enough in all conscience, like a piece of time out, and on Friday he lay long in bed, being dragged out only at ten by a persistent noise on the stairs. The shop often left the downstairs door open by day, and this was a gipsy, ineptly picking at the store-room lock.

'Tell your future, gentleman?' she cried, with the air of one who had been hurrying up the stairs all this time, most legitimately.

'I wish you could,' said Richard. 'Ma, you want to stirk out for the rozzers: they will be on the tullock in half a mo.'

He closed the door behind her, but when he had climbed the stairs, up to the very top, he was called down again by the repeated postman's knock.

'Here is your future, gentleman,' the postman said. 'Sign here.'

It was a lumpy envelope, tied up with wool and sealed with violet sealing-wax. It held Valerie's sapphire ring and a letter blotched with tears. 'The ring is my own,' she said, 'Uncle Fred gave it me.'

He was profoundly touched, and although he did not finish the letter he mentally sent her a firm promise of the kindest portrait she could imagine, later (for somewhere he had caught the words 'this cannot last for ever . . . shall meet again'). But almost

at once his defences were overwhelmed; they were elaborately
organised against despair and unhappiness, and he had never
thought it worth while to prepare any secondary line against
excessive joy, if that was quite the word. He looked intently at
the ring, with his heart beating so that he could scarcely form
an intelligent opinion: a cloud of anticipations filled his mind,
and he abandoned thought for emotion. The predominating idea
was that he must act *quickly*, before the danger from Torrance
could arise; or any of the thousand other dangers. If the police
had come now, rather than the other morning, he would have
attacked them without a word.

Hurriedly he began to shave, then with the lather still on his
face he hunted for his best clothes, and while he was tearing
feverishly through his suit-case for a clean shirt he heard a sound
on the stairs. Silently he padded across the boards and turned
the key in the lock. The steps mounted, and passed the store-
room door. Tense and motionless he listened, and the knock on
the other side of the thin wood sounded like the blow of a ham-
mer. Silence. He heard breathing on the other side. Then the
double knock again, loud, authoritative; and the rattle of the handle. Had he really locked the door? Silence again, and ominous.
He moved a little and disturbed a pinned-up sheet of paper. It
took to flight, planing this way and that, and at last hit the floor
with a loud grating noise. On the other side there was a cough,
and a movement of feet. His fear was now so extreme and mas-
terful that it was like being trapped in the same room with a mad
wild animal.

Then the first step, slowly on the bare top stair. *Go on, go on*,
he urged. They went down reluctantly, and at last he caught the
change in sound from stairs to passage-way; after another
moment's listening he tiptoed over to the window and looked

cautiously out. There was no one; only traffic and quickly walking people: but then, with a shock that cut his breath he saw a
man on the other side, almost concealed by the awning of a shop,
a man in a soft hat and a drab mackintosh looking up. The usual
uniform. Then the man in the soft hat waved and smiled, obviously looking at a window next door, and almost immediately
after a girl crossed the road and they walked off.

'Don't be such a *bloody* fool,' he said, sitting down on the bed,
and he was recovering his poise when he put his hand on his
cheek and felt a cold leprous wound, insensitive. It was only the
forgotten lather, however, and as he shaved it off he began to
impose some limits upon himself, and to comfort himself by reasonable soft talking. Why should there be any more danger this
day than any other? He was surely letting his irrational feeling
about Torrance seep into his rational caution. Yet indeed as each
day passed there was less need even of that; today was less dangerous than yesterday, yesterday than the day before.

It was a comforting thing to say, but he knew that it was false:
the slow army against him moved with an incalculable tide, nothing much to do with time. There was no statute of limitations in
this case.

His hands trembled as he put on his coat, but he was getting
over it. It was a silly panic: it quite often happened, and that was
what wore men out, so that one day, when the panic was not silly
but well-founded, they went quietly, almost thankfully now that
it was all over; they fraternised with the enemy and one kind
word and a cigarette at the right moment and they 'co-operated
with the police'. They welcomed the rod at last and kissed it with
passionate relief, giving themselves, their friends, everything, as
a freewill offering.

There are few pawnshops that can deal with coloured stones,

because they are so liable to fraudulent imitation; and at one time or another Richard had been to all these few.

'Good morning, Mr Temple,' said the manager. 'It is a long time since we had the pleasure.'

It was disturbing to be known by name. It had not happened before. He said something vaguely amiable.

'It must be six months,' said the manager. 'Your ring will be coming up.'

'What ring?'

'Square emerald with pearls, if I do not mistake.'

Richard sensed a trap. He thought he remembered, but he could not be sure. He shook his head and said, 'No,' dismissing it as a thing of no importance.

'Perhaps it was for a friend?'

'Perhaps. I really don't remember. I have pawned things for friends in the country, sometimes.' The man seemed friendly enough, but Richard felt that he was not far from the end of his endurance, and if this went on he would get out. 'But it is another sort of business that I have come about today,' he continued. 'I want this valued.'

'A nice looking stone,' said the other. 'I wonder if it is reconstituted – what we call a scientific stone. They are very tricky things, these coloured stones. Is it yours?'

'It is part of an inheritance. That is why it must be valued.' He blew his nose and thrust his hand into his pocket; but catching a side-view of himself in a double mirror he saw, to his surprise, that he looked quite natural and unaffected.

'I will just look at it through the peepers for refraction. Do you understand refraction, Mr Temple?'

'No,' said Richard, as pleasantly as he could under the reiterated goad of his name.

The man went away, to the back of the shop; he could be heard talking to an assistant in the pawning part, but the words were indistinguishable. Richard lit a cigarette and asserted to himself that he had taken far worse than this, far worse. There was a telephone-bell far inside the office: he heard the single ring as a call was made.

The manager's form appeared wavily through the glass partitions. 'Well, yes, Mr Temple, it is a sapphire all right. But it has been badly knocked about. Do you see the chip here, Mr Temple? Take the glass. And the scratch on this facet. But the scratch on the table – that is what we call the table, Mr Temple – that is the worst; and I am afraid it takes a lot of the value away. I am afraid the lady as wore this ring must have been a little heavy-handed, Mr Temple.'

'How clever of you to know!' said Richard.

'Aha, Mr Temple, in our trade we get to know a lot of things,' said the man. He looked full into Richard's face. 'It would surprise you.'

This was horrible. He could think of no countenance or reply.

'However, we must come to figures. I could lend you . . .' he paused, tossing the ring in his hand. 'I could lend you – but you said it was a valuation, didn't you, Mr Temple?'

'Yes.'

'Not a pledge?'

'No.'

'Well, in that case, I should say – what is it, Harris? Excuse me a minute.'

There had been a ringing of the telephone in the office, and now Richard, alone again, furtively brought out his handkerchief to wipe his lips. The cigarette, when he picked it up, was so short as to be unsmokable and he walked across to the door to throw it out. The door was locked, and although the long handle turned under his hand, the massive glass and bronze affair remained quite still.

'Dear me, Mr Temple,' cried the manager, 'I must have touched the jigger by mistake. So I had. But there is an ashtray on the counter, Mr Temple. I had no idea . . . we have to have these things in our trade, because some queer customers come in sometimes; but really, I'm sure. Now as I was saying, I reckon it should be worth about one forty-five. Say a hundred and thirty to be on the safe side. I am sorry I can't say more, but the scratches . . . Would you like me to write it down for you, Mr Temple?'

He was in the street again, breathing the keen air. He had paid his half-guinea, and the manager had opened the door for him with renewed apologies – 'We must not keep you locked up for ever, like a pledge, Mr Temple.' The free air was so exhilarating that although he had meant to take a prudent rest he found his urgent feet taking him up Bond Street, where he said, 'I have a sapphire that I wish to sell.'

Upstairs the man seemed dubious, none too civil – or was that imagination? Already there had been far too much waiting about, coming and going, private words: the excellent feeling of relief had all gone and was replaced by the same wild, trapped boil of emotion.

'What is this?' said the man on the other side of the desk, and with his tweezers he plucked a little curl of paper from the socket in the ring-case. He read it with a discreet smile and handed it over. *For Richard with love from V.* she had written, in tiny letters. He blushed, and looking down said that he had not noticed it.

The man became more agreeable at once, and five minutes later Richard was in Piccadilly, with brilliant triumph in his eye, and for once the look of a man with a hundred pounds in his pocket.

'Lonely?' asked a tart, attracted by this look, and his apparent drunkenness.

'No, love,' said he. He was not lonely. He had a hundred pounds for company. He hurried down the hill at a furious pace, and the thoughts raced through his mind, coming much clearer now; he was much more capable. 'I shall cross tonight,' he thought, stepping off the pavement at Hyde Park Corner, 'and that should bring me in—' His thought was interrupted by the shriek of brakes and a voice, and he leapt forward directly in front of a curiously skidding car, that was still travelling much too fast. Its sharp-angled bonnet hit him on the left side, at once breaking three ribs, which he felt, and driving a part of one into his lung. He was then flung on to the car's low windscreen, which stunned him as it shattered, and in spite of its special properties, severed a number of blood-vessels in his neck and forearm: a convulsive jerk of his body, together with the centrifugal force of the car's last eccentric curve, threw him to the ground, where the near rear wheel passed over his foot, twitching him from sideways to flat on his face, where he lay quiet in a welling pool of blood and a thick close crowd gathered to watch him die, pressing closer about the dark blood.

CHAPTER ELEVEN

I N THE HUGE darkness that followed his recording mind came into operation now and then, sometimes to register such statements as 'Three ribs, I said, and perforation; a spontaneous pneumothorax: and now of course this pneumonia. Much undernourishment,' or the authoritative 'Stand back there,' of the policeman that must logically have dated from the very beginning, although the record, defective only in this, supplied no relation in time.

Indeed, time did the strangest things; once or twice, anaesthetised, he recaptured not only the reversal that had come about at the moment of the accident and which was already familiar, but a new dislocation in which things happened in no recognisable sequence, not first and second, but according to some other dimension or arrangement that could have an unbelievable and revolutionary effect in painting if only it could be retained. Yet all that could be retained was the memory of the existence of the thing, not the thing itself, which had never been crystallised before some fool spoke, saying 'Stand back' or 'Ask sister if we can have the other trolley' or even his own voice saying in a harsh whisper, 'His mother's name was Valadon, and that is why I sign Utrillo V.'

On the whole, the record was an arbitrary list of sounds – the noises of a ward set down in haphazard moments for example, or an animal noise of breath and moaning, which was himself – and of impressions such as the wine-like revivifying stream of oxygen, or the inhuman cold of a metal pipe searching down his throat, and of the innumerable fragments of pain, discomfort, the racing of delirium and the consciousness of delirium that go to make up the experience of a desperate illness. Yet he had one or two more complete memories as well: at one time his mind cleared to a remarkable degree and he found himself aware of inhabiting his snorting, gasping body, propped up in the attitude of pneumoniac death, with rubber tubes in its nostrils, stuck by adhesive plaster; he was not suffering in any way, for not only was he somewhat apart from his body but his body too was below suffering now; and he knew that if he chose to make no effort he could die – that death (at least this death) was not what he had expected or feared, and that it was in fact rather friendly than otherwise, a profound quiet.

After that time, however, clarity was very rare; for although he was obviously very much better and although he obviously accumulated knowledge and memories (he knew the nurses and the disposition of the ward) he was much troubled by fancies. The simplicity of the old battle was gone, when he plainly had to fight for life; and it being apparently won, his forces disarmed or deserted and left him so wandering and stupid and weak that he could not always grasp his own identity for long. Sometimes he talked all day very sensibly, but only in French, and to people who were not there; sometimes his mind, wandering at large, became stuck in his own pictures so that he himself was that triangle of verdant green; or, what was more confusing by far, in the pictures of other men, from which it was very difficult to return, the return being a complicated way among a crowd of shapes and sometimes people whom he more or less recognised. Occasionally the loss would be in a book: he would be astray among its characters: but much more often it would be necessary to escape through the oranges in Uccello's silent battle or wind with all civility among the Graces, dancing in a ring. It was not necessarily unhappy – far from it sometimes – but it could be very distressing and hopeless to be pinned up in some foul pre-Raphaelite affair or a pseudo-Braque, and quite a small unhappiness would make him weep. And as well as the pre-Raphaelites there were some creatures that got in out of pictures or from no source at all, and it needed patience and a great deal of cunning to count and circumvent them all: a great silly devil, from a Temptation of St Anthony, whose tail could always be seen below its dimity skirt, and a very small pale semi-human rather like Gay who would race in behind the trolley screaming like the trolley's wheels and who would do something very unsuitable if not closely watched.

They came and went, came and went, and people said, 'Do not excite him.' There was an infinite procession of trolleys; trolleys eleven times a day.

'Do not excite him,' said the nurse, and there was a scraping of chairs. Almost immediately afterwards a trolley came in, followed not by the usual tiny Gay, but by two of them, racing about like children, superhumanly nimble and transparent, imitating railway engines.

It was a populated day, and on his right a whispering said, 'My God, do you think we ought to ask him how he is? He is sort of conscious. Go on, James. You ask him.'

This might well be Ugly James, the poltergeist, and Richard, who had been rapidly counting the grey panes in the window above the screens that surrounded him, cut in upon him with the instant reply, 'Very well, I thank you.'

'He can talk,' said a man's voice.

'How clever you are, darling!' And in a louder voice. 'I say, are you really feeling better?'

One of the pale creatures had darted away to the right, where it might easily find an unwatched corner. He followed it with his eyes and saw a young woman dressed in black sitting on the shiny chair. He thought *Now who the hell will she say she is?* and as so often happened now the thought spilled.

'I'm Philippa Brett,' said the young woman.

'So you say,' thought Richard.

The man's voice coughed, and seemed to wish to insist, but the woman hushed him. 'Shut up, darling. You're not to excite him.'

'Your wife, your wife, your wife,' said Richard, 'your wife, under pretence of keeping a bawdy-house, is a receiver of stolen goods.' He wished to explain the bearing of this, but the page-number escaped him, flickering among the windowpanes.

'He has not *got* a wife,' said the voice, reasonably.

'When Adam delved, and Eve span, who was then the gentle-man?' asked Richard, by way of finishing with them.

'We had better go,' said the man.

He had a good many encounters with them: they were far less trouble than the little pale screamers, but they were pertinacious, and more than once they reduced him to tears.

The pale screamers made their last appearance, were finally unsuitable, and he reverted to the commonplace world, reaching it permanently one morning with a vile headache and in a vile temper. It was visiting day, and the desert of hours that lay between that time and five o'clock, when the ward had been inhumanly woken, had been filled with tedious and peevish scrubbing, twitching, polishing that had vexed the convalescent patients into as much fury as their strength would permit. They would find fault with their visitors, and as like as not send some away in tears.

Here they came, a flood with baskets, books, flowers; creak-ing and grinning in their best clothes – why their best clothes? To do honour to their friends, no doubt: the ward was very conscious of status. Very well, but they would have nothing whatever to say in five minutes' time, thought Richard sourly: it is like an eternal train, that never will depart. They filed past his bed with their eyes fixed beyond him, already making little signs and nods, wasting their small stock of communication. A remarkable young woman came walking up the ward alone, obviously used to the place; she appeared to be looking at the next bed, whose occupant, however, had died the night before.

'Good morning,' she said. 'How wonderful to see you sitting up!'

He made a polite noise, and watched attentively as she sat down, flicking her mink coat aside. She was not the sort of woman he expected to see in the ward, and if it had not been for the cold, prosaic, everyday nausea that now bound him so close to the common ground he would have suspected her of being illusory – of having escaped from a Reynolds that he could not quite remember, although her face was certainly familiar. They looked at one another: for the first moment she looked closely at him with the liberty of an old acquaintance peering for signs of improvement or perhaps of understanding; almost as one might peer at a baby; but then, meeting his look of weak surprise and only too human petulance, her face showed a certain embarrassment and confusion of feeling. Blinking rapidly and looking very grave she said:

'Are you *really* feeling better? They told me downstairs that you were sitting up and taking notice, and that next week I could bring you a pear, or a grape, but I could scarcely believe it. You know, I am so terribly sorry about it all: I have told you every time, but I don't think you understood. I think it is perfectly wonderful of you not to die. Thank you so much. I kept my fingers crossed, and made vows, and prayed, you know, but I never believed it, and they all shook their heads and I have been feeling like a murderess.'

There was a pause, in which he looked at her with the same attention. He had seen women like her before, principally in galleries, staring with no enthusiasm at the paintings, dressed with the same elegance, moving in the same way; but this one was human; and not only human, but kind.

'I'm afraid you have had a perfectly foul time,' she said solemnly, and then repeated that it was wonderful of him not to die – 'I do not know what I should have done if you had.' The sister interrupted her at this point and screened off Richard's bed, on the ground 'that he was getting excited'. But when next she appeared they took up their conversation at the same point and after she had asked after his condition – better – she said, 'Do you know who I am?'

'No.'

'I thought not. Isn't it a scream? I know you frightfully well. I have washed your face – how much better it looks without that foul beard – and blown your nose – I mean as well as that, apart from nearly doing you in. And we have gossiped away for hours, when you were–' She paused, as if looking for something between mad and raving, but could find nothing better than 'off your crumpet. But you don't even know who I am, which must make me seem very bold and forward, I suppose. I am Philippa Brett: I ran you down. I am so sorry about it – I have felt so miserable and guilty.'

'Yes, they said it was an accident; I remember a bang. But there really is no need to take on. I dare say I was on the wrong side: in any case I am perfectly well now.'

'I have seen you looking like something in Madame Tussaud's,' said Philippa. 'And in the very beginning it was even worse. I was coming round by Hyde Park Corner, meaning to cut in before a cab, when you suddenly appeared out of nowhere *rushing* towards Apsley House. We were going pretty fast, because of getting in before the cab, but I might have managed it if James had not made a mad lunge at the wheel, and we went into a skid. My dear, I've never been in such a teewee in my life. One moment you were there, through the windscreen, and practically nestling in my lap, and the next you had shot out again and were *writhing* in the most dreadful way. Then when I got out you were absolutely dead, in an ocean of blood. My God. The place looked exactly like a slaughter-house. And everybody was furious: while I was howling and roaring and trying to find my handkerchief an old woman hit me with her shopping bag. I thought the end of the world had come.'

'It was not your fault.'

'My dear, it is perfectly sweet of you to say so; but they all behaved as if I had done it on purpose. Daddy was utterly livid. He said that I should be sent to Bridewell and severely whipped: he said it was exactly the sort of thing the Communists loved, and he hoped they would flay me. He made me read the pieces out of the *Daily Herald* and the *Worker* aloud at breakfast and I wept for shame: it sounded dreadful, because apart from anything else James had got his step that morning and he was absolutely stinking already, or if not absolutely stinking at least he could hardly stand when he got out of the car, and just after you had been carted off he tripped over the gutter and fell down.' She paused, and rather hesitantly added, 'Of course, the Communist papers were quite right; and frightfully *interesting*. I don't mean to be rude about them.'

'I think they are horribly dull.'

'Oh? I thought for a moment that you might have been a Communist – all sorts of people are Communists now. You can't tell by their looks any more. A lot of the clever ones who were at school with James are roaring Communists. And I thought you might possibly be, because I suddenly remembered that when you were delirious – you were a madly funny delirible, although it was all so shocking and I wept buckets – you asked James the one about Adam and Eve and which was the gentleman. That floored him. My dear, you should have seen his face when you told him that his wife kept a bawdy-house. He hasn't got one – not one of his own, anyhow – but when he does marry, she will be exactly like that. I thought of it last night when I saw him *dancing*, as he calls it, with Nancy Trafford, leering away as he thundered round, and she was smirking and bridling in spite of the agony, and my God if ever there was a woman like the one you predicted for James it is Nancy Trafford. Laugh? I was nearly sick. You must have been inspired – in a sort of prophetic trance.'

+

RECOVERING FAST FROM one disease, or complication of diseases, Richard fell directly into another, and in this case (like so many other sufferers) he loved to read about the symptoms, prognostics, other examples and history of his malady. He found, in Partition 3, section 2, member 2, subsection 1 of Burton's classic work, that 'Idleness overthrows all, *Vacuo pectore regnat amor*, love tyrannizeth in an idle person. If thou hast nothing to do – *Invidiâ vel amore miser torquebere* – thou shalt be hailed a-pieces with envy, lust, some passion or other . . . 'Tis Aristotle's simile, "as a match or touchwood takes fire, so doth an idle person love."'

Nothing could have been more idle than his life at this time. He was washed, fed, woken and told when to sleep by an impersonal authority; and his mind was idle in most of its aspects, for he was spiritually contained within the antiseptic walls of the ward – his remote and squalid room had only the smallest far-off existence, and his dread of Torrance had no meaning here. He was idle, and therefore by the book he was ready for some passion or other: envy was disqualified, because a hundred bloodstained but still negotiable pounds lay within hand's reach of his bed and he did not envy anyone; lust was incompatible both with his condition and the hospital's chaste and insipid diet; but he was hailed a-pieces with love.

Not that idleness was necessary: she was beautiful, and beautiful in a way that would at any time have moved his heart – dark hair, pale blue eyes, and she held her small fine head magnificently – but idleness contributed, if only because it allowed him to lie there all day, watching the door to see her walk in with her high-heeled grace and to see the friendly and almost boyish smile operate its incredible change: the difference between Philippa in repose and Philippa smiling was the difference between the moon and the sun – Galatea many times a day. And if any additions to beauty and grace were wanted she had them nearly all, poise and style, an agreeably cynical hardness of mind and if not exactly wit at least a great capacity for being amused; and wealth, position and family were far from indifferent to him, very far, poor soul, but he was far too earnest and besotted to reckon with the force of these considerations. The cleanliness of his surroundings, the lack of worry, his own weakness, did a great deal to renew his youth, or some of its outlook, as if some of his hard experience had rubbed off.

She brought her father one day, a strikingly handsome man, with a blue, unmeaning eye; there was little likeness between them, except that he too walked very straight, but there was obviously a great deal of liking, even if it was somewhat overlaid at the time.

'I tell you what I should do, Temple, if I were you,' he said, in the kindest and most considerate voice, 'I should sue her. Sue her. Make her smart for some of your broken bones. I said to the magistrate, "If that girl of mine comes up before you, Chandos, you send her to prison. You have my full authority and consent." It was a monstrous thing to do: might have crippled you for life. We were all very much concerned to hear of it, I assure you, and very glad that it has turned out so well. Though I am sure it has been damned unpleasant; and very inconvenient too, I dare say. As I was saying in the House only yesterday, it is all part of this modern craze for speed. However, you can read all that in *The Times*. You have a book, I see?' – looking rather discontentedly at Burton.

'He has finished it,' said Philippa.

'Did it end happy? I hate a book that don't end happy.'

'It was riotously happy,' said Philippa. 'Everybody got married.'

Mr Brett smiled, and said, 'On my way here I stopped at Pochard's, and asked them for a book for someone interested in art. They asked whether you were interested in *modern* art, and I said, "No, no, he's not one of these *modern* fellows," and they showed me a whole shelf of books. I found this one myself. They don't make books like this any more. It is an illustrated catalogue of the Academy of 1905, the year of the horrible Liberal disaster – we are paying for it yet.' In the momentary hesitation he showed a trace of his daughter, and more in the intonation of 'Though I dare say there are some excellent Liberals'.

'Do you think so?' said Richard.

Mr Brett shook his head, and continued, 'But for all that it was a very good Academy. I went with your mother, my dear, and we nearly bought this picture. Amazing picture. You can't see in this because it is too small, but in the original oil-painting if you went up with a reading-glass and looked at the hay in the manger here, you could see every piece, and you could see what it was – timothy, fescue, clover, and so on. They had to rail it off, there was such a crowd. I don't suppose that this Jew they make so much fuss about could do that, eh, eh?'

'Not the sculptor?'

'No, no. You are thinking of Epstein. I mean this Picasso.'

'He's not a Jew,' said Philippa.

'There are a lot more Jews than you might imagine, my dear. However, we will give him the benefit of the doubt. But he is a foreigner?'

'Oh yes.'

'Could he paint anything like this? You tell us, Temple: you understand these things.'

Richard looked at the stable and the fabled hay, and replied, 'No.'

Mr Brett smiled and nodded kindly. He took the book back, and as he turned the pages he murmured, 'I would love to see a pogrom; beginning in Whitehall. But you mustn't say anything like that in the House. Here we are. I knew it would be here. Cousin Muriel as a girl. Do you see the likeness, my dear? It was considered very like; and indeed you can still make out something in the nose. It was painted by Duroure: I met him several times. Do you know him at all? Scipio Duroure. French, or Italian, or something like that, you know – very much the foreigner, with prominent lips, flat nose, et cetera; et cetera; but not at all a bad fellow, all things being considered; and a very clever artist, as everybody said.'

When he was going he said, 'As soon as you can get about, I

hope you will come down to Churleigh for some country air: set you up again. There is a capital ruin in the park, and some damned picturesque nooks – ivy, bowers – it would be just the thing for you. My wife will write you a note.'

Mrs Brett, it seemed, preferred the country; but Philippa's brother came with her from time to time. He was a tall, broad young man, with protuberant pale eyes and colourless or faintly yellow close-cropped hair over a florid face, and whatever Mr Brett might say his son's lips were conspicuously thick: he sat there looking Hanoverian and soldierly, in an amiable silence. He brought obscene illustrated magazines.

Nearly always, it was Philippa alone. It was she who brought the heralded note of formal invitation. 'I do hope you will be able to come,' she said. 'I am sure it would do you a world of good. Besides, I should love to show you Churleigh: it is madly dull, but quite lovely in its tedious way. And Georgiana has furnished the south room with genuine Great Exhibition nonsense from the attics, which will make you laugh like a drain.'

'Who is she?'

'My step-mother. She was at school with me, and Daddy married her four years ago. That's what makes him look so furtive when he's not triumphing about the car – about my running you down. And *she* will never believe I don't hold it against her, which makes her frightfully humble. I always have a wonderful time when I go down there, and they always think I'm so magnanimous. My dear, I don't give a damn: Georgie has to cope with Mrs Raffald now, which always used to petrify me, and I just lie in bed and laugh.' Then, as if she had to persuade him, she spoke of Churleigh's varied delights, and added, 'Then we have some screechingly funny neighbours, who have not heard about Queen Victoria yet. There are the Dammerleys, who give the hunt ball every Christmas, with a rope across the middle of the room.'

'What kind of a rope?'

'A plush rope.'

'What for?'

'To separate the sheep from the goats. The sheep dance away like mad on one side, drinking claret-cup, and the goats do the same on the other, with shandy-gaff.'

'Don't the goats mind?'

'No, I can't say they do. Of course it would be rather upsetting to find yourself on the side you had not expected; but I suppose the in-betweens stay away. Anyhow, they have a tremendous time, dancing the polka and shrieking all night. But there are lots of other things, besides the Dammerleys. I do hope you will be able to come.'

'I should like to, very much.'

'I'm so glad. Write to Georgiana now, and I'll post it.'

When the letter was written she said, 'You have not stuck it.'

'No,' said Richard. 'Because I am giving it to you to post.'

'Must I stick it?'

'Certainly. I was always taught that you must never seal a letter that you ask someone to post: Monsieur Durand called me a grossier personnage for doing it, once.'

'Were you educated in France?'

'Yes.'

'That is why you speak French so well.' He suddenly felt tired, too tired to deny that he spoke French, and he only smiled. 'They thought you were French for quite a long while, because you delired in number and gender. My dear, it was a terrible trial trying to reply, with nothing more than a shaky memory of Mademoiselle.' She weighed the letter abstractedly and said, 'Now I am beginning to get cold feet. You will be bored, cooped

up with the family. There is no one else coming. Would you like
me to ask someone clever? The family is not really startlingly
brilliant, not so that you would notice. We do *The Times* crossword after dinner, if Mrs Raffald has left it for us, and then we
stare at the fire like cats until ten o'clock, when we go to bed. I
will ask Nancy Trafford: she's frantically vicious, but she can talk
about Modigliani and Brancusi for hours.'

'No, no.'

'Besides, it's a shocking place, really; there's no running water,
or electricity. And you have to get used to the awful examples . . .
Daddy had a very eighteenth-century turn of mind when he was
young and he fairly peopled the countryside. He was the younger
son, you know, and he would not have inherited if it had not been
for the war; and he was allowed to be so mediaeval that now wherever you go you see his likeness waving at you from behind a
haystack. Yokels with six-days' beard and Daddy's eyes peer out of
hedges, and as most of them are half-wits they gibber.'

'Most painters do the same. It is nothing, once you know.'

✦

IT WAS TRUE: Churleigh was quite lovely. And if from one side
it looked so very like a lunatic asylum, that was because so many
a big country place has been turned into a madhouse. They
approached it from behind, up a deeply rutted lane and past a
horse-pond, because Philippa wanted to show him the old part
first, with the wistaria stretching right across, in blue flower against
the grey stone. The back, three sides of a square, was much as the
monks had left it when an earlier William Brett had mustered
enough parliamentary influence to displace them; not unlike one
of the less sanitary Oxford colleges. But the front was Palladian,
with a magnificent flight of steps that rose ten feet the whole width

of the centre, effectively depriving the kitchens of what little light they ever had, but supporting a splendid double row of pillars. The asylum part was really an independent structure, built in James the Second's day; it must at one time have been charmingly mellow, but a Brett who married a coal-mine in the forties had had every brick scrubbed and repointed with pink cement, restoring and even adding to its primitive aggressive barbarity.

It was a very large house, built piecemeal and without any notion of domestic economy or convenience or even the right true end of a house; but Mr Brett was a rich man, and his grandfather, seeing the beginning of the end in 1832, had looked to the comfort of the future generations. He had cut up seven handsome farms into uneconomic smallholdings, and this had ensured the continued existence of the army of servants whose incessant and often devoted labours made most of Churleigh not only habitable but tolerably comfortable. Some of them were still working away at the age of eighty, and proud of it; but even so it was impossible to keep the whole of the house in current use, and part of the lunatic asylum was shut up, and unsheeted only for very grand occasions.

Inside the house the confusion of the exterior was repeated: a door might open on anything from the austerest Gothic bower, with all the original agony, to a pure Edwardian smoking-room. Women are the culture-bearers of the race, and presumably the Bretts had at one time found a way of perpetuating themselves without the aid of wives, for somewhere between the eighteenth and the nineteenth centuries culture (never very steady at Churleigh) had fallen with an irrecoverable crash. The big drawing-room was Adam, and Chippendale considered the Chinese bedroom and the library his happiest creations; there was also a little Regency boudoir that could not have been bettered; but the hall and the windows of the main staircase were filled with the most appalling glass. It was a Brett over-excited by Sir Walter Scott who had done this, and he had splashed coats of arms and mottoes all over the place – *Sic vos non vobis* over the servants' hall was a sample of his taste and wit – and peopled the breakfast-room windows with a perfectly mythical set of crusading Bretts in early Victorian tights. And some of them were not even real stained glass, but a despicable kind of paper, that could be peeled off. It was shockingly unpleasant, like a baronial hall in a Scotch whiskey advertisement, but none of the succeeding Bretts had ever minded the darkness or the vulgarity enough to scrape even the paper off, let alone have the glass removed. These generations bought furniture from time to time: mahogany and fumed oak from the big London stores.

The reader of Scott was also the last reader of his race. Chippendale's magnificent shelves now contained, by way of new books, nothing but rows and rows of Hansard together with a few almanacs and government publications. Nothing else, unless bound *Punches* and gardening catalogues are to be counted. The ancients and the moderns slept undisturbed, very gently collecting dust, in spite of the efforts of Chippendale and Mrs Raffald, the housekeeping generalissimo.

But it was a friendly house. Philippa was welcomed by a cloud of dogs who made conversation impossible and who dug their scaly feet into shins, thighs or loins, according to their height as they leapt up; and a very pretty young woman who appeared from a side door, eating a piece of bread and butter, shrieked with delight, kissed Philippa and shook him warmly by the hand, looking solicitously into his face. Above the shouting he learnt that this was Georgiana, his hostess, and that she had put him in the bachelor's tower. 'I thought he would like the well,' she said.

A very large black old dog came in, did not see Richard directly, but when it did it narrowed its eyes and walked silently round behind him. The tumult, the necessity for keeping watch upon Hell (the dog's name was Hell) without seeming to do so, and the anxiety of first arrival made Richard stupid and tired, and he missed the reasons why he would love the well: he was very glad when they roared out in their piping voices that they were sure he would like to see his room. Philippa led him through a corridor and a stone arch to a staircase that wound up and up past slit-windows that gave on to totally different glimpses at each turn, and so into an agreeable Victorian five-sided room. His bag was already there, and a bright fire threw its welcoming light and warmth upon it as it stood there on a flowered carpet.

'I do hope you will have enough on your bed,' said Philippa, plucking at it. 'But if there is not, or if there is anything you want, ring the bell very hard. Ring madly and go on for about ten minutes, and then if nobody comes, shout down the well. Mr Luke will hear you, and his bell always works.'

'My God, what a view!' said Richard, who had been looking out of the window at a maze of tiled roofs with here and there a square – a stable yard, with Philippa's little car and a horse standing head-on to one another; then white-railed grass and beyond it a rolling wood with a stream shining through the trees, and farther than the wood, where the vale rose again at a distance too great to see men or houses, the downs rising and rolling in an unimaginable variety of whale-backed curves, with the shadow of the clouds moving over them.

'That's Pog Hill,' said Philippa. 'Come and look at the well.'

It was an ordinary room; its dim walls were wainscoted to the ceiling and painted brown, and everything had a comfortably used and cared-for air – nothing conspicuous or surprising in it, but when you opened a door in the shorter of the five walls you found yourself face to face with an immense pale well, a stone shaft that rose into darkness above and sank into darkness below.

'Isn't it sweet?' she said, leaning over the worn yellow edge, shining with the rub of generations of bellies before. 'Listen to the echo.' She howled, 'Oo-hoo-hoo,' and a fainter, deeper 'hoo-hoo' returned, followed by a click and the words 'What is it?'

'It's only me, Mr Luke,' she said. 'We were just trying the echo. This is the bachelors' part,' she said, closing the door. 'It used not to be, but the well led to goings-on. My dear. One Christmas party, when the house was full, there was a girl in the room below, where Mr Luke is now, and an admiral I think or anyhow someone very respectable and who should have known better, tried to get at her by lowering himself down the well, but he slipped; and she either didn't know or didn't like to say, and he was not missed until Boxing Day, poor soul. They found some wonderful old spoons down there, and a bottle that someone must have let down on a string to keep cool with the wine still in it: and quite a mass of relics and baubles. But this part is an archeologist's paradise; which is rough on the maids: they wouldn't do it at all if it was women, but they hurry about with cans of hot water and buckets of coal for bachelors. Mr Luke lives better than any of us. He is the steward. That door is the lavatory; on the same principle. You will take care, won't you, because one false step and you fall two hundred feet. Do you know how to work these things? You turn up the wick . . .' – showing him the oil lamp.

'Yes. I was brought up with them.'

'Then you'll be all right? You had better lie down for a bit, hadn't you? I will come just after the ten-minute bell so as to show you the way, so don't be anxious.'

Yet anxiety filled the room as soon as she shut the door: he had felt it coming into the remoter parts of his mind as soon as they had left London, driving soberly towards Hampshire in Philippa's reined-in, frustrated car, and between moments of amazement at the brilliance of the world and at their airy passage through it, and in the few moments when they were not talking, he had realised the particular strength of feebleness. In his bed he had been fortified behind his frail but invincible sheet: he could do nothing, he was responsible for nothing; his existence was almost absolute and uncontingent – he had no antecedents; and if anything he was on his own ground. The road was neutral ground; but at Churleigh he was a stranger – he felt that he might not be recognised as the same person who had so composedly (at times) inhabited bed 23, dressed in an official nightshirt, none of his choosing, soft with many washings and common, if you thought about it, to a great many past and present prisoners.

Yet this anxiety could not survive very long, at least not the reasonable part of it, in the absence of all nourishment. Nothing could have been more friendly than his reception, nor than the way they eased him into the position of a rather privileged member of the family. At the breakfast table he had his place, clearly marked by a little basket of what presently came to be known as 'Richard's bread' or 'the French bread', believed to be baked according to his fancy and in any case *good for him*, rather as native air is good for one; and once, when it was not there because of a fire in the kitchen chimney, everybody, including Richard, felt a distinct sense of grievance, as of good old ways needlessly abandoned.

'Why the hell can't she be consistent?' cried Mr Brett. Dog Hell thumped his tail, as he always did when hell was mentioned

– so often that his tail was nearly bald. 'It is not too much to ask, Georgiana. One day there is bread as there always had been, and the next day there is none.'

He was no burdensome intruder, they said, by means of the frank way in which they continued to disagree with one another, as soon as he had settled down: breakfast was usually a most agreeable slow browsing meal, unceremonious to the point of wandering about and reading letters, and the best-cooked, most lovingly-prepared meal of the day; but breakfasters were human and sometimes petulant, obstinate and positive, and although their disagreements were rarely anything beyond the mild wran-glings of any family, occasionally Mr Brett would break out in a very eighteenth-century manner, using terms of a rare violence and a fruity ring – *whoremaster*, for the chief of the Opposition, and *damned ill-looking jade* for either his wife or the house-keeper, one could not be certain which. And once there were words between Philippa and Georgiana that did in fact go beyond ordinary breakfast-time maundering.

'Archie Brocas is to marry Anne Charrington,' cried Mr Brett, from behind *The Times*. 'Eh?' he exclaimed. 'What?' staring about, very much as if his wife had kicked him under the table.

A little after this Philippa asked Georgiana why she had let Trimins wreck the rose garden, which was now such an utter shambles that she was ashamed to show it to her friends; she had always been particularly fond of it before, but now it was like nothing so much as a bloody Ideal Homes display or a municipal park – quite unrecognisable. Georgiana, whose per-sonal plan it was, joined battle at once with remarkable spirit; Mr Brett and the dogs looked apprehensive and low, and Richard took his cup for a long, long survey of the picture opposite. It was worth looking into, for it foreshadowed many techniques

that had not so much as a name at the time when it was painted
– somewhere between 1860 and 1875, and presumably in
France. The person had begun by covering the canvas with two
or three good coats of Vandyke brown, as was only right and
proper, and above this he had depicted seventeen dead fish and
some slime; but these were only the background to the real body
of the work, which was a swag of shells, starting with winkles at
the top corners and increasing to great things the size of your fist
in the lower middle. They hung there, stuck to the canvas, or
possibly sewn to it, and as they had been very deeply covered by
several coats of an oily yellow varnish, together with some brown
and viscid green paint in places, they had more or less coalesced
into one gleaming, undulating, bloated tube. Only a single whelk
was clearly recognisable as itself, and it sent back the strangest
umber light.

'What patience, eh?' said Mr Brett, coming and standing
behind him. 'There is another one like that in the long gallery. It
is shut up, now we are so poor, but Philippa must show it to you,
when they have stopped fripping. There are dozens of pictures
there, some of them very good, I dare say: I know my old gover-
nor thought the world of the portrait of his Tip.'

Dinner, of course, was not the same kind of a meal, particularly
when there were people invited; but it was a mild ceremony at
this time of the year, and when there were no other guests Mr
Brett and Richard sat long over their port like a couple of old
cronies. Richard knew tolerably well how to behave in such circumstances, and how to conciliate Mr Brett's good opinion; after
all, he was in a world not very unlike that which he had partially
inhabited as a boy – richer, but not essentially different. There
was the same unchanging conversation, in which a thing said three
thousand times was very true ('We are the salt of the earth; we are

indeed,') and the same wild eccentricities flourishing in a calm eternal conformity; Lord Cohorn was more than a little mad about Bolsheviks and he was trying to rally support for a bill to frustrate their knavish tricks by gas, but he presided over the quarter sessions in their immutable solemnity. Mr Crowthorne, their nearest neighbour, was the image of Mr Holden of Plimpton Hall, and the rector might have been transplanted from Easton Colborough. There were the same manners, a mixture of roughness and great urbanity, which were familiar to him, the same mania for protecting some animals and killing others: *The Times* was the parish magazine here, as it had been there – the same parish. And although nothing in his experience had prepared him for the young women (in whom London predominated over the country) he knew how to get along with Mr Brett and the dogs. When Hell bit him he was the first to say that the *poor old dear* had been unfairly startled; he was scrupulously polite to all the other dogs and to Tib, and he bribed them with secret morsels; he spent long evenings with stinking Tory on his knee, which Mr Brett noticed, when he was in a condition to notice anything after dinner, and which pleased him, for he had great faith in the intuition of dogs. 'You can't fool a dog,' he used to say. And in more human conversation Richard knew the necessary reticences: he recoiled before no sacrifice, and threw over the Jews, modern painters, sculptors, poets, foreigners and the working class without a qualm, and, which is perhaps more curious, without any conscious hypocrisy: he listened attentively, intelligently, to Mr Brett's anecdotes and opinions, drank with him glass for glass, and more than once helped him up the stairs.

Moving from the dining-room to the drawing-room after a tête-à-tête with Mr Brett was a movement of two clear centuries; and sometimes Mrs Brett seemed a little aware of this: she seemed sometimes to pine for contemporary conversation. Mr Brett had wrought too much havoc among his neighbours long ago to have many unattached young men in the house, or to let Georgiana come to London often: that very day he had referred to their annual ball as the Hampshire Horned Cattle Show, and he spoke with authority. One evening, when she was dressed in red velvet and Philippa in a severe black tube – both looking wonderfully contemporary: but Georgiana had never looked virginal at any time – Richard let in the distant sounds of Mr Brett's singing as he opened the drawing-room door.

'I suppose he has gone to bed,' said Georgiana. 'I have kept your coffee hot on the little stool,' she added, looking at Richard with a kindness that was perhaps wasted on him, but not at all on Philippa, who was sitting on the other side of the fire with the crossword on her knee.

'Come and help me with this anagram, Richard,' she said, moving to the sofa. 'George, isn't it marvellous to have someone who can cope with an anagram after dinner? Usually they come in bolt upright, scarlet in the face and tittering.'

In general Philippa's language was not adapted for the expression of any direct, unironical sentiment or emotion, but when they were taking a last turn by the tobacco-flowers before going to bed she said flatly, 'I hate drunkenness. It is perfectly *dreary* to see how James is becoming more like a sponge every day: and there is this idea that it is all so madly funny . . . It was that that smashed things up between Archie Brocas and me: we were engaged – I dare say they told you? – when I was all dewy, and he more or less raped me one evening – in a ridiculous little revolving summer-house that was teed up in the rose-garden before Georgiana spoilt it. He was stinking at the time, of course: he nearly always was.'

But when he thought of Churleigh it was a perpetual break-fast that he remembered: the breakfast-room no longer dread-ful because of custom, the delightful smells of bacon, toast, coffee and methylated spirits; the green of the lawn outside where you could see through the panes; the gentle noise of cups; the rustle of *The Times*. Churleigh was a wealthy house, but it only had one copy, and this was usually divided, not with-out some discussion, into imperfect shares. On the morning of the sixth, the rector, who often dropped in for breakfast after fishing the early rise, had the cricket news, Philippa the court page and Richard the correspondence, where Lord Cohorn exposed his views on the restoration of the whipping-post. Mr Brett read the financial part with a shrewd, contented smile, for it was devoted to armament shares, and even the least commer-cial mind could see that they were now a capital investment. Georgiana had her own whole paper, the *Mirror*, bought nomi-nally for the kitchen but never released until the little supple-mentary meal at eleven o'clock.

'Oh, no,' cried the rector, with real pain, 'Glamorgan have fol-lowed on.'

Nobody replied with more than a grunt; for to tell the truth nobody cared about Glamorgan, being attached to Hampshire exclusively.

'Is there going to be a war?' asked Philippa.

'No,' said her father. 'But fortunately a good many people think there is.'

'This Hun is making a great deal of noise.'

'Yes, my dear, I know. But it don't signify.'

'Odo,' said Georgiana, after a pause, 'You won't have the Bishop of Cleobury's vote.'

'We certainly shall,' said Mr Brett. 'It is promised, in return for what we did in the Easements bill, and even Cleobury could not rat on a thing like that.'

'No you won't. He has been eaten.'

'By whom, pray?' asked Mr Brett, in an incredulous tone.

'I can't pronounce it. Somewhere in Africa, I suppose. It gives that he went back to see his flock: he had been there before.'

'It is not in *The Times*,' said Mr Brett.

'Was it on the wireless?' asked the rector, who had a natural interest in a vacant throne. But nobody knew; nobody could make the wireless work.

'It says here,' said Georgiana very positively, 'that he went back to see his flock. It says *flock*. And they ate him. Pretty black sheep, I must say: most ungrateful.'

'Not Limbobo?' asked Richard.

'Yes,' said Georgiana, looking narrowly at the paper: she was short-sighted, but would not wear spectacles.

'Oh,' said Richard, with almost as much feeling as the rector had shown for Glamorgan. He put down his fork: it was as indecent to eat as to laugh: and they looked inquiringly and anxiously at him. He said that the bishop was, or had been, his uncle, and as they did not know how he was taking it they all at once adopted the grave, most considerate, attitude of entire condolence. Mr Brett said what kind words he could manage about the bishop and told Georgiana that they should cancel their luncheon-party. 'They were all very upset,' he was sure. 'A damned thing to happen – a vote and an uncle in the same day, is *pretty stiff*.' But this was not meant for Richard's ear.

It was perhaps something of the decent gravity which must accompany even an unlamented death that prompted Philippa to show him the long gallery, which was mournful enough, in all conscience, and carpeted with a thin, fine, grey dust that had set-

tled like snow in spite of shutters, curtains, dust-sheets and quantities of newspaper. Two eighteenth-century Bretts had made conscientious purchases abroad – debased Venetians and copies of
Guido – but it was less a collection than the kind of haphazard
accumulation that happens in any family that stays rich and in
the same place long enough without a fire. Favourite terriers still
guarded their rats, water-colours of Lausanne jostled Flemish
boors; but among all these and the samplers there were three
Coxes, a Girtin and a Crome. A probable Lawrence had been so
damaged by the improving zeal of a Victorian aunt that he could
not make up his mind about it – in any case, it could scarcely be
seen. And other pictures had been treated with no more ceremony;
Philippa herself had once decorated a boiled red general with a
beard and a top-hat and the traces of the chalk still hung about
him; and a Hoppner had been thrust through with a billiard-cue,
or perhaps a walking-stick. He manoeuvred to see it in the mixture of gloom and glare, serpenting his neck from side to side;
eventually he stood on a chair, and saw with the strangest shock
Philippa's own eyes looking back at him: a more diffident Philippa,
meeker and comparatively subdued, but unmistakable. The girl's
magnolia face and the poise of her head were quite exquisite.

'It is a shame to leave it like this,' he cried passionately,
'stretching and sagging. It is a lovely thing.'

'My dear, you sound quite passionate,' said she. 'They all look
like hell to me.'

'It is exactly like you,' he said. 'Won't you let me at least mend
the hole? Re-back it and put it on a decent stretcher?'

'Do, plum, if it would make you feel happy. I am sure you
could take it away and boil it, for all anyone cares, unless it is
one of the entailed things.'

When he had taken it down she looked at it with real attention, however, and said, 'It is true that she has the same ghastly pale eyes, poor pet. She is the one who came to such a sticky end.'

He was too anxiously engaged in taking the picture from its frame to ask about the end, for somebody in the past had transfixed it with nails in every direction, in a blundering attempt to keep it in for ever: when he had got it out she said, 'How naked the poor thing looks! Tell me, Richard, why do you think they painted all these boors?'

'I don't know. I never have known,' he replied, looking at some of the boors, sleeping, carousing, being boorish in odd corners of a brutal landscape. 'I have never wanted to do a boor.'

'Darling,' she said, 'I am so glad. I could not have borne it if you had done boors.'

She did not like boors, and she did not like the things she saw at the Academy: but she had nothing much to say for modern painting, either.

'Cousin Windham is always trying to make me understand them – he is the cultured one of the family: you will meet him in London. But it always seems so earnest and bogus and solemn to me, so horribly *solemn*. He says "Look at this terrific statement about Life" or a chair or that rotten sunflower, and everybody looks serious and dreary and mutters something about *values*, and all I can see is a mess. It is the solemnity that I can't bear – a silly girl looking glum with a most shocking hair-do and two eyes on the same side of her nose, God forbid: but *glum*. The only ones I like are the surrealists. They are madly amusing sometimes – they make you nearly sick with laughter: and really some of them are very clever. Such *perverted* ideas. Don't you think Dali is really very good? I adore him.'

Richard laughed vacantly.

'Well, anyway, my dear, they make all this sort of thing look like old hat,' said Philippa, walking away down the gallery, whistling like a blackbird.

She was filled with contradictions: she had a brilliant sense of colour in her clothes and he would have sworn that she would have liked Dufy, for example; but he must always have had his doubts, because from the beginning he had hesitated to talk about his own painting, and he had temporised in his own mind by saying that it would be better for her to see it all at once and in the best circumstances: then she would certainly like it – she was, after all, the essence of the present day. It would be impossible if she did not.

She was far more complex than he had thought, and with each new aspect of her that he discovered, good, bad, or indifferent, his emotion became more complicated and various: he had supposed that no emotion could be greater than that which he had felt sometimes when he was painting at his best, but now he thought that this perhaps equalled it, perhaps exceeded it.

It was an emotion made up of an incalculable number of factors, and although her beauty was no doubt the first of them – Philippa riding away in a cold rage after her quarrel with Georgiana, high and straight on a tall, burnt-umber horse, was the loveliest thing he had ever seen – there were a great many that he surmised, but could not define.

In coming to Churleigh he had expected to grow more intimately acquainted with her, to come to know her far better; but this had not happened. He had seen her under a great many different lights, and in different appearances, but his knowledge of her was not much advanced. One reason lay in him, because in coming to Churleigh he had reverted to an earlier life – church on Sunday and Mr Crowthorne blundering through the lesson exactly like Mr Holden or Colonel Apse – and what with the weakness of convalescence, the diffidence of a lover and of a poor person in a rich man's house, and the diffidence of his recaptured youth, he was less apt to judge. He grew younger, and shedding his hardness and arrogance he tended to accept rather than to criticise: judgment in Richard had come late and only in the years during which he had abandoned diffidence, cleanliness and civility: resuming them, he lost his acuity.

Yet nevertheless it seemed to him that she was a very difficult person to know, partly because she did not choose to be known, and partly because underneath her remarkable self-possession and poise she herself had no great amount of information about what went on.

Self-possession was the important word: she might resent being possessed by anything more than affection and he could only pray without any certainty that she would not resent the burden of being loved. She certainly resented any control, and at times she certainly resented being a woman, although she was such an excellent one. (Talking of the coming war she almost wept because she was not a man, and could have little hope of killing many Germans.) She was most affectionate, where her liking lay; and although she disguised it she had the strongest sense of duty: but as for love – would she undergo the violation of love?

He had once copied Colleone's Diana and although his notions of the myth were vague he knew chastity when he saw it; and it was not impossible that because he had lived so long in a milieu in which a girl who remained a virgin long was either a fool or hideous he now overvalued the virgin state.

She was somewhat older than himself, he collected, and he thought that she had been engaged to be married more than once: but Churleigh was a comfortable place and one of its great comforts was the kind reticence of its people; it was not a place for sudden confidences or unbosoming; you were not questioned there, and he had no more precise information about her than she had happened to strew about. This was not a little, however, because she had at once admitted him to one particularly valuable kind of intimacy; she had shown him such stupefying objects as her collection of birds' eggs (stupefying when he thought of her swaying on stilt-like heels down a London pavement, clothed in mink) and her stamp-album, with the ridiculously forgotten and instantly remembered images of the Frenchwoman sowing on a twenty centime field, the embossed double eagle of a vanished Russia, and the magic words Magyar Kir Posta; and he knew, for example, that she too had undergone the agonies of mumps.

He knew a thousand little facts, from her telling or from his own observation: he knew that she could go cherry-pink with anger, and that she could behave beautifully under enormous boredom; he knew that she could cast a fly with remarkable skill under the branches that overhung the Dribble, and that she could play a daring and often successful hand at bridge, and that she could hold a cigarette in the corner of her mouth, with one eye partially shut, until either the hand or the cigarette was finished.

He knew these things and a great many more, and perhaps they should all have pointed towards some central, knowable character: but for him they did not; she could continually surprise him by some new and totally unexpected facet of herself. There was an indecency in handling, weighing, and as it were valuing his mistress's natural essence by any kind of a conscious intellectual effort, however; and if ever he did so – a timid synthesis – it was not so much a questioning of her perfection as an attempt to find out by this criterion what perfection was.

Perfection could be rather obtuse on occasion. When they were hurtling northward at the end of his holiday, she said, after some fifty miles or so, 'Daddy says I am to find out, in a very clever and roundabout way, whether you have any money – need it, I mean. He particularly said I was to be subtle and not go blundering about like a Shire stallion – really, my dear, he has the oddest images – trampling on your feelings and when I asked him how he said *Oh, I must use my mother-wit*, with great complacency.'

He said he was quite well-off, and thanked her very much: but although he was deeply changed by love he could not help feeling that his assurance was too easily accepted – he would not have been sorry to be pressed, to resist again; and for a few fleeting moments he wondered what she knew about money, if anything, to accept any statement about it lightly. Probably nothing: how could she? But it was certainly not her fault: no rich people could have any notion of reality.

It was not a happy ride. In its nature it could not be and as well as that there were many little things that added to the misery – a grey, low, uncertain sky; a cruel east wind. Philippa drove very fast, which is generally more fun for the driver than the passenger, particularly in a small car that leaves the ground from time to time; and as the London road was well inhabited that day she had to concentrate too much on overcoming the others for more than scraps of conversation. Between Lyndhurst and Romsey she had a furious race with a small unknown foreign car, and after that a hopeless duel with a Bentley, and all the time his mind was free to grope anxiously forward to the end of the journey and taste beforehand the moment when he should step out of the car and say, 'Good-bye, and thank you very much.'

Churleigh was fading as a dream fades, and as they ran up past Sutton Scotney, now on the familiar Stockbridge road, he felt many of those kinder youthful habits of his mind fade too: the harsher ways came back one after another as the harsher realities drew closer at eighty miles an hour. He grew older as the miles flicked by; not less loving, but more desperate.

In the twilight they hummed past Camberley and a low café that he knew, and almost immediately afterwards Philippa said that she was sure they could catch the Lagonda ahead and beat it into London.

'Why not?' she shouted, learning her head sideways as she slid up past a boorish lorry in the middle of the road. Was he nervous? Was he not feeling well? Did he want to stop for a minute? She was not pleased.

'Well, no, darling,' he said, 'it is just that it might belong to a man I know that I do not want to see.' The word darling in his mouth was wrong, he never said it, he did not know how to say it, and although Philippa used it continually to him, it made the wrong noise, sounded a false note, from which the journey did not recover.

The harsh sordid light of a garish roadhouse that he knew too well lit them green and red, and he felt something like a steel probe in the region of his heart. She started the windscreen wipers against the drizzle, and silently, rather slowly, they drove into London, past scattered factories, huge heaps of metal waste and empty smoking lots.

CHAPTER TWELVE

What shall I do to be saved? What shall I do to be saved? For the Salvation Army band in the street below there were no doubts upon the matter; but Richard had no useful information. He was sitting in the accumulated filth of his room and its associations and memories, and he could see no way of extricating himself. He was part of them, they formed part of him; there was no way of separating the one from the other: and as if by way of marking the point the physical dirt in his room, particularly an all-pervading soot from the open window, had come off on to him from everything he had touched. The window had been left open wide for these months past and high wind-blown leaves, scraps of paper and bus tickets had piled in a sopping bank between the window and the wall; a few had come to settle on the table, among the crocks of his last meal. Cockroaches had come up from the basement to eat the remnants and to make their way into his larder. There were several of them drowned in the milk jug, now quite dry: he had met them first on the stairs, underfoot, as he came up; and on opening the door he had found the room full of them, and the air full of their stench, instead of the smell of paint. His bed, well within reach of the drifting rain, had moulded, and either through the rotting of the cover or from the scrabbling of a rat some of the grey stuff of the mattress had spewed out.

For some time he had known that this reckoning would have to take place and he had known that it would be painful, but he had not known what form it would take nor how painful it would be; he could not have known, because many of the emotions involved were new to him, or at least new to him as an adult. His procrastinating mind had remained deliberately vague: he had been determined not to let anything spoil Churleigh and he had used the future as a rag-bag for all the considerations that rose in his mind from time to time – as, for example, when Georgiana, looking at the *Tatler*, had said, 'Here is Paula Crichton. Do you ever see her brother?' James, down for a week-end, had not replied except by shaking his head; but some minutes after he observed 'We used to call Jack Crichton *Stinker* at school, which shows that we were not such clods as some people say' – glaring at his sister – 'He has gone completely down the drain.' Richard, with his heart beating faster (such an unexpected injection of fear) had calmed it by saying that he would come to that in time, and in London.

He was in London now. He had supposed that he would have to grapple with immediate physical difficulties and to take his measure in regard to Torrance, and that was true enough – these things had to be done – but that was not all.

As far as it went it was an absorbing, worrying preoccupation. His room had been silently entered and silently left; he would never have known it if he had not still been pedantically exact in the arrangement of his colours – the catch of the window might have been his own mistake (it was a defective catch), but he could never have left burnt sienna next to raw sienna. The searcher might have been a policeman, but he did not think so: the man in the shop downstairs, seeing him come in, had waved and called out 'Been away?' quite cheerfully. He would have been closed and secret if the police had been.

He felt that all this happened long ago: there were two brief notes from Torrance in his letter-box, making appointments for that pre-historic time when he was lying senseless in St George's, and nothing after; and he supposed that Torrance, having grown suspicious then, had made his way in to find out what he could. Richard wondered whether he had brought Crichton with him; and wondered what would have happened if they had found him there – even now, when he was utterly free from Torrance's domination, he had to clear his mind deliberately before he could get rid of the idea that Torrance naturally knew every turn of his present disposition. He wondered, too, that Torrance should not have opened the letter-box and taken away his own letters (a complete silence would have been more sinister) as well as the others that lay there. These were invitations from various galleries – he looked through the names distractedly – and a card from Gay, holidaying in Williamsburg with one Doll Tearsheet, with *Pure Hell* scrawled on the back, together with a long fat letter, in which he said he would be back in London before the autumn.

It was a friendly letter; but Gay, although he was an excellent and witty talker and although he could write an intelligent minute, fell into a facetious, labouring style for his particular friends, and this not only disguised Gay but also grated upon Richard at this juncture, when, standing in the cold irreparably sordid stye which he had provided for himself, he tried to avoid the most unpleasant confrontation of his life.

To put it off a little longer, or to diminish its impact, he began to put some decency into the room: there was not much he could do at this time of the night to make his bed inhabitable and for a moment he had the strangest idea (almost like a hallucination) that he would go to Pamela's flat and sleep there. Love eats friendship and no one has less to say to one another than dead

lovers, he knew very well; but in this odd momentary lapse out
of his context he thought he would not have to speak. However,
he spread his good blanket over the electric fire and made it
steam, and he did something towards throwing the wind-bank
out of the window and sending the black-beetles down. But he
tired very easily still (he had been much injured and reduced)
and he soon gave it up – it was an impossible task without zeal
and daylight, and he had neither. For some reason that he could
not define, and for the first time after an absence, he did not
turn his pictures round (they were all facing the wall) for comfort and company; he only looked in an objective business-like
manner to see whether the drawings and gouaches were injured
or needed moving from the damp, and finding that they were
unhurt he left them alone.

His long holiday was over: his mind was filling fast with the
confused fears and obscure hurrying associations that had before
made it so distinctive a place for him; he would be obliged to
deal with them, and with the new emotion that kept piercing up
through them, which he supposed to be the remorse of conscience that he had heard of from time to time. He took his
warm-damp blanket, and wrapping himself in it up on the model-
throne with his feet on a box, he waited, watching the pale window for the morning.

Churleigh was flitting away, receding and vanishing with an
extraordinary speed: he was in his own element again, and the
gap that Churleigh had torn in its continuity was closing of itself.
When he stretched out his hand without thinking it found the
electric switch, and when he went on to the roof to piss down
on to the dark world he moved with all his old habits guiding
him; his confrontation was not with a somewhat hypothetical
Temple, removed in time, his qualities the subject of more or

less accurate recollection and recounting, but with himself as closely and immediately as if they had met face to face, unavoidably, in a narrow passage.

For a very long time now he had divided his world: his world had been habitually divided (painting apart) into the sharps and flats, and, by a somewhat different division, into the poor and the rich; he belonged to the sharps – he belonged with much more certainty to the poor; and the people on the other side of the barrier were his natural enemies, his natural prey.

But there was no conceivable doubt about where Philippa stood; and there was no question about the mutual enmity of the two worlds. Once he had spoken of Crichton, putting the case of a possible change in him.

'Is he a friend of yours?'

'I have met him. Not a friend.'

'I don't really know him, either; but from what his people say the only thing for that young man is a stable bucket.'

'No hope?'

'But my dear, he's dis*honest*,' said Philippa with a lift of her nostril, as if this entirely finished the matter. She looked wonderfully handsome.

'No hope for thieves?'

'Oh, no: once a thief, always a thief. But darling, are we to wave flags for Jack Crichton? Good old Crichton?'

'No, no, no. I was only thinking.'

'Besides, he is such a howling bore, like all those wrong 'uns – Avon's son and the rest of them. I don't want to be a Christian Brother, plum, but the only improvement that fellow can ever hope for is enough sense to put his head in the bucket himself, and keep it there. The sooner the better.'

There was no doubt of the enmity between the worlds, and

there was no doubt that one had to belong to one or the other. Yet it was inconceivable that he should regard Philippa as the enemy.

All his heart was on the far side of the barrier: but it did not appear to him that an emotion, however violent, could alter the place in which things stood. An overwhelming desire to be of another kind was not magically efficient. No tears have ever yet restored a maidenhead, and his loss was more complicated.

He had lost enormously, and although he had not gone so far as some (Torrance and Mowbray were incapable of affection any more) still he had parted with a fair share of his humanity. A man is a man only because he feels like one – his identity is in his emotions – and when he is obliged by some inhuman army or religious order or hag-riding virtue or factory to feel like a social insect he is no more than a white ant upon two legs: and when he has been feeling like a rat for a long time much the same thing happens. For a great while Richard had been almost continuously afraid or at least aware of danger not far away. He was still afraid and on the stretch – afraid very much as a rat is afraid, of countless known and unknown pursuers: and the fear had many of the same effects, if a rat is indeed hard, untrustworthy, savage and full of hate. He had not been alone in London for five minutes before the sight of a policeman had sent the habitual wave of enmity through him: recognising the prick of fear he had crossed the road. The rat, the figurative rat, was a somewhat base and object creature, although it might turn dangerous; but above all, it was an unhappy one.

And then as for morality, he had already defected to the flats, if for no higher reason than that their life, even at its stupid worst, appeared to him a happier one. Most of them had no intellectual or experimental right to condemn dishonesty, but they reached the right answer because they instinctively knew how to live, as some people can draw as soon as they pick up a pencil. There is not much to be done in the arts without instinct: no intellectual effort will paint a picture, but perhaps after years and years of anxious plodding a man might come to the point at which the true beginners start. Philippa and her kind, with their natural and highly-developed sense of *how to behave* in an infinity of finely differentiated circumstances, were artists in living, and they had begun with an understanding of the fact that he was now reaching, with a mind appalled by its truth and significance.

With an earnest solemnity that might have been as ridiculous as it was naïve if it had not been so racked out of him, he had discovered many undoubted, uncontested truths – that it was wrong to steal, because it turned you into a thief; that dishonesty was to be condemned (could not be too much condemned), because of what it did to the dishonest man; that crime is its own punishment; that the criminal builds his own prison and locks himself in; that the touch of pitch defiles – and he sat there with these maxims running through his head, to end with the terrifying shout *and the wages of sin is death*.

But it was one thing to assent to a code of religion, and quite another to belong to the people who practised it. Instinctively and in many of his ways he belonged among the wrong 'uns, the improvers of fortune: he belonged among them partly by nature and partly by long living in that country; he knew it, and he knew that at any moment this might be made obvious to the world in general by some commonplace misfortune. But with a sudden horror it occurred to him that perhaps no revelation was called for, no denunciation, no police; by now the thing might be written on his face, clear to any observer more acute than, say, old Mr Brett. He was almost persuaded that this was the case, and he felt far away, very far away, on the wrong side of the barrier between Philippa and himself.

And yet it was not until he came to ask how he came to be there that the full bitterness of the night began; for a multitude of answers instantly replied. He was in the best condition of long wakefulness for total recall, and the answers, in exact brilliant images and words, spared him nothing. His memory supplied him with all the details of his illegal doings, the things that underlay his fear; and his various prostitutions; but very much more than that it laid open all his legal crimes, the things for which he could not be punished because there are no laws against dryness of heart. Some of these recollections were atrocious, and he had succeeded in burying them; some, the more commonplace betrayals of love and kindness that happen to men who have prided themselves on lying around, had long been the subject of some degree of explanation and regret; but now all of them presented themselves without any reserve of half-truth or gloss. A day of judgment with the whole of a man's private, secret, discreditable life ripped up before an omniscient judge and the whole world might have been more painful; but it could not have caused more sadness.

The light came, and with it the full day: it had little effect on him, although he moved about, paying some attention to the necessities of living. It was not a state of mind that could pass that day or the next, for he was a person then who moved (like some insects) from stage to stage of his development by violent prolonged new labours. But towards the end of the paroxysm, seeking not so much justification as more knowledge, he turned his paintings about and walked up and down the line. Some he turned round again; some he put on the easel to judge them better. The colour flooded the unhappy room and warmed him, and he held each side of his St James's Bridge with great affection, as something that he might cling to; but still, tapping its tight canvas from behind, he said, 'It's very well. It's very well. But you might pay too much for it.'

+

THIS WAS A strange thought for him, one that had never occurred before: it was obscurely connected with a sense of liberation, not unlike the eventual blurting-out of some blasphemy that has been pushing up in the back of one's mind for a long time against one's will. The whole process was obscure, for painting had nothing to do with the things for which he reproached himself; but however devious it was it led him on to a further liberation – he was not obliged to stay in this horrible place. He had felt (as if it had been written in a book) that he was either to go to Paris, as he had prayed, or he was to stay; one or the other. Yet as he was now deter-mined not to go to Paris or indeed a yard further from Picton Square than he was forced to go, and as it was clearly impossible to ask Philippa to this swill-tub of associations, it was an unusu-ally pleasant surprise, a liberating surprise, to find that he was not obliged to stay – that there was a third and obvious course.

Pleased, revived, exhilarated by this discovery, he washed, shaved, put on a clean shirt and went to call on Philippa in Picton Square.

'My dear, where have you been?' she cried, clutching his arm with the most affecting pleasure and concern. 'What have you been doing to yourself? Have you been ill? My God. Come and sit down. What have you been doing?'

'Oh, I don't know,' said Richard, very pleased to be there, now that he was past the discreet, discouraging anonymity of the hall and stairs. 'Thinking, mostly.'

'My dear. Well, never think again, darling, if it makes you turn dull grey from head to foot. Sit down, and I'll make you a nice strong cup of tea. There are cigarettes in the thing.'

It was a very feminine flat, but not uncomfortable: it looked out on to the trees of the square – a formal square with informal trees glistening under a light drizzle, a square such as a home-sick Londoner of a certain kind might compose to console himself in Kano or Sokoto. The room also had a curious air of having been composed. It had something of the unity of a picture, and after some thought he called Zoffany to mind, a muted Zoffany: perfectly modern, however; there was no blundering about in pursuit of George III. It was a little like living in a frame, and he sat with bumpkin primness until Philippa came back with the tray; but by pulling the door closed with a foot hooked behind her she turned the place from an exhibition-piece to a room, par-ticularly as it was clear that she did this every time she came in with her hands full.

'Do you like it?' she asked, meaning the room.

'I have never seen anything like it,' he replied.

'David Banbury did it ages ago,' she said indifferently, 'and everybody still shrieks when they see it for the first time. Aunt Sophie stood me the whole thing for a birthday present the year she backed Hyperion for the Derby. It sounds ungrateful, but I must say I am getting sick of those bogus stripes; and besides, the curtains are filthy. I was going to ask David to do something else – less bleeding good taste – but he has turned very *missish* on account of something Ninian Crawshay said Aunt Sophie said about him. I had thought perhaps Victorian: but a horsehair anti-macassar costs a fortune now . . . so does David. Do you know him?'

'I have heard of him.'

'Who hasn't?' said Philippa, with a nasal giggle. 'Such a *roar-ing* queen. But he is madly clever. Aunt Sophie launched him, you know.'

'Is she Prudence's mother?'

'No, that is Aunt Sophie Kilmore. This is Aunt Sophie Manton, the fashionable one of the family, and the only one who can spell, apart from Cousin Windham: she is rolling in money, and never leaves London for a second except when people drag her away by force. She loves launching people – very artistic. God knows where she gets it from. She is frightfully excited about you and I am sure she will buy hundreds of pictures – when may I come and see them? Have you got a match? This—ing lighter never works. My dear, aren't you smoking? You used to smoke like a chimney.'

He said he had given it up.

'Is it your chest?' she asked anxiously – having, after all, bashed it in – 'You were supposed not to, at Churleigh: Dr Box said so.'

'Parsimony,' he said, with the intention of doing away with her anxiety; but immediately after he regretted his candour and tried to overlay it with some poorly contrived falsehoods, which to his mind had the repulsive air of denying to affirm. Parsimony was the fact, however: if he was to remain within walking reach of Picton Square for any length of time he must take up his old monastic ways: a more obviously pagan monastery or hermitage this time, but not less acceptable.

After a silence in which she appeared to be listening she said, 'My dear, I wish you were a decorator instead of a painter. I could *hurl* money into your lap. Now that Aunt Sophie and David have quarrelled – and anyhow David is booked up two years ahead and even if he weren't he has soared right through the ceiling, I

mean in prices; which goes for Ninian too . . . But there is not
so much difference really, is there? I mean Dufy and Léger and
all those very clever ones do curtains too; and Derain and Picasso
for the ballet. But anyhow, I am sure your pictures are quite
lovely, and I am longing to see them.'

'You won't like them,' said Richard, crossing the fingers of his
unseen hand. 'But I do very much want to show you one or two.
As soon as I am in you will have to come and praise them.'

'When?'

He waved his hand evasively and said that he hoped it would
be very soon.

'But why not now?' asked Philippa in a sort of indignant
whine. '*I* don't mind where the hell they are.' He was immovable
on this, however. Philippa was not used to being thwarted, particularly in London, and for a moment he felt the approach of
polite acquiescence – that she accepted the rebuff, and abandoned the right she had assumed to break into his privacy, and
that now she would make a graceful retreat to the far side of the
line between intimate friendship and intimate acquaintance. He
had seen her being *affable* to Young Conservatives at Churleigh,
with the same deadly affability that he knew from his childhood;
and something in the poise of her head reminded him of it now:
he was too frightened to say anything to remedy the situation.

It was only a second, however, and her kindness returned: she
was already beginning to speak with her old expression when the
telephone interrupted her. The machine was in another room,
but she presently appeared in the doorway at the utmost stretch
of the flex, still speaking into it, sometimes nodding to Richard
or winking at him with private (though mysterious) intelligence
and at other times addressing the unseen with the face appropriate to her words: it was obviously a person she knew very well.

'. . . but if you would let me get a word in edgeways,' she was saying, 'I was *telling* you; he is here now, at this minute, and I will
ask him.' And nodding with great vehemence to show him that
he was to say yes, she asked, 'Can you dine on Friday?'

'That was Cousin Windham,' she said, 'being rather tedious. I
do hope you will like him: but I don't know . . . he can be so
bloody tedious. He is the cultured marvel (I told you) just as dear
Aunt Sophie is the wealthy one. I suppose every family has one
of each. But while Sophie is madly gay, a marvellous advertisement for having lots of money, as if anybody needed one,
Windham is enough to put you right off culture for ever, sometimes. Not that I was ever on it, much. I mean, it's a very good
thing and where would we be without it, but as far as I can see
it has just made Cousin Windham sicker and sicker of more and
more. He despises practically everything now. I have to hide all
the books in the house when he comes: he used to make me read
dreadful poems rather like washing lists by people who said *earth*
and *blood*, but he doesn't like even them now. And then Cousin
Windham about the newspapers and the BBC – laugh. I don't
know which he loathes more, the *Mirror* or *The Times*. But he
does grow tedious now and then: I mean everybody loathes the
dreary little refined man who reads the news, and Children's
Hour, but you don't have to go on about it for hours and hours,
staring straight ahead of you in a sort of furious trance, livid and
gently frothing.' She gestured with the tea-pot, and went out of
the room, still talking backwards, loudly, through the open door.
'The only thing he really likes any more are brass band contests,'
she shouted from the room with the telephone in it, 'and those
weird cup-ties.' Coming back she said, 'But listen, Richard, if
you won't show me your pictures – which is pretty swinish, I
must say – please tell me about them, the ones you said I might

come and praise. That was what I was going to say when the telephone went – have you got a telephone? No, of course not, if you are moving. But what *kind* of pictures are they? Not abstract?'

'No,' said Richard, and he looked for the words to define himself. Pomposity, unintelligible jargon, facetiousness, false humility and some others all edged in closer to jump on his back, and while he was still gazing at his enemies she laid her hand upon his knee and said, 'I shan't be a minute.'

Returning with an anxious, worried face she said urgently, 'It's Mrs Payne's cat kitting. She had to go away today – she's my housekeeper – so she brought her here. But she's not really *used* to the place, and she's not happy. Poor little soul, she's not really used to this kitchen at all.'

Nine kittens will check the most devoted self-observer in the exposition of his views; and if that had not been enough (though one kitten would have sufficed for him) he was required to take seven of them away and drown them in a nightdress bag. They were both much shattered by this experience, and obliged to be recovered with brandy and further cups of tea and they neither of them mentioned pictures again; but in these latitudes and under this light he did not dream of resenting it, however umbrageous he might have been in another world – in this light it seemed to him natural. It was a light with particular virtues, and it was a light very much charged with her presence – how much so he had not realised until, walking away from Picton Square, he crossed Sloane Street, which was the beginning of the no-man's-land between their worlds; nor how much that light sustained him. He crossed by Pont Street and entered a grey, colourless world, with no savour in it, and the people seemed anxious, hurrying under a disagreeable compulsion: he did not see one good-looking face. At Sloane Square the sun went out; and in fact the shop-windows began to light as he went past their too-well-remembered faces. In the tobacconist's he saw – he thought he saw – Torrance's back. He walked on steadily, neither to provoke the encounter nor avoid it, but his face was clamped shut with the effort, and long before he had reached his own door he had reverted to a state in which a continual effort was needed to keep hard and calm.

On Friday he telephoned Philippa to ask when he should come, and with a secret delight there in the public booth he noticed how the slightly nasal, training quality of her voice was accentuated by the earpiece, together with the just distinguishable common and even bucolic overtones that she had caught from servants in her childhood: it sounded faintly colonial, and it melted his heart, which, unaccustomed to the machine and still alas in its native territory, was at that moment somewhat hard and constricted.

Many of his old suppositions had been backward, provincial, plainly mistaken, or (more often) based upon observation of the more careful middle class; Philippa's voice contained inadmissible vowels, and at Churleigh, in spite of its many points of identity with Easton Colborough, he had heard some criticisms of the royal family that would have made a republican stare. There were many things in which experience was challenging his earliest and sometimes most painful – unnecessarily painful – tenets: *these* people did not give a damn whether you had been to a public school or not – they were less imprisoned by their caste, he observed, as he walked eastward, carefully avoiding the dirt.

The nearer he came to Picton Square in the course of these reflections the happier he felt: he loved the people there, and he looked forward very much to meeting Aunt Sophie, who might look in after dinner if she had time, but with whom he was to drink tea in any case on Tuesday: she was no other than the Mrs Manton of whom he had heard so many hushed rumours in his former days. Her favour was said to have launched two poets, one man-milliner and a little host of people connected with the ballet, music, food, decoration and portrait-painting: the entrance to her house was very carefully guarded, and her followers fought passionately to keep each other from the golden spoils.

He reached Philippa's flat in a fine glow of charity with his fellow-men, and although Philippa introduced him to Cousin Windham with the words *I hope you will like one another* (a hopeless beginning and one that Philippa would never have used if she had not known that Mrs Payne had muffed the bouillabaisse, and that Windham was already in a vile temper) he was not in the least prepared for the cold eye with which Windham stared at him. The other guest was to be Nancy Trafford, of whom Richard had heard: she was late, and after half an hour of desultory, unsatisfactory conversation and far too many slightly warm martinis Philippa said, 'Perhaps we won't wait for Nancy: she must have got hung up. Nancy Trafford was supposed to be coming, Richard – I told you about her.'

'Yes,' said Richard; and feeling it necessary to say something into the cold room and perhaps also to assert his intimacy he added, 'She is the vicious one.'

'No,' said Philippa with a meaning glance, 'You are thinking of someone else.'

At this moment the bell rang, and five minutes later the assembled dinner-party sat down, with Nancy Trafford still explaining the accident that had made her late (her flat had caught fire). There are some parties that should never begin, however, doomed parties, and this was one of them: apart from the spontaneous dislike between some of the guests and the irritation between others, disaster and war had broken out in the kitchen; the food was lamentable, from the coal-tar soup to the chalky Camembert and the Dead Sea apples, and whenever the frightened, pink-eyed maid opened the door she let in the sound of battle or hysteria.

If it had not been for Nancy Trafford, Philippa would have said, 'The hell with it. Let's go and buy some fish and chips,' but as it was she sat there with a pleased expression, conversing, while the food went from bad to worse: and all this while the men competed barbarously for the women's attention – vainly, in Philippa's case, though she turned her bright smile from one speaking face to the other.

Throughout their glutinous struggle with the bouillabaisse Windham held forth on painting in England – not whether it was dead, but what it had died of. It had died with Turner and the last gleam of the old order, said Windham, who had a way of never finishing a sentence until Richard had a fish-bone or the claw of a lobster in his mouth, and so held the field: since then, with the rise of industry and the total embourgeoisement of the country the pursuit of beauty had been an impossible thing to avow openly. Good taste and craftsmanship, yes: antiques, silver, gardens and dead architecture, yes: but embroidery and water-colours and any pictures for that matter were effeminate. The English painter believed this, in his heart of hearts. 'Most of his energies are taken up with fighting against his own convictions. And then the criticism is in the air he breathes; all his surround-ings tell him a thousand times a day that his is not a *man's* work, not a lifetime's pursuit. So he cries louder and louder and gets more shrill and extreme, anxiously watching what goes on over the Channel. They order these things better in France: but to expect the same kind of painting out of a totally different culture, to go through Parisian gestures in London, is as stupid as trying to make sense out of the squiggles that represent Chinese writing in eighteenth-century chinoiseries, or to expect English school-children to speak French because they have smelt the irregular verbs. It is mere irrelevance and falsehood and they end up by more or less faking or even deliberately forging the work of men from another hemisphere: they say, "mum-mum-mum-mum: behold, I am speaking perfect French."'

'What do you think they ought to do, poor things?' asked Nancy Trafford. She had enough female solidarity, in spite of her vice, to try to make Philippa's party go, and she had been helping it along with drops of oil and merry laughter whenever the exchanges between Richard and Windham seemed likely to stray over the boundaries of social incivility, 'You can't expect them to suddenly stop *pursuing beauty*, though it is a repellent thing to say and rather like church, don't you think, Phil?'

'The people here must dose it – the beauty – according to their patients. Over there they can fling in the cantharides and as much of the absolute as they can conveniently get hold of, but here, to get it down, to make it of any use, they have got to work through respectable craftsmanship. No, I am perfectly serious,' he said, staring round the table. 'The painter has got to paint out of happiness, and so he has got to be in decent standing with his nation, whatever his nation is. The older I get' – he was pushing forty-five and he was terrified of fifty, – 'the more I count the thrust of the world: one man is nothing against fifty million. He must have the support of the tribe if he is not to be a pariah, or in the painter's case a wretched spiritual outcast.'

'You forget that a painter is necessarily an exception,' said Richard.

'No more so than a plumber,' said Windham, reverting to his

shrewish expression. 'Not many people plumb, probably fewer than paint. A plumber is an exceptional man. Every man is an exception. That is what vexes me so about modern painters: in the days when they dosed their beauty according to their customers you heard nothing of these high-falutin' attitudes. It was not a small thing to make an Adam drawing-room and civilise generations by it; no, and it was not a small thing to paint like Stubbs or Cox, and make an acceptable, profitable dose of beauty sink in by way of craftsmanship, but in those days no one carried on in such fluting tones about the all-importance of art. These exalted hysterical claims do more harm than anything. Take painting – any picture, any valid picture, is in some degree a statement about life, don't you agree?'

'Yes,' said Richard, feeling rather stunned, and watching Windham's hand as he poured.

'Then which is more important, the thing itself, or a remark about some infinitesimal corner of it?'

'The thing itself,' said Richard.

'Well there you are. There you are!' cried Windham. 'You say the same thing as I do. You agree with me.'

'I take it,' said Richard, after a momentary pause, 'that you are in favour of Life?'

Windham flushed, and lowered his head over the sodden pudding that Mrs Payne had dropped and wept into some time before; and Philippa hastened the end of the interminable meal.

The men were left alone – an odd sensation, because all the tensions at once altered, and Richard, for one, could feel little enmity; but Windham, leaning back his huge face as if he were still addressing an audience, spoke about a young painter he had known. 'He didn't really speak the language here – he was all adrift. And I advised him to go and live in France, where no one would expect him to speak the language. Some simple little place on the Mediterranean – all foreigners, no one more foreign than the rest.'

'We shall have to get a cab that doesn't mind drunks,' said Philippa, in a cold fury. 'I shall never speak to Windham again in my life.'

'Oh, I don't know,' said Richard. 'He was entirely right, in a way.'

✦

FINDING A NEW place had never been so difficult, but at last, in Ebury Street, a district almost unknown to him and prettily balanced between Heaven and Hell, he found a studio, a very well-lit studio, on the top floor of a quiet house. The rent was beyond anything he had ever thought of as a possible figure for himself or any other Christian. The payment of the first month's rent ripped a terrifying hole in his accounts; he would more gladly have given flesh and living skin than the notes that passed from the pocket next to his heart. And yet in a way the greater the pain the greater the satisfaction: as in another sphere sick men can offer their pain as a sacrifice or as it were give their patience under agony to another being, so he looked for mortifications that he could lay on his private altar. He had never been far from a kind of regarding religion, a piety towards fate, (nor from a set of gross private superstitions and fetishes): he was deeply convinced that he must pay, and he was always pleased to be allowed to pay in small, bearable instalments; but there was also this kind of voluntary payment, outside all account and with no relevance to it. So far, however, he had found nothing that could even begin to count in comparison with his happiness; and as for direct payment, he could think of no existing or conceivable coin – no adequate draught on futurity.

During this long interval they had been about a great deal together; he had been most kindly received by Mrs Manton and invited twice to dinner; he had drunk innumerable cups of tea with Philippa, had taken her to some very mean and tawdry cinemas – she chose the films – and to a notorious cellar in Bloomsbury; he was thoroughly used to her presence. Yet when he was installed, when the place was scrubbed and drilled into the rigid, antiseptic order of a spring-cleaned prison awaiting a royal inspection, and when his calendar of cryptic squares of colour marked the day when she was to come and see his pictures he found himself uncontrollably nervous – convinced of disaster.

He was ready much too soon, and he left himself hours in which to feel his uneasiness. The day was kind enough, with some fleeting sun and a breeze, and he opened all the windows on the street to get rid of the damp reek of soap: the middle window provided him with a box to view the pageant of Ebury Street and to stare himself into a calm, if he could. Besides, the wind was grateful on his bloody face, double-shaved to agony. The pageant was moderate enough: a delivery-van, striped yellow and black, bowled silently up to the house with green window-boxes over the way. Half a dozen people walked either up or down, and on the road between them a boat-shaped coal cart towed by a horse and a coal-man in a boat-shaped leather hat that reached his middle. Every few steps the coal-man gave a melancholy cry, putting his left hand far behind his ear. From the extreme left of this scene a policeman appeared, pedalling a cumbrous, upright official bicycle. He looked from side to side as he approached, as if he were looking at the numbers in the street, although this might have been interpreted as curiosity, or professional interest: but when he arrived at the height of Richard's new dwelling he wheeled ponderously in a half-circle to the near pavement, and dismounted. He propped his bicycle against the kerb directly under the window and stood there fiddling for some moments with the top pocket of his uniform; then, turning, he looked straight up at Richard and nodded.

'Good afternoon,' he said. 'If there is anything you would like a hand with, don't hesitate.' He was interrupted, and directing his voice into the railings of the basement he said, 'All right, all right. I was just telling the gentleman. Anything I can do, or the missis,' – speaking upwards again with an expressionless red moon that opened and closed – 'A pleasure, I'm sure.'

'Thank you very much,' said Richard.

He retreated into the room, and softly closed the window. 'My God, my God,' he whispered, but he allowed himself no other outlet – formulated no emotion – and at once he began to draw. At first he made nothing but geometrical shapes, cones and cylinders and arrangements of innumerable interlocking cubes, but as the need for this died away he took to drawing Cousin Windham's large grey face. He had the slick trick of superficial likeness to a degree that he had always found a little disgusting, and when he was doodling it often came out: in much the same way his vacant mind would produce hopelessly vulgar little dance tunes and repeat them indefinitely, although in fact he knew a good deal about music, and loved it dearly. He drew Cousin Windham talking, talking, talking; Cousin Windham mocking Christ in something of the close dreadful manner of Bosch; Cousin Windham damned in scores, being received by a hell-full of more Cousin Windhams; hundreds of very naked Windhams, some being eaten by thin pointed Gothic dogs, fed carrion by birds, butchered – a busy butcher's shop on Saturday night all hung with hollow pieces of Cousin Windham; Windhams hunted, flayed and stuffed, loved by a baboon, deathly sick.

He was coming back into an excellent warmth of mind when a noise froze him, a little furtive scratching outside: the former tenant of the studio had painted a great many nudes and the boy downstairs had formed the habit of watching through the keyhole and a crack in the panel of the door; he was on the landing now. Richard could not know this: for him the faint animal movement, the breath, were something far more sinister. After they had moved secretly to and fro on each side of the trifling leaf of wood for some moments – the leaf separating such very different emotions – Richard whipped it open. The boy, half kneeling for the hole, half up, saw him huge and bitter and almost threw up his heart in terror: he looked so pitiable and white that Richard did not move until with a sort of gasp the boy managed to turn and scuttle down the stairs.

He walked out on to the landing and saw not only the flying boy spiralling away in continual diminution, to vanish at the first floor, but also Philippa, let in by the policeman's wife, walking up.

'What's the matter with Pimples?' she asked. 'My dear, you aren't on fire?'

'God knows,' he said vaguely. 'How glad I am to see you!'

He had every reason to be: she was wearing a black suit and a pale blue blouse, and she looked astonishingly lovely. But she was not in form; she was pale, and under her perfectly calm exterior there was a feeling of intense irritation. Her car had developed some complaint, and the fool at the garage had probably wrecked the timing with his ham-handed interference.

'For Christ's sake don't pace about like something behind bars, darling,' she said, throwing down her paper and burrowing in her bag. 'Sit down. Relax. You haven't got a cigarette, I suppose?'

'No,' cried Richard, shocked at the omission: he ran down the stairs, plunging terror and guilt into the wretched boy below; and presently ran up them again.

Philippa had been looking at Cousin Windham: she was enchanted. 'Really, plum,' she said, drawing the smoke in deep, 'I had no *idea* you were so clever. It's quite adorable. I would never have said you had such a filthy, *filthy* mind, either. But I thought you said surrealism wasn't the thing?'

'That is only nonsense,' said Richard, uneasy, but delighted with her pleasure. 'I was just assing about. It is not surrealism, either.'

'What is it, then?'

'Huh, if it is anything,' said Richard, looking at it, 'I suppose I had Bosch in mind.'

'Should I know about this Bosch?'

'A very old party: fifteenth century.'

'Well, it's what *I* call surrealism: I think it is sweetly pretty, particularly the lewd baboon. Are you going to show me some more? I hope they are like this.'

He showed her some more, putting the pictures that he had arranged beforehand one by one on the easel, moving it up or down so that they should lose no scrap of advantage. Her chair was in an excellent position; the light was even, strong and pure; the pictures could not have asked for more. But he could not tell what she thought. Perhaps they were not what she had expected; perhaps she had to get over some preconceived idea: it was a pity that she had seen the stupid drawing first. He knew he must be brief and calm; brief because painters easily over-estimate receptivity and endurance in others, and calm because agitation and talk would destroy the right atmosphere. But did it exist to be destroyed? She said very little, just a few words dropped into the void '–what a sweet pink sort of cloud in the corner – I love that red – my dear, what a cunning mauve blob!'

Was it possible that she hated them, or was bored, and did not know how to say so? Very well-poised people, if a rare chance throws them off their balance, can become as furious as cats surprised: Torrance had been the same.

Once at the Bracken Gallery with Philippa and Nancy Trafford he had hurried them to a Miró: 'I love the colours,' Philippa said, 'but what is it meant to represent?' Forgetting the other girl he replied, 'It is not *meant to represent* anything. A rose does not represent anything, for God's sake: why should you expect a picture to?' He had peered far into the picture, and absently asked her, 'How can you be such a–' He was three parts taken up with the picture, and his mind, fumbling among his stock of names unhappily came up with *lout*. 'How can you be such a lout?' That, and Nancy Trafford's horse-laugh, had knocked her off her balance: he had thought the world was going to end.

But all that was a trifle in comparison with this. He became more and more nervous, and in order to force the atmosphere into being before he should show her his last, his St James's Bridge, which was to be her present, and to delay the moment of final decision, he put up several pictures that he had not intended to show at all. In spite of his principles he lengthened the afternoon, and when he came to the bridge far too much time had passed.

He watched her face, in silence. She looked steadily at the picture, smoking and fanning the smoke away with her hand.

Eventually he could not bear it any longer and he started to talk about the need for the vermilion on the right and the difficulties he had had with the blue. In a stupid, dull, unconvincing tone he said, 'It was most important that the blue should hold the centre.'

And after a pause she said, 'It is perfectly lovely, darling: but as for abstract painting, I am only one of the beasts that perish – I am not up to it. Too loutish,' she added, trying to make him smile.

'But it is not abstract,' he cried, interrupting her in the beginning of some polite deprecation and rushing pell-mell into an explanation of the point of departure and the intention of the picture. He showed her the sketches, drawings, gouaches and other versions, trying to make her see the progression: they impressed her. But then borne on in his spate of words he tried to explain the nature and function of painting and the whole thing degenerated into a straggling inconclusive and rather stupid wrangle.

'But darling I am not trying to make you paint mid-Victorian academy pictures, God forbid, but what is so ghastly immoral about painting things that look like something?'

'I never said–'

'I may be naïve and limited,' she said, raising her voice so that it quelled his heart, 'but it is just not true to say that I am all caught up in whimsy: and I do *not* love coloured photographs. I don't mind your mauve grass a bit: in fact I think it is a lovely colour. I am *not* trying to make you paint quaint nooks or kittens. It is only that I think this drawing and that gouache are ever so much better than the painting – if that is old-fashioned, all right so I am old-fashioned. But I am *not*, because I adore some modern painting.'

'Surrealism–' Richard began, but his throat choked him.

'Oh well,' said Philippa, looking round for her gloves, 'I suppose it's just one of those things. Thank you very much for–'

'Don't go yet,' said Richard. 'Please don't go yet.' He pushed her back into the chair: she looked startled into his face, and after a moment lit a cigarette without saying anything.

He clamped the picture to his usual height and with extraordinary despatch he was at work. The bridge came violently to earth, precisely modelled, lunging into a remarkable trompe-l'oeil depth; the trees broke into a mass of leaves: the picture had jerked back fifty years. Now, working very close and calligraphically, he jerked it forward again, and to a very different plane; the trees turned into one shining rounded marble column, verd-antique, and the bridge, even more precise, now depended upon girders made of wool; its nearer foot rested upon a flat white jar ajar, from under which another Cousin Windham crawled.

'It is Gentleman's Relish,' she whispered, just behind him.

And across the bridge moved a number of figures, some almost human, under the glare of a huge eye that had replaced the sun. He stepped back again, and saw that he had gone even beyond his aim; the various objects stood in weird relation to one another, on planes still connected by the picture that had once been there; and the extraordinary slickness of the drawing was something that he had never accomplished before.

'Don't touch it,' she said. 'It is quite perfect now. Richard, you must promise me always to paint like that.'

'Do you like it?' he said. 'I am so glad.' And with the utmost precision, just where the red-haired figure would make nonsense of the bridge's curve and complete the sacrifice he painted a grey Judas walking towards a tree. 'I had meant the thing,' he said slowly between strokes, retreats, and narrow-eyed sharp staring in the fading light, 'as a sort of present, if you liked it. The only intention of the picture – the present has no sense otherwise – my only intention is to please you.'

With this and the last stroke of red he turned away and automatically began to clean his brushes.

'May I really have it?' cried Philippa. She was very much moved; she looked at him with respect and affection. He had no doubt that she liked the picture: and it was decorative enough, in its way.

'I shall hang it in the drawing-room, over the fire-place,' she said, with intense satisfaction. 'We shall have a party for it.' She kissed him, looking at her watch and screamed – she would be late for a very holy dinner, she said, grabbing at her belongings. 'Thank you for such a lovely, lovely afternoon – I've never enjoyed anything so much as the second part. My dear, you are so clever.'

But when they were on the pavement, waiting for a cab, she said in an altered tone, 'Oh, I meant to tell you when I came in. Jack Crichton – I'm afraid he broke his neck: I wish I hadn't said that about him.' She gave him the paper, and when she had driven away he read it there before he walked into the dark stairway. Torrance and Crichton had been killed on the Great West road: their car had been travelling at between eighty and ninety miles an hour when it overturned.

He walked slowly up to his studio: he was aware of nothing but an overwhelming sense of loss.

CHAPTER THIRTEEN

W HEN PHILIPPA HAD said 'I could hurl money into your lap' she had not exaggerated: in the few months before the war began he made more money than he had ever handled in his life – more money than had ever kept him up to that time. He had a car; he lived in a clean, soft, warm, dry flat; he ate regularly and very well.

Aunt Sophie Manton, like so many rich people, had an excellent head for business; she was experienced, pleasantly cunning, and at that time largely unoccupied. She undertook most of the launching, which had been determined upon by the family long before Richard came to grapple with his soul (it was perfectly typical that the Bretts, without the slightest tinge of hypocrisy, should have envisaged a gentlemanly form of compensation in which all the payment should be made by society at large); but it was clearly understood that this was Philippa's young man, and Philippa herself did a great deal. She had all her aunt's energy, a good deal of her natural ability, and an even greater determination to get her own way: and she was, if possible, even less scrupulous in putting the bite on her richer friends.

He was exceedingly busy, and he had little time for examining his conscience; but in any case it did not reproach him unbearably, because although it was true enough that in the empty coldness of the next morning he had said *I have sinned against the spirit and I have offended the comforter, who is gone for ever* yet even then he had known that he had done it not only to retain

Philippa but also because this particular integrity was the only possession that he had retained and that it was the only sacrifice that he could offer for a restitution of virtue.

And in addition to this feeling of ultimate justification he was conscious of a liberty that he had never known since he was old enough to recognise himself: any artist who aims high must put himself into a disciplinary prison more severe than most people would willingly bear; and he had aimed very high. Now he had much more time for living, much more perception of it: and with the passing or burial or death of his talent he seemed to acquire much more worldly poise – he seemed to grow right up. It may have been coincidence or the possession of money; but talent might also be the reflection of a certain childlike innocence – not childishness, but the quality of 'little children'. But in any case, it was far more comfortable to be without it.

Nevertheless he had some very disagreeable moments before use, money and time hardened him. Gay came back: Richard was very glad indeed to see him; but he was obliged to show him his pictures.

'I have given up painting,' he said in a voice as unaffected as he could manage, but still pretty surly, 'and I have taken to decoration.'

'Oh,' said Gay, looking solemn.

'This is what I was doing before I stopped: and these are the sort of things I do now; but most of them are on walls or ceilings.'

After a long pause Gay said, 'You aren't serious, are you, Richard?'

'Yes.'

Gay laughed, in his very cheerful way, and said, 'Well I can't see any difference. I mean it is obvious that these are lightweight, but they don't pretend to be anything else, do they? I like them very much indeed – full of light – charming.'

'The trouble with you, Charles,' said Richard angrily, 'is that you are all taken up with lively colour and competence. They are only decorations – props.'

'The more like this the better,' said Gay, turning them over. 'Are you sure you are not fooling yourself? There is nothing to be tragic about here.'

'I am not being tragic,' cried Richard, 'and if you had any decency–'

'I suppose this is Iphigeneia,' said Gay, holding up a big bistre monochrome.

'Yes,' said Richard, and after a moment, 'They are a-doing of her in.'

'Do you know that this is exactly like the Under-Secretary?' asked Gay. 'It is almost libellous. And this is Beresford.' He gazed wonderingly at Richard.

'Yes,' said Richard. 'Philippa tells me about them and points them out. This is for the Cormorhams' place.'

'Oh, I *see*,' said Gay, enjoying the picture far more now. 'Well, it is quite true that he is the great one for doing evil that good may come of it, which I suppose is what you mean. Your Philippa must be pretty well-informed,' he said, looking over some more sketches. 'You don't mean this Philippa?' – holding up a drawing of her head – 'Philippa Brett?'

'Yes,' said Richard, turning aside to hide the silly smile. 'Do you know her?'

'You are flying pretty high, aren't you?'

Richard laughed. 'I hope to marry her soon.'

'So do plenty of other people.'

'Who?' cried Richard.

'Oh, I don't know,' said Gay, finding that Richard was in earnest. 'I have been out of touch for so long. I only mean you can't go around looking like Philippa Brett without having people try to marry you at every turn.'

'Charles,' cried Richard, struck by a new thought, 'would you come one evening? I should love to show her a respectable friend. You could wash, and put on a decent suit; and you might do quite well.' But when Gay was going, with a date fixed for their dinner, Richard said, 'You won't give her the impression that I have given anything up, will you? I do this because I like it, entirely for my own amusement and the money. I like it.'

He had an unpleasant moment with Drome, too, meeting him at one of Mrs Manton's huge parties. Drome could not have been more obliging, more civil, and when he said that he had seen Richard's ceiling at Cormorham House he let no kind of particular intelligence come into his eyes; but it was a bitter thing to undergo his congratulations.

However, the morning's post brought the thumping great Cormorham cheque, as well as a semi-literate note from Philippa asking him to help her look at some dresses in the afternoon: the envelope also contained a flattering piece about him from one of the shiny papers, which she had cut out and improved.

He drove her as far as Grosvenor Square, and there she suggested that he should park the car. 'Darling,' she said, when the echoes had died away, 'it is all very well plunging into the thick of it with your head down and your eyes tightly shut when you are on a horse, but it is too courageous altogether in a car.'

'It was *joie de vivre*,' he said.

They went in through the grey glass doors, and Richard looked at the enormous room. Grey and silver, crystal chandeliers; a competent genteel piece of work, terribly dull. While Philippa was talking to her vendeuse he wondered what he would do with the vast bare expanse of wall, but presently he was interrupted by the approach of a mannequin, a tall, slim girl, but somewhat less elegant than Philippa, who bore down on them with the ritual pace and the haughty stare of her trade. She came up, turned twice with a swing of her skirt, and swept away. Another, in black faille, took her place, strode over the carpet with the same forbidding face, and arriving at the height of the little grey table and chairs, placed a wink and a leer somewhere between Richard and Philippa, before swishing herself about and mincing back to the changing room.

'Did you like that dress?' asked Philippa. 'My dear, you look quite consternated; it wasn't all that good. Or are you admiring Sally? She is still quite fetching.'

'Do you know her?'

'Of course I do. She's Sally Mander. She was a house-prefect and captain of hockey. I used to plait her hair: laugh. You must have seen her about; she was at the Pelhams' last week. A frightful bitch.'

'So it was you she was winking at.'

'Yes, plum, it was me: now do pay some attention to the dresses.'

In the changing room the smaller mannequin said to Sally, 'Who is that young man with the green face? The one with Philippa Brett.'

'He is Mrs Manton's new painter. You must have heard of him.'

'That's him, is it? I have always wanted to see him,' said the small one, peering curiously through the curtains. 'Why is he sitting so very close to Philippa Brett?'

'Because he likes it, I suppose,' said Sally, pursing her lips. 'She picked him up in Piccadilly, and he has never been the same man since. She knocked him down and secured him when he was helpless; now he likes it.'

'He is quite good-looking, in a depraved sort of way. What did she knock him down with?'

'God knows. A life-belt, probably. She was absolutely desperate when Archie Brocas married Anne Charrington.'

'But I thought that was on again?'

'Oh, I don't know. She was always a sly little thing, but I don't know. People say these things: I think it is just because Anne Brocas makes scenes. She hates every woman under ninety in London and the home counties. No, I think Philippa is quite fond of her prey.'

'He is really very good-looking.'

'She says he is wonderfully pure.'

'My God. He doesn't look it.'

'She says she can trust him absolutely anywhere.'

'Dear me.'

'She says it is great fun being with him, and you feel quite safe, like being with a eunuch.'

'How *quaint*! He is all right, I suppose?'

'I've no idea: but I can't imagine Philippa within a hundred miles of anybody who was not – not her cup of tea at all.'

'Where does he come from?'

'He is the son of that bishop who was eaten.'

'Perhaps it won't last. Archie Brocas didn't last, nor did Charles Salkeld; and there was somebody before him.'

'Well, I don't know; but it has been going on for a long time now, and he still runs briskly round after her with his tongue hanging out, adoring her. He worships the ground for miles around, and kneels all night outside her flat, clasping the dustbin.'

'It must be nice to be adored.'

'Yes, my sweet: I must admit it's very flattering. But only for a while: you get awfully sick of doggy eyes after a month or two.'

'All the same, I think I could put up with it. He doesn't look like a eunuch to me.'

The idea that devotion might be boring had also occurred to Richard: there were times in that last blazing summer when everything seemed too good to last and by way of averting the evil chance he imagined that he was a bore, that she was engaged much more often than she used to be although so many people were leaving London early: he asserted (for the sake of this argument) that being now comparatively fit, launched and well-to-do he was lost in the sea of healthy, rich, established contemporaries, and of no interest. And partly because of this, partly because he was afraid of pestering her, being an ever-present nuisance, he hesitated over an invitation to Churleigh.

He had a fantastic amount of work to do: he had refused to go to the Pyrenees with Gay, very much against his heart, and he knew that from the sensible point of view he ought to decline Churleigh as well, quite apart from the stroke of lover's strategy. But when he heard Philippa's nasal voice on the telephone, asking him quite plaintively to go he dropped everything and drove down that afternoon.

He could only stay six days; but they were days that might have been picked out of all the hundred last years as their best. He walked with Philippa; they fished together, and by iron determination and the kind good will of his mount he rode with her through woods suffused with green light: there were two families of little cousins staying, with mothers and women who talked of nothing but school uniforms and disease, and apart from one day when they drove the whole band to the distant sea, they were left very much on their own.

When he said good-bye on the broad steps, with the children all roaring and hooting farewell, he felt that he had been there all his real life; and at the last moment, when they looked at one another, smiling, he had the strangest impression of seeing an infinitely transformed version of himself, as if they had been married for years and years and had come to form one person in two aspects.

There was no way that he could find to formulate this thought without its sounding intolerably vain or presumptuous, although he turned it over in his mind for the whole length of the London road, the switch-back hills, the remembered towns, cricket-matches and a vast sky filled with soft warm light.

In London he postponed all thinking and set about his trade, for it was at this season that the people who could afford to agree with Mrs Manton's value of him left their flats and houses empty. The days packed down one upon another, a series of accurately planned hours, business details – Mrs Manton had a young woman who helped him, but even so he found that he had a great deal more common sense than he had ever supposed – and consultations with decorating firms and craftsmen, as well as his own direct labour. He was a quick worker, but he longed for twenty-five hours in the day, and he was obliged to farm out more than he cared for: he supplied the Monteiths with a starred blue heaven at ten guineas a constellation and a zodiac at so much a sign that he almost blushed to take it, particularly as he sold the drawings immediately afterwards to a firm of glass-engravers for as much again. He began the first half of Philippa's flat, and cov-ered one entire wall of her bedroom with leaf gold to make the ceiling glow, and upon it he painted the rural joys in green.

He did not see her again until the day the war broke out: the sirens were howling as she ran up the stairs. 'Darling,' she said, kissing him without thinking about it, 'Isn't it exciting? I came up in three hours flat, just in time for the sirens. Have you had any bombs yet? Have I missed anything?' she asked, staring anxiously up at the sky.

London turned into a uniformed camp overnight, and those who had no uniforms pinned arm-bands on themselves: Philippa had one as an ambulance driver, and she vanished into a fetid underground garage for twelve hours of the day or the night. It was a time of indescribable confusion, excitement and exaltation, and although nothing happened after those first unearthly, Martian sirens there was no sense of anticlimax: the general vitality of the people had been jerked up to an extraordinary level, and it stayed there.

Richard was extremely interested; he watched and listened with the closest attention; but he did not feel himself involved – he had no uniform. He had altered himself almost beyond recognition, but he had not completed the transformation and at this time he had no particular patriotism: indeed, he never felt the true stirrings of it until the fall of France. Just as formerly it had never occurred to him that he should work so now it did not occur to him that he should fight: he did not understand the issues involved, and at this time the fighting was very remote and theoretical, the authorities unbelievably inept and pompous.

He had no uniform, and he might have stayed indefinitely on the sidelines if it had not been for Philippa. But there was never for a second the slightest ambiguity in her attitude. She and all her friends, all her kind, were entirely for the war, the bloody and total annihilation of the country's enemy. She could not conceive knowing anybody who had any reserves about the matter. She spoke with furious indignation about his chief rival, David, who had been exempted from military service on cultural grounds.

'*Cultural grounds,*' she said, with her nostrils flaring. 'Fiddling about with a paint-brush. Poor pet, you wouldn't do such a thing for a million ballet-dancers, would you?'

He now sought for a literal uniform with more zeal than any but the most committed, for it was not that he had any contrary principles to overcome; but no uniform was to be had. The three services told him to go away, the third saying that he was wasting their valuable time, coming with a chest like that: he could pass no medical examination. A great deal of wire-pulling went on at this period, and both he and Philippa as well as Mr Brett used all their many contacts. There were many telephone calls, many arrangements, much waiting: many people who spoke with a protecting air turned out to be quite powerless: but there were others, and of these Charles Gay was perhaps the most promising. He had something to do with one of the many branches of intelligence but which or what naturally remained vague: he had taken Richard for an interview with some military and civilian people in Kilburn (a surburban house in the best tradition) and the interview had been conducted in French. There was an almost equally promising colonel to do with camouflage, and a cloudy department to do with the enemy's fine arts; but they were all unendingly tedious, muddled and slow.

Between the scrappy finishing of his contracts and his search he saw Philippa in brief glimpses, often at strange, twilit morning hours. But sometimes they both had the day off: just before the huge German offensive that smashed France they had tea together in her flat. The servants had gone to Churleigh at the very beginning, and they had the place to themselves: she was dressed in trousers and a jersey, and her hands were still oily from her ambulance.

'My poor darling,' she said, 'I'll give you another note to the

Admiral. It's just no use telephoning. Peter assured me that you could get into trawlers without any sort of trouble at all with his good word. My dear, how I should love to see you in bell-bottomed trousers!'

The bell rang, and Richard, toasting a crumpet by the fire, heard the murmur of voices. Then Philippa came back, followed by a tall, thin soldier. Six months before he might have looked loutish, too straight in a town suit, but this was the hour of the fighting man and now he seemed splendid – Sam Browne, decorations, gleaming buttons here and there. Philippa said, 'Major Brocas – Mr Temple.'

Richard got up, at a disadvantage with the toasting-fork; but Brocas did not offer to shake hands. He nodded and said, 'I have heard a lot about you.'

'I hope you two will keep one another amused,' said Philippa, lighting a cigarette, 'but anyhow I am afraid I must leave you together, because my bath is running over.'

They had little to say to one another while she was gone, saw little to like in one another, and parted at length without expressing or feeling any desire to meet again: *at length*, because there seemed to be an inclination to outstay.

Philippa came back, bathed and dressed in a pretty frock; she poured out tea and single-handed, or almost so, maintained a long conversation: but at last, after a brooding silence, Brocas said, 'Well, I must be getting along to the War House. Are you coming my way, Temple?'

'No,' said Richard, with an open smile, 'I am taking Philippa out to dinner.'

They dined at a place with a band and a floor-show, and in the entrance they ran into a party who were celebrating an engagement; they were invited to join them, although they hardly knew the girl and the man not at all. It was a brilliantly cheerful party, with a great deal of noise – the best kind of unexpected vinous gaiety – and when they were obliged to leave it still in full cry, because Philippa was on night duty, they found they were both somewhat tipsy.

They crept through the blacked-out streets, singing, and when they tripped and bumped into things they laughed uncontrollably. By the lamp-post just before her garage door he kissed her passionately and when she had gone in through the faintly blue-lit oblong he stood there for some time before he turned. He had never embraced her before, and it made him tremble: he walked away without any notion of where he was going.

He must have walked for miles in that quiet windless darkness, for at one time there was the river on his left; but he took no notice of his direction or indeed even of the fact that he was walking until after a long passage of darkness he found himself standing silently in front of the door of his old lodgings in Chelsea, as if his body had been a horse that had carried him there, a sleeping rider. Now, with a nervous hatred of the omen, he hurried back to his flat, picking up a late-night taxi on his road.

There was a message for him from Gay: *ring me up as soon as you come in; triple urgent*. And this he did. Gay was still awake, facetious, but with an undercurrent of an odd gravity: he had got Richard *in*; he was to come to lunch and would be introduced to his chief afterwards; it was all that he could have hoped for.

A little while before tea the next day he had taken a great oath of secrecy; and after it, with an invisible but sustaining uniform on, he rang her up. But the machine burred and burred in her empty flat; and so it did at hourly intervals for the rest of the day.

They were supposed to meet at the Leighs' house the day

after, and as he had little time left in London he spent it all in making the necessary arrangements, which he regretted very much when they sent him a note to say that the party had had to be put off. He regretted it still more when Gay came through to tell him that it must be Friday and not Saturday.

'But I have not told Philippa I am even going yet,' cried Richard, shaking the receiver.

'Oh, that doesn't matter,' said Gay, a tiny, maddeningly certain voice in the earphone. 'I'll tell her myself, if you like. Come to the Office at seven, and there will be an official car to drive you down. Seven a.m., you understand, Richard?'

Richard knew Philippa's rota, and he saw that this would be just half an hour before she would be on duty: he hated to wake her early, particularly at this time of change-over between night-duty and day, because she was a sleepy creature, who loved her bed; but clearly there was no help for it, and at half-past six in the grey morning he hurried round to Picton Square. Ignoring the slow lift he went up the stairs three at a time: his mind was so elated, and his heart was pounding so when he rang insistently on the bell that he did not hear the growling oath on the other side, and when the door opened he was inexpressibly surprised by the tall, unshaven figure of Brocas, in a dressing-gown.

'Oh; oh,' he said, 'I beg your pardon.' And turning, 'I am very sorry.'

CHAPTER FOURTEEN

WITH THAT RECOLLECTION his mind went white: from the earliest days he had set himself to stop thinking or remembering at that point, and by now the discipline was so strong that although he had actually provoked her image on this exceptional holiday of mind and all the train of memories, yet still he stopped.

His intention had once been to account for himself in every particular, to complete the chain between the little boy and the boy's physical continuation, himself in that cell; and still there were years to go to bring his account to this date, the crowded, dangerous years between, which had equipped him with the hardness and the fierce, brutal unscrupulous kind of intelligence needed to keep alive in this atmosphere of heroic illegality – quite apart from the recent months of forced development. But he was very tired now; and in the automatic silence of his mind he felt the waves of sleep coming up all round him. With a heavy consent (as a careful householder celebrating a victory might for once go to bed without locking up the house) he let himself go – no mental reserves, no spiritual precautions, no part of himself told off for a sentry.

+

THE FIGHTING IN the lower part of the town was growing now: a new force of maquisards from La Bastide had pushed between the small German holding force (elderly worried men, most of them handier with a filing cabinet than a rifle) and the miliciens in the town hall. The miliciens had let themselves be separated into three bodies, and unless the German commander thought it worth his while to cut his way through the narrow streets there was little hope for them. He had a few lorries, scarcely enough for his own men, and now they were drawn up with their engines running, on the north side of the Place Gambetta, where the road to Paris ran over the river bridge: he sat there, waiting for leave to abandon the town, and determined to take it by sunset, whether HQ came through or not. He gave no thought to the miliciens, whom he had always despised, but concentrated all his attention on making sure that the bridge did not go up before he could get out.

The miliciens and the few other extreme collaborators presently became aware of their situation, and those in the ancient town hall began to run about like wild beasts. Barricaded behind the five-foot stone walls, they heaped the town records into the inner court and set fire to them; they smashed furniture, pictures, glass cases; and all the while their comrades at the windows and the mediæval arrow-slits fired at anything living they could see. A single milicien, in a state of complete exaltation, ran the length of the attics, soaking the beams with oil.

The other bodies, somewhat less engaged, were retreating from the school and the disused tannery towards the prison; it was the noise of the attack and their retreat that came down to Richard Temple's cell like the sound of a distant, uneven typewriter, just stirring him as he slept, changing the visions that moved across his mind. They followed one another in an arbitrary disorder and yet there was no apparent want of logic as he dreamt, dreaming with all the vivid brilliance of starving dreams.

Sometimes dreaming, sometimes waking into those very short

waking dozes that are so filled with living memory that they are as lively as dreams, but more controllable, he lay there, drifting in and out of the world. There were the ridiculous aspects of his war: the overgrown eternal adolescents in the training school, with their throwing-knives and the Robin Hood stuff; the parachute-tower from which you were dropped with the thing already open, but you were always supposed to go through the motions of pulling the rip-cord and if you did not (you wished them all to hell) the fat man in charge would cry, *it isn't cricket, Temple*, in real distress. The sleepy Levantine, who was supposed to drop pamphlets over North Africa, in the languages spoken there, and who was found to have dropped nothing but advertisements for his own green tea, and little samples of it.

He felt again the unearthly stillness of the descent after the blind rush of his fall in the slipstream of the plane, when under the umbrella of his parachute and the peaceful face of the moon he drifted imperceptibly towards a moonlit haze, under which lay a bare alpine moor, invisible.

And here he had a complete and perfect dream of Philippa – himself a disembodied spectator while she walked (she had a most distinctive walk) along a lawn by the side of a long blue flower-bed, arguing with some unseen person or perhaps only to herself, about a trivial point of housekeeping; whether it was better to make hot-cross buns with iron or death. And then in his dream he was on the turf of an alp again, but not that alp beyond Grenoble where he had dropped. It was the alp or more exactly the grass-covered mountain that runs between France and Spain, the ultimate rim of France where the land breaks and, as a cliff, plunges far down to become Spain a great way below among the trees – a visibly different country.

It was an atmosphere and a feeling that he lived through

again, and although some of the feeling was that of total nightmare so that his sleeping face was distorted with effort and agony
yet some of the atmosphere had the nature of the keen air of the
mountain and its clarity.

On the day he was taken he was walking along this rim, from
the hidden camp at Mollo to Olot; it was a journey that he often
made, for it crossed two little-known and unguarded passages
(or rather scrambles) into Spain, where he sometimes had
appointments, and ended at the terminus of an escape route.
Usually he preferred to make it at night whenever the moon
served, for although the high bare slopes were lonely enough for
an army to exercise there unseen and although walking through
some of the country in between was awkward except in daylight,
yet he preferred the dark: he liked the restfulness of invisibility,
and he felt larger, stronger and more at home in the night. But
the way from Mollo, before it reached this high remote country
beyond the trees, passed through a forested valley, and in this
forest he had often heard, and sometimes glimpsed, the wild
boars that lived there. The last time, coming back from a con-
ference with two different organisations, the one Catholic and
the other Communist, where the passionate volubility of all concerned had kept him late, he had surprised a boar in the broad
daylight and he had followed it along its own beaten track for
half a mile. If he had been armed he could have shot it easily,
and that great hulk of trotting pork would have been welcome in
a camp of hungry men: so, having a rendezvous on the other side
of the mountains within a week of this he took a rifle with him,
and timed his journey to reach the trees at dawn.

The camp was in a deserted hamlet on the dry hills, a country
that had been less arid once, and had supported the little farms
that stood here and there, roofless now, in the more sheltered

valleys: he left it in the darkness and made his uncomfortable
way up and down slopes and ravines towards the high ridge that
dominated them all by two thousand feet. The old farm tracks
still existed and some of the goat paths were still used, but the
maquisards took care never to clear them or smooth them at all,
and they, as well as his short cuts, were overgrown with the harsh
and often spiny growth of the garrigues; thistles, Judas thorn,
scrub-oak, asphodel, cistus.

By the time he was half way up the ridge it was growing light,
and when he reached the top he found that Venus had already
risen, a splendid star, and in those days half an hour before the
sun. He was out of breath with the last scramble, and the rifle
hung heavy on his arm; he unslung it, and sitting with his back
against a rock he gazed out over the country that he was about
to leave. It was still grey, and the light was not strong enough for
him to see the details, but in a very short while now the sun
would come up and bring the colours into the hills that went
rounding away one after another to that distant coast he had
once visited with Fifine when he was a boy. The wind would certainly rise with it – it was a wonder it had been calm for so long
in this country of incessant winds – but in spite of the wind the
sun would presently make all those valleys shimmer and rever-
berate and if there was any moisture left in them it would dry it
out. From a human point of view it was a discouraging landscape,
ravaged by the wind and poisoned by the sun: on the barer hills
the shale spilled down in harsh colours, acid green and ochre,
slag-heap red. Everywhere on the lower slopes where there was
any earth men had tried to live, and everywhere they had failed.
They had tried very long, from the Romanesque chapel to the
nineteenth-century farm below: the laborious terraces of the
dead vineyards still followed the contours of the hills – every-

where there were the proofs of huge vain effort for hundreds of years, by anxious generations slowly beaten.

Behind him, over the bare ridge, there was a completely different world. Nobody had ever tried to live there except a few odd fugitives – and yet it was a country filled with streams, fresh, glad of the sun, and sheltered from the wind. It was a high country, and in a way it was a guarded country, for to the north, where the complex of valleys sloped to the plain, there was the tumult of old earthquakes, masses of piled rock, narrow breakneck gorges, too tortuous for even a charcoal-burner to make a profit of it. It was said that there were still bears up there.

The sky was growing brilliant in the east, and he crossed over the ridge: the forest began at once, with flattened hoary junipers at the top and then a little lower down beds and rows of rounded wind-combed dwarf hollies separated by perfect turf, like a ducal park; then holm-oaks, and so down through mixed trees to the innumerable host of beeches that formed the main part of the forest. It was virgin forest, untouched, and in its windless depths down by the stream he was surrounded not only by magnificent silver trees soaring up out of the night that lingered there, and by the long saplings of the next generation, but by the solemn and whitened death of hundreds of ancient trunks. The ground was littered with gleaming branches, and the living trees upheld the dead.

If he were to follow the main stream to its head-water, a place called the Seven Springs, he would be able to climb up to the alp above the tree-line, and so walk on almost level high ground to within a mile or two of Olot; but he had allowed some hours for hunting, and in order to increase his chance of a boar he took the first tributary on the right hand and shaped his course to cross a much larger stretch of the forest.

Coming down through the oaks he had already seen the ground turned and worked by them in their rooting, and he hoped to get a sight of one quite soon. He knew nothing about hunting, except from war and from having been a quarry, and although he had spoken to men in the neighbourhood who had killed boars he had not learnt much to the point, because their experience had all been in the regular way, in numbers and with dogs, whereas his was a private war. Besides they all said that there were no rules for the boars of La Palaresa (the name of the high country) – they were so fierce and so undisturbed that they did not behave like others: they were thought to belong to another race. He had always known that a boar was a dangerous creature –

> The great wild boar of Cossa's fen
> That ravaged fields and slaughtered men

– particularly a wounded one; and a local expert confirmed this by insisting upon the needles and gut that he and his friends always took with them, to sew up the dogs.

He knew nothing about hunting, but perhaps no man is devoid of a predatory instinct, and anyhow he would have been a fool indeed not to understand the meaning of the tracks that went down to the brown stream in front of him and emerged on the other side, to go up the bank and into the trees by a recognisable path. They were the tracks of a boar, and each foot had left two long half-moons with a little mark like a knob to one side; he had seen them several times before and he had no doubt of their nature, but he had never seen them quite so large and deep, nor so distinct. While he was staring at them the mark nearest the stream slowly filled with water, and a moment after a little piece of mould fell from its side.

The beeches stood wide and clear; there was almost no under-growth, and he could see the tracks leading away through the trees. He stood listening, with all his animal senses on the strain. Far behind him there was a noise of something moving among the still heaps of leaves and branches – a vague, distant noise that was often confused with the varying sound of the running water – and beyond that there was the cackle of a jay waking up. But in front of him there was nothing, no hint of the hurried noise of a boar going away.

He followed the tracks into the wood, darting his eyes from them to the trees, continually hoping to pierce the shadows and see a movement before he was seen: on and on along the bottom of the valley, moving fast and with the sinuous perpetual caution of one who must not make a sound, immensely alive, but quite blind to anything outside his chase.

A great while later he was still following, scratched, very hot and tired, impeded by his clothes and his rifle. He was almost ready to give up, although he had once caught a sight of his boar: but that had been long ago, and in the open wood. He had not been able to shoot, being straddled between two fallen trunks with his rifle still slung, but he had seen it very clearly, a huge grey compact triangular hairy strong thing, very nimble; and it had stopped for a moment to listen before moving composedly on, along its habitual path. That was long ago, and since then he had climbed the far side of the valley, through close-tangled wood and even scrub. There were paths, but they were paths made by four-footed animals, sometimes like low tunnels where the growth was thick, and they were almost impossible to follow: besides, once the beech wood was left behind the ground was often dry, and although at first a few muddy patches showed him that he was in the right direction, it would have needed a dog's nose or the gift of prophecy to have felt more than a faint hope that he was anywhere near the boar now.

The line had led up to the edge of the forest, towards bare country, rock-speckled grass interspersed with a few low thorns, a stretch of mountainside that waved in gentle valleys originating in a high ridge before him – small valleys about a mile from crest to crest. According to his notions this was no place for a boar, which he conceived as a beast of the low, dark, muddy bottom of the forest, and he looked at his watch and at the high ridge, which would probably lead him straight up to his old regular way: and when he saw the boar he was for an instant so amazed that he might never have been hunting it at all. The eager ferocity had died out of him; but it came flooding back, with an audible thump of his heart. He was now on the edge of the scrub, just shielded by a leafy birch: straight ahead of him one of these side valleys ran up towards the high ridge, finishing in a little half-round or dell a quarter of a mile away, with one last clump of trees in it, as if it had a spring. The boar stood at the opening of this valley, standing there in the full sunshine and scraping its back under the bare limb of a thorn. The bush moved rhythmically with the repeated urge of the boar's back, and it was this unnatural movement in the calmness that caught his attention.

It was a long shot for a rifle all unsighted and muffled by a home-made silencer, and the boar was turned three-quarters from him, but it was possible, and he might never have another. At the sound of the bolt the boar stopped. Glaring through the leaves and along the barrel while his finger began to squeeze on the trigger, he saw the boar's ears come up, pointed, not flaps, and its whole body became attentive. The shot parted: a puff of dust and hair sprang from the boar's shoulder and it was thrown forward on to its knees. Then it was up, its head turning quickly from side to side, the whole animal poised. He broke out of his shelter, running fast towards the boar and working the bolt as he ran; but before he had run ten yards he realised that the shell had jammed. He stopped, and for a moment they stood head on: then the boar wheeled in a quick neat turn and moved up the slope in a stiff-legged canter towards the dell at the top.

He levered the shell with his knife, ejected it; sliding the new round home he followed the boar to the dell. It was a sudden dip in the ground, with a cliff behind it; a few trees came up out of it, growing round the edge of the little pool that could be seen under the dense tangle of tall fern down there in the shelter. It was a dell not ten yards across, and it was some ten feet deep against the cliff – much less at the nearer end.

He had walked round and round its rim, plumbing it, measuring it, calculating the risks, doing everything but go down. He was afraid to go down into that impenetrable green: when the boar had turned, its tusks, but even more the bulk of its head, its little fiery eyes and its enormous high shoulders, had shocked and daunted him; he dared not go down.

He thought sometimes that he was going to risk it, and at other moments he thought that he was going to go away: the indecision enraged him – the prospect of walking off after all this, disappointed and blamed, was very bitter; the prospect of walking in to meet the charge of a boar, with only one shot, instantly and perfectly delivered, to prevent a long ripping-up in the mud and water, was very horrible.

He came and went, and in the end he hardly knew his own mind, but stepped down at the shallow end, step by step, with his gun held high under his heart, and his whole being wrought up to the highest state of immediate violent expectancy; he

walked the thirteen paces to the end, to the dark cliff-face. There
was no boar.

He walked round each side, making the circle, treading down
the cover, but there was no boar and eventually he climbed out
and after a slow and dull re-orientation he set himself to climb
to the ridge and so reach the alp of the frontier, before darkness
should come down and find him still in a strange country.

The fact troubled him very much. Even when he was right up
there on the familiar way to Olot, with the high thin air round
him and the enormous stretch of Spain away under his left hand,
with minute silver rivers creeping through it, the fact distressed
and preoccupied his mind. It seemed to him a terrible sign: it
seemed to him to mean that there was no victory; not that he
had been deceived or beaten or that he had failed, but that there
had at no time been any possibility of winning because victory
did not exist – there was no victory. He had had this same nightmare of discovery once in the Haute-Savoie, when he had
stopped the lorry to decide which road to take at a fork, and on
the road that he was to take the signpost said *Route sans issue*.

He was still turning this round and round in his mind, walking very fast and automatically (he was fit and tough) when he
came in sight of the Cami d'en Pau, a mule-track that led up
from Spain over to Olot, and which had a Spanish post halfway
down. At this point he usually made a detour, taking a smuggler's
path a quarter of a mile further on, which would lead him, in the
darkness, to Olot: but here today, just before he reached his turning and while he was still looking down on the evening as it darkened over Spain he ran straight into a German patrol, cleverly
spread out among the jutting rocks of the topmost ridge.

At the first shout he knew what he had done. He dived to the
left, a jump of fifteen feet, and raced under the cover of a line of

rock towards the mule-track. But there on the track itself were three field-grey soldiers. He swerved and reached the track below them: he was flying down the hill, and if he could reach the white frontier stones and the Spanish post he was safe. He jigged, although at such a pace it was mortal to slip: the unseen rifles bored into his back, between his shoulder-blades. The Spaniards and their police-dogs came out to watch, and darted in again as the firing started. Running, running, with his feet hitting the ground in huge flying strides, he hurtled past the stones and flung himself sideways behind the cover of the little house, where the Spaniards seized him and frog-marched him with the blood pouring out of his nose right up the hill again to their German friends.

That was not the nightmare, however: the nightmare was the mad running under the compulsion of the silent, pointing guns before they fired; and far more, far deeper, the horror of the bottomless world which he found in that pretty dell.

But now his dreaming mind, as if it were better informed about the nature of victory, began to glow, and passing through one of those marvellous visions of colour that had once been usual with him, but which had stopped for years, he came to a dream that took the form of print. He was reading the words as they were printed, and although they did not always, nor often, make ordinary sense, they conveyed a profoundly important statement about painting; things that he had never known were now distinctly proved, and things that he had felt and suspected ran out on the page in clear and certain terms, sometimes as errors, sometimes as part of an enormously important truth.

This dream, because of the speed at which he had to read and understand as well as guide the writing (for he was in the end the thing written and so both reader and writer) grew very tiring, and he was glad when the pace slackened and a voice, or a series of kind intimations from outside, replaced the hurrying print.

The dream of print had been in the light, of course, but the voice was in the profound darkness; and one of the things it said, *Love is never lost*, filled him with a piercing happiness. It was a low voice, perfectly clear. Somewhere in his mind a question arose and a need to know whether that meant even erotic love, but the calm certainty of the voice overlaid everything; and besides in the changing current hundreds of things were all borne in upon him one upon another, several together, in a crowd of prophecies, huge colours, revelations and throughout everything a promise of great happiness; and the whole took on the sound and crash and thunder of explosions as the bridge over the river shot up into the sky and at the same moment hundreds of feet rushed clashing down his corridor and everywhere the doors slammed to and fro.

He was on his feet and torn between the two worlds as the cell burst open and an intolerable light blinded him: the furious thumping rattle of the firing-squad burst in with the light, and with his blind white face straining towards the door he cried out, 'What? What is it?'

'Come out, come on out,' they bawled. 'This is the liberation.'